T0069363

# Secrets of Cavendon

Books by Barbara Taylor Bradford

Series

THE EMMA HARTE SAGA

*A Woman of Substance*

*Hold the Dream*

*To Be the Best*

*Emma's Secret*

*Unexpected Blessings*

*Just Rewards*

*Breaking the Rules*

THE RAVENSCAR TRILOGY

*The Ravenscar Dynasty*

*Heirs of Ravenscar*

*Being Elizabeth*

THE CAVENDON SERIES

*Cavendon Hall*

*The Cavendon Women*

*The Cavendon Luck*

*Secrets of Cavendon*

Others

*Voice of the Heart*

*Act of Will*

*The Women in His Life*

*Remember*

*Angel*

*Everything to Gain*

*Dangerous to Know*

*Love in Another Town*

*Her Own Rules*

*A Secret Affair*

*Power of a Woman*

*A Sudden Change of Heart*

*Where You Belong*

*The Triumph of Katie Byrne*

*Three Weeks in Paris*

*Playing the Game*

*Letter from a Stranger*

*Secrets from the Past*

Ebook-only novellas

*Hidden*

*Treacherous*

*Who Are You*

# Secrets of Cavendon

Barbara Taylor Bradford

HarperCollins*Publishers*

HarperCollins*Publishers*
The News Building
1 London Bridge Street
London SE1 9GF

www.harpercollins.co.uk

Published by HarperCollins*Publishers* 2017
2



A catalogue record for this book
is available from the British Library

ISBN HB: 978-0-00-750335-3
ISBN TPB: 978-0-00-750336-0



Set in Sabon by Palimpsest Book Production Limited,
Falkirk, Stirlingshire

Printed and bound by CPI Group (UK) Ltd, Croydon CR0 4YY

MIX
Paper from
responsible sources
FSC™ C007454

This book is produced from independently certified FSC™ paper
to ensure responsible forest management.

For more information visit: www.harpercollins.co.uk/green

For Bob, with all my love always

# Contents

# Characters

ABOVE THE STAIRS
THE INGHAMS IN 1949

Miles Ingham, 7th Earl of Mowbray, aged 50. Owner and custodian of Cavendon Hall. Referred to as Lord Mowbray. He is married to Cecily Swann, 48, who is the 7th Countess of Mowbray.

THE CHILDREN OF THE EARL AND COUNTESS

David Ingham, heir to the earldom, aged 20. He is known as the Honourable David Ingham. Walter, 18; Venetia, 16; and Gwen, 8.

Lady Diedre Ingham Lawson, sister of the Earl, aged 56. She is married to William Lawson, 56, and lives in London with him and her son, Robin Drummond, 22. She works at the War Office. They come to Cavendon at weekends where they have their own house, Little Skell Manor.

Lady Daphne Ingham, sister of the Earl, aged 53. She remains married to Hugo Ingham Stanton, 68. They live permanently at Cavendon Hall, in the South Wing. They have five children who live in London and visit at weekends. They are Alicia,

35; Charles, 31; the twins Thomas and Andrew, 28; and Annabel, 25.

Lady Dulcie Ingham, youngest sister of the Earl, aged 41. She lives in London and at Skelldale Manor at Cavendon. She is married to Sir James Brentwood, 56, one of England's greatest actors, who was knighted by King George VI. They have three children: twins Rosalind and Juliet, 20, and a son, Henry, 17.

The three sisters of the Earl are now referred to affectionately as the Three Dees by the staff.

BETWEEN STAIRS

THE SECOND FAMILY: THE SWANNS

The Swann family has been in service to the Ingham family for almost two hundred years. Consequently, their lives have been intertwined in many different ways. Generations of Swanns have lived in Little Skell village, adjoining Cavendon Park, and still do. The present-day Swanns are as devoted and loyal to the Inghams as their forebears were, and would defend any member of the family with their lives. The Inghams trust them implicitly, and vice versa.

THE SWANNS IN 1949

Walter Swann, aged 71; father of Cecily and Harry. Head of the Swann family, and in charge of security at Cavendon Hall.

Alice Swann, his wife, aged 68, the mother of Cecily and Harry. Alice runs most of the village events and helps to run the Women's Institute alongside the Dowager Countess.

Harry, son, aged 51, a former apprentice landscape gardener at Cavendon Hall. He is now running the estate. He has also created beautiful gardens which draw the public.

Cecily, daughter, aged 48. She is married to Miles and is a world-renowned fashion designer.

Paloma Swann, 38, wife of Harry, and mother of their children: Edward, 10; Patricia, 8; and Charles, 6. She is a well-known photographer.

## OTHER SWANNS

Percy, younger brother of Walter, aged 68. Head gamekeeper at Cavendon.

Edna, wife of Percy, aged 69. Does occasional work at Cavendon.

Joe, their son, aged 48. Works with his father as assistant head gamekeeper.

Bill, first cousin of Walter, aged 63. Head landscape gardener at Cavendon. He is widowed.

Ted, first cousin of Walter, aged 74. Head of interior maintenance and carpentry at Cavendon. Widowed.

Paul, son of Ted, aged 50, working with his father as an interior designer and carpenter at Cavendon. Single.

Eric, brother of Ted, first cousin of Walter, aged 69. Head butler at Cavendon Hall. Single.

Charlotte, aunt of Walter and Percy, aged 81. Now Dowager Countess of Mowbray. Charlotte is the matriarch of the Swann and Ingham families. She is treated with great love and respect by everyone. Charlotte was the secretary and personal assistant to David Ingham, the 5th Earl, until his death. She married the 6th Earl in 1926, who predeceased her during World War II.

Dorothy Pinkerton, née Swann, aged 66, cousin of Charlotte. She lives in London and is married to Howard Pinkerton, 66, a Scotland Yard detective. She works with Cecily at Cecily Swann Couture in London.

## CHARACTERS BELOW STAIRS

Mr Eric Swann, Head butler
Mrs Peggy Swift Lane, Housekeeper
Mrs Lois Waters, Cook
Miss Mary Lowden, Head housemaid
Miss Vera Gower, Second housemaid
Mr Philip Carlton, Chauffeur

OTHER EMPLOYEES

Miss Angela Chambers, nanny for Cecily's daughter Gwen, addressed as Nanny or Nan.

THE OUTDOOR WORKERS

A stately home such as Cavendon Hall, with thousands of acres of land, and a huge grouse moor, employs local people. This is its purpose for being, as well as providing a private home for a great family. It offers employment to the local villagers, and also land for local tenant farmers. The villages surrounding Cavendon were built by various earls of Mowbray to provide housing for their workers; churches and schools were also built, as well as post offices and small shops at later dates. The villages around Cavendon are Little Skell, Mowbray and High Clough.

There are a number of outside workers: a head gamekeeper and five additional gamekeepers; beaters and flankers who work when the grouse season starts and the Guns arrive at Cavendon to shoot. Other outdoor workers include woodsmen, who take care of the surrounding woods for shooting in the lowlands at certain times of the year. The gardens are cared for by a head landscape gardener, and five other gardeners working under him.

The grouse season starts in August, on the Glorious Twelfth, as it is called. It finishes in December. The partridge season begins in September. Duck and wild fowl are shot at this time. Pheasant shooting starts on the 1 November and goes on until December. The men who come to shoot, usually aristocrats, are always referred to as the Guns, i.e., the men using the gun.

# Part One

# A Rip in the Fabric
# 1949

Yesterday's weaving is as irrevocable
as yesterday.
I may not draw out the threads, but I
may change my shuttle.

Muriel Strode-Lieberman,
*My Little Book of Life*

# One

Cecily Swann Ingham, the 7th Countess of Mowbray, was on the steps of the office annexe, looking out across the stable block, her eyes focused on Cavendon Hall perched high on the hill in front of her.

It was a lovely June morning, and the luminous light particular to the north of England cast a sheen across the soaring roof and chimney tops, which appeared to shimmer under the clear, bright sky.

How glorious the house looks today, she thought: stately, grand, strong and safe. She smiled wryly to herself. It wasn't safe at all, in her opinion. Not in reality.

Sadly, as grand as the house looked this morning, it was facing serious trouble once more in its long life, and she was genuinely worried about its future, the future of the entire estate, including the grouse moor, as well as the Ingham family itself.

Cecily sighed, closed her eyes, shutting out the view. Cavendon had bled them dry for years, and taken an enormous amount of their time. They had each made huge sacrifices for it, and all of them had at one time or another poured money into the bottomless pit it had become, particularly Cecily herself.

Opening her eyes, straightening, she wondered how on earth they would manage to stave off the encroaching trouble, which was slowly but steadily moving forward to engulf them. If she was truthful with herself, she had to admit she had no idea. For once in her life she felt entirely helpless, unable to create a fool-proof plan of action.

The clatter of hooves cut into her worrisome thoughts, and she opened her eyes. Her brother, Harry, was crossing the cobbled stable yard, accompanied by Miles, who walked alongside the horse.

Her husband spotted her, raised his hand in greeting, smiled at her – that special smile reserved for her alone. Her heart tightened at the delighted look that crossed his face, because he had seen her unexpectedly.

Harry waved; she waved back, and watched her brother leave the yard. He was off on his Saturday morning rounds of the entire estate. Harry revelled in his job as the estate manager and had made such a huge difference in numerous ways. The new gardens he had created after he had been invalided out of the Air Force were startlingly beautiful and had drawn many visitors.

Miles joined her on the steps, putting his arm around her. 'I missed you at breakfast. As adorable and entertaining as our children are, they can hardly take your place, my love.'

'I needed to get to my desk, go over the latest figures Aunt Dottie sent up from London. Before going to the meeting.'

'Bloody hell! I'd forgotten about the Saturday morning meeting,' Miles exclaimed, sounding annoyed.

Cecily gave him a nod and grimaced.

Miles said, 'Come on then, madam, buck up at once! Gird on your sword and prepare to do battle. You have no alternative, you know. The die is cast!'

'Indeed it is.' She laughed. 'I'm off,' she added, 'there won't be a battle, maybe a bit of grumbling, and whining, but that's all.' She blew him a kiss.

'I know *that*. Still, just think, next week we'll be all alone with our little brood and Aunt Charlotte. The rest of the family will have gone off on their holidays, thank God.'

'Like you, I can't wait,' she replied, and left him standing on the steps of the annexe. She made her way across the stable yard, heading for the terrace which ran along the back of the house, facing Cavendon Park.

When she stepped onto the terrace a few seconds later, her three sisters-in-law and aunt had not yet arrived for their regular weekly catch-up. She sat down in a wicker chair, her gaze resting on the lush park which flowed to the edge of Little Skell village.

On the left side of the park was the lake where the two white swans floated, a matched pair, bonded for life, as were all swans. It had been the first Earl, Humphrey Ingham, who had decreed there must always be swans at Cavendon to honour his liegeman, James Swann.

The spectacular view had not changed over the many years, not since the 1700s, in fact, when the house had first been built. But everything else had. Things were different now . . . nothing was the same any more. Anywhere.

Cecily sat drifting with her thoughts, thinking of the last four years. In 1945, when the war had ended in victory, the euphoria of the public had been high. Unfortunately, that sense of pride, triumph and relief had soon drifted off, and the rot had set in. The country was broke, the Great British Empire was creeping away, disappearing into nothingness, and everyone grumbled, complained and couldn't wait for things to get better. *They didn't.* The worst thing of it was that Churchill was out of office; the Labour Party had won the election and Clement Attlee had been made Prime Minister.

City councils without funds were unable to function properly. Bomb sites, great gaping holes in the ground, eyesores in every big city, had been left untouched for lack of money and materials. It was the same with ruined buildings; there were piles of rubble everywhere, making everyone miserable because they were constant reminders of the war. And the country was still suffering rationing on much of the food and day-to-day goods they needed.

It seemed to Cecily that Britain had just stood still. Now, in 1949, she hoped things were improving: people were becoming more optimistic once more and there was a sense of cheerfulness in the air. Princess Elizabeth's wedding eighteen months earlier had helped lift the country's spirits.

On the other hand, Britain was still a country mostly made up of old men, women and children. Hundreds of thousands of young men had not returned from battle, had died in foreign lands. She knew how much this had affected Cavendon. They were a large estate and had lost many of their young men from the tenant farms and the villages, the families devastated by loss for the second time in a generation. And Cavendon was an agricultural estate that needed sturdy men to till the land, harvest the crops, tend the cattle and sheep.

Miles said they were lucky that two of the Land Army girls had stayed on, and were running several of the tenant farms; by advertising in local newspapers, Harry had managed to hire three families to move into tenant farms in the nearby villages of Mowbray and High Clough.

Hearing voices, Cecily swung around and immediately stood up. Through the French doors she saw Aunt Charlotte, who was talking to Eric Swann, head butler at Cavendon.

Cecily went into the library to greet her aunt, exclaiming, 'Good morning, I didn't expect you to come today, Aunt Charlotte.' Like her, her great-aunt was a Swann who'd married an Ingham – though in Charlotte's case not until later in life. Now the Dowager Countess of Mowbray, the older woman retained the poise and upright bearing she'd had from girlhood. Her face was lined with her years now, and her hair white.

'Hello, Ceci – and why not? It's the last of the meetings for the summer. I should be here.'

Looking across at Eric, Cecily said, 'I see you've brought in coffee, Eric. I'd love a cup, please. And what about you, Aunt Charlotte?'

'Yes, of course, I'll join you. We can have a chat before the others get here.'

'Right away, my lady,' Eric said, and turned to the tray on the table.

Charlotte walked over to the fireplace and sat down, and beckoned for Cecily to join her. 'There is something I must tell you . . . privately.'

But before she could say anything else, the door of the library opened and Lady Diedre came in. The eldest of the Ingham sisters, she was an elegant woman of fifty-six, her blonde hair now streaked with grey, but dressed as usual in the most up-to-date fashions. Today she wore the chic, wide-leg trousers she adored, teamed with a relaxed silk blouse.

Cecily raised her eyebrows at Charlotte. Their private conversation would have to wait. She stood up to welcome her sister-in-law. Diedre was widely regarded as the brains of the siblings, having worked for years at the War Office. She didn't suffer fools gladly, but her razor-sharp intelligence always livened up any gathering. Cecily gave her an affectionate kiss and pointed her towards the coffee.

She was followed by Lady Dulcie, the youngest Ingham sister, now in her early forties. Dulcie might be slightly plumper and a mother of three, but she was still the baby of the family in all of their eyes. As they got themselves settled, Diedre leant across to Cecily and said, 'I just want to congratulate you on the success of the gift shop. You've done a marvellous job, and certainly the income from it is proving very useful.'

'Thank you,' Cecily answered, and smiled gratefully at her. It was Diedre who was usually the peacemaker when any problems arose and squabbles started. 'I honestly had no idea people would be interested in so many small things related to Cavendon.'

As Dulcie sat down, Cecily turned towards her.

'How long will you be away in Hollywood?' she asked. 'Miles said James has two films to make for MGM under his old contract.'

'Yes, that's correct, but I think we'll be back in time for Christmas. At least that's what we're planning. Also, James wants to do a play in the West End next year.'

'That's good to know,' Cecily said. 'Christmas wouldn't be the same without you.' She adored her glamorous sister-in-law, who remained as funny and down-to-earth as she'd always been, despite her husband's Hollywood success.

At this moment the door opened and Daphne, the last of the Ingham sisters, stepped into the room. Cecily blinked with surprise. It was obvious that her sister-in-law was dressed for travelling rather than the weekend at Cavendon.

Walking forward, Daphne greeted them coolly. 'I just came to say goodbye. I'm not staying for the meeting.' She looked around at the other women, her face set. 'Nobody listens to me anyway.'

Cecily recoiled in shock. Daphne was, to all intents and purposes, the chatelaine of Cavendon. Ever since her mother had left them, she'd run the place; she'd lived here all her life.

A wry smile twisted Daphne's mouth briefly, and she went on. 'Hugo and I are leaving very shortly. We wish to have supper with the children in London this evening. Then we are off to Zurich tomorrow, as you know. What I want to tell you now is that we won't be coming back for a long time. Perhaps not for another year.'

Diedre looked startled. 'Goodness me, Daphne, a whole year!' she exclaimed. 'Why ever would you, of all people, stay away from Cavendon for so long?' Her face betrayed her bemusement.

'Because I can't really bear it here any more,' Daphne answered. Her voice was level, steady, 'I can't live here with the public milling around the house and gardens any longer. They seem to be everywhere. I keep stumbling over them. It's perfectly ghastly.'

Daphne paused and stared at Cecily for a prolonged moment. 'It's become far too commercial for me, Ceci. Almost like a giant store, an extension of Harte's, what with the shops, the café, and the art gallery. I'm afraid you've turned it into a rather horrid tourist attraction.' She shook her head, her beautiful face suddenly grim, and without uttering another word she left the library, closing the door quietly behind her.

There was a stunned silence.

Diedre and Dulcie looked at each other. The amazement on both sisters' faces proclaimed that this was as much of a surprise to them as it was to Cecily.

Aunt Charlotte spoke first, her voice quiet. 'I think we must excuse Daphne and what she's just said. She's been exhausted for a long time and has put a lot into Cavendon. I do believe a few weeks of quiet and tranquillity in Zurich will help her feel better.'

'She blames me,' Cecily said in a low tone. 'Ever since the end of the war she has been saying I have been making Cavendon too commercial. She and Hugo have never stopped grumbling – about the house tours, in particular. She's been very off with me lately.'

'But it's the money we make from the public that keeps us going!' Dulcie cried, her voice rising slightly. 'And she blames me too, because you let me create my little art gallery. But all of the profits go to Cavendon, not to me.'

In a soothing voice, Diedre interjected, 'Don't let's get excited about this. Frankly, I agree with Aunt Charlotte. Daphne's been bone tired for years and I think she deserves a long rest. She loves the villa and Switzerland. She'll get her strength back, soon be her old self again.'

Dulcie, looking from Diedre to Aunt Charlotte, asked, 'What do you mean, bone tired? Do you both think Daphne has some kind of *illness*?'

Aunt Charlotte shook her head. 'Not really, but she has put so much of herself into the house, she's sort of, well . . .' Charlotte paused before finishing, 'A little *possessive* of it, should we say?'

Diedre nodded in agreement. 'The public does get on her nerves, but if we didn't have the house and garden tours, and the shops . . .' She broke off, her hands raised in a helpless gesture. 'I don't know where we'd be.'

'Broke,' Cecily said. 'Well, not quite, but almost.'

'And aren't we lucky the public are so terribly fascinated by Cavendon Hall and the gardens,' Dulcie remarked. 'Especially since they pay through the nose for the privilege of touring them.'

She laughed, and so did the others, breaking the dour mood.

'Perhaps we should just skip the meeting, go on about our own business,' Diedre suggested.

'If there's nothing else to discuss, I think I'll go and finish packing,' Dulcie announced, rising. 'There are lots of my clothes here which I want to take with me to Beverly Hills.'

Diedre remarked, 'Talking of packing, I'd better go and do the same thing. Will and I leave for Beaulieu-sur-Mer early next week.' Glancing at Cecily she went on, 'Will's brother Ambrose is letting us have his house in the south of France for six weeks, and we'd love you and Miles to come down and stay, Cecily. And why don't you come along as well, Aunt Charlotte?'

'That's a lovely invitation, Diedre, and I just might do that, providing Cecily and Miles are coming. You see, I do prefer to travel with someone these days. I'm getting to be an old lady, you know.'

'Nonsense!' Diedre exclaimed. 'You don't look or act your age, and you're as fit as a fiddle. But I know what you mean about travelling alone. Just let us know when you can come.'

Cecily gave a distracted smile. Her emotions were running high. She said nothing until her sisters-in-law had left the room, then walked to the window, looking out at the grounds.

'What do you wish to tell me, discuss with me?' Cecily asked her great-aunt, keeping her voice calm.

'The estate,' Charlotte answered. 'As you are aware, I was the personal assistant to David Ingham, the Fifth Earl.' She glanced at her. 'And, as such, I know more about the entire estate than anybody else, even Miles. It struck me about ten days ago that Great-Aunt Gwen had no right to leave Little Skell Manor to Diedre, because she didn't actually own it. Neither did her sister, who had left it to Great-Aunt Gwen. You see Cavendon Hall, all of the buildings on the estate, the thousands of acres of land, the grouse moor and the park belong to whomever is the earl. However, for the past fifty-five years or so, the last few earls have allowed family members to live at the two houses *rent free*.'

Cecily looked at her great-aunt. 'Do you mean that James and

Dulcie should be paying rent, because they live at Skelldale House, and so should Diedre and Will, because they are occupying Little Skell Manor?'

'That's correct,' Charlotte replied. 'To be absolutely sure, I checked in the files I created years ago and came across the relevant documents, which confirmed what I've just said.'

'It will, but we must convince Miles to accept the idea. He might not want to do it.'

'There are the papers I found to prove my point,' Charlotte reminded Cecily. 'I know they were overlooked by the Fifth Earl, because I worked with him, and obviously the Sixth Earl did the same thing. Now the Seventh Earl can put it all straight.'

Cecily wasn't so sure. She knew her husband would loathe the idea – especially as his sisters believed the houses had been given to them. And it was going to seem, once again, that the Swanns were meddling with the Ingham ways.

She stood up wearily and excused herself.

# Two

In moments of sorrow, or when she was troubled, Cecily went to a special place at Cavendon to be alone and calm herself.

It was no longer the rose garden, which she had used as a sanctuary for years, although she did still visit it occasionally. These days she usually went down to DeLacy's grave, where she would sit and talk to her dearest friend. DeLacy Ingham had been tragically killed in the war, when the South Street house had been struck by a flying bomb, and Cecily continued to miss her childhood companion, the missing sister of the 'Four Dees', as they'd been known.

Leaving the house, Cecily walked to the cemetery, located across the park near the woods. When she arrived she saw at once that someone else had been there before her. The vase on the grave was filled with late-blooming pink roses.

Instantly, she choked up, touched that another member of the family had also recently felt the need to visit DeLacy. That was the way she always thought of these visits – *going to see DeLacy*, never going to DeLacy's *grave*. Because she couldn't bear that thought. Cecily sat down on the grass and leaned against the headstone. In her mind's eye she could see her friend as clearly as if she were standing there, could hear the lilting voice telling her something special, their laughter echoing in the air . . .

She missed Lacy so much it was a physical pain, an ache inside, a terrible longing for someone she had loved and lost, whom she would never embrace or laugh with ever again. DeLacy's untimely death in the Second World War had been the biggest loss of her life.

Cecily thought now of the years they had grown up together, here at Cavendon, always close, never far away from each other. They were the same age, with the same needs. While DeLacy was an Ingham, one of the Earl's four daughters, and Cecily a Swann, who served the aristocratic family, the social divide had meant nothing to them. We were like one person, Cecily suddenly thought, all twined up together, interwoven like a fine fabric, thinking and saying the same things.

A small sigh escaped her and she closed her eyes, unexpectedly remembering their terrible quarrel. They had not spoken for several years. It was Miles who had been able to bring about a reconciliation, which Lacy had begged for, and Cecily had agreed to forgive and forget, and she had done that with all her heart. When they had come back together, were friends again, it was so easy, so natural, as if they had never been apart. In an instant, they had become one again.

To Cecily, DeLacy had always been the most beautiful of the four Ingham sisters, even though Lady Daphne had been singled out as the beauty of the family by their father.

Her husband's sisters were all blonde with sky-blue eyes. Diedre, Daphne, DeLacy and Dulcie, each with their own honorary title of Lady, as the daughters of an earl. Her sisters-in-law, her friends. Daphne's words earlier had hurt Cecily very deeply.

There had never been a serious rift between the Inghams and the Swanns until after the war. It was *then* that the fabric of the family had suddenly and unexpectedly been ripped. All because of the need for money for new government taxes and the proper running of the estate. Miles fully understood he was the guardian of an ancient line, one of the most important earldoms in England. Still, his birthright was a heavy burden to carry, Cecily knew that. Many of the ancient estates had been put up for sale over the years since the First World War, and now the Second World War had made it harder still. An old world order had ended for ever: a world in which the big houses were full of servants and the money flowed had disappeared.

Aunt Charlotte had told her as they had parted earlier that it was the first time in living memory there had been issues between the two families. And she ought to know. Aunt Charlotte had been the keeper of the Swann record books all of her adult life. They had been written since Cavendon was built, started at the time of the 1st Earl by James Swann. In those books were all the secrets of the Swanns *and* the Inghams; they were absolutely private and for Swann eyes only.

The Inghams had never been allowed to read those books. Now they were in her hands, and Cecily would keep the records, write in them, and they would not pass to another Swann until the day she died.

Cecily focused on Aunt Charlotte. She held a unique position in the two families, as the matriarch of the Swanns and, as the Dowager Countess of Mowbray, matriarch of the Inghams. Aunt Charlotte's work for Miles's grandfather, David Ingham, the 5th Earl, long before she married the 6th Earl, Charles, late in her life, meant there wasn't much she didn't know about the two families. How lucky for them that she had now remembered that the two houses, Little Skell Manor and Skelldale House, belonged to the 7th Earl, and not the different women who had lived in them over the years.

She hoped Miles wouldn't be silly and get on his high horse, and say his sisters must continue to live rent free.

Daphne lived rent free, come to think of it. She and Hugo and their children had occupied the South Wing of Cavendon for all of their married lives. Did they pay rent? Had they ever? Should they now start? She had no answer to that.

Cecily felt a sudden rush of resentment. Daphne blamed her for the visitors who intruded on Daphne's private haven, and she had to admit she was hurt, considering the efforts she had made over these many years. She had saved Cavendon from disaster time and again, shoring it up with money from her own fashion business.

Unexpectedly, tears again began to leak out of the corner of her eyes and trickled down her cheeks. She was weeping for the loss of her darling DeLacy, but also because of the accusations Daphne had levelled at her, words that had been most unfair.

She remained seated by the grave for a short while longer, pulling herself together, taking control of her emotions. On her way back to the house Cecily saw her mother hurrying along the path from Little Skell village. They spotted each other at the same moment, waving. A few seconds later they were embracing. Alice Swann said, 'I was coming to look for you, Ceci. Your father told me that Lady Daphne and Mr Hugo have gone off to Zurich, and that she didn't even attend the family meeting.'

'Oh gosh, the Swann network does move fast,' Cecily shot back, but there was humour in her tone. 'I suppose you also know that she blames me for the commercialization of Cavendon, opening it to the public and all that stuff.'

'I do,' Alice replied. 'When I think of all the money you have given to the family to maintain Cavendon, my blood boils. Thousands. Even when Swann Couture was starting to take off you chipped in, and later you bought that pile of Ingham jewellery and then gave to the Earl annual cheques from your collection of copies.' Alice shook her head and let out a long sigh. 'Poor Daphne, she's not well, in my opinion. Or perhaps she's just overtired. I know deep down she loves you dearly, Cecily. You look as if you've been crying. Not about Daphne, I hope?'

'No. Missing DeLacy. Anyway, I'm a bit hurt at the moment,

but it will pass.' Quickly she changed the subject and said, 'Aunt Dottie is looking forward to seeing you and Dad, Mam.'

Alice smiled. 'And I can't wait. She's always so cheerful and loving.'

Miles swung around and jumped up when he saw Cecily coming into his study. 'There you are, darling!' he exclaimed, his engaging smile filling his face with love. 'I've been wondering where you were.'

Taking hold of her, he led her over to the sofa.

'There was no meeting,' she began. 'Daphne—'

'Daphne's been here to see me,' he cut in. 'With Hugo in tow. He indicated they would be living in Zurich for quite a few months. A short while later, Aunt Charlotte showed up and told me all about her little scheme. Not so little, actually.' He paused, reached out and gently wiped a damp cheek with his fingertips. 'You've been crying. Not about Daphne, I hope?'

'No. I went to sit with Lacy for a few minutes. Missing her.' As she spoke, Cecily swept both hands across her face, sat up and offered her husband her brightest smile.

Miles studied her. She was forty-eight and still beautiful, with her luxuriant, russet-brown hair, those unusual lavender-tinted eyes and a clear complexion. If there were a few wrinkles around her eyes, he hardly noticed them, and neither did anyone else. She was his woman, his wife, his partner, his soulmate, and his saviour in so many ways. Without her he would be lost.

He was fifty, but he had worn quite well. There were many grey hairs now, and frequently bags under his eyes, and sometimes he was ready to collapse from exhaustion. On the other hand, fifty was fifty, after all. Certainly he made sure nobody knew how tired he felt half the time, although he suspected this woman he had loved all his life knew this. Cecily Swann. The girl he had loved from childhood. Now Cecily Ingham. His. There had only ever been her. His brief marriage to Clarissa, a forced marriage at that, had been a sham. Thank God he had his Cecily by his side, loving and loyal.

Miles leaned closer and kissed her forehead. 'I won't permit anyone to blame you for turning Cavendon into a commercial enterprise. We all supported that. And we had to do it in order to survive, to save all this.' He paused, waved his hand towards the window, indicating the entire estate.

'Did Aunt Charlotte tell you Daphne *does* blame me?'

'She did. And Daphne more than likely blames Dulcie for opening her art gallery; Harry for creating gorgeous gardens that lure the public here; her son Charlie for writing a bestselling history about us that titillates everyone and brings more visitors; Paloma for producing a coffee-table book about Harry's gardens that sells so well for *us*. And I am positive that the greatest blame goes to me. Her brother, the Seventh Earl, who has allowed all this horrific stuff to happen.' He smiled gently, shaking his head. 'Please don't take her words to heart. You've saved us, not ruined us. And we've all aided and abetted you.'

'Oh Miles, you do make me feel better. I was a bit down in the dumps earlier. I'm afraid Daphne's attitude has been troubling me for the past year. She and Hugo have been . . . well, grumblers, to say the least. So, are you going to do what Aunt Charlotte suggests? Charge rent for Little Skell Manor and Skelldale House?'

'She persuaded me I should think about it.' Miles wasn't giving much away.

Cecily nodded. 'They can both afford it. James and Will are wealthy men, and Diedre still works.'

'She's always been keen to help out, and actually those two houses they live in are taxed by the government as part of the estate taxes.'

'Then you have no choice,' Cecily answered emphatically.

Miles stood, walked over to the window and looked out at the moors. There was a prolonged silence before he finally returned and sat down with Cecily. Taking hold of her hand, he said,

'Daphne's departure is going to be a burden for you in some ways. I think we must discuss the problems now, get them dealt with.'

'I have to be at Cavendon all the time, to run it myself now, don't I?' Cecily replied, detecting the seriousness in his voice.

'You do, darling. You must take on the full responsibilities as chatelaine. After all, you are the Seventh Countess. And you must manage all the village events and be part of village life. The three villages.'

'I have been doing quite a lot of that over these many years,' Cecily protested, her voice rising slightly. 'I realize Daphne always had a hand in supervising Cavendon Hall, especially when it came to keeping the room décor up to par, checking for leaks, making lists of any other tasks that needed doing. And keeping Ted and Paul Swann informed, showing them any damage.'

'That's not a difficult task, Ceci. We will ask every family member to keep an eye open for such things. I'm afraid Daphne could be overzealous about upkeep in a sense; she was always on top of the carpentry shop, pushing Paul in particular.'

'I know that,' Cecily replied. 'Let's not forget that Eric and Peggy haven't left with her for Zurich.' There was a sarcastic edge to her voice when she added, '*They* run the domestic side of Cavendon. Daphne didn't do that any more, and hasn't for years. Eric inherited Hanson's mantle well. He's a wonderful head butler, and Peggy Swift is an amazing housekeeper. I don't think they need my hovering around them.'

'That's true. But you have spent a lot of time in London, and when it comes down to it, the Countess should be here on a regular basis.'

'I've been in London for my business, not having a good time!'

He took her hand in his again, squeezed it. 'Let's not bicker. What we have to do is make a plan, work out how you can do both—'

Cecily interrupted him peremptorily and said in a brisk, business-like tone, 'I shall have to learn to delegate, since I will have to run my business from here. I'll promote Aunt Dottie and Greta Chalmers.

They can do it, I'm sure. They'll both handle more responsibility for the business well.'

'And you won't mind that?'

'Of course not. I have to do what's practical.'

His pleasure showed on his face. He was beaming at her, and his eyes held the sparkle that had been missing for so long.

Cecily's heart sank. Her being here full time as Countess was what Miles wanted – and needed. But as she considered the serious problems she had with her business, the debts, the lack of money, she knew that spending less time on it could be disastrous. She was almost on the point of confiding in him, but changed her mind.

She would not be able to give him any money for Cavendon this year. Her business was in the red. But would Cavendon survive without her contribution? She was not sure.

Now she thought: Why spoil the weekend? I'll talk to him on Monday, give him the bad news then.

'We'd better go to lunch,' she said, standing up, offering him a loving smile. But her heart was heavy with worry, disguise it though she did, knowing that Cavendon could go down.

# Three

Alicia Ingham Stanton, eldest child of Lady Daphne and Hugo Stanton, stood staring at herself in the bathroom mirror, startled by her appearance. Her blue eyes were red-rimmed, there were dark shadows underneath, and her delicate pink and white complexion had a strange greyish tint to it today.

But she was not really surprised she looked so awful. She and Charlie had drunk far too many cognacs last night, and later sleep had eluded her. Now, at six o'clock in the morning, she felt totally exhausted.

A small shiver ran through her as she thought of the evening she had spent with her parents and her siblings. The farewell supper at the Savoy Hotel had started out well enough, but had almost disintegrated into a huge quarrel. Knowing she was the only one who could prevent this from happening, she jumped up and threatened to leave immediately. Knowing that she always meant what she said, Charlie had backed off and their mother had instantly shut up.

After that their father had managed to quell the imminent storm, and had reintroduced a measure of peace around them. But, for Alicia, the dinner before their parents' departure for

Zurich had been a disaster, ruined by her mother's bitterness about Cavendon.

Peering at her face once more, Alicia reached for a face cloth, ran ice-cold water on it, then pressed it against her cheeks. She did this several times, patted herself dry and slapped on layers of Pond's cream.

She was not particularly vain about her looks, but she knew she must take care of them, since she was an actress who worked in films. The camera could perform magic but it also highlighted flaws. In two weeks she was starting a new film and must look her best, be in good form.

Once she was back in bed, she pulled the covers over her, determined to get a few hours of sleep. She was having lunch with Charlie later and knew she must be rested and alert before meeting him.

Alicia did not blame her brother for last night's debacle. Rather, it was her mother's fault. Everyone had been shocked to hear Daphne's critical comments about Cecily, including their father. Of course Charlie, as usual, had been unable to hold back, had spontaneously blurted out a heated defence of Cecily before she could stop him. As always, this verbal fight-back was like a red rag to a bull as far as her mother was concerned. He had been doing it since childhood.

Though it was justified, Alicia now thought. Charlie was correct to defend a woman who had saved their family from catastrophe more than once. Their mother had been wrong, the attack misguided. Why on earth had Daphne spoken like that?

Although she had not said anything to a single soul, Alicia was worried her mother was ill. She had noticed certain little things lately. A tremor in her hands at times, a hesitation when trying to remember something, an irritability Alicia had never seen displayed before.

Did her father know the truth? Was he keeping something from them? Maybe. Hugo would never reveal a thing to his children about his wife. He loved them, she knew that, but his main priority in his life was his beautiful Daphne. He had always been her knight in shining armour. That was the way it had begun – love at first sight for him – and ever since he had been mesmerized by her beauty and charm, devoted and supportive.

It suddenly struck Alicia that she ought to confide in Charlie, pass on her worries about their mother. She knew she must also exonerate him for speaking out; she needed to reassure him he had been correct. At the back of her mind, she was positive her brother was still harbouring that anger from last night.

At thirty-five, Alicia was four years older than Charlie, and had been his protector since childhood, forever looking out for him. They were joined at the hip, more like twins than their siblings, Andrew and Thomas, who *were* twins.

The shrill of the phone cut into her thoughts, and she reached for it. 'Hello?'

'It's me,' a gruff male voice growled at the other end.

'Brin? Is that you?' she exclaimed.

'Who else would ring you at this ungodly hour?'

'What's wrong? You sound strange.'

'I've been up all night. I'm about to collapse, drop dead perhaps. I'm coming over. Okay?'

'You sound bad. I'll come and get you. Where are you?' she cried, her alarm spiralling.

'Just left Albany, Jake Stafford's place. I'm in Piccadilly, in a phone box.'

'That I realize—'

'Say you'll let me in . . . Do you want me to be arrested for loitering with intent?'

'Get into a taxi at once. Oh, do you have money?'

'Sure.'

'I'll be waiting.'

'I bloody well hope so.'

The phone went dead. She stared at it for a long moment, then put it back in the cradle. In the year they had been involved in an intense and passionate love affair, nothing like this had ever happened before. He did like to drink, that was true, but he could hold his liquor, was always in control. Now he sounded out of control, weird. She couldn't help wondering if he was still drunk?

Alicia leapt out of bed, went to the kitchen, and put on a pot of coffee. She then hurried into her bedroom, pulled on a silk dressing gown, continued into the bathroom, removed the cream, washed her face, cleaned her teeth and brushed her hair. Ready for anything, she muttered.

Returning to the kitchen, Alicia set a tray, but was interrupted by the doorbell. Bracing herself, she went to let him in, not quite knowing what to expect.

She called him Brin, an invention based on a favourite toy from her childhood. His real name was Bryan MacKenzie Mellor, born thirty-one years ago, in Edinburgh of a Scottish mother and an English father. A fellow actor, he was tall, handsome, dashing, and considered to be the second best-looking man on the West End stage. The first was her uncle, James Brentwood, still thought of as the greatest matinee idol of all time.

Brin coveted his Savile Row clothes, was proud of his stylish appearance and looks, and did not usually have a hair out of place.

Not this morning, she thought, shocked by what she saw standing before her. He looked like a tramp who lived permanently on the streets; someone who had just risen up from the gutter.

His navy blue pinstriped suit, a piece of perfect Savile Row engineering, was crumpled and his jacket was stained. A blue silk tie dangled out of a side pocket; his white shirt had dark bloodstains on the front and the collar was torn. Then she noticed the cut above his right eye and bruises on one cheek, just visible under his growth of stubble. He lolled against the door-jamb and it seemed as if he was about to slide down onto the floor. He almost did.

Reaching out with both hands, she grabbed his arms and pulled him inside the flat. He tripped and almost fell, but managed to somehow stay upright. Then he staggered towards the bedroom, muttering, 'Bathroom.'

Alicia followed him, stood waiting for him. Once he came into the bedroom, she took hold of his arm and said firmly, 'Come on, darling, let's get you comfortable.'

He didn't protest as she led him into the living room, just allowed himself to be propelled over to the sofa. He flopped down, a look of relief crossing his face as he sank into the soft cushions.

'Do you want a glass of water? Coffee might be better.'

'Whisky.'

'No way. You smell like a brewery.'

'Hair of the dog,' he muttered, and tried to smile, but winced, and a small shiver ran through him.

'Have you been in a fight, Brin?' she asked, leaning forward, peering at the cut above his eyebrow and the puffiness on one side of his face, her puzzlement apparent.

He shook his head, then closed his eyes, a deep sigh running through him.

Alicia went to the kitchen and prepared the coffee. She then took a fresh loaf of bread out of the bread-bin. After cutting a thick slice, she spread on butter, then peeled a banana and cut this into rounds, laying them on top of the bread. Taking the tray into the living room, she put it on a low table, bent over Bryan and shook him lightly.

'Drink this coffee. It'll help a lot, and so will the slice of bread.'

With a bit of an effort he roused himself, and sat up straighter, took several long swallows of the coffee. 'I'm hungry,' he said, 'I don't remember having dinner.' As he spoke, he reached for the slice of bread.

'What happened to you last night?' she asked, sitting down in a chair.

'Nothing. Lads' night out – a pub crawl. Too many pubs, I suppose.' He then ate the remainder of the bread.

She asked, 'How did you end up at Jake Stafford's?'

'Tony Flint and I took him there. He was more the worse for wear than we were. Very drunk. We ended up sleeping on the sofas in his posh drawing room, too tired to drag ourselves home.'

She nodded. 'Are they both all right?'

'Dead to the world when I left, but alive.' A faint smile formed on his mouth, and there was a sudden amused look in his deep green eyes, which, she noticed, were also bloodshot.

'Sorry . . . to come here like this, Alsi. But then where else could I go?'

She went over to the sofa and sat down next to him. 'You did exactly the right thing. I'm not angry, just worried about you.'

'I'm okay, the coffee helped and the bread.' He put an arm around her shoulders, drew her closer.

Instantly she pulled away, grimacing. 'You stink, Brin. Of stale beer, whisky, smoke and sweat. It's into the shower for you.'

She jumped up and took hold of his arm firmly. Once again he didn't resist, just let her manoeuvre him into the bedroom, where she helped him out of his clothes.

When he was finally standing under the shower, she sighed with relief. She had come to realize he wasn't drunk, just hungover. That in itself was reassuring, but it was out of character for him to be in this kind of dishevelled state. He was so finicky about his appearance and proud of his sartorial elegance. Once the water stopped running, she picked up a large towel and handed it to him as he stepped out of the bath.

'Thanks,' he murmured, 'I do feel better.'

She nodded and went into the bedroom, glancing at the clock on the bedside table. It was almost eight. No point in her going back to bed now. Last night she had promised to go over to Charlie's around eleven o'clock today to read some chapters of his new book, and she wasn't going to disappoint him.

When she realized Brin was standing behind her, she turned and looked up at him. Alicia was tall at five feet ten, but he was six feet one, broad of chest, a big man, but without an ounce of fat on him. The sunlight now coming in through the window gave a hint of radiance to his blond-reddish hair, and as he drew her towards him his eyes were full of tenderness. She realized the cut over his eyebrow was nothing serious.

'Let's go to bed,' he said softly against her hair.

'I can't,' she murmured. 'I promised Charlie I'd help him with a couple of chapters this morning.'

Standing on her tiptoes, she kissed Brin's cheek. 'But *you* ought to get some sleep. Right over there.' She waved a hand at the bed. 'You did say you were spending the weekend with me.'

He grinned. 'You owe me for last night . . . you skipped out on me, to see your parents for dinner instead of eating with me.'

'A big mistake.'

His eyes narrowed. He glanced at her swiftly. 'Problems? Not with Charlie, I hope.'

'How well you know us. But it wasn't Charlie's fault.' She took hold of Brin's hand, led him to the bed. 'Get in, get some sleep, and I'll be back as soon as I can.'

# Four

Cecily Swann Ingham knew that she was facing the greatest crisis of her life.

She was at her wits' end. For days she had turned over in her mind a thousand thoughts about the immense problems facing her. Cavendon was at its lowest ebb ever, truly on the brink of disaster. She kept thinking that even the lightest breath of wind would blow the house off the edge of the precipice where it teetered dangerously. Gone in a puff. It was that easy. She shivered involuntarily.

Her beloved business, the one constant in her life, her mainstay, was facing financial trouble, and because of that she could not help Miles pay the government taxes and so help save Cavendon. She had managed to do so many times in the past; she could not help him any more. Not now. *Sadly.*

Every time she had been about to confide in him, tell him the bitter truth, she had lost her nerve. Instead she had simply promised him that she would now do her full and proper duty as the 7th Countess of Mowbray.

She would remain at Cavendon Hall indefinitely; she would not go to London to run her company. She would do that long distance. She would take on the duties her sister-in-law had shouldered. Daphne was gone. Cavendon was now in her keeping.

If Miles had expected her to fight him about this, or quibble, or endeavour to make some sort of compromise, he would soon discover that her acquiescence was genuine, and she would keep her word.

Cecily had agreed to do what he wanted because she was realistic enough to know she had no choice in the matter. This was the family tradition in most stately homes. The Countess ruled. She would do the menus for the meals, and supervise the running of the house. She would turn up for all the activities in Little Skell. She would open the garden fêtes in all three villages, give prizes at the village schools, and take part in Women's Institute activities.

Once, long ago, Emma Harte had warned her not to sacrifice her marriage on the altar of ambition. 'Husband first, business second,' Emma had instructed. 'And just be glad you have that option. Some women have had to discover, the hard way, that a cash register doesn't keep your cold bottom warm at night.' Cecily half smiled to herself as she walked through the park, remembering those wise words.

It was now Wednesday morning and early, not quite seven o'clock. Cecily had crept out of the house, needing to walk, to be in the fresh air, to clear her head. And to think. Miles still did not know of her dilemma, was unaware that she was on a rack, crippled with despair. If nothing else, at least she knew how to push a bright smile onto her face, and look as if everything was all right and under her control.

Glancing around, she couldn't help thinking how beautiful Cavendon Park looked this morning. The huge spreading trees, centuries old, were full and luxuriant under a sky of palest blue, filled with scudding white clouds. There was no sun this morning, but no sign of rain either, and the northern light was crystal clear.

She grimaced to herself as she walked on, thinking how little the weather mattered to her when she had such immense issues to deal with.

The problem was, she had no solution for anything, and that was so unlike her. For the first time in years her head was totally empty, without inspiration or a game plan.

*I've completely run out of steam.* This terrible thought brought her to a sudden stop. What's happening to me? It was then she saw the door to the rose garden; pushing it open, she went down the steps, and headed for her preferred garden seat. Sitting down gratefully, she closed her eyes.

The peacefulness enveloped her, the fragrant scent of the late-blooming roses a balm for her weariness. How could it have come to this, she wondered? And knew at once the answer. *The war.* The war had not only killed off their men, ruined their cities, left their country broke, and the British Empire in disarray, it had destroyed her couture business and even her ready-made line. Clothing had just come off rationing but there was no way back to the pre-war days. Only her accessories were selling, and the White Rose perfume.

Many other businesses, as well as her own, had been affected. Money was short, very tight. People weren't buying. Yes, the war they had won had left its imprint in more ways than one. The country was ruined.

The loud fluttering sound of many birds rising up into the air caused her to stand. She glanced around. But no one was there, nothing had disturbed them. They had just decided to leave the trees in the park. *She wanted to leave. She couldn't.*

Scattered, as they flapped their wings and flew up, they became, within seconds, a true formation, totally aligned, as if directed by a hidden hand. They formed a huge V and remained in position like a squadron, flying towards the grouse moor, balanced, absolutely perfect, every bird in place.

Amazement filled her face. How do they know how to do that, she wondered? Well, it's inside them perhaps, in their genes. They were born knowing how to form these squadrons and when to fly to warmer climes. How extraordinary nature was.

*Born knowing.*

Her son David, now twenty, had been born knowing he was the heir, would one day become the 8th Earl of Mowbray. Her son, Miles's son: part Ingham, part Swann. The two families, united in her children, for the first time carrying that joint bloodline forward under the name of Ingham.

She could not fail him. She must find a way to solve the problems facing her. She had to win. For David, for her son. The future.

With this thought came an unexpected new vision. Her eyes were suddenly wide open and clear. Everything around her stood out in the brightest of colours. How lovely the mixture of varied pink roses was against the ancient red-brick walls; as she went out of the rose garden and into the park, she glanced up at Cavendon Hall standing high on the hill. It looked pure white, appeared to shimmer in the brilliant morning light. The trees were a mixture of deep greens, and the lawns dropping away from the long terrace looked like rolls of emerald velvet spreading out towards her. To her left the white swans floated on the blue lake.

*Technicolour*, she thought. Everything is so vivid this morning. She blinked, aware that she was seeing everything in a different way. It was as if a veil had been lifted from her eyes.

In a month, when August came, the moors ahead of her, a dull brown now, would be covered in heather, flowing like a purple sea along the horizon. And on the Glorious Twelfth, as it was called, the grouse season would begin. There is so much to save, and I must do that, she told herself.

Automatically, she began walking down the path which led to the small wood and the Romany wagons.

'Don't cry, liddle Ceci,' the gypsy woman said as Cecily hove into view. She was sitting on the steps of her wagon.

'I'm not crying,' Cecily answered as she walked into the clearing near the wood where Genevra's wagon was parked.

'In yer heart yer crying,' Genevra told her. 'But there's no rhyme or reason – no need for yer tears. Swann rules, yer knows that, I've allus told yer.'

Cecily nodded and sat down in the chair which Genevra usually had waiting for her. 'You have told me. And I've always believed you, but we're not ruling too well at the moment.'

'Big mess, aye, I knows, my lass. But yer gifted, liddle Ceci, yer've got many talents. And like no person I knows of, anyway.'

Cecily remained silent for a moment, pondering on Genevra's words. The gypsy was fifty now, the same age as Miles, but had retained her exotic looks and a certain youthfulness in her appearance.

The Romany said, 'Five ways ter skin a cat, yer knows.'

'I don't even know *one* way.' Cecily shook her head. 'My mind is blank.'

'No, it's not, Countess Cecily. Yer blinded by worry. *Swann rules*. I have the sight. Remember. *Swann wins*.'

'I don't know what to do . . .' Cecily's voice trailed off; she felt quite helpless at this precise moment.

Genevra sat very still, staring at Cecily before speaking, saying in a firm voice, 'Go to Swanns. Yer need yer Swanns.' An amused smile flickered on Genevra's face, when she added, 'More Swanns than Inghams these days. Go see Eric . . . he'll help yer, liddle Ceci.'

Genevra is right, there are more Swanns than Inghams at Cavendon at the moment, Cecily thought as she walked slowly back to the house.

Miles was the only born Ingham in residence with his sisters gone: Lady Daphne to Zurich, Lady Dulcie to Los Angeles, and Lady Diedre to France. Aunt Charlotte and she were Inghams by marriage, and her four children were half Ingham, half Swann.

Cecily had great belief in Genevra, knew she had the sight. Her predictions had usually been correct over the years. So she *would* go to Eric Swann, her father's first cousin. Now head butler at Cavendon, he had worked for them all his life. His sister Laura had, too, and it had been Laura who had died with DeLacy at the South Street house when it was hit by a flying bomb in the war.

But it was Percy Swann she ran into a few seconds later, as she came up the dirt path leading to the house.

'Good morning, Your Ladyship,' Percy said. Like all the other Swanns, he always addressed her formally. Head gamekeeper at Cavendon, he was her father's younger brother.

'Morning, Percy,' she said, smiling at him. He was one of her favourites, and a mine of information about the estate. 'How's the grouse moor doing?'

Beaming at her, Percy exclaimed, 'Never been better, thriving. We've kept it in good shape all through the winter, coaxed it along, treated it well, coddled it really. Birds'll be good in August.'

'That's wonderful news,' Cecily said. 'Congratulations. I know how valuable the grouse moor is to the estate, and I'm glad you and Joe are in charge. I hear we have some Guns coming for the Glorious Twelfth.'

'That's correct, m'lady.' Percy took a step closer, and said in a low voice, 'This is just a tip, to use if you can. Tell His Lordship that many other stately homes with grouse moors are making money out of them. Inviting people to shoot, but charging them.'

Cecily gaped at him. 'Charging them! Who on earth are *they*?'

'Rich Americans,' Percy answered. 'They stay as guests – you know, bed and board. Business is growing. We should do it.'

Flabbergasted, Cecily nodded, then exclaimed, 'Now I remember something, Percy. I've heard about this before, from Mrs Harte. She told me some American tycoons she knows often came to shoot in England in the season. Thanks for the tip. I'll speak to Miles, have no fear.'

He hoisted his gun onto his shoulder, and winked. 'Good lass,' he murmured in a voice so low she hardly heard him. She smiled to herself as she went up the terrace steps to the house.

* * *

Five pairs of eyes stared at her as she walked into the morning room, and four voices cried in unison, 'Good morning, Mummy!'

Miles stood up and went to kiss her, his eyes sparkling as he brushed his mouth against her cheek.

'Good morning,' Cecily said to her children and, turning to Miles, she whispered, 'I love you. And good morning.'

'Likewise,' was his only comment, but he held her arm tightly and led her to her chair.

Once they were seated, Miles said, 'I went looking for you in the annexe, darling. Where have you been?'

'I went for a walk. I needed the fresh air.'

Gwen said, 'I'm sorry I started to eat before you came, Mummy, but I was hungry.'

Laughter bubbled up in Cecily as she looked across at her youngest child, her wartime baby, she called her, who was now eight years old. 'Well, you know me, I'm always late somehow. And it doesn't matter that you didn't wait, Gwen.'

The others laughed with Gwen, and Venetia said, 'Shall I pour you a cup of tea? And do you want any breakfast?'

'The tea would be lovely, thank you.' Turning to David, who so resembled her, she said, 'You're looking very smart this morning. Are you going somewhere perhaps?'

'With Father. He has to see his solicitor in Harrogate, and he invited me to go with him.'

Cecily nodded, and looked down the table at Miles, raising a brow.

'Just for company, nothing special,' Miles explained, seeing the worried look in her eyes. 'David's going to drive us.'

Before Venetia could pour the tea for her mother, Eric arrived and took over. As he put the cup and saucer in front of her, she thanked him and then asked in a low voice, 'What time could we have a short meeting this morning, Eric?'

'Whenever you wish, Your Ladyship,' the butler answered. 'Around eleven? Is that all right?'

'It's perfect. I'll come to your office.'

'Can I serve you breakfast, m'lady?'

'Nothing to eat, but thank you.'

Eric retreated to the small butler's pantry behind the morning room, and there was a silence as everyone ate their breakfast.

It was Walter who spoke first, when he said in a rush of words, 'I took a message for you, Mummy, from Aunt Dottie in London. She said she was returning your call, and she would be at the shop all day.' Walter grimaced and added, 'I'm sorry I didn't tell you immediately when you arrived.'

'That's not a problem, Walter,' Cecily said warmly, eyeing her second son. At eighteen, he was tall for his age, and good looking, all Ingham in his looks, with their blue eyes and blond hair. He was athletic, loved sports, and seemed totally unaware of the extraordinary effect he had on girls. 'I'm hoping Aunt Dottie and Greta are confirming their travel plans for their visit. I must ring her back after breakfast.'

His sixteen-year-old sister, Venetia, who teased him unmercifully, now said, 'But Mummy, it's rather nice to be here, just the six of us.'

'Seven!' Walter exclaimed. 'You're forgetting Aunt Charlotte.'

'Seven, then, but I'm glad it's just us,' Venetia murmured, looking at her father, whom she adored. 'Don't you think so, Daddy?'

Miles swallowed the sudden laughter bubbling inside, and nodded, 'It's a change,' he answered noncommittally.

Before Cecily could make a comment, Gwen said, 'I agree with you, Venetia. Now that the cousins have left, I only have you to boss me around.'

'I never boss you,' Venetia protested, her voice rising indignantly.

'Yes, you do,' Walter shot back, smiling at Gwen, as usual in cahoots with her. 'You think you're the bee's knees.'

Gwen said, 'The American cousins are *very* bossy.'

'They're not American,' Venetia corrected her sharply. 'They just live there part of the year.'

'They're still bossy!' Gwen exclaimed. 'Like you.'

'Don't be a big baby,' Venetia began, and stopped abruptly when she saw the look on her father's face.

Miles said, 'Enough of this. We're going to be here alone together all summer, and we should enjoy ourselves at the moments when we have visitors. No more squabbling. Or I'll take your mother on a holiday, and leave you all to fend for yourselves.'

Cecily smiled to herself, sneaking a look at Gwen, who had flushed bright red. Her youngest child might look like her, with her features, her russet-brown hair, but she reminded Cecily of Dulcie when she had been Gwen's age. Spirited, independent and able to defend herself. Cecily had no worries about Gwen, or who she would become when she grew up. Most decidedly her own woman. A warrior woman like her aunt.

Later that morning, Cecily went down to Hanson's old office, now occupied by Eric Swann. Her face was thoughtful as she tapped on the door, opened it and looked inside. 'Can I come in?'

'Of course,' Eric exclaimed, jumping up, going forward to greet her.

'This room always reminds me of Hanson,' Cecily said as she sat down in the chair Eric had pulled out for her.

'I know what you mean,' Eric replied, sitting down at his desk, facing Cecily. 'I haven't touched a thing. When I was installed here, I felt this place was sacrosanct.'

'I know we had a frank talk and went over all the routines on Monday, after Lady Daphne . . . left for Zurich,' Cecily began, 'but I have a couple of questions, Eric.'

'I'll answer them as best I can, m'lady.'

'I know that the public visit all the main reception rooms in the East and North Wings, and the Long Gallery where all the paintings are on display. And a couple of dining rooms in those wings. But obviously they don't go upstairs to the bedrooms. Or do they?'

Eric shook his head. 'No, they don't. Just the rooms you mentioned.'

'I think we should close up the North and East Wings, only on the upper floors, of course. Why keep them open to be dusted and cleaned all the time? Why not cover the furniture in sheets? We don't use the rooms much, if at all these days. Let's close them off.'

'I've often thought the same thing,' Eric answered. 'It would certainly take a burden off the maids, and make them available to do other things. More help for Peggy too.'

'Hanson used to keep a log of the wine cellar and our stock. I'm sure you've kept it up to date,' Cecily said.

'I have indeed. It's essential to know what we have.'

'It's rather a lot, isn't it?'

'Enormous, Your Ladyship, and it worries me sometimes.'

'Why?'

'I'm afraid that some of the wine might turn. Go off. The Fourth, Fifth and Sixth Earls purchased a great deal of vintage wines over the years. Quantities. Now not enough wine is drunk here, even when the entire family is in residence.'

'I know that. I was thinking of bringing a wine expert up from London, to do an inventory. And perhaps we could auction off some of the vintage wines.'

Eric gaped at her, a startled expression flashing across his face. 'Do you think His Lordship would agree?' he asked, his voice going up an octave.

'I'm not sure. But an expert opinion is worth listening to, and I'm sure His Lordship would take advice, especially if an expert thought the wine might turn. That would be such a waste. I think it's worth a try.'

'I agree about getting an opinion, but I still think His Lordship might balk at an auction,' Eric persisted.

'Perhaps.' She gave her second cousin a long, thoughtful look, and said in a very low voice, 'When I talk to Miles in a certain way, he always listens, Eric, and we could use the money. We're strapped for cash.'

'I know that, Your Ladyship. Which brings me to something

else. There's a large wooden box in the attic, which I happened to look in yesterday, when I was installing the new trunk for the Swann record books. There are some paintings in the box. By Travers Merton . . .' Eric paused, knowing the sensitivity involved, and finished quietly, 'I think they belonged to Lady DeLacy.'

'He did give her some paintings,' Cecily began, and stopped, staring at Eric. Their eyes locked and they exchanged knowing looks, both of them remembering the night Travers had died. Together they had gone to Travers's studio to rescue DeLacy, to take her away from that terrible scene.

It took Cecily a moment to settle her flaring memories, and she noticed that Eric was struggling for composure himself. It had been such a bad night. Poor DeLacy's life had not always been a happy one.

Cecily said, 'Those paintings are very valuable, but I'm not sure who they belong to in the family. I will have to seek out DeLacy's will. I know where it is.'

'When I saw them yesterday I thought they had come from Lady DeLacy's flat in London. They seemed familiar,' Eric confided.

'She probably left them to Miles. Or to the Cavendon Restoration Fund,' Cecily murmured, thinking out loud. 'How strange to think she might come to our help after her death – but lovely, in a way.'

# Five

The four women sat together in the gazebo in Cavendon Park. It was a warm morning, but the position of the gazebo near a shady old oak tree and its open walls made it a cool and pleasant spot for their meeting.

It was Friday, the first day of July, and Cecily Swann Ingham had named it D-Day in her mind. She was going to set about finding a way forward for her troubled business and she knew she had a hard fight on her hands. Nonetheless, she understood she had to win. She had no other choice. Failure would be a catastrophe in many different ways.

As she glanced at the three women she smiled inwardly. They were of various ages, well-dressed women, whom some might dismiss as being normal, ordinary, and probably not particularly interesting. She knew differently.

Each one of them, like her, was full of ideas and ambitions. They had nerves of steel and an iron will. They were her mainstay. With them at her side she knew she couldn't lose. They made the best team. A winning team.

Her eyes flicked to Aunt Charlotte, born a Swann, an Ingham

by marriage. Her father's aunt, Charlotte had lent Cecily the money to start up by herself all those years ago.

Aunt Dottie, also a Swann, was now sixty-six, but like Charlotte she looked much younger and was in great health. Married to a Scotland Yard detective, she'd been Cecily's advisor and helper since the very first day they had opened their little shop.

Then there was Greta Chalmers, her personal assistant, with whom she had bonded the first day they had met, when Greta had been a young widow. Greta, now forty-two, had worked by her side for many years and they had never been out of step. They were always on the same wavelength, had the same goals, and similar attitudes about life. Taking a deep breath, Cecily beamed her brightest smile, and then glanced at Dottie and Greta. 'Thanks for coming up last night, and for listening to me gabbing on ad infinitum.' She turned to the Dowager Countess sitting next to her, and added, 'And I'm glad you insisted on being here, Aunt Charlotte. After all, without you, there might not have been a business called Cecily Swann Couture.'

'Oh yes, there would!' Charlotte shot back encouragingly. 'You would have eventually done it on your own, Ceci dear. I just helped to make it all happen a little bit quicker.'

'I'm jumping right into the deep end,' Cecily announced. 'We all know Cecily Swann Couture is in real trouble, and could go down at any moment. I have bad debts, but I don't want to declare bankruptcy. I want to make a lot of good moves very quickly, and they will have to be drastic if I'm going to pull out of this mess.'

'We're here to help you,' Aunt Dottie assured her. 'And as you suggested last night, we must speak the truth to you, no holds barred. I have certain ideas, and so does Greta, and what we do *must* be drastic. There's no other way.'

'The first thing you have to do is get rid of the two factories in Leeds,' Greta said, leaning forward slightly, her eyes focused on Cecily. 'One is empty, and the other we don't need. Because the ready-to-wear line is not selling.'

'I agree,' Cecily instantly replied. 'I'm going to speak to Emma Harte on Monday. She will be at Pennistone Royal. I told her I needed her to help me find a buyer for the Leeds factories.'

'Putting two linked factories on the market together is essential, in my opinion,' Aunt Dottie volunteered. 'Ever since the end of the war, when we stopped making military uniforms for the troops, the big factory has been a financial burden. Renting it out from time to time hasn't filled our coffers, and it has to go. Without ready-mades we don't need the other.'

Cecily nodded her agreement, and looking over at Greta she asked, 'Why do you think the ready-to-wear line doesn't sell any more?'

'At first I was as baffled as you,' Greta replied. 'When I spoke to my sister about it, Elise said she thought it was *staid*. The clothes were well made, but a bit out of date, in her opinion. They worked in the Thirties, and even the war years, with all the problems of rationing, but let's face it, *1950* is only six months away. We have a different world now, and a different market. Women's lives have changed.'

Aunt Charlotte, who had been listening attentively, now interjected, 'And I think you must adjust the name of the couture clothes, Cecily. The line should be called Cecily Swann, or perhaps better still simply "Swann". Like Chanel in France. Or Hartnell here in England. He's dropped Norman. There's also Hardy Amies, another competitor of yours, who is mostly using only his last name.'

When there was silence, Aunt Charlotte asked, 'Well, what's the verdict?' She glanced at her companions, frowning.

'Yes!' Cecily exclaimed. 'The word *couture* puts people off, I think, because it spells MONEY in capital letters. It will be couture, of course, but we don't have to announce it. What do you think, Greta? Aunt Dottie?'

'I'm all for it,' Greta answered.

'As am I,' Aunt Dottie concurred.

'So we sell the two factories, because they're not needed, since we are dropping the ready-to-wear line. That's the first step. Change our name to Swann. I prefer it to Cecily Swann. And then I concentrate on the couture.' Cecily's eyes swept over them. 'What else should we do?'

'Lower our overheads. *Dramatically.*' Dottie stared hard at Cecily, and went on in a brisk voice. 'Close the smaller shop. Keep the original one, of course. It's brand recognition, and it's become . . . well, sort of an institution. And we have to get rid of the offices. Find a smaller space, and let some of the staff go.'

Cecily took a piece of paper out of her pocket, and glanced at it, then grimaced. 'Getting rid of the offices and reducing the number of staff is at the top of my list. It seems we're thinking along the same lines.'

'Just as we should be,' Greta said. 'After all, we've been working together for years now, usually very successfully. But, like so many other businesses, we got into trouble after the end of the war. The public was not ready to splurge on clothes. And speaking of that, Cecily, I think after we leave on Sunday, you should start to design a new couture line. Since you now have to live up here most of the time, it's an ideal place to be inspired, don't you think?'

Cecily stared at her. 'There's a hint there. Isn't that so? Do you and Elise think the couture line is *staid* also?'

'As a matter of fact, yes,' Greta responded in a steady voice. She did not want to sound critical. 'Your clothes are fabulous in their cut and line, but there's a new mood now. People want frills, and flounces, and pastel colours, florals, and chiffon fabrics. Listen, I don't mean you should copy anybody, but you need to create a line that has the same appeal of the Christian Dior clothes that came out in 1947. The New Look.'

'I know his clothes, and I love them,' Cecily said, her voice suddenly growing enthusiastic. 'And I will get inspiration here, from Harry's fantastic gardens. If I start working next week, I can probably have a collection ready for next spring—'

'No!' Aunt Dottie exclaimed sharply, cutting in. 'Design a collection for *next autumn*. We need to get the business in order first, which Greta and I can do, with your advice and help. Remember, we may have to hire a few more women who are good at making couture, and there will be fabrics to hunt down, and all the usual things you'll need. Don't rush this, Cecily.'

'Dottie is correct,' Aunt Charlotte remarked. 'Remember that old saying, "Make haste, make waste." Let's not do that. Put everything you've got, all that brilliance and talent, and take as much time as you need to create a totally unique, fresh collection. One that is spectacular. And don't forget, the Festival of Britain is currently being planned. Next year may well be a turning point for the country. *And for us*. Now let us discuss the debts. A great worry indeed.'

Cecily sat up straighter in her chair, and looked carefully at the other three women. After a moment, she said, 'I need at least fifteen thousand pounds to be free and clear of everything the business owes, and be ready to start afresh. I will also need money for that. There are such things as rent for the shop, the office, wages for the staff. We need money to buy fabrics, and all the items needed to make the clothes. Wages for the dressmakers making everything by hand. That is a necessity if they are to be sold as couture.'

Cecily shook her head, her face suddenly turning gloomy. 'The war has been over for four years, and in that time we have been rapidly losing money, customers and clients.' After taking a deep breath, she finished, 'Because of this failure on my part, I am unable to give Miles the money he needs for the government taxes on the estate. But he doesn't know that yet. I'm sorry to say I haven't had the heart to tell him the bad news.'

There was a silence. No one spoke. Each woman settled back in her chair, obviously thinking of the financial problems facing Cecily – and indirectly them – in regard to the business.

It was Greta who broke the silence, and spoke out, 'If you would consider this, Cecily, I would like to become a partner with you, you see—'

'Goodness me, no!' Cecily cried, interrupting Greta. 'I won't let you do that. What if you lose your money, I'd never forgive myself. Elise and Kurt are dependent on you, I know that.'

'Please, Cecily, just listen for a moment. When my father died, he left his money to Elise and Kurt. You see, he knew I would inherit from my grandmother. My mother was an only child, and after her death when I was young, I became my grandmother's only heir. As you well know, Grandma died last year, and I put her house in Hampstead on the market. It's taken a while, but I could afford to wait until I got the right price.

'Last week it finally sold. The contract is in the works right now. So, you see, I can afford to invest in Swann.' Greta cleared her throat, and added carefully, 'But only in Swann. I can't invest in Cavendon.'

'I would never let you do that,' Cecily answered softly. 'And thank you for offering to invest with me. But I will have to think hard about it, Greta. It is a responsibility, having a financial partner.'

Dottie said, 'Have you told Miles about Howard's suggestion? Regarding an auction of the wine?'

'Not yet, no.'

'When are you going to tell him? About *everything*, actually?'

'I'd planned to do that tomorrow. Saturday is his day off, and we get to spend more time alone together.'

'Auctioning the wine?' Aunt Charlotte said, sounding astonished. 'What a brilliant idea. Howard *is* rather clever, Dottie.'

'It wasn't really Howard's idea,' Aunt Dottie answered. 'He read about a wine auction, which was held by the Earl of Overshed. It was in *The Times*. Howard suggested I pass on this information to Cecily, because he knows there is an *enormous* cellar here. Hanson took him on a tour of it. In 1938, in fact, when Hanson was converting the basements into . . . dormitories, I suppose we should call them. In case the country was invaded by the Nazis.'

'I certainly think Miles should consider the idea. Do you think he will?' Aunt Charlotte looked at Cecily, a brow lifting eloquently, a quizzical expression on her face.

'I feel sure he will, but if he hesitates, I will persuade him. And you've just reminded me of something.' Cecily went on swiftly, 'I ran into Percy, earlier this week. He told me that some aristocratic families who have shoots like ours are taking paying guests during the shooting season. Mostly rich Americans, who apparently enjoy staying at stately homes and mingling with the toffs.'

Cecily had sounded so droll when she uttered those last words, the other three women burst out laughing. And she joined in.

A moment later, Eric arrived at the gazebo with lemonade and glasses on a tray. Cecily relaxed for a moment, her mind calmer. Charlie and Alicia were also arriving for the weekend, and she needed to check on lunch, but just for a moment she allowed herself to enjoy the July morning, her mind lighter than it had been for weeks.

# Six

Cecily stood at the bottom of the grand staircase, listening. In the distance she could hear footsteps, and she knew immediately who was coming along the corridor to the front hall. It was the slightly uneven step that told her it was Charlie.

Moving into the hall, she stood waiting for him; suddenly he was visible as he left the corridor and walked into the hall. He waved. She waved back. He had always been her favourite of Miles's nephews and nieces when he was a child; after he was wounded in the war and tragically had to have a leg amputated, her heart had gone out to him.

And yet she had known that he would handle his disability well, and he had. He used a walking stick for proper balance, but few people realized he had lost a leg. His limp was almost imperceptible; he stood tall, and at thirty-two was a good-looking man.

When he stopped next to her, she put her arms around him and gave him a huge hug. They were both smiling when they stepped away from each other. There had always been a special bond between them, and they had often relied on each other for many things over the years.

'I'm sorry we arrived so late last night,' Charlie apologized. 'All my fault. I was on a special story, and it just took longer, was more complex, than I'd realized.'

'No problem,' Cecily replied. 'I'm glad you and Alicia are staying until Monday, and I understand from Paloma that your books are doing well. Congratulations. And thank you for sharing them with us. Your contributions do help to pay some of the staff in the shops.'

He grinned. 'Our pleasure. And I must say, I am rather chuffed that my little history of the Inghams and the Swanns is sold out. Who'd have thought it, eh?'

'I knew the history book would work. It's a very well-told story, rather intriguing. Like a novel, in a certain sense.'

'Thank you, Aunt Ceci, and listen, I'm so sorry about Mama. Alicia and I were really upset that she blamed you for what she calls "the commercialization of Cavendon". We know she loves you, and deep down she is probably very appreciative of everything you've done over the years, to save the estate and the family. We believe she's just worn out. We do hope you can forgive her one day. You can, can't you?'

Cecily linked her arm through his, and said, 'I've already forgiven her. Daphne has put her heart and soul into this house, and she'll come back refreshed, her old self. Now, let's go to the library for a few minutes. It's a bit early for lunch.'

Within moments they were sitting together on a sofa near the fire, which burned year round because this room was always icy cold.

Cecily said, 'I understand from Eric that Bryan didn't come with you after all.'

Charlie nodded as he leaned back against the cushions, stretching out his artificial leg. 'He had to beg off. His father is sick, and he felt he had to go to Brighton to sort things out. Bryan's mother is dead, as I'm sure you know, and I don't think Bryan's younger brother is all that good about taking care of their father.'

'I understand. I like Bryan. He's an awfully nice man and such a good actor.' She laughed. 'I rather thought we might be getting yet another actor in the family, actually. Alicia and he seem like a good fit. What do you think? Is Alicia finally going to tie the knot?'

'I hope they make it permanent. He's a fine chap—'

'Hello, Aunt Ceci!' Alicia exclaimed as she floated into the room, looking lovely in a summer frock of checked lilac and purple cotton, which Cecily had given her last year.

'I'm so glad you both came up,' Cecily replied, smiling at her niece.

'About our mother,' Alicia began, and then stopped abruptly when she saw Charlie shaking his head, warning her off.

Looking at his sister, Charlie said, 'I've already apologized to Aunt Cecily, and she fully understands about Mother being exhausted, Alicia. There's no problem here.'

'There certainly isn't!' Cecily exclaimed. 'I know Daphne will come back, sooner than we think, and everything will be back to normal. Cavendon is her home, and Hugo's and yours. This is where you all belong.'

'Goodness me, am I late?' Aunt Charlotte asked from the doorway, walking in, coming to join them near the fireplace.

'I think we were a bit early,' Charlie replied, standing up to greet the Dowager Countess. He went over to Charlotte, escorted her into the room; Alicia joined him, welcoming her as well.

They all sat together talking for a few minutes, when Charlie suddenly focused on Cecily and asked quietly, 'Isn't Greta here? I thought she was coming to see you this weekend?'

'She is at Cavendon, yes, Charlie. She and Dottie are here for a meeting about changes we're planning in my business. But my mother invited them both to lunch.' Greta's half-sister, Elise, was best friends with Victoria, the young girl who had been taken in as an evacuee by Walter and Alice Swann when she was ten years old. Now almost twenty-one, Victoria was working as a photographer in London.

Poor Greta. She was going to get quite a grilling about how Victoria was doing in the big city.

A faint smile played around Cecily's mouth, then she laughed, as she added, 'As you well know, my mother is forever wanting news of her little evacuee, whom she and my father love very much. She's like a second daughter to them. Mam's missed her since she moved down to London.'

'I've no doubt Greta is getting quizzed at this very moment. I know how Mrs Alice feels,' Charlie answered. 'But she has nothing to worry about. Victoria is doing well, and because Elise works in the reporter's room at my place, I get constant updates about her friend all the time.' The mischievous grin he was well known for suddenly surfaced. 'Surely you must realize by now that both girls treat me like their big brother.'

'More like their great hero,' Cecily shot back, knowing how the two young women felt about Charlie. They were in awe of him, almost worshipful.

'You know, Aunt Ceci, the next time you want to have some of your clothes photographed, you ought to try Victoria,' Charlie said. 'I've seen some of her pictures and she's extremely talented. I know she's still young, but Paloma is very proud of Victoria's talent, which she helped to nurture. She thinks she will go far.'

'That's a very good thought. I'll keep it in mind.'

At this moment the door opened again and Eric entered the library. Looking at Cecily, he said, 'Lunch is served, Lady Mowbray. His Lordship is waiting for you in the dining room.'

It was one of those lunches where everyone was friendly, warm and chatting to each other continually. Obviously, they were happy to be with family.

Charlotte sat at the right of Miles, and was engaged in a long conversation with David, his eldest, while Miles was questioning Alicia about her new film, due to start soon.

Walter and Venetia were focused on Charlie, wanting to know what it was like to work on a newspaper, asking questions. And Gwen was taking every ounce of Cecily's attention.

'Can I help you design the clothes?' the eight-year-old was begging her mother. 'You said I was very good at sketching.'

'Yes, you are, my darling,' Cecily replied, not wanting to discourage her youngest child, who was indeed talented when it came to drawing. 'I shall be starting the new collection soon. You can help me to do my research.'

Gwen gazed up at her mother, a smile of adoration flooding her face. 'Oooh,' she sighed, 'thank you, Mummy. What will I research with you?'

'The gardens – the ones designed by Uncle Harry. That's going to be my theme for the collection of 1950.'

'A garden collection,' Gwen said.

Cecily stared at her intently, and then laughed. 'Why, of course it will be a garden collection. I shall call it Autumn Garden. You see, you've helped me already, Gwen.'

Deep within the inner recesses of her mind, Cecily knew that Miles would be angry with her when she gave him the bad news. Not because she didn't have the money to give him for the estate taxes, or because her business was in trouble. He would be angry because she hadn't confided in him earlier, shared her worries.

Miles expected her to tell him everything. He had been that way since their childhood, wanting every piece of her, every little bit, every thought, every feeling. Even when they were apart, after his unhappy marriage to Clarissa, she was aware he was still involved with her emotionally, in love with her. She knew because everyone told her he asked questions about her constantly. 'He's very possessive of you,' her brother had once told her. 'He'd control your life from a distance if that were at all possible.'

At the time she had not been impressed. In fact, she had been angry, disdainful of Miles when answering Harry. And she had made sure she never ran into Miles at Cavendon, or anywhere else for that matter. She believed he would want her as his mistress if she so much as gave him a half smile.

Now she looked down the table at him, staring at him with intensity. He noticed her fixed scrutiny as he turned away from Alicia and picked up his glass of water.

He smiled at her, love suffusing his face.

She smiled back.

Their eyes locked and for a moment neither could look away from the other.

It was always like that between them . . . They had their quarrels and disagreements, and sometimes became angry with each other, but their little spats were over in a very short time, and about nothing of great importance, in actuality.

What she had to tell him was important. She decided to take a wholly different approach, and she would do it tonight. After dinner, they usually had a little quiet time together in their upstairs sitting room before they went to bed. Her thoughts continued to turn about this matter through the latter part of the lunch, and by the time it was over she was fully prepared, everything in place in her mind. She was armed and ready to deal with him.

Once everyone had left the table, and gone off to do other things, Cecily went downstairs to the kitchen, heading for Eric's office. She found him behind his desk, and he jumped up at once, welcomed her, pulled out the chair so she could sit down.

'Thank you for the notes about the wine cellar and the stock, Eric,' Cecily began. 'I am going to mention the possibility of an auction, in passing, to Miles tonight. However, Aunt Charlotte will take it up with him later in more detail. Along with several other things.'

'Perhaps she should be the one to mention the idea of paying guests during the grouse season,' Eric suggested, throwing Cecily a quizzical look. 'I did ask Percy if he could make a few enquiries and find out which aristocratic families are inviting Guns who pay for the privilege of shooting at a stately home.'

'That was a good move, and knowing that others are doing it would perhaps influence Miles.'

Eric said, 'About the wooden box up in the main attic, m'lady. I took the liberty of opening it, and bringing down the contents. They are paintings which belonged to Lady DeLacy, from her flat in London. I took them to Lady Diedre's old room and stacked them in there.'

'Thank you very much, Eric.' She gave him a small smile, which faltered, then added, 'It was thoughtful of you not to take them to Lady DeLacy's room . . .' She broke off, blinking back unexpected tears, swallowing hard, pushing back a sudden rush of emotion.

'It struck me that having them there would have been too much for you to bear . . . a neutral room seemed the best under the circumstances,' Eric explained. He knew how close they had been, understood it might be painful.

'Some are by Travers Merton, aren't they?'

'Yes, and very beautiful.' Eric unlocked the top drawer of his desk, and took out an envelope, handing it to her across the desk. 'This is the key for the new steamer trunk you bought. Actually, there are two keys, m'lady, and you should put both of them in your private safe in your bedroom. Better they're locked up.'

'I will do that. Aunt Charlotte kept the Swann record books under lock and key all her life, and I must do the same. And thank you again for helping me to fit so many notebooks into the trunk. It was quite a task.'

'And an amazing record of the Swann family, and the Inghams, and things that happened to them over the centuries. Full of secrets, too, I've no doubt.'

If only you knew, Cecily thought, you'd never believe it. But she remained silent. After a moment, she went on, 'Now that Lady Daphne has gone to Zurich for an indefinite period, I think Ted can relax a little, concentrate on repairs more than redecorating, Eric.'

'I agree. By the way, the bedrooms not in use have all been closed. I've put dustsheets over the antiques in the North and East Wings, attics as well. But obviously the South Wing is open. Even though Lady Daphne and Mr Hugo are away, I'm sure their wing should be open. After all, their children will keep coming up for weekends.'

'Two are already here,' Cecily answered. 'And quite right, Eric, the South Wing has always been Lady Daphne's home since she married Mr Hugo, and their children grew up there. We must welcome them always.'

After discussing the menus, wines and activities for the next few days, Cecily left Eric to go about his duties. She took the back staircase up to the bedroom floor, and walked along the corridor to Diedre's bedroom, not used since Diedre had moved to Skelldale House with her husband Will Lawson and her son Robin. Cecily was due to have a cup of tea with Aunt Charlotte but had taken a quick diversion.

She hesitated for a moment before going in, and then took a deep breath and did so. Eric had arranged the paintings around the room, propped up against chairs, the desk, and a chest of drawers. Several had been placed on a sheet on top of the bed.

The one which instantly caught her eye was the portrait of DeLacy which Travers had painted years ago, commissioned by Lawrence Pierce to give to DeLacy's mother one Christmas before the war.

It leaned against the legs of a chair, and Cecily went to it immediately, picked it up and placed it on the chair.

She stepped back to view the painting, and her heart missed a beat. She caught her breath in surprise. It was so lifelike; it seemed as if DeLacy were sitting right there in front of her. The painting was magnificent. Travers had captured something unique in DeLacy, a delicate beauty, a certain fragility, and yet her bright blue eyes sparkled with life and energy.

This painting of DeLacy had hung in the former Countess's sitting room in her house in London. After her death, the Four Dees had not taken very many of their mother's possessions, since they were all estranged from her.

Now Cecily remembered how DeLacy had asked her sisters if she could have the painting of herself. It was one of the last paintings ever executed by Travers Merton, and of course, they had said she could.

Cecily felt a cold chill running through her and shivered involuntarily. Goose flesh sprang up on the back of her neck and her arms; memories of that horrendous night were suddenly at the front of her mind.

The night Travers had died in his studio, with DeLacy beside him in his bed. Not understanding at first that he *was* dead, she had called Cecily for help. Cecily, in turn, had phoned Eric. They had gone together to rescue her from the scene, recognizing from DeLacy's hysterics that something was wrong.

They had been flummoxed, not known what to do. Finally they had phoned Uncle Howard at Scotland Yard, who had come to their rescue, taken the matter into his hands, and dealt with the problem.

For a few moments, Cecily was totally mesmerized by the painting, and then she went over to the chair, picked it up and took it down the corridor to their upstairs sitting room.

Last night she had mentioned the large box of paintings in the attic to Miles. In their pain and misery after DeLacy's death in the war, Miles and Cecily had been far too beleaguered and grief-stricken to even think about her possessions, most of which had been brought from DeLacy's flat in Mayfair and stored in the attic at Cavendon. Where they had remained untouched, until now.

Once Cecily was in the sitting room, she moved a large blue

and white vase from a chest, and put DeLacy's portrait in its place. Then she took several books, and placed them in front of the painting to stop it from sliding.

There you are, my darling Lacy, she said under her breath. Now I can see your face every day for the rest of my life, my lovely.

# Seven

'I wish you had confided in me, Ceci,' Aunt Charlotte said, her voice growing more sympathetic as she added, 'You've obviously been going through an awful time with all your many worries – on every level, unfortunately.'

Leaning back in the armchair, Cecily made a *moue*. 'It's been hellish, to be honest.'

'I can just imagine. But remember what Churchill said, in reference to that. "If you are going through hell, keep going." It does work, you know.'

Laughing, Cecily nodded, remarked, 'He also had another saying which I've always loved. KBO. Which stands for "keep buggering on". And that's what I've tried to do. But I am glad we had the meeting with Dottie and Greta this morning. They are very dedicated to the business. And it's given me more incentive than ever.'

'I know that.' Getting up, Charlotte walked over to the window, looking out at the park for a few moments, lost in her thoughts.

They were in Charlotte's upstairs parlour, a small room that Cecily had always liked. It was restful, tastefully decorated in soft green velvet and silk fabrics at the windows and on the loveseat and chairs, with a dark rose carpet on the floor. She knew that many of Charlotte's favourite things were gathered together here, meaningful mementos of her life, and photographs of loved ones, mostly Inghams when they were children. There were also pictures of her and other Swanns. With no children of her own, the extended family was her family; all her nephews and nieces, both Swann and Ingham.

Turning around, Charlotte caught Cecily unawares and noted the oddest look on her face. She asked quickly, 'What is it? You seem puzzled. Or bemused? You're wearing a very strange expression.'

'Am I? Well, I was just thinking how much your life has been tied up with Cavendon. And with two of its earls . . . How you stepped in and helped to bring up Dulcie, looked after all of them really, when Felicity ran off.'

'What else could I do? I loved them, you see – the Four Dees. And I loved their father, although no one knew that at the time, except me.'

'You've been the protector and mainstay of this family, and in so many different ways. We all owe you a lot, Aunt Charlotte,' Cecily said, her voice full of sincerity.

'Nobody owes me anything, except perhaps to be courteous, and hear me out when I've something compelling or important to say.'

'That's absolutely true. Do you now need to tell *me* something?'

'Not especially, Ceci dear. It's just when I was gazing out at the park I thought how beautiful it was and so well worth saving. But Miles must do that. *Not you.*'

'He is trying, you must know that. However, he does have a huge task.' Cecily blew out air and sat up straighter. 'We have income from some investments, and from the house and garden tours, and the shops and café. But that money pays the wages of staff and helpers.'

'I realize that. Look, I want to talk to Miles about the taxes. I think I have a plan that will help him.' As she spoke, Charlotte walked across the room. Cecily couldn't help thinking how well she looked today, more like a woman in her early seventies than her eighties.

Sitting down, Charlotte explained, 'If Miles agrees, I am going to introduce him to Leslie Parrish, the managing director of my bank in Harrogate. I believe Parrish will give Miles a loan for the taxes, if I become the guarantor. I thought of it as we were listening to Greta and Dottie, when we were drinking our lemonade outside.'

'It's wonderful of you to suggest this, Aunt Charlotte. I'm not sure Miles will agree, though. You know how proud he is.'

'He can't afford to be proud at this particular moment in time! He needs help. And it isn't coming from you. Not ever again, in fact. I won't permit it. As it is, you've worked miracles for this family.'

'If Miles says he'll meet Mr Parrish, will *he* agree, do you think?' Cecily asked swiftly, a brow lifting.

'Well, yes, I believe he would. Because we've got some financial backup now, possibilities of making real money.'

'What do you mean?' Cecily sounded surprised.

'All the new ideas. The wine auction, for one thing. There is a good point I'll make to Miles. It's this. Half that stock might have turned already, because we've had it for years. So now is the time to rescue what's left. There is also the idea of tycoons from America, and anywhere else for that matter, coming to shoot and paying for it. *Let's turn privilege into profit.* That is going to be my motto from now on. And he might have to sell one or two paintings from the Long Gallery.'

'You may find it a hard task to convince him. Miles has never wanted to let any of the art go to auction,' Cecily pointed out. 'His father didn't want to do that either. You know that better than anyone else, Aunt Charlotte.'

'Yes, I do know. And the Ingham men can be very stubborn. Let me see if I can persuade Miles.

'Now, about Greta and her offering to be a partner,' she went on. 'I think you might wish to think about this seriously. It would help you, give you start-again money, and be an incentive to her, having a stake in your business, I mean. Here's a point. I don't want Dottie to feel slighted. She might want a stake too. So, if you agree to take Greta into Swann, as we're going to call it, then you must invite Dottie to be a partner as well. Give her the option . . . she might well refuse. I am not sure they would have that kind of money, but I think you should offer.'

'Yes, I see what you're getting at. But don't you think I ought to be free of debt before taking their money? If they want to give it to me, of course.'

'I do, indeed. And I would like to suggest the following. I will pay off half your debt over the next six months, on a monthly basis, which will satisfy the bank, I'm sure. But I—'

'No! I won't let you take this on! It's not fair to you, and you've done so much for me in the past,' Cecily exclaimed, her voice rising in protest.

'Here's the thing. It's money I would be leaving you in my will,' Charlotte pointed out. 'So let me finish my point. I know you still have the collection of Ingham jewellery you bought from Charles in the late 1920s, the collection you based your copies on. You do, don't you?'

'Yes. It's here in the vault. Why do you ask?'

'Put it up for auction. Get money for it, in order to pay off the other half of your debt. You don't need the collection any longer, since it's now available in your fake collection of Cavendon jewels that you sell around the world.'

Cecily began to laugh, filling up with mirth in a way she had not done in a long time. As she continued to chuckle, she wondered why she had never thought of that herself. A mind clouded by worry, she thought, which has blocked me lately.

Charlotte laughed with her, and finally Cecily sputtered, 'Only you would think of a jewellery auction, Aunt Charlotte.'

'And *you* can make it sound very enticing, exciting. *Now you can have the real thing*, that sort of selling point,' Charlotte said.

'And I know the head of Bonhams Auction House, and I will introduce you to him.'

'What an amazing number of ideas I've had thrown at me this week. If only a couple of them work, we'll be in clover,' Cecily murmured.

'Not quite,' Charlotte said. 'But I do believe you need to free up your mind, so you can start designing next year's collection.'

'That's true. And I will.'

'I'd like you to do something else for me, Ceci. I want you to give the bad news to Miles as soon as you possibly can. Because I want to take him to the bank on Monday morning.'

'I will tell him tonight or tomorrow,' Cecily promised, feeling much more confident about confiding her troubles to her husband. She dreaded to think what Daphne would make of all of this: not just letting in the public but now selling off all Cavendon's assets. But it was that, or go under.

As she looked at herself in her dressing-table mirror, checking her face and hair, a phrase was running through Cecily's mind: *Let's turn privilege into profit.* It would be her mantra from now on.

What a relief it is, she thought, not to feel so alone any more. Greta and Dottie, as usual, had been on her wavelength, and had been plotting and planning in the office annexe, attempting to streamline their ideas for finding smaller offices, and letting certain staff members go.

That was always the hard part. Cecily balked at doing it, but at the moment she had no option. They had to cut their overheads. Dottie had told her she already knew of a two-room suite near Burlington Arcade, and would try to secure it.

It would be tough going, she knew that already, but by lowering their overheads, selling the factories, changing the whole theme of the couture line, and making Greta a partner, she would be on the right track. Starting again, they would succeed. Fingers crossed, she added to herself.

Rising, she left her bedroom and went downstairs. Everyone would be assembling in the dining room for dinner at any moment.

# Eight

The happiness of the evening was still with her, wrapped around her like a soft silk shawl, and she felt better than she had in a very long time. She had a sense of peace, of quiet contentment.

As Cecily undressed and got ready for bed, she knew this feeling of joy stemmed from the presence of Charlie and Alicia at dinner, and Greta had added much to the evening's enjoyment as well. She and her assistant were as close as ever.

As he had done at lunchtime, Charlie made them laugh with his stories and comments about his life as a newspaperman; Alicia was her charming and loving self, and the two of them brought the true meaning of family to the table. Aunt Dottie was staying with Cecily's parents, Alice and Walter, in Little Skell.

Even Miles, often so dour these days, had smiled and chuckled and joined in the fun.

What was so important about the evening was the way Daphne's tirade of last week had disappeared, just gone away. No one mentioned her, and they were the happy clan again, united in all things, at ease with each other.

As Cecily slipped on her silk dressing gown, and crossed the bedroom floor, she braced herself. She had promised Aunt Charlotte she would tell Miles about her troubles tonight, and there was no way out. *She must do it.*

Their upstairs sitting room was empty when she went in, and she walked over to the chest upon which she had propped up the painting of DeLacy earlier, stood gazing at it. A moment later, Miles came out of his dressing room and joined her.

'Isn't it beautiful, darling?' he said, glancing at her after staring at the portrait of his sister for a few seconds. 'How could we have forgotten about it?'

Turning to face him, Cecily said, 'I never really forgot it, Miles. I knew very well where it was, since I put the box up there in the attic when DeLacy's possessions arrived years ago.' Her face changed, and she sighed. 'I simply couldn't bear to bring it out, not then, so soon after she had been killed. And I thought you would feel the same.'

Miles nodded. 'I did, and I understand. It was a terrible time for all of us.' He paused, took a sip of cognac. 'But why *now*? What made you finally bring it down?' As he spoke he walked over to the sofa and sat down.

Cecily gave the painting a lingering glance and joined him. 'I bought a new steamer trunk, a big one to hold the Swann record books,' she explained. 'And Eric noticed the large box which contained DeLacy's portrait and others by Travers Merton. I suddenly understood that *now* was the right time. So I told him to bring it down to the bedroom floor. Being sensitive to our feelings, Eric put them in Diedre's old room, rather than DeLacy's. I brought the portrait out earlier, and I'm glad I did.'

'So am I.' He smiled at her, and changed the subject. 'It was a nice evening. I was happy to see Charlie and Alicia still in such good form. Incidentally, I'd like to take a look at the other paintings by Travers. Why don't we do that tomorrow?'

There was a moment of silence. Taking a deep breath, Cecily said, 'I can't tomorrow, I'm afraid. You see—'

'But we always spend Saturday together,' he cut in, sounding put out.

'Yes, I know. However, I need to meet with Aunt Dottie and Greta to discuss a few more of my business plans. Greta is staying on until Monday. In fact, they both are.'

'Oh, I see. I suppose you do have a bit of planning to do, now that you will be in Yorkshire most of the time.'

'Yes, I also have a lot of problem-solving to do. Anyway, Aunt Charlotte would like to speak to you tomorrow morning, Miles. She asked me to tell you she'll be available any time it's convenient for you.'

'*Aunt Charlotte?*' He frowned. 'Is there something wrong? Do you know what it is about?'

'I do. She wants you to meet the managing director of her bank in Harrogate on Monday. To arrange a loan for you. She will be your guarantor.'

Miles stared at her nonplussed, frowning. 'A loan? Whatever for?'

'The government taxes, Miles. They'll be due soon.'

Once again he gaped at her, surprise and puzzlement still filling his face. 'But you always give me the tax money . . .' he began, and then his voice trailed off when he saw how serious her expression was.

'I don't have the money to give you, I'm afraid. I have a lot of business problems, which is why Aunt Charlotte has now stepped in.'

'I can't borrow money from a bank! The whole world will soon know the Inghams are in trouble!' he exclaimed, his voice rising.

'But everyone knows that already, Miles. All the aristocratic families have been in trouble financially since the end of the war. Because of the tax increases and lack of men on the land. It's not a secret.'

'Why didn't you confide in me?' he demanded, anger echoing in his voice. He glared at her. 'We share. Always.'

'I didn't want to worry you. I believe I can solve my business problems by selling the two factories in Leeds, finding smaller offices in London, closing one of the shops in the Burlington Arcade, and dropping the ready-made clothing line. Greta wants to buy in as a partner, and also, Aunt Charlotte will give me half the money to pay off my bank debts . . . She explained I am her main heir, and it's part of the money she would be leaving me in her will anyway.'

There was total silence in the room.

As she looked at Miles, Cecily noticed his face was as white as bleached bone and there was a look in his eyes she couldn't read. Anger? Bafflement? Bewilderment? Shock, she decided. He was in shock.

He said suddenly, 'Well, it seems the Swanns have been very busy these last few days, doesn't it?'

Startled by those words, infuriated by them, Cecily snapped back, 'More like a couple of hundred years, wouldn't you say? And where would the Inghams have been without the Swanns?'

Standing up, she walked over to the fireplace, and stood there, appreciating the warmth coming from the dying embers. 'We've looked out for the Inghams for centuries,' she announced in a cold voice.

Miles was furious with himself. He had made a silly remark, and she had taken umbrage. Of course she had. It was a rotten remark, and totally uncalled for.

Before he could apologize and say something nice to her, Cecily spoke. 'You might as well know that a few other Swanns have come up with some ideas that might help us out. Uncle Howard recently read in *The Times* that Lord Overshed auctioned off his wine cellar, or rather the contents thereof, and made money. Mind you, a lot of wine had gone off. I told Eric to check the wine logbooks started by Hanson, and which he has continued to keep. A wine auction might produce money.'

'I see,' Miles said, now determined to watch his words, not wanting to upset her further.

'And I ran into Percy the other day. We talked about the grouse moor. He told me that many aristocratic families with shoots are actually taking paying guests during the grouse season. Mostly American tycoons.'

'I don't quite know how that would work, here at Cavendon, I mean.' Miles took a long swallow of the cognac, and put the glass down on the small table.

After a moment he said quietly, 'You've given me a lot to think about, Cecily. I will consider your suggestions. And I haven't forgotten the one about charging rent.'

'And will you have a meeting with Aunt Charlotte tomorrow?' she asked, keeping her voice soft.

'Of course. I'll listen to what she has to say, but that doesn't necessarily mean I'll take a bank loan.'

He let out a long sigh, and stood up, walked over to the fireplace, kissed her on the cheek. 'Why don't you go to bed? It's been such a long day for you. I'll join you shortly, I have quite a lot to mull over, and I do need to have a quiet think alone.'

'I am a bit tired,' she admitted, and touched his arm lightly. 'Don't stay up too late, Miles. And tomorrow afternoon we can look at the other paintings in Diedre's room,' she promised, by way of a peace offering.

Cecily found she was unable to fall asleep. She was very tired, just as Miles had suggested, but her brain would not stop working.

His remarks about the Swanns had infuriated her, but within herself she realized it was just a thoughtless, throw-away line. He had not meant to hurt. He knew only too well how much the Swanns had done for the Inghams. And what she herself had contributed to the welfare of the family. She had saved them several times. Everyone knew that.

Despite his anger and shock, Cecily believed she had been correct in telling Miles everything at once. Knowing him as well as she did, she was certain he would not come to bed until he had puzzled everything out. He was no doubt drinking another brandy in the sitting room, and 'getting his ducks in a row', as he called it.

One thing she was sure of was his ingrained practicality. However distasteful something might be to him, he would, in the end, do what was best for Cavendon and its future.

After a while, she managed to ease herself into a better frame of mind, to let go of her worries, and concentrated on her youngest child. Gwen had been unhappy for quite a while now, because she wanted to have a kitten. Miles had not liked the idea of animals in the house. Now Cecily decided she was going to buy Gwen that cat. Once it was there, Miles would find it extremely difficult to take it away from Gwen, whom he adored.

Cecily smiled at this decision, and fell asleep at last, filled with loving thoughts of her wartime baby who had brought her so much happiness.

# Part Two

# Les Girls

I have spread my dreams under your feet;
Tread softly because you tread on my dreams.

W. B. Yeats, 'The Cloths of Heaven'

# Nine

Victoria Brown, the shy and somewhat wary little evacuee, whom Alice Swann had taken into her heart the moment she had first met her, had grown up to be a lovely young woman. She had arrived at Cavendon in 1939, just before her eleventh birthday, and she would celebrate her twenty-first birthday later this year.

In the ensuing years she had become strikingly pretty, with a mass of shiny brown hair shot through with golden streaks, and unusually deep green eyes. Tall, even as a child, she had a lithe, willowy figure, and a graceful energy when she moved.

Alice was not at all surprised she had turned into a unique young woman, who made heads swivel when she passed people on the street. And neither was Walter. They knew, too, how talented Victoria was as a photographer, and had permitted her to move to London to pursue her passion. Her love of taking pictures had started when Walter had given her a Kodak camera as a child. Ever since then she had never had a camera out of her hands. But over the years they had grown more intricate and expensive.

It had been Harry Swann's wife, Paloma, who had noticed Victoria's budding talent; a photographer herself, she had taught

Victoria everything she knew about the art. Victoria's forte was portraits, but she also enjoyed helping out on fashion shoots and had started to do a few of her own, which she managed to make unique and very different.

On this warm Saturday afternoon in July, Victoria walked around her small flat in Belsize Park Gardens, checking the tiny rooms. Alice had told her to make Saturday her household day when she had first come to London a year ago; it was when they had found this flat. And this she had done. She went shopping for her weekly groceries first, then returned home to clean the bedroom, bathroom, sitting room and galley kitchen. Despite its small size it was comfortable, and she liked its cosiness.

Nodding to herself, satisfied that everything was 'spick and span', as Alice always called well-cleaned rooms, she went into her bedroom. Walter had made a closet for her when she had first moved in, with a rail and curtain. It was in a small alcove, and held all her clothes – not that she owned very many, with rationing having been in place for a decade, and Alice being a great believer in make-do and mend. She slid hangers along the rail, picked out several skirts, blouses, cotton shirts and cotton frocks. These were her selections for next week; they were her work clothes.

Alice had advised her to do this every Saturday: 'being prepared', Alice called it. It was yet another rule from Alice, but then Alice had been the centre of her life since she had arrived in Little Skell village ten years ago.

Bright and very clever in a variety of ways, Victoria was aware Alice and Walter had helped to make her who she was today. It was their influence and love which had shaped her, their help that had supported her scholarship to Harrogate College.

She hardly dared think what would have become of her if she had not been sent to them as an evacuee. She might well have been dead. They had saved her life, of that she was absolutely certain.

It was to the Swanns that she always turned when she needed advice, or had a problem, and they had never failed her. And she knew they never would. Victoria was determined to make them proud of her.

By the end of the war she had so settled in with them she was scared what would happen to her when peace came. Victoria knew she was where she wanted to be, where she belonged: in Little Skell village on the edge of Cavendon Park.

But the Pied Piper Organization, in charge of the Evacuee Programme, might take her away and send her back to the frightening house in Leeds. That had truly made her shudder at the time. And she had finally found the courage to confide in Alice about her terrible childhood and her horrific mother. Alice had been upset, angry and shocked.

After the war, Alice had gone to Leeds to see the head of the agency in charge of evacuation. They informed her that Victoria's mother, Helen Brown, had died of leukaemia in 1943, and her maternal grandmother, Bessie Trent, of a heart attack that same year. Her father, William Brown, who was in the Merchant Navy and was on the Russian convoys, had gone down with his ship in 1944.

Alice had asked why this information had never been passed on to them before, but the organization had been unable to give her a proper answer. One kind woman working for Pied Piper said there had been a mix-up and directed her to the correct government department so that she and Walter could fill in the papers to adopt Victoria. This soon happened, and Victoria was adopted by them almost immediately.

They were all immensely pleased – overjoyed, in fact – and Victoria had felt secure at last. She was aware that their loving care had made her more confident over the years, and was grateful to them.

But even now in 1949, various childhood traits lingered in Victoria's personality. She was still a trifle shy, and always cautious, even a bit wary, in fact, and she certainly kept many people at arm's length. However, for the most part, she was genial and had made several friends. It was Elise Steinbrenner and Charlie Stanton who were her closest friends, though, and she spent as much of her free time with them as she could.

Victoria had known Elise and Charlie since her childhood, and it was Alice who had asked them, in a discreet way, to keep an eye on Victoria in London, and they had willingly agreed. What they had done at first out of family ties and a sense of duty had soon become a pleasure.

Elise and Charlie had grown to love and admire Vicki, as they called her, and they were both in awe of her talent. Despite her youth, her portraits of people were almost like paintings, and they seemed to capture and reveal the souls of those who posed for her.

She had photographed Charlie for the cover of one of his history books, and he was staggered by it, and recommended her to everyone. So did Greta Chalmers, Elise's sister, who was a big fan, and was determined to try to use her to give a younger feel to the autumn collection that Cecily Swann was about to design for next year.

Her chores finished, Victoria stood in front of the cheval mirror in her bedroom, checking her appearance, the way Aunt Alice had taught her. She liked the way she looked this afternoon; she was wearing a white dirndl skirt, a blue and white striped blouse and ballerinas. Neat but chic. Alice made her clothes and gave her Cecily's hand-me-downs.

Satisfied that she was properly dressed for a simple supper with Elise, Victoria picked up her black patent shoulder bag and the small overnight grip, and left her flat, going downstairs to the entrance hall of the converted four-storey Victorian house.

When she stepped outside she saw the grey car parked across the street and instantly went back into the house and closed the door swiftly. Her heart was suddenly clattering and she was filling with dismay.

She had recognized the Vauxhall at once. It belonged to Phil Dayton, who worked in the office at Photo Elite. He had asked her out several times, but she had never accepted his invitations. Despite her efforts to discourage him, he had become something of a nuisance, pestering her to go out with him. *Now this*. He was spying.

Leaning against the wall, her mind racing, Victoria understood that Phil Dayton had become a threat. Instinctively, she smelled trouble. She would have to find a way to deal with him. Right now, though, she considered her options, wondering what to do.

If she left the house, he would see her. She might manage to get a taxi quickly, but he would follow her. Perhaps she could make a dash for the Tube station nearby. He certainly couldn't do that, because he wouldn't leave his car unattended. Her last option was to go over and confront him, and imply she was going to report his behaviour to their boss, Michael Sutton.

But she wasn't too thrilled with that idea. There might be repercussions, and who knew whether she would be believed. She must be careful.

She jumped, startled by the banging of an upstairs door and the clatter of heavy feet running down the stairs at high speed.

Quite unexpectedly, her neighbour Declan O'Sullivan was calling her name, and a moment later smothering her in a big bear hug in the hallway.

Then he held her away and looked at her intently, his black eyes full of sparkle. 'You look smashing, Victoria! You should be in pictures.'

Victoria couldn't help laughing; Declan was always full of good cheer and bonhomie. 'How was your mother's birthday party?' she asked, happy to see him.

'A good time was had by all, and Mum loved every minute, being the centre of attention, and all that jazz. We partied until dawn.'

'I'm glad. And I'm also relieved you're back,' Victoria said, and meant it. She missed Declan when he was touring in rep, or off making a film. He was one of her good friends, and reliable.

'I see *you're* off now? Going to Cavendon, are you?' he asked.

'No, I'm not. I'm about to have supper with Elise tonight. Nothing special, but tomorrow I'm going to see the flat she wants to take, so I can give her my opinion. Since I'm in north London and she's in Chelsea, it's always better if I sleep over at her sister's house in Chelsea.'

'That's in Phene Street, isn't it?'

'Yes, why?'

'Because I'm going that way. I'm meeting a mate at a pub in the King's Road. So I can give you a lift. My car's parked just down the street. Come on, let's go.' As he finished speaking, he picked up her overnight bag and opened the front door for her.

It was with some relief that Victoria fell into step with Declan and clung to his arm as he led her to his Morris Minor. It was parked further down in Belsize Park Gardens.

She couldn't help hoping that Mister Phil Dayton was watching them in the mirror of his car. Then he would think she had a boyfriend and might leave her alone. No one had warned her that being a single career girl in the big city might carry this risk. But she wouldn't give it up for the world.

# Ten

Elise Steinbrenner stood on the landing between the two attics at the top of Greta's house. She had suddenly felt the urge to walk around it a little earlier, and now her heart and mind were flooded with memories, filling her with happiness, and also a sense of sadness as well.

She loved this warm and welcoming place. *Eleven years*. That was how long she had lived here in Phene Street with her older half-sister, who had received them with open arms. They had arrived on a Sunday, weary, tired and a little scared, and yet relief and joy had soon replaced these other emotions. Her father and brother and she were *safe*. At long last.

They had escaped Berlin and the terror of Nazi Germany by the skin of their teeth.

They were in England at last. It was the red, white and blue Union Jack on flagpoles that whirled in the wind in London, and not the German flag bearing the dreaded swastika, that symbol of danger and fear to her.

A sudden memory flashed: the Union Jack billowing above the front door of the British Embassy on the Wilhelmstrasse. It had spelled SAFETY to her, and she had always thought how ironic it was that a few buildings further along was the Reichstag, where Hitler and his cronies sat plotting their heinous deeds in their headquarters, envisioning their conquest of the world.

They had been lucky, she and her brother Kurt and their father. They were Jews. And Jews in Germany were being killed by the thousands in 1938. Their escape had somehow been secretly arranged by Lady Diedre Ingham, who worked at the War Office. She had a contact at the British Embassy in Berlin, who knew someone who knew someone else. And their escape had been cleverly and carefully planned; and once they had their valid travel documents they had been able to leave Berlin. Elise knew she would never forget the moment they had crossed into France, and finally arrived in Paris. It was a strange kind of shock to realize she was *free*. That her brother and her parents were *free*.

A small involuntary shiver ran through her as her mind filled with thoughts of her mother. Heddy Steinbrenner had not travelled with them to London in the end. She had remained in Paris. And now, as an adult, Elise knew the reason she had stayed, having gone back to Paris and Berlin in 1946, wanting to find out about her mother's fate.

Pushing these thoughts to one side, Elise walked into the attic that her brother Kurt had called his lair. Years ago, Greta had furnished it with a desk and chair, several comfortable armchairs, bookshelves, and a chest of drawers. He had spent a lot of time in here.

Now, staring at the corkboard above the desk, Elise smiled to herself. There had always been a small Union Jack flag and a bright red poppy for Poppy Day, in remembrance of the First World War, pinned to the board. His special keepsakes. Those spots on the board were empty. Kurt had taken his flag and his poppy with him when he had left for New York to continue his medical training to be a brain surgeon at a hospital in Manhattan – New York Presbyterian.

Kurt, independent and determined by nature, had always had his sights set on what he termed 'the new world'. He loved

London, but the other shore beckoned, luring him with its modernity.

When their father had unexpectedly died from a massive heart attack in 1947, Elise had known Kurt would start making his plans. And he did. He had been gone for almost two years already.

Turning, leaving Kurt's lair, she glanced in the other attic, which had been her brother's bedroom, and sighed to herself. At the moment Kurt was having romantic problems, but he was far away and all she could do was offer advice . . .

The ringing of the doorbell cut into her reverie, and she ran downstairs to the foyer, smoothing down her dark hair. Seconds later she was greeting Victoria and Declan on the doorstep.

'Won't you come in for a drink?' Elise asked the young actor, whom she'd met before. Her musical voice still had the hint of an accent, despite all her years in London.

Declan shook his head, smiled, then explained, 'I'm running late, but another time perhaps?' He smiled again, eyeing her appraisingly, and raised a brow.

Elise laughed. 'Of course. Vicki will give you my number.'

Declan nodded, looking pleased, placed Victoria's bag on the foyer floor and said his goodbyes.

Once they were alone, Victoria and Elise hugged, and then went upstairs together. Elise said, 'I know you like the green and white trellis bedroom, so I've put you in there, as usual.'

'I do like it, yes. Thank you. But you know I love the feel of this house. Greta's a great decorator. She would have been a huge success at it.'

'She would, but she's dedicated to Cecily and the business.' Pushing the guest-room door open, Elise went in, followed by Victoria, continuing, 'Greta told me this morning that Cecily has promoted her. She is now general manager of Cecily Swann Couture, and Dottie is now joint managing director with Cecily.'

'That's great news!' Victoria exclaimed. 'I heard from Aunt Alice that Cecily will be spending most of her time at Cavendon now . . . because Lady Daphne has gone to Zurich, and anyway Cecily *is* the Countess of Mowbray.'

'Greta's a real career woman, you know, and I suppose we are too.' Elise sat down in an armchair, as Victoria began to unpack her small bag. She looked thoughtful.

'I love my job, but sometimes I think about getting married and having a family. Don't you, Elise?'

'Gosh, yes I do. Don't forget, I'm twenty-eight. Quite the old maid. I should be having babies. But I can't bear the thought of leaving the *Daily Mail.* My job as a reporter is important to me, but sometimes I do yearn to have a baby; I feel very broody at times . . .' Elise's voice trailed off and she shook her head. Her thoughts from earlier returned, and suddenly she found herself confiding in Victoria. 'I'll never really understand how a mother can abandon her children, as mine did.'

Picking up on the sorrow in Elise's voice, Victoria turned away from the wardrobe and came and sat down in the other chair. Leaning forward, she touched Elise's hand affectionately, and there was sympathy in her voice when she spoke. 'It *is* hard to comprehend, and I must admit it baffles me, too. After your visit to Germany in 1946, I thought you seemed less troubled.' Victoria stared at her friend. 'Were you just putting on a good face?'

'To a certain extent,' Elise answered truthfully. After a moment's reflection, she continued, 'What I managed to find out gave me *her* reasons, but I realized later they did not excuse her behaviour. She was selfish.'

'You've never told me about her reasons. I don't want to pry, Elise, but I am happy to listen, if it helps you.'

'I think it might do me good to get it off my chest. I never confided in anyone other than Papa, Kurt, and Greta, because they had a right to know.' Her dark eyes brimmed with tears suddenly.

Victoria nodded, leaned back in the chair, giving Elise time to sort out her thoughts.

After a long silence, Elise said, 'My mother had a childhood friend, a boy, called Heinrich Schnell. Their families lived next door to each other in Dresden. As teenagers they became very close and apparently fell in love. But my mother was Jewish and the Schnells weren't. Actually, they were adherents of Hitler, ardent Nazis, members of the Party. And Heinrich was in the Nazi Youth movement, but he got sick and couldn't join the army. My mother's parents, Esther and Hans Mayer, moved away. To Berlin. Eventually, my mother met Papa, after his first wife had died in London – that was Greta's mother. They married. I was born, and then Kurt. But at some moment, Heinrich found my mother in Berlin and they became lovers again and it never stopped. That's why she abandoned us. She refused to come to London. Remained in Paris for a few weeks and then went back to Germany.' Elise paused and closed her eyes for a moment, her emotions churning. She wasn't sure she could continue.

Victoria sat very still, knowing she must give Elise a chance to gain control of her feelings. Perhaps she even regretted what she'd just told her.

After a while, Elise opened her eyes and sat up in the chair. 'My mother finally returned to Dresden and Heinrich. He had never married. They moved in together.' Elise let out a long sigh and shook her head. 'He was apparently more important to her than we were. And they died together. When Dresden was consistently and heavily bombed by the Allies. And that's the story. Most of it.'

'I'm so sorry she left you all, her family, and in the way she did, Elise. Really so very sorry. I know how painful it must be. Things like that don't go away. They stay inside.'

Elise nodded. 'Finding out helped me a lot, and Kurt too. And I'm glad I went to Germany and dug up the true facts, as hard as it was to endure.'

'That's what you do as a reporter. Charlie has always said you're a natural, a born journalist. You just dig till you get the facts.'

Elise smiled but it suddenly faltered when she added, 'And guess what? Papa had suspected everything anyway. You see, he'd always known about her affair, had turned a blind eye.'

'Everyone has always said Professor Steinbrenner was a brilliant man, and Aunt Alice once told me that a spouse usually knows when there's hanky-panky going on.'

'What on earth made her say that?' Elise asked, puzzlement echoing in her voice. She stared at Victoria.

'She was explaining something to me that happened long ago, when I was little. Nothing of real importance; nothing about you.'

'Thank you for listening, Vicki. Confiding in you has helped me, and will continue to do so, I think. Now, let's go down to the sitting room and you can tell me all about Declan O'Sullivan.'

Victoria jumped up and so did Elise, and they went down to the next floor of the tall, book-lined house.

The room was the width of the house, and two tall windows filled it with light. It always seemed airy and sunny because Greta had had the walls painted yellow, and silk drapes, floor length, hung at the windows. There was a polished wood floor partially covered by a large cream and yellow area rug. Several modern paintings added bright colour to the walls, and pink and pale green pillows enlivened the sofas: it was full of the vivid colours that were the fashion these days.

Victoria sat down on a sofa, and glanced around admiringly. She loved rooms full of light; dark rooms alarmed her, bringing back frightening memories.

Elise, walking over to the Queen Anne chest, asked, 'Would you prefer lemonade, Vicki? I made some earlier and it's very refreshing.' Glasses, sherry and the lemonade stood on a silver tray.

'Thanks, I'd prefer that. I'll have something stronger with dinner.' She watched Elise, thinking how attractive her friend looked in her red dress, with her dark wavy hair, dark brown eyes and pale complexion. She was slender, petite, but her posture was so good she appeared taller than she really was.

Victoria knew men found Elise beguiling, her hint of an accent and dark beauty attracting them. She had an unmistakeable sexual allure, and yet she hadn't settled down with any of those men she had dated. She was very particular. And very devoted to her career.

Returning to the seating area near the windows, Elise took the chair opposite her friend. After a sip of the lemonade she fixed her attention on Victoria. 'First of all, was Declan flirting with me, do you think?'

'Yes, he was. I'm sure he wants to see you again.'

'Does he have a girlfriend?'

'Not that I know of, Elise, and he's a wonderful person. He's always been helpful to me, especially when I first moved in, hanging my photographs, that sort of thing.'

'He seems to work a lot. I've seen him in a few movies – small parts, of course. He's from Dublin, isn't he?'

Victoria nodded, and then laughed. 'And he's as Irish as Paddy's pig. But listen, go out on a date with him, have some fun. He's charming.'

'If you say so,' Elise responded, pulling a wry face, and changed the subject. 'And what about you, Vicki? Have you met anyone lately . . . anyone who interests you?'

'No, I haven't. Too much work, actually.' She suddenly smiled. 'Too involved with a camera and what I see through it to notice a man.'

Elise laughed, and the two of them turned to discussing the flat that Elise had found nearby in Margaretta Terrace. And what her move would mean to Greta. Elise was worried her sister would be lonely without her.

# Eleven

'It takes a lot of courage to be brave,' Alicia said, staring across the table at Constance Lambert. She shook her head, and muttered, 'Oh, sorry. That does sound ridiculous, doesn't it?' Her eyes suddenly brimmed with tears.

Constance reached out, took hold of Alicia's hand. 'I know exactly what you mean. It takes a great deal of *strength* to be brave in this kind of situation, darling.'

'It was just so unexpected and he was, well, *brutal*, really, in the way he told me, so blunt, unfeeling.' Alicia rummaged around in her bag for a handkerchief, tears sliding down her cheeks.

'So it seems,' Constance murmured, her voice sympathetic, gentle. 'And you're not the first woman to weep over a man. Or the last. Women have been doing that for centuries.'

Constance looked off into the distance, as if recalling something, her face contemplative. Then she said in a low voice, 'Men can be real sods at times.'

Alicia wiped her cheeks, blew her nose and attempted to smile at Constance, but it faltered almost at once. Once again, Constance took hold of the younger woman's hand, held it comfortingly.

The two of them were sitting in the lounge area of Brown's

Hotel, having afternoon tea. They were very close; Constance and Felix had been Alicia's theatrical agents since the beginning of her career in British films. She had not become a big star, but she was an actress of some standing. Beloved by the public, she worked on a regular basis and always in good movies. They had established a successful career for her, and looked after her interests scrupulously. And she relied on them, trusting them implicitly. However, it was Constance she had turned to in her upset over Bryan Mellor, knowing how well Constance understood her on an emotional level.

Constance broke the silence, when she said in a slightly puzzled tone, 'There's one thing I do find strange, and that is Bryan's decision to do Victor Chapman's Shakespearean tour of Australia. That's certainly not going to embellish his career in any way at all. In fact, it's a bit of a comedown, in my opinion. And by the way, Felix agrees.'

Leaning forward, Alicia confided, 'I'm glad you said that, because that was exactly what I felt. On the other hand, he is a bit odd, sort of quirky, and he's stubborn; he wants to do his own thing.'

'He's a man, what do you expect?' Constance remarked, a bleak smile flashing across her face. Then she added, 'But let's look at it in another way, Alicia. Bryan could have just broken it off, walked away. He didn't have to put thousands of miles between the two of you . . .' Constance cut her sentence short, looking thoughtful yet again. 'Unless he did it to prevent himself from coming back to you; in case he'd be tempted to reconcile, knowing he was unable to resist you.'

A startled look flickered in Alicia's blue eyes, and she exclaimed, 'Why would he want to have me back? I just told you how . . . *harsh* he was. Here's the thing, Connie. I believe he had been planning to break up with me for a while. Just consider how sneaky he was about his clothes, saying he was taking them to the cleaners. He was probably packing his suitcases.'

'True enough. Look, if he left anything behind, be it a tie, a book, anything at all, just get rid of it. Send it back or, better still, throw it away. Reminders of a man can be bothersome.'

'Thank you for thinking of that. There are a few bits and pieces. I'll mail the stuff to his flat.'

'Don't waste the postage; he's gone, sailed away. Throw the things in the dustbin. Get him out of your life. You've got to move on. Now. At once.'

'I've decided to go to Cavendon, get out of the flat. There's too much of Brin there at the moment.'

'Good idea. And stay there for the next ten days. Now that the picture has been postponed for two weeks, for those important rewrites, you can relax, go over your lines – although, knowing you, they're already committed to memory.'

Alicia smiled for the first time that day. 'Yes, they are.'

'You must think of the future,' Constance announced, her voice suddenly firmer, more decisive. 'I know Felix told you that the associate producer is a big fan of yours. He's hinted to Felix that he might want you for his next production. There's a lot to look forward to, darling. And you mustn't moon over Bryan Mellor. He's a lost cause.'

At the other side of London, at Photo Elite's office on the Fulham Road, Victoria stood in the office of Michael Sutton, owner and head of the agency, listening to him carefully.

When he had finished, she exclaimed, 'I don't like what you're saying, Mike. You're actually suggesting that you're troubled by the fact I'm living with a man because you promised Paloma Swann you'd keep an eye on me. That's it, isn't it?'

He nodded. 'I also promised your aunt the same thing, and these rumours I've been hearing are worrisome. I do feel a certain sense of responsibility, you know.'

'You can stop at once. Aunt Alice and Paloma have Charlie Stanton and Greta Chalmers keeping an eye on me, and that's already too many people.' Throwing him a cold, hard stare she added, 'I am disappointed in you; I thought you knew what kind of girl I am. Someone's spreading bad things about me, things which are not true.'

Michael went bright red, the flush starting in his neck and flooding up into his face, and he looked chagrined. 'I ought to know better – shouldn't listen to a bit of odd office gossip,' he muttered, feeling like an idiot.

'The man I was seen with, well over a week ago now, was Declan O'Sullivan, the actor. He happens to live in the flat above me. The other Saturday he and I were leaving at the same time and he gave me a lift, since we were both coming down to Chelsea.'

Michael knew she was extremely angry and he didn't blame her. He'd been foolish to listen to a disgruntled member of staff, never mind bringing it up with her. Taking a deep breath, he said contritely, 'I'm very sorry, Victoria. I made a mistake. I hope you'll accept my apology.'

'Yes, I will,' she answered at once, not wanting any problems to linger with her boss. She wondered if she should tell him about Phil Dayton watching her building at times, and decided against it.

Michael said, 'I have an assignment for you which I know you're going to like. That was the real reason I wanted to see you today.'

'Oh.' She paused, giving him a quizzical look. 'What is it?'

'Photographing Alicia Stanton for *Elegance Magazine*. It's your big chance. Your first solo job.'

A smile settled on Victoria's face. 'When? I know she's about to start a new film.'

'Apparently shooting starts a bit later now. I've been told there's some rewriting on the script to be done. Shall I accept? Will you do it?'

'Of course I will . . . I've known her since I was a little girl.'

He grinned, glad that her anger had subsided. She was his

favourite. Everybody's favourite, in fact. How could he have been so foolish? Listening to pettifogging gossip like that. I'm stupid, he added under his breath. Plain bloody stupid.

It was seven when Victoria left the agency. She glanced up at the sky as she went out onto Fulham Road and saw that it was heavy with dark clouds; rain threatened. After developing negatives for several hours, she was tired, and pleased to climb on to the top deck of the bus, where she relaxed and turned her thoughts to photographing Alicia. She was aware it would be a wonderful project, that she could get some unique shots because she knew Cavendon and its secret places so well.

As the bus wound its way through the London streets, past the gaping holes and the endless rebuilding that had begun, she couldn't believe that she had earned her first proper assignment. Her thoughts were still on the new job when she walked slowly up Belsize Park Gardens. It was a long commute from the Fulham Road to here, especially on a rainy evening. Suddenly she stiffened. There it was again. Phil Dayton's grey Vauxhall parked a little further up the street.

Immediately caution kicked in. She turned and ran back down towards the main road, where a cab with its light on was passing. Hailing it, Victoria opened the cab door and jumped in. 'Quick! I need to be somewhere else right away,' she exclaimed to the driver.

'No bovver, miss,' the Cockney said. 'Where to then?'

'Phene Street,' she answered. 'The far end.' Then she sat back, crouching down a bit as they passed the grey car.

She was not only infuriated but a little bit afraid. Phil Dayton's obsession with her, for that was what it was, was abnormal. And tonight it had become troubling. She didn't relish the idea of being in her flat knowing he was sitting out there. It was too creepy.

As a child she had not only learned caution and wariness, but also to anticipate trouble, and therefore to be on her guard, always prepared. These traits were now ingrained in her.

# TWELVE

Greta Chalmers sat staring at the bottle of Dubonnet, and put it down on the table. She had been about to open it, so that she and Elise could have a celebratory drink together, and then remembered that Elise was at the paper, working tonight.

And, even if she had been off, would she have been here? Of course not. She lived in her new flat now, in Margaretta Terrace. It was just around the corner, a tiny single girl's place up under the eaves, and she would have rushed over immediately if she hadn't been working. Greta shook her head, and a sad little smile slid onto her face. She lived alone here now.

At twenty-eight, Elise had wanted to stretch her legs, move on, feel more grown up, live her own life, in her own place. Greta understood that. Nonetheless, she already missed her sister. The house felt empty, strange without her.

For eleven years this house had been a family home, once her father and her half-siblings had arrived from Germany. It had been perfect for them, fitted them all in, with Kurt tucked into an attic bedroom; it had truly served them well. Once they had finally arrived in 1938, Greta had been able to find a real sense of peace, eventually managing to put aside her sorrow about her husband's untimely death in 1933. Her family had given her a fresh start. She knew she should be glad of the time she'd had here with them, time that could so easily have been denied to them by the Nazis. Greta sat up straighter in the chair, her thoughts rushing back to the conversation she had had earlier with Cecily. And the end result of their long phone call. *This was a fresh start.*

That thought grabbed her, wiped the sadness from her face. It's a new beginning, she told herself. I can forge ahead, do so much more, fill my life with new activities. The business needs so much work if it is to survive. And I might even meet a nice man.

Sitting back in the chair, Greta's thoughts ran on as she pondered about Life with a capital L, and what surprises it held. The unexpected was never far away. Sometimes Life rose up and bashed you in the face, almost destroyed you, but occasionally it gave you a bit of happiness, a sense of joy, however fleeting.

The trilling of the doorbell brought Greta to her feet, and she hurried down the corridor wondering who was there. When she opened the front door a look of total surprise filled her face.

'Victoria! Hello!' For a split second Greta stood gaping at the young woman who was smiling at her, still taken aback at Victoria's unexpected arrival.

'Can I come in please, Greta?' Victoria asked quietly. She looked pale and tired, her hair flat under a hat that was damp with rain.

'Of course you can, Victoria. How stupid I am.' As she spoke, Greta ushered her inside and closed the door behind them. 'I was startled for a moment.'

As they walked down the corridor to the kitchen, Greta went on, 'I'm always glad to see you. But Elise is at the paper.'

'I know. It was you I came to see, Greta. I realize I should have phoned first, but I was in the street and I just made a snap decision and jumped into a cab. You see, I want your advice. I need to tell you about something strange. In confidence.'

'I'm always here for you and, oddly enough, I have something I'd like to confide in you, too, Victoria.' Greta studied Victoria's face for a moment, as they both sat down at the kitchen table, and said, 'You said *strange*, and you look a trifle worried. Catch your breath and let me give you a drink. My story is more celebratory, I think. So shall I go first?'

Victoria nodded. 'Mine is a bit complicated. So yes, do that. I think you're going to tell me something happy, aren't you?'

'I am indeed.' Standing up, Greta opened the bottle of Dubonnet, took the two glasses from a cupboard and poured.

Sitting down again, passing a drink to Victoria, Greta leaned across the table, a wide smile on her face when she announced, 'I became Cecily's partner in Swann today . . . We finalized the agreement, meaning I will invest in the company, and I'm thrilled.'

'How wonderful! Congratulations.' Victoria picked up her glass, touched it to Greta's before taking a sip.

'Thank you, darling. It's sort of . . . well, given me a new lease on life; it's like a fresh start in a way. Before you arrived I was sitting here wondering who I could share my good news with, so thank you for showing up right on time.'

Victoria couldn't help laughing; Greta had a wonderful sense of humour. She had always admired her, and the way she had looked after the professor, Kurt and Elise. There was something fine about her, and she had real integrity.

Aunt Alice always said that Ceci had been lucky to find her, that Greta was honest, reliable and had backbone. The latter was most important to Alice Swann. Backbone counted. Victoria thought Ceci and Greta were somewhat alike in certain ways; they had both been born in the first week of May, although Cecily was six years older than Greta, who was about forty-two now.

After sipping her drink, Greta said in a more serious voice, 'Ceci and I made a verbal deal over the phone today, Victoria, so what I've told you is very confidential. No one else knows about the partnership yet.' And Greta would not be mentioning to anyone the trouble the business was facing, and the changes they were having to push through to save it.

'I won't say a word, I promise. Aunt Alice taught me years ago

I must keep things to myself, never gossip.' She knew that it was Alice's credo. Victoria suspected that Alice herself must know many sensitive things about the Ingham and Swann families, stretching back years, that she would never tell.

Greta nodded. 'Now, explain why you need my advice.'

'It is a bit complicated, as you'd guessed.' Slowly, speaking in a steady voice, Victoria told Greta all about Phil Dayton, from the evening he had given her and another girl from Photo Elite a lift home in a thunderstorm, to his pestering her for a date, and lately parking near her flat. 'Seeing that grey Vauxhall tonight was just one time too many.'

'I would say three times too many!' Greta exclaimed, looking appalled at what she had just heard. 'You did the right thing, coming here. And you're going to spend the night here.'

'But I—'

'No "buts". He might well have seen you arrive in Belsize Park Gardens, and then jump into the cab and ride off. He could still be parked there, you know. He might get out of the car, try to accost you, or speak to you anyway, when you got home. Imagine if it's late at night.'

'Yes, you're right, he could. I have this dilemma, Greta. I want to confront him, tell him off. I also want to report his behaviour to Michael Sutton. I think I even might want to leave the agency. That strange man makes me feel uneasy.'

'I would feel the same way about him. But tackling this Phil Dayton would be the worst thing to do, in my opinion. A weird man, which he really is, might take umbrage, get angry, I think. My advice is to keep your mouth shut and do your own thing, which is to leave the agency, and as soon as possible. Put yourself out of reach.'

'Michael Sutton told me tonight that *Elegance Magazine* would like me to photograph Alicia, and I accepted the assignment. I do want to do it. It's my biggest assignment yet – my first proper solo one.'

'You'll still be in close proximity to Dayton.'

Victoria shook her head. 'Mike told me the magazine has suggested I should photograph her at Cavendon, so I wouldn't be in London.'

'I see.' Greta looked thoughtful. 'Melinda Johns, the editor-in-chief of *Elegance Magazine*, is a friend of mine, a close friend, as I think you know, Victoria. She might well want to steal you away from Photo Elite. And, once you've done this Alicia piece, you won't have trouble finding a job. I'll speak to Melinda whenever you wish. It's up to you, just say the word.'

'Thank you, Greta, for listening, and for your advice.' Victoria looked at her friend's big sister with imploring eyes. 'Please don't tell Ceci about Dayton, because she'll tell Aunt Alice, who'll be worrying about me all the time.'

'I won't tell a single soul, I promise,' Greta replied, and sat back in the chair, sipping her drink. After a moment, she ventured, 'I've often wondered why Alice and you chose that flat. It's cosy and nicely appointed, but Belsize Park Gardens is so far north, now that you work around here in Chelsea. You're miles away from us all.'

'You're right, it's not the best place because of its location. The journey is a bit of a bore. But Mrs Skelton, the owner of the house, and Aunt Alice have a friend in common, and the flat was newly done and available.' Victoria shook her head. 'I suppose we didn't think it out properly, to be honest; no other reason really. It was convenient then. I know Aunt Alice and Uncle Walter were happy it was owned by someone they knew of. It took a lot of persuading for them to let me move down here at all.' She paused. 'But perhaps I also have to think about a new address as well as a new boss.'

'I believe you do. In the meantime, I want you to promise me you'll stay here with me until you go to Cavendon for the shoot. I won't be able to sleep at night, worrying about this man Dayton.' Greta had spent a decade looking after Elise and Kurt. It was second nature for her to want to look after Victoria.

For a moment Victoria did not respond, taken aback by Greta's suggestion. When she looked at Greta's face and saw the worry in her dark eyes, she instantly nodded. 'I'll do that, Greta. I'll just go back there to pack a bag the day I leave for the shoot.'

'Thank you, Victoria, that eases my mind considerably. Now, Nina always leaves something for my supper, as you well know.' Rising, Greta walked over to the pantry, and looked inside. 'Ha ha! Here we are – she's left me a cheese and potato flan, and a tomato salad. Or there is a piece of ham. What do you fancy?'

'I can't resist the flan,' Victoria answered. 'I'd love that, please.'

'I'll join you. All I have to do is pop it in a hot oven for thirty minutes to reheat. And in the meantime – let's put some music on and set the table.'

As she busied herself in the kitchen, turning on the oven, taking various foodstuffs out of the cupboard, Greta spoke casually to Victoria, chatting about the Festival of Britain, planned for the coming year, and other things. She had decided to let the matter of Phil Dayton drop. Why chew over the problem all evening? At one moment, as she put the supper in the oven, Greta wondered whether Elise might like to share her new flat around the corner with her friend. As the food was being heated, Greta and Victoria set the table. 'I love the way you have decorated this house,' Victoria told Greta, as she placed white linen mats on the little kitchen table. 'One day, when I'm married and have my own home, I shall have a blue and white room like your dining room. Or perhaps a sitting room in these colours.'

'I've always loved them myself,' Greta said, smiling at Victoria. 'I've found a really wonderful French *toile de Jouy* fabric, white with a blue pattern. I find the stories the *toiles* tell quite amazing – sort of amusing, in a way.'

Over supper, Victoria told Greta some more funny stories of her working life, and confided, 'I love being in London. I couldn't go back to Yorkshire now. And I like working for Melinda Johns a lot. When I've assisted before, she never tells you how to shoot a story. I just get a short memo . . .' Victoria paused, laughed. 'She gives me the barest instructions.'

Looking over at her, Greta asked, 'What do you mean?'

'A one-line message most of the time, such as "*This is a profile. Serious*" or "*Have fun with these clothes.*" Sometimes she wants "*Edgy*" or "*Fantasy*". And I love it, because she leaves it up to me.'

Greta nodded. 'I understand, and you have that marvellous opportunity now to shoot the most innovative and unique pictures. Actually, I think you must have a very vivid imagination, which comes into play a lot.'

'I try,' Victoria answered, sounding modest but looking pleased at Greta's praise. 'I look for crazy places for backdrops.'

'I bet you've already planned the Cavendon shoot, haven't you?' Greta remarked, her eyes twinkling knowingly.

Victoria laughed. 'A little bit. Obviously, I don't want to do the standard shoot. You know, the Honourable Alicia Ingham Stanton at Cavendon, her family's stately home. Too staid, I believe. And there are some really odd, even dramatic spots on the estate. I'll probably choose mostly outside settings, and perhaps only a couple of indoor pictures, but even they have to be . . . offbeat in some way. It's 1949, after all. I think we need a fresh approach.'

Greta lay propped up against the pillows in her bed, as usual reading for a while before going to sleep. But she found her concentration diluted tonight, and finally laid the book on the bed. She glanced around the bedroom, as always enjoying its clean contemporary lines and simplicity. She had decorated it in pale colours, and the effect was relaxing and comforting, creating a sense of tranquillity.

A small sigh escaped as her thoughts settled on Victoria, glad that she had come to see her earlier, and that she was safe and sound across the corridor in the guest bedroom.

This man pestering Victoria was troublesome, but Victoria was practical and instinctively cautious, and Greta was confident they could sort the problem out. She should find another flat. It was the right kind of disappearing act, and would put an end to his access to her. She doubted he would hurt her; on the other hand, no one ever really knew what might happen.

Greta lay back, closed her eyes, drifting with her myriad thoughts for a while, and as she became drowsy, she sat up, turned out the bedside lamp and settled down to sleep. It had been quite a day in more ways than one. And, with her new life as a business partner in Swann in front of her, she had no doubt there would be more days like it ahead.

The following morning, Elise arrived promptly at seven o'clock, bright and breezy and full of happy smiles. She always came to share breakfast on her day off, and found Greta in the kitchen. After hugging her sister, kissing her cheeks, she said, 'I wrote a really good story last night. I even got a congratulatory nod from the news editor, who actually smiled at me. Rather proudly, I thought.'

Greta laughed. 'Congratulations, darling. I know those gruff men sitting around with their sleeves rolled up, working hard at getting out a paper, can be awfully tough, and especially with women journalists.'

Elise nodded, laughing hollowly. 'Who are very few and far between. You don't see many skirts in Fleet Street. But I must say, the chaps I work with treat me nicely, don't give me a hard time. I think perhaps because they realize I'm serious about my job, and I've always got my head down typing, anyway.'

'If you looked up sometimes, you might see an interesting man.'

'Listen who's talking! You've never had time to find a man, because you're the Career Woman Supremo.'

Greta burst out laughing. 'I've never heard that expression. *Supremo* indeed. But I do have some wonderful news.'

Elise sat down at the kitchen table. 'Tell me. You sound very excited.'

'I am. I became Cecily's partner in Swann yesterday. We made a deal on the phone. And by the way, nobody knows, so we must keep it quiet for the time being.'

'I understand and I'm thrilled for you,' Elise exclaimed, jumping up, hugging her sister tightly. 'I know you've been hankering after this for a long time. How did it suddenly come about?'

'We've discussed it on and off for the last few weeks, ever since that trip I made up to Cavendon, but I thought Cecily had shelved the idea. It would be a big change for her to have a partner.' Greta didn't mention the reason it had become so vital. 'Then she brought it up again yesterday when we were discussing next year's summer collection. She suddenly said that if I wanted to invest in Swann I could become her partner. I said, "yes" so loudly I think she was startled. Anyway, she's putting it in the works, and we'll sign the papers in a few weeks. Imagine, Elise – I'm going to actually own part of a business, and the one I love. Swann Couture, now to be called just Swann.'

Elise beamed at her. 'I think this calls for a celebratory dinner, even a small party. Can I organize something?'

'Thank you, that's so sweet of you. But not just yet. Once it's signed, sealed and delivered, maybe. However, I'm far too superstitious to celebrate before those dotted lines are covered with signatures.'

At this moment Victoria came into the kitchen. 'Good morning, Greta! Elise!'

Elise swung around, a startled expression on her face. 'Victoria! What a nice surprise.'

'I spent the night here. Greta was being motherly,' Victoria said. 'I'll explain everything in a minute. Obviously you've just heard the great news about Greta and Ceci becoming partners. But strictly hush-hush for now.'

'Yes, I have, and I'm over the moon about it.'

'So am I.' Victoria sat down next to Elise, kissed her on the cheek. 'Have you seen Charlie?'

Elise shook her head. 'He wasn't in the office last night. Actually, I think he's taken a few days off. He's got a tough deadline for his new book.'

'Oh that's right, he mentioned that to me recently,' Victoria replied.

Greta turned around from the stove, and asked, 'Do you both want a bit of breakfast? I have a couple of eggs – scrambled with fried tomatoes?'

'That sounds scrumptious,' Victoria answered.

Elise grinned at her sister. 'You know I love everything you cook.'

Within minutes Greta had served them their plates of food, and joined them at the table. They chatted about unimportant things as they ate, relishing their breakfast. It was only when they had finally finished their food that Victoria explained to Elise why she had stayed one night at Phene Street.

Elise looked shocked as she listened to Victoria. When the tale was finished, she exclaimed, 'I met Phil Dayton once, when I came to pick you up at Photo Elite. Don't you remember?'

'Yes, I do. You chatted to him about Merle Oberon, as I remember. He's a big fan of hers.'

'He seemed quite pleasant, just an ordinary kind of young man, not particularly good looking, but not unattractive, average sort . . . well, that's the impression I got.'

'You've described him exactly, Elise, but he's a pest, and his interest in me has become somewhat creepy.'

'It is, yes,' Elise agreed. 'And I fully understand why you don't want to confront him. It could set him off in some sort of way. So what are you going to do? Report him? Leave the agency?'

'Yes, I think I am. I like Mike but I bet he won't fire him – I can't prove anything, and I've seen other girls sidelined for complaining about being hassled. I have one assignment I want to do, photographing Alicia at Cavendon, then I'll give Mike my notice.'

'The shoot sounds exciting. I bet it's for *Elegance Magazine*.'

'It is.'

Greta said, 'I've suggested she moves out of her flat, finds something around here, so we're all closer together.'

'You can always camp out with me until you find a new place,' Elise said warmly, smiling at Victoria. 'It would be a bit cosy, but you're welcome.'

'Thanks, Elise, but I promised Greta I'd stay here for the moment.'

'Nowhere better,' Elise answered, and squeezed Victoria's arm. 'We'll help you find somewhere nice and I'll help you to move. That would be exciting – we girls all in the same area.'

'Thank you.' Victoria was grateful for her friends' support. She would have to tell Aunt Alice about the flat. 'Now, changing the subject, you haven't said anything about the date you had with Declan. How did it go?'

Sitting back in her chair, Elise looked at her friend slyly. After a moment, she said, 'I loved every minute of being with him. He's loaded with that irresistible Irish charm. He's warm, funny, and, frankly, if I keep on seeing him, I'm going to fall for him. And hard.'

Before Victoria could comment, Greta pushed back her chair and stood up. 'I've got to go to the office, girls. I'll see you both later, whenever.' And with a cheery wave she left the kitchen.

Victoria leaned closer to Elise and said, 'That's how I thought it would be. You're just made for each other. I bet he was all over you, wasn't he?'

When Elise remained silent, Victoria said, 'Well, wasn't he?'

'Of course. We both were. We just clicked from the first minute. We've made another date for later this week, but I think I won't see him again after that.'

Victoria frowned. 'Why not? I don't understand.'

'The few times I've met him before with you, I had a certain sense of him. I was aware of his immense confidence. It's a unique kind of self-assurance. The other night I spotted that again. It's as if he knows he's someone special. And he is, actually. It's not that he's arrogant, I don't mean that. I can't quite explain it, Vicki.'

'I've seen that in him too,' Victoria answered. 'He doesn't swagger, nothing remotely like that. But he sort of . . . fills a room.' There was a pause and Victoria searched her friend's face. 'Why does that put you off?'

'It doesn't, Vicki. But I realize that Declan has big plans for himself. I don't know how good an actor he is, and he's only had small parts until now. Apparently, he's the second male lead in his new film, and there's already a lot of noise about his performance. There's talk on the street about him.'

'That's good, isn't it?' Victoria stared hard at Elise, looking puzzled yet again.

'*Absolutely*. I'm happy for him. However, I've never met anybody so focused, so relentless about making it. He's tremendously driven and furiously ambitious. You'll see, he'll end up in Hollywood. Declan aims to be a big movie star.'

Victoria was silent for a few seconds, and then she reached out, took hold of Elise's hand. 'I understand. You're worried you'll become involved with him, and he with you, and then when Hollywood calls, he'll go at once.'

'I'm afraid you've got it right, Vicki. There's a strong attraction between us, and we're on the same wavelength . . .' Elise stopped, shook her head, and sighed. 'I know, and without the slightest shred of doubt, that his career will always come first with Declan. Marriage is the last thing on his mind. I'll even make a prediction, he won't marry until he's at the very top of his career.'

'Why do you say that? How can you know?' Victoria's voice rose slightly.

'I just do. He wants the fame, the glory. All of it. That's more important to Declan than anything else in the world.'

'I hope you're wrong, Elise. That sounds awfully sad in a way. Fame isn't so great if you've no one to share it with.'

A small smile flickered around Elise's mouth. 'I agree. And I suppose you could say I'm a coward. It's just that I know I'll fall hopelessly in love with him, and then have my heart broken when he leaves. So you can call me "No-Risk-Elise" if you want, but that's the way I feel.'

'I'd never call you "No-Risk-Elise" because I think you're very brave, venturing into Fleet Street the way you have, pursuing your career in a predominantly man's world. And you've been through a lot of pain and sorrow about your mother.' Victoria gave her a huge smile, then put an arm around her friend. 'You're being self-protective, and no one understands that better than me.'

Elise nodded, and looked at Victoria, half smiled. 'Better to get out now, don't you think?'

'I'm afraid I do. And I trust your insight into Declan. I've always known about that driving ambition of his.'

'Let's change the subject. When are you going to Cavendon?'

'Fairly soon, before Alicia starts filming. I'll phone Cecily this morning, just to . . . well, ask permission. I need to alert her that it won't be just me and a camera coming. The magazine sends a stylist to look after the clothes, and people from hair and makeup. It's quite a bunch.'

'I'd like to be a fly on the wall.'

'Come on, come with me,' Victoria said, a smile in her eyes.

'I can't. I have a career, you see.'

They both laughed, as always enjoying being together.

# Thirteen

The special bond between Alice Swann and Alicia Stanton had begun in babyhood. Even before the child's birth, Alice had been focused on the baby. The bond had remained constant and strong over many years. It was Mrs Alice, as everyone called her, who was Alicia's only other confidante, after her brother Charlie.

Lady Daphne, Alicia's mother, had been helped by Mrs Alice when she was in trouble as a young girl. Daphne had relied on her throughout her difficult pregnancy. And so she had honoured Alice by calling this first child after her, and the two of them were still close.

On this sunny August morning, Alice and Alicia were seated in Alice's lovely cottage-style garden at the back of her house in Little Skell village, under the shadow of the moors. Looking across at them, Alicia said, 'I love it here at this time of year, when the heather starts to bloom. What a sight it is . . . a line of undulating purple against the rim of the horizon.'

'The view is wonderfully comforting, I always think. I suppose because it's constant, sort of reliable, always coming back, like the changing seasons.'

Moving closer to the younger woman, taking hold of her hand, Alice said quietly, 'I'm glad you told me about Bryan leaving. And I'm sorry. I thought you and he were developing into something serious. Why did he have to go away on the tour?'

Alicia let out a long sigh, and gazed at Alice. 'I can't answer that, I have no idea.' She tried to smile but her face was sad. 'Of course, he could have just broken up with me. It's a bit of a puzzle.'

'He might have become involved with another woman who was set to go on the Shakespeare tour, and decided to go along with her.' Alice couldn't imagine why any man would find another woman more attractive than her favourite. Alicia was busy with her career, of course, but Alice longed for her to find happiness in love too.

'I must admit, I hadn't thought of that, but you're right. Anyway, I just know I can't dwell on it any more. I just have to throw myself into this new film and put it behind me, Mrs Alice.'

At this moment Victoria came down the garden path, waving a piece of paper. 'I've found my list, so let's go and look at the spots I've picked out, and then review the clothes.'

Alice and Alicia stood up, and Alice said, 'I suppose we're going to High Skell, since you told me to wear comfortable shoes.'

Victoria grinned. 'Yes, we are, and let's go there first, get it out of the way. I thought of the maze in one of Harry's gardens as another spot, and also the water gardens. What do you think, Alicia?'

'Wonderful choices, Victoria.'

It took the three women twenty minutes to walk across Cavendon Park, through the stable block and up the hill past the church. Once they reached the heather-covered moors, High Skell came into view.

The monolithic rocks were formed in a kind of semicircle, so that they created a protected area that was also secluded. Alice remembered that Charles, the 6th Earl of Mowbray, had often climbed up to this outcropping of rocks, which she knew dated as far back as the glaciers that had covered Yorkshire at the time of the Ice Age. Charlotte had once told her that Charles thought of it as his private place, where he could sit and think, and sort out the problems in his head.

'I know there are flat stones set against the wall of rocks in the circle,' Alice informed them. 'We can sit there for a minute. I'm out of breath.'

'So am I,' Alicia exclaimed, and followed Alice, adding, 'But my God, what a place! I'd forgotten how fantastic it was up here, and the view of Cavendon from here is fabulous.'

'I thought the huge rocks and the strange shapes would make a perfect background for the tulle evening gown, Alicia. What do you think?' Victoria asked as she followed them into the semicircle, starting to snap photographs of the rocks.

'You're just brilliant,' Alicia replied, sitting down.

'I'm glad you liked the clothes the fashion editor selected, and that they all fit,' Victoria murmured, still wielding her camera.

'They do, and they're lovely. But are you going to get me to wear them all? There are quite a lot.'

'I think the fashion editor will decide that when she arrives tomorrow with the rest of the crew. You know, the stylist, hair and makeup women. But I pretty much know which ones will work for the shoot from my instructions from Melinda Johns.'

'What did she tell you to do?' Alice asked curiously, rather in awe of her little evacuee who'd grown up to be so clever.

Victoria laughed. 'Not much, as usual. I generally get one line. Yesterday I received it. *Glamour. Drama. Glamour.* That was it.'

Moving away from the semicircle, Victoria roamed around the area, snapping away. She had always enjoyed being up here on this vast empty moorland, which stretched for miles towards the North Sea. Basically, there was nothing here but an arc of blue sky and the monoliths. Plus the wind, she thought, hoping it wouldn't be blowing too hard tomorrow; that was when she planned to start the shoot.

As they walked back down to the house, Alicia stopped suddenly and looked at Victoria. 'I suppose I'll be coming up here in a dressing gown? Or trousers and shirt? I can't very well wear the tulle evening gown, climbing up to High Skell.'

'You can't, that's true. Aunt Alice is lending us a folding screen. Ted will bring it up tomorrow morning, and you can change behind it.'

'Don't worry, your Little Imp has thought of everything,' Alice said, reverting to Alicia's nickname for Victoria when she was a child.

Their next stop was the water gardens, behind the West Wing of the house. They were beautiful, and dated back to the eighteenth century. They were on lower ground behind the house, and Victoria went ahead of Alice and Alicia, her eyes glancing from side to side, taking everything in as she went down the hill.

This part of the parkland had a tranquillity to it that was genuinely calming. There were manicured green lawns at the bottom of the hill, and in the centre of the lawns, straight ahead of her, was a large ornamental pond.

Four canals branched out from the pond like spokes, and these narrow waterways were surrounded by a circular canal. The effect was like a giant wheel. Harry had never tampered with these canals and the pond, but had put water lilies in the ornamental ponds and added several white stone statues of women here and there, which he had found in storage in the basements. They added to the overall effect of antiquity, as did the white stone temple, which was called the Temple of the Moon. This was an elegant structure, with pillars at the front and steps into it. Victoria headed down the flagged path, making for the white temple, thrilled at the thought of photographing Alicia in these unique gardens.

The two other women were also looking pleased. Alice exclaimed, 'Isn't it strange? I've seen these water gardens all my life, and yet today they somehow look different. So beautiful.'

'And Harry's added to them,' Alicia remarked, 'reinforced what they were. Somehow made them more . . . *exciting*. That's what I think.'

Victoria was in her element, walking around, taking more photographs. Alicia and Alice were following her, as she spoke of the clothes which would work so well here, explaining what she was after.

Eventually Alice broke up the tour when she said, 'I think we should go and have lunch. I've prepared some finger sandwiches, and we can relax. Then later we can look at the clothes that arrived yesterday.'

'That's a good idea,' Alicia said. 'Come on, my Little Imp, let's go.'

Victoria nodded, and followed them up the hill.

Later that afternoon, Alicia sat in her bedroom in the South Wing, going over the script. She knew her words by heart now, and finally put the script on the ottoman and leaned back in the armchair. Being at Cavendon comforted her. It had been a wise move, coming home. She glanced at her old teddy bear, a bit ragged now, but much loved when she was a child. *BRIN*. That was the name of the bear, and she had given it to Bryan Mellor, because he was a teddy bear of a man at times.

The odd thing was he seemed like some distant object now, not like a person. This past week here she had managed to expunge him from her mind. And she didn't cry about him any longer. Common sense had kicked in; of course, Constance and Alice had helped her no end, in their different ways. In a certain sense, once she had got over the shock of his nasty departure, his very behaviour had turned her off him. She wasn't used to being treated in such a brutal and rude manner, and being spoken to with such vehemence – disregard, almost. Charlie, who had phoned her every day, had muttered something this morning about Bryan having no class, and perhaps her brother was right.

Anyway, her eyes were now focused on the future and her career. And she was looking forward to the magazine shoot tomorrow. Victoria and she had chosen the clothes they preferred earlier, and her Little Imp had told her not to worry about anything at all. 'I'm in charge,' she had explained. 'Melinda Johns always makes that clear to the crew.'

# Fourteen

Cecily Swann Ingham sat at the desk in the upstairs sitting room, staring down at the four Swann record books, two of them very old indeed. For the last few weeks she had been attempting to read parts of them, and still had not finished. There were a few things she needed to understand better, puzzling entries, but she had been so occupied with her business and her new responsibilities that she just never had time.

She glanced at her watch and realized she and Miles had agreed to meet the people from the magazine around ten fifteen, when they would have all arrived. Alicia had suggested using the South Wing for the shoot, and they had agreed. Daphne and Hugo were away in Zurich, and Alicia had grown up there. It was her home and the perfect place for everyone to assemble.

Realizing she did not have time to put the record books in the safe, Cecily slipped them into the top drawer of the desk, locked it, dropped the key in her jacket pocket and left the sitting room.

As she went downstairs she decided to talk to Aunt Charlotte later today and ask her a few questions regarding several curious things in the record books. She was quite certain that Charlotte must have dipped into the books at different times. Who could possibly resist?

As she went into the library, Miles glanced up, waving a letter he was holding. 'Good news, Ceci!' he exclaimed. 'The wine expert in London has just suggested three dates when he can come and look at the cellars. I shall pick the first.'

Touching his shoulder affectionately, she went and sat in the chair on the other side of his desk. 'And when would that be?' she asked, thinking how well he looked this morning.

'The middle of next week. Wednesday, to be exact. I'll give him a ring later today and set it up.' Miles shook his head, then grimaced. 'I'm afraid there might be quite a mess down there. Eric and I have been doing the odd check, and a lot of wine has turned, gone sour.'

'Oh no, Miles, that's terrible. Why didn't you tell me before?' she asked, her expression troubled.

'No point, really, darling. Can't be helped. However, no worries. There is still a lot that will be all right, I'm sure. And, I must admit, my antecedents really stocked up on it. Wine lovers, most obviously. Enough for an auction.'

'I took your advice, Miles, and offered a partnership to Greta, and the good news is that she did accept. I've just had her letter confirming it in writing. I think it was a good move.'

A wide smile spread across his face. 'Congratulations. Her investment will help, will ease some of your worries – and it was a nice thing to do, actually. She wanted it so much, and it gives her an incentive, an investment in the future. Besides which, she deserves it.' Miles got up and walked around the desk, gave Cecily his hand and pulled her to her feet.

'We'd better go and do our duty, welcome the magazine group to Cavendon, support Victoria and Alicia in this endeavour.'

Cecily nodded, and then looked at him intently as he drew her into his arms and held her close. Against her hair, he said, 'We're a good team, you and I, Ceci. Sorry I've been grumpy at times.'

He kissed her forehead, then looked down into her face. 'You were right about the bank loan. I know Aunt Charlotte had to practically drag me to Harrogate kicking and screaming, but I am relieved I took the loan, to be honest. At least the government taxes are off our back for this year.'

Cecily said, 'Thank you, Miles.' Slipping her hand into his, she went on: 'We've made a good start, and there's more to come if the auction works. Now, we'd better go to the South Wing, darling. They'll want to get started.' As they walked through the main hall and down the Long Gallery, Cecily was smiling inside. She understood that his last few words had been a genuine apology. He had been more than grumpy for some time – very bad-tempered, in actuality – but it had slowly dissipated of late. She wondered if she dared mention the cat. Gwen was still pestering her for one.

Miles and Cecily stared at each other as they approached the dining room in the South Wing, and Miles raised a brow. 'How big is this crew?' he asked, staring at his wife.

Cecily shook her head, laughing at the alarmed expression in his eyes. 'I don't know, but it sounds like an army, doesn't it?'

Laughter, chatter, squeals, shouts: a cacophony of sounds were emanating from the room. The door stood open, and when they went in Alicia was standing right there, obviously awaiting them.

'Aunt Ceci, Uncle Miles,' she exclaimed. 'Here you are. Come in and meet everyone.' After greetings were exchanged, along with hugs and kisses, Alicia led them forward.

The room had gone silent at the moment of their arrival, and a bevy of young women were standing there, expectant looks on their faces.

Victoria hurried forward and hugged and kissed Miles and Cecily. 'Thank you again for letting me do the shoot here and, by the way, don't worry about anything being damaged. Everyone's careful, and anyway the magazine is insured.'

Miles put an arm around Victoria and brought her closer,

hugged her. 'My clever Victoria, always so practical. And because you're in charge, I know we've nothing to worry about.'

He grinned at her and she laughed, then said, 'Alicia is going to introduce the girls to you.' Lowering her voice, she explained, 'They're all very excited about meeting an earl and a countess.'

One by one, Alicia brought them forward to shake hands with Miles and Cecily, who greeted them warmly and welcomed them to Cavendon. Seven young women altogether: Catherine, the fashion editor; Hannah, the stylist; Mavis and Carrie, who did hair and makeup; Brenda and Flora, who were in charge of the clothes. The last was Trigger, who helped Victoria.

After the introductions, Alicia explained, 'Brenda and Flora were here at seven thirty and, guess what, Aunt Ceci? They brought their own irons and ironing boards, and various other useful implements.'

'So I noticed,' Cecily replied with a smile. 'And hopefully it was Ted and his decorating team who moved the dining-room furniture. It's all very heavy for you girls to handle.'

'Yes, of course. And Ted and one of the men will take a folding screen and various other things up to High Skell. We've plenty of help, thank you.'

'Are you going to shoot up there?' Miles immediately turned to Victoria. 'It can be very windy, you know.'

'It can. And so I went up yesterday with Aunt Alice and Alicia, and it wasn't too bad. I'll work inside the semicircle of monoliths, if necessary. It's quite protected.'

'Where else are you going to shoot?' Cecily asked curiously, now understanding this was a much more important assignment than she had realized.

'The water gardens definitely, and I thought of Uncle Harry's maze as well as the flower gardens.'

'Perfect.' Cecily glanced around the dining room, noting the many racks of clothes which had apparently arrived yesterday in a large van. But she made no comment.

Once again, Miles addressed Victoria. 'I think this question might be redundant, because I know how well you plan things, but what about the general public? The estate and house are open today. Are they going to be a nuisance, get in your way?'

Victoria shook her head. 'I don't mind if they stand and watch if we're in the water gardens or the flower gardens. I spoke to Uncle Walter about it, and he said his outdoor men will look after any situation that might arise.'

Cecily said, 'Anyway, visitors are not allowed to go up to High Skell, and the maze is a puzzlement to everyone.' She began to laugh. 'I for one will never go near it, knowing I'd be stuck in there forever.'

Everyone laughed, and after a few more minutes chatting to the young women, Miles and Cecily left them to get on with their jobs of attending to Alicia, preparing her for photography.

Victoria walked them to the door. 'I thought of calling the shoot "Eternal Serenity", after the water gardens. Is that all right?' She looked from Cecily to Miles, and added, 'Melinda Johns, the editor of *Elegance Magazine*, asked me to come up with a title.' When they didn't immediately respond, Victoria said, 'Well, what do you think?'

'I love it,' Miles answered quickly. 'I was just impressed that you thought of it, Victoria.'

'And so am I,' Cecily added. 'It's a beautiful title for the story.'

Later that afternoon, Cecily went in search of Aunt Charlotte, wanting to chat with her. Her thoughts were still on some of the pages she'd seen in the notebooks. This was the first opportunity she had had, but the Dowager Countess was nowhere to be found.

Cecily rang for Eric; instead it was Peggy Lane, the housekeeper, who appeared in the downstairs parlour. 'Can I help you with something, Your Ladyship?' Peggy asked, hurrying across the room.

'Yes, Peggy, you can. I've been looking for the Dowager Countess and haven't been able to find her. Is she outside with Victoria at the shoot? Or did she go to Harrogate?'

'Neither, m'lady. She is talking to Eric. She needs to get into the vaults. I think they will be here any moment to ask for the key.'

'Eric has his key,' Cecily answered, but when she saw the look of surprise flash across Peggy's face, she quickly thought to add, 'Of course he would never use his key without asking my permission.'

'That's correct, Your Ladyship.' As usual she was extremely proper and aware of the rules and their duties, having worked at Cavendon for over thirty years.

At this moment the Dowager Countess appeared in the doorway of the parlour, accompanied by the butler. 'There you are, Ceci,' she said. 'I need to get in a vault, darling. I have some of my own jewels stored there, which I want to discuss with you. We need the key, please.'

'Oh,' Cecily said, wondering why Aunt Charlotte wanted to speak with her about them. Then she glanced at Eric. 'Use your key, Eric, would you, please? Mine is locked in my safe upstairs.'

'Certainly, Your Ladyship.' He turned to the Dowager Countess. 'If you will accompany me, Lady Charlotte, I will open the vault and carry the items up here for you.'

'Thank you,' Aunt Charlotte said, and the two of them left.

'Are you sure I can't get you anything, m'lady?' Peggy asked. 'Maybe a cup of tea or coffee? Eric told me His Lordship cancelled afternoon tea today, because he was very busy, and also because of the photographic shoot. Victoria wished to keep taking pictures until the light fades.'

'Thank you, Peggy. I don't need anything right now. Unless you know of someone who might have a kitten available.'

'How odd you should ask, Lady Cecily. My friend Annette Green in the village has a cat that had a litter about four months ago or so. Shall I put Lady Gwen's name on one of the kittens?'

'*Absolutely*. And I will pay for it, of course. Do tell her that.'

'I understand, m'lady,' Peggy said with a smile. 'I know it will make the little one happy.'

'It will indeed. But we won't tell anyone about this for the moment. Most especially His Lordship.' Cecily gave Peggy a pointed look.

Peggy nodded, did a little bob, and hurried off, happy to have been of help. Cecily smiled to herself as she took the small notebook out of her pocket, and flipped to one page in particular.

A cat, she thought. A cat for my little wartime baby. How happy she will be.

Twenty minutes later the butler returned. 'Lady Charlotte asked me to take her boxes upstairs to her parlour, m'lady, and she would like you to join her there, if you don't mind.'

'That's not a problem,' Cecily answered, slipping the notebook into her pocket. She walked out of the room with Eric, giving him a few more details about the dinner that night and lunch the following day.

'I was thinking it might be a good idea to sell some of my pieces,' Aunt Charlotte said, indicating the jewellery boxes open on the low table in front of the sofa. 'I would give the money they fetch to Miles, to help with next year's taxes.'

'No, no, that's not necessary, Aunt Charlotte,' Cecily said swiftly. 'However, it is very, very kind of you to offer to help Miles. Such a thoughtful thing. Thank you so much for being unselfish, being prepared to give up jewels you love.'

'I don't wear these things very often, and even if I sell them or give them away now, I do still have quite a lot left, you know.'

Cecily smiled at her and looked down at the pieces. 'They're all lovely, exquisite, Aunt Charlotte.'

Sitting back against the sofa, stretching her legs, Aunt Charlotte said, 'Long ago I picked out these pearls for you, Ceci. They were given to me by Miles's grandfather, David, for my twenty-first birthday, and I've worn them for years. I always loved them, and still do. But they're for you, and I want you to take them now. *Today*. Because they shouldn't be sitting in a box in a vault. It's important that pearls are worn. They need air and light.'

Lifting the three strands of pearls out of the box, Aunt Charlotte held them up to the light. 'Just look how lustrous they are, absolutely beautiful.'

Leaning forward, she handed them to Cecily, who also held them up to the light. She was about to say thanks but no thanks, then instantly changed her mind. Aunt Charlotte genuinely wanted her to have them, so why not accept them now, and with grace. It might appear churlish otherwise.

'How can I refuse, Aunt Charlotte? I *will* take the pearls, because they belonged to you, and were given to you by an Ingham. And we're both Inghams now . . . I shall treasure them always. Thank you for such a lovely gift.'

'You've made an old lady very happy,' Aunt Charlotte said, smiling up at Cecily. 'And look at this, a tiny silver arrow pin, with a few aquamarines along the shaft. I thought I would give this to Gwen, either today or tomorrow. I've had it since I was eighteen.'

'Oh goodness! How sweet of you, but I think she's a bit young for a real piece of jewellery. She is only eight,' Cecily protested.

'Do let me give it to her, and I will tell her she can only wear it on Sundays. How's that?'

Cecily laughed, and laid the three-strand pearl necklace in its box. 'I'll make a deal with you, Aunt Charlotte.'

'Oh dear, Ceci, you and your deals! I've never known anyone like you.'

'Come on. Be a good sport. Make the deal, let's shake on it.'

'You haven't said what the deal is,' Aunt Charlotte pointed out.

'I'll allow you to give Gwen the brooch today or tomorrow, whenever you wish, but you also have to give her a cat.'

'Goodness me, a *cat!* Where on earth would *I* find a cat?' Aunt Charlotte was staring at her in astonishment.

'I think *I'll* be the one getting the cat – well, the kitten – and any day now. I just want you to say it's a gift from you to Gwen. Miles won't dare object . . . because you're *you*.'

'He doesn't want her to have a cat? That's it, right?'

'Yes. He says animals are not meant to be in the house. He's afraid she'll have the cat with her all the time, and that it might even sleep on her bed, God forbid. He's really serious about this, so the cat, if he lets her keep it because it's from you, will have to live in the kitchen most of the time. Although I'm hoping I can persuade him to let her take the cat to the old nursery, where she usually plays. I'll explain it will sleep in the kitchen near the warm stove.'

Stretching out her hand, Aunt Charlotte said, 'It's a deal, Ceci. Shake on it.'

They both laughed and then Cecily said, 'I was looking for you today because I really do want to speak to you about something quite important. The record books. At least a few of them. There's a lot of inflammatory stuff in them. Dynamite stuff.'

# Fifteen

Charlotte Swann Ingham gazed at Cecily Swann Ingham, thinking how elegant Ceci looked. They were the only two Swann women ever to marry into the aristocratic Ingham family.

Settling herself comfortably on the sofa, the Dowager Countess said, 'Dynamite? Inflammatory? Well, yes, you're right, in a sense. They were exactly that when they were happening, but that was about a hundred and eighty years ago. Frankly, Ceci, I don't think anyone gives a fig about those things today.'

Cecily gasped a little and laughed. She was of a mind with her great-aunt – but she knew that the Inghams might struggle to agree. The famed record books were considered sacrosanct.

'I agree with you, Aunt Charlotte, probably only me, because I'm the keeper of the Swann records, and I suppose I'm curious about my ancestry.' She paused. 'But I'm really intrigued by James Swann. I know he worked with Humphrey Ingham most of his life, travelled with him, helped him to make deals, and was a sort of personal assistant. Their relationship was obviously very close. But what I also think is that it was really James who was responsible for so much that happened here; that Cavendon became what it is today because of him, as well as Humphrey, the First Earl.'

When Aunt Charlotte was silent, Cecily continued, 'In many ways you have an advantage over me, because you also have access to the Ingham papers.'

'That's true. I worked for David Ingham, the Fifth Earl, for twenty years. And I wasn't at all surprised to discover that the Inghams as well as the Swanns kept records. I did tell you they were available to you, any time you wished to look at them.'

'I know you did.' Cecily laughed as she said this and added, 'Until very recently, I wasn't here all the time. I was in London, and I never really had a free moment to go browsing into the past.'

'And now you do?' Charlotte raised a brow quizzically.

'Not exactly, but I have been peeking into the record books now and then. I have a few questions – will you answer them if you can? Then I won't have to keep digging.'

'Of course I will. It's quite a complicated story, though.'

'We've plenty of time to chat,' Cecily answered. 'Miles cancelled afternoon tea today, as I'm sure you know, because of the photographic shoot, and he and Harry are extremely busy working on a special project anyway.'

Charlotte nodded. 'We can always ask Eric to bring a pot of tea and some scones up here, if you should feel peckish. So go ahead. Ask me any question that comes to mind, and I'll do my best. You certainly know I will tell you the truth as I know it to be.'

'Was Marmaduke Ingham, Humphrey's first son and heir, illegitimate?' Cecily's eyes rested on Charlotte, her gaze intense, penetrating.

'Actually, he was,' Charlotte said without hesitation. 'But Humphrey was Marmaduke's biological father, and he was born at Cavendon Hall. James saw to that. And he was brought up by Humphrey. Moreover, there was never any question about his legitimacy. He was the heir.'

'Why was that? How do you know?'

'There is a strange paper, a sort of birth certificate, in the Ingham papers. It looks . . . doctored, shall we say? Humphrey is listed as the father, and his first wife Marie is listed as the mother. I don't think it would stand up to much scrutiny nowadays, mind you,' Charlotte finished, shaking her head. 'Humphrey and James had a way of manipulating things to their advantage, it seems to me. They managed to get away with everything they did.'

'But how was that possible?' Cecily frowned. 'Were they so very clever? So brilliant?'

'I think they were, yes, but let's look back to those times. Cavendon Hall was finished in 1761. Whilst it was being built, the park was being created, and James was managing the plans for Little Skell village. A local builder was hired to create the main street with cottages on both sides, and James personally overlooked the erection of the church. What I'm trying to explain is that there weren't many people around when Humphrey was moving into the West Wing, and James and his family were settling into the East Wing, which Humphrey had insisted on. Basically, there were only a few house servants and a cook to begin with, along with a number of outdoor workers. Once the cottages were finished, they were able to hire new people to work in the hall and on the estate.'

'There are quite a few references to that particular period of time in the Swann records, as you know. It always strikes me how scrupulous James was about his notes, Aunt Charlotte.'

'Yes, he was. He had many talents, I believe.'

Cecily sat back in the chair, a reflective expression settling on her face. Eventually she said, 'So they got away with anything they wanted to do, because there was no one in higher authority to challenge them or question them. Actually, they were the ones in charge. It was their own little fiefdom. They ruled the roost. Certainly servants aren't going to risk losing their jobs by speaking out of turn. Although they probably gossiped amongst themselves.'

'Quite true, Cecily. And you're correct about the fiefdom. Humphrey had been elevated to the peerage some years before, and was lord of the manor and an extremely rich man by then.

He had gone to London at sixteen and made his fortune when he was young. In my opinion, James saw to everything, ran everything. He and Humphrey were practically joined at the hip, it seems to me, and they were partners in many different things.'

'What?'

Aunt Charlotte sat up straighter on the sofa, and her gaze was fixed as she stared at Cecily.

'Cavendon holds secrets, my dear. If you want to know them all, you have to be prepared to keep them as your ancestors have. And now that you are the Countess, and are the one with the key to the record books, you will want to read more.'

'And he needed a real countess to reign over this pile. I can't help thinking James probably found one for him.'

Aunt Charlotte burst out laughing. 'That's just a guess on your part, because there's nothing in the Swann records about that. But you are correct. After Humphrey's first wife Marie died, James did indeed find him just the right woman. One who needed a husband *fast*, who wanted to please and was attractive.'

'Who was she? All I know is her name. Wasn't she called Helen Lester Latham?'

'That's right, she was. In fact she was already titled. She was the Dowager Countess of Latham when James met her, and she was only about thirty-three. The important thing was that she accepted Humphrey's children, took rather a fancy to Humphrey and agreed to anything he wanted. According to Humphrey's mother, he had made a good choice. She approved of Helen, and so wrote in a letter to her son. It's still in the Ingham papers.'

'So James Swann brokered yet another deal for his great friend, Humphrey Ingham, and that's why, among other things, we must always have swans on the lake that James built at Cavendon.'

There was a knock on the door, and Eric came in with Peggy, both of them carrying tea trays. And the conversation was curtailed.

* * *

It was only later, after Eric had removed the tea trays, that they returned to their discussion about the Swanns and the Inghams in the eighteenth century.

It was Cecily who started it up once more.

'So, all's well that ends well,' Cecily murmured and, giving Aunt Charlotte a searching look, she asked, 'When you were talking about Humphrey Ingham and James Swann, you said they weren't bad men, that they were *nice* men. What did you mean?'

'They may have manipulated many matters and people to suit their own ends, their needs and desires, but as far as Cavendon was concerned, the two of them ran it extremely well,' Aunt Charlotte told her, and then went on to explain.

'Humphrey kept good logbooks about everything that was happening in his various businesses and on the estate. When he travelled, he was very open about where he was. He could always be reached if he was needed in an emergency. James ran the estate with enormous efficiency, and both men treated the staff well . . . both their personal servants in the house and the workers on the estate. They were known for their reasonable attitudes and understanding.'

'Yes, I gathered that,' Cecily said. 'James makes lots of references to Humphrey's fairness in certain situations and his generosity to the staff. I found one notation that was interesting. James wrote that he and Humphrey made sure they gave every man they employed his dignity and his due.'

Charlotte nodded. 'David also told me a lot about his ancestors, things that had been dutifully passed down from earl to earl. Fairness, justice, dignity and safety were the words he usually mentioned. He said anyone who had worked at Cavendon had been safe, protected, and that they had had two strong and clever men to defend their rights. That was important to the 5th Earl, and he maintained that the 1st Earl of Mowbray, Humphrey, set the standards which were scrupulously adhered to by the following generations. They lived by those rules. And they still do.'

'And then there was Great-Aunt Gwendolyn, who fell in love with a Swann and bore him a child,' Cecily suddenly said, remembering that well-hidden secret.

A warm smile spread across Charlotte's face. 'Lovely Great-Aunt Gwen, who longed for all those years to see her only child, given up for adoption at birth, and whom I found quite by accident.'

'Some might call that a fluke, Aunt Charlotte, but, using your favourite phrase, I believe *it was meant to be.* And certainly it gave Great-Aunt Gwen a new lease of life, not to mention the last chance for a bit of happiness, getting to know her daughter.'

The Dowager Countess looked off into the distance for a moment, and then turning her head, gazing at Cecily, she said, 'I must go over to Harrogate next week, Ceci, and see Margaret, take her out to lunch. Will you come with me?'

'Of course I will. I like her, and she does remind me of Great-Aunt Gwen, there's no two ways about that.'

'And *Diedre.* Don't forget, Margaret has quite a look of her.'

'She does, and talking of looks, there's something I'd like to do, right now.' As she spoke, Cecily jumped up, went over to Aunt Charlotte and helped her out of the sofa. 'I want to go and look at them.'

'Who?' Charlotte frowned, seemingly puzzled for a moment.

'The ancestors! At least the Inghams – many of them are hanging on the walls above the double staircase. Come on, let's go and look at Humphrey, Marie, Marmaduke, Elizabeth and Helen. They're all out there, you know.'

'And there is a portrait of James Swann, his wife Anne and their children. At one end of the Long Gallery. What a good idea, Cecily.'

The two of them stood on the landing at the top of the double staircase, staring at the painting hanging on the wall above. 'This is the First Earl of Mowbray,' Charlotte said. 'The famous

Humphrey, painted by Thomas Gainsborough. What do you think?'

'What I've always thought, that he was a rather handsome man, and now, as I'm really scrutinizing it more carefully, I must admit he looks like Miles's father, Charles, the Sixth Earl.'

'Right on the mark, my dear. And this is Marie.' Charlotte glanced at Cecily. 'I don't think she's that ugly, do you?'

'No. Perhaps Humphrey's mother was prejudiced, you know, because Marie was older than him. Though she is a bit plain,' Cecily finished, wrinkling her nose. 'Also painted by Gainsborough, I see.'

'I agree. Helen, his second wife, is rather pretty, don't you think? Quite glamorous, but George Romney tended to give women who sat for him a really gorgeous look.'

Cecily nodded, and then grabbed hold of Charlotte's arm, and exclaimed, 'Look at this portrait. It's Marmaduke, the Second Earl. But if it weren't for the awful wig, I'd say it was my own firstborn, David.'

An amused smile played around Aunt Charlotte's mouth. 'I've often thought that. The portrait is very well executed. It's by Reynolds. Look, here is Elizabeth, Marmaduke's sister. She has a look of you, Ceci. It's by Romney, and a beautiful rendering of her.'

'Do you really think I have a look of her?' Cecily asked, not really seeing the resemblance.

'Yes. Haven't you ever noticed that?'

Cecily shook her head. 'Perhaps Ingham men always like the same type of woman. Let's go to the Long Gallery and look at the portraits of James Swann and his family. And be careful walking down the stairs, Aunt Charlotte. Hold onto the bannister.'

'I will. I'm quite steady on my feet, Cecily.'

A few seconds later they were walking through the main hall heading to the Long Gallery, where many of the great paintings by famous artists were hanging.

At the far end, near the East Wing, there was a grouping of

paintings Cecily knew well. The two main paintings were of James and Anne Swann, and there was another of James's sister, Sarah Swann Caxton, and her children.

'I've looked at these paintings since I was old enough to understand that I was descended from James and Anne Swann, Aunt Charlotte. And I've always thought what a good-looking man he was. But having read parts of the Swann record books he kept over his lifetime, his portrait means so much more to me now. I feel as if I really knew him.' Cecily's eyes were glued to the painting.

'Yes, it sort of sinks in, doesn't it, knowing that he was our founding father and that we carry his genes . . . And that we live at Cavendon because of him, and everything he did to make it great is stupendous, actually.'

Unexpectedly, Cecily's eyes filled with tears. She brushed them away swiftly, and her voice wobbled slightly when she said, 'I feel so very proud of him, and proud to be a Swann.'

'As do I, darling,' Aunt Charlotte murmured and took hold of Cecily's arm. 'This has been worth fighting for, hasn't it? Because of Humphrey and James, and what they created through their vision, which is quite marvellous. Cavendon is one of the greatest stately homes in England, and hopefully it will stand forever.'

## PART THREE

# Magic and Make-Believe

Come live with me, and be my love,
And we will some new pleasures prove
Of golden sands, and crystal brooks,
With silken lines, and silver hooks.

John Donne, 'The Bait'

# Sixteen

In the end the new script book took longer than expected to finally arrive, and Alicia had spent the whole month of August feeling restless and frustrated.

As she waited at Cavendon, whiling away her time by cleaning her clothes closets and sorting items, she cursed the associate producer under her breath. His name was Adam Fennell, and she hadn't met him, but his constant requests for additional rewrites seemed endless. When the approved shooting script finally did come, it was sent up from London by messenger, no less, and she changed her mind about him.

She knew at once, after one quick read-through, that he had been right. This script was excellent, and so much better than the others. It now had dramatic force and swifter pacing, and it struck her immediately that her part had been enlarged. She had the female lead, which was now well written, and the character she was playing was well defined. Felix Lambert had agreed with her, told her that the rewrites gave her greater prominence in the storyline, and that if she was clever and put her heart and soul into the part, she could quite easily steal this picture.

'Adam admires your work,' Felix explained on the phone. 'He'll make sure you get plenty of exposure and publicity when the film's released.'

He told her that her new starting date was Wednesday 14 September, at Shepperton Studios in Surrey, and the producers hoped to wrap the picture in ninety days. He reminded her that she must be available for a week after that for post-production, looping, and whatever else was required.

Once Alicia had the screenplay in her hands, her mood changed. She curled up on the sofa in her bedroom at Cavendon, reading her lines, committing them to memory. She was at her happiest when she was working, and her excitement about the new movie kicked all thoughts of Brin and his bad behaviour out of her mind. Work gave her comfort, courage and confidence in herself again. She couldn't wait to begin.

In the past, Alicia had enjoyed working at Shepperton Studios. There were some big sound stages and a spacious backlot. She was walking across the backlot on her first day at work, when she heard her name being called in a low, masculine voice.

Swinging around, she saw Sir Alexander Korda waving to her. He was not only an extraordinary film producer and director, and the creator of some magnificent films, such as *The Fallen Idol* and *That Hamilton Woman*, starring Vivien Leigh, but he also had the largest financial interest in Shepperton Studios. He practically owned it.

His companion that morning was Orson Welles, the American actor, and she hurried over to greet them. After Sir Alex had introduced her to the actor, she congratulated both men on the success of *The Third Man*, in which Orson Welles starred. The picture, recently released, was a huge hit.

Sir Alex chatted to her for a few seconds, and seemed to be aware that she was the female lead in *Broken Image*, being made by Mario Cantonelli and Adam Fennell. He added that her director,

Paul Dowling, was one of the best in the business, as she no doubt knew.

A few minutes later Alicia was looking around the dressing room which had been assigned to her. It was one of the best, and quite large, with a window looking out onto the backlot. Obviously it had been recently repainted and spruced up. Aside from the dressing table and several straight chairs, there was an armchair and sofa, and the lighting was excellent.

Alicia smiled to herself, knowing she was getting special treatment. She could not fail to miss the enormous bowl of flowers on an end table, and the white envelope propped up next to it. Opening the envelope, she read the card. It welcomed her to the production, wished her luck, and was signed Mario and Adam.

She walked over to the dressing table, turned on the lights which surrounded the mirror, and sat down. Everything sparkled, and she could see herself very clearly. It was obvious to her that there had been a big effort to make the dressing room comfortable. Glancing down, she saw her call sheet for that day and the following one on the table. A glass vase on top of the two sheets was holding a single white rose.

Immediately, she knew it was from Anna Lancing, undoubtedly the best makeup artist in the picture business. Anna always gave her a white rose at the start of a production. Alicia jumped up and walked across the room. She would go to Makeup to greet her long-time associate and friend.

Pulling open the door, she then stepped back swiftly.

The two men standing there, about to knock on the door, looked totally startled. One was Mario. She assumed the other one was Adam Fennell.

Recovering himself at once, Mario greeted her warmly, stepped forward and kissed her cheek. He then introduced his companion. It was indeed Adam, who thrust out his hand and smiled. 'I'm so glad you're part of the production,' he said.

He held onto her hand a moment too long. It was Alicia who let go of his. Smiled in return. She was surprised by his looks;

she had imagined he would be a much older man. He appeared to be in his thirties, and he was extremely good looking. In fact, he might easily be mistaken for a film star himself, and he was impeccably groomed.

'We came to welcome you,' Mario now said.

Alicia opened the door wider. 'Please, do come in. And I want to thank you both for the flowers. They're lovely.'

Mario immediately zeroed in on Alicia, sitting down next to her on the sofa, and he did all the talking.

Adam sat back in the armchair. He said nothing. He listened. He had learned that listening was a gift.

Adam Fennell had started listening acutely and very attentively, when he was a child. It had saved his life time and again, and had taught him a lot about people and the world at large. Being a good listener had given him an edge.

Long ago, when he was ten, he had overheard someone say that he was nothing, a nobody from nowhere, a piece of rubbish only worth pissing on.

He had ruminated on those words for many months, and one day he had made up his mind to become somebody from somewhere.

His endgame was to be an important man with money and power: those were the great protectors. And so he had dragged himself up out of the gutter, out of poverty, starvation, abuse and disregard by using any means he could.

This enormous effort had made him stronger, brought out his natural drive, and then a sense of ambition had kicked in. As he became older, he had grown relentless in his determination and ruthlessness, and it had delivered success.

He was thirteen years old when he had decided he must run away. His father had been a volatile and dangerous drunkard, living on the dole; his mother a terrified and quaking battered wife, with no spirit, life, or love left in her. His older brother, Andy, had been blindly following in their father's tracks, with no real purpose in life.

When Adam had left the ramshackle cottage in Manchester, he had set off to walk to London. Instinctively, he had realized that was where he was meant to be, where fortune and fame awaited him. Well aware, even at his age, of the hopelessness of his life with his family, he had understood that he must put that behind him as fast as possible.

That night Adam Fennell possessed only the clothes he wore – shabby grey trousers, a dark green jumper of Andy's, and his father's only jacket. In his pockets were a pound note he had stolen from Andy when he was in a stupor and reeking of booze, two apples, and a penknife he had found in a gutter months before. He treasured that knife.

It was midnight, in the summer of 1924, when he had gone. He felt no regret, only profound relief as he walked away from the despair, drunkenness and doom.

Plodding along, heading for the main road to London at a steady pace, he had made another vow to himself. He would not touch alcohol, not as long as he lived. And he never had.

Once he had felt tired, he had found a hedge and gone into it, burrowing into the hedgerow, had eaten an apple, and eventually he had fallen asleep.

The next morning he had begged for food from the kind woman who opened her kitchen door to him. Taking pity on the boy, she brought him inside, fed him bacon and eggs. He had repaid her by stealing her purse from the kitchen dresser when her back was turned.

Nights spent in hedgerows, haystacks, barns and fields; days stealing food and anything else he could find. He had turned out to be a good little thief. He had managed.

On the last leg of his journey, Adam had hitched a lift with a young man driving a shiny new car. But it turned out to be a disastrous mistake. When Adam had asked the young man to stop alongside a wood so he could relieve himself, the man sneaked after him and had tried to rape him.

Adam had reacted angrily, had had no alternative but to use the penknife. He had stabbed the young man in the arm and neck to prevent the sexual attack on himself. Struggling to his feet, he had taken the man's money and run off. He knew he had only wounded his assailant.

Understanding that he must put distance between the wounded man and himself, Adam had turned off the main road once he had noticed a signpost pointing towards Harrow. It was not quite London, but Adam was aware the city was very close.

Although he did not know it then, this was the best choice Adam could have made. He had been out of breath and panting when he had seen the public house. It was called the Golden Horn. He had seated himself on a wooden bench outside the pub, which was not yet open, trying to catch his breath, hoping to regain his strength.

Closed though it was, the publican, the keeper of the tavern, had spotted the boy through the window. He had come out to question him, and immediately noticed that the young boy looked worn out, impoverished, and very dirty. When he had asked him if something was wrong with him, Adam had answered that he was exhausted, thirsty, and needed a drink of water.

The publican, Jack Trotter by name, had gone back into the pub, swiftly returning with a tankard of fresh water. After pushing it towards the boy, he had introduced himself and had asked his name.

Adam told him and then he had launched into a sad and touching tale of despair, poverty and abuse. He had explained he was running away to London.

Trotter had quickly discovered Adam had no relatives or friends in the city, and no job to go to, and impulsively he had decided to take him in, if only for a few weeks. He had felt the need to help get the boy on his feet.

Before he could do that, Trotter had had to go and discuss this unexpected matter with his brother Timothy, who ran the tavern with him. The Trotter brothers had returned, after mulling it over, and had invited Adam into the public house.

After he had listened to their offer, Adam had accepted it. He had agreed he would clean the brass decorations hanging on the walls, mop the floors and clean the bar. In return, he was told he could live in the small barn and that they would provide food. They had promised him a small wage.

The bonus, as Adam had soon discovered, was the clothes Jack Trotter had offered him. Jack's son, Tommy, had been killed in a road accident a year before at the age of sixteen, and Trotter had still been grieving. This was one of the reasons the publican had decided he must help this poor young boy, in memory of the son he had so tragically lost.

Adam had never forgotten Jack Trotter and how he had helped him when he was a boy. And eventually, as the years passed, he had also come to realize that Jack had done something else of major importance, quite aside from taking him in.

One night, just after he had arrived at the Golden Horn, Jack had taken him to a picture house in Croydon. It was the first time he had ever seen a film. And, in so doing, he had changed Adam's life, put him on the right path, however unwittingly. Adam had fallen in love with the moving pictures he saw up there on the screen. Nothing would keep him away from films ever again.

Patient listener though he was, Adam now noticed that Alicia was looking nervous, and he said swiftly, 'Sorry to interrupt, Mario, old chap, but I think we must go now. Leave Miss Stanton alone. She will have to go to Makeup soon . . .' He let his voice trail off, and smiled at Mario, never wanting to offend the older man.

Alicia, filled with relief, immediately exclaimed, 'I must do that, Mario, as much as I've enjoyed talking to you. I start shooting around noon. My first scene.'

'My goodness! I *am* taking up too much of your time. So sorry, my dear.' Mario rose and gave her a peck on the cheek.

Adam stood and so did Alicia. He walked towards her, smiling, and shook her hand. 'Break a leg,' he said in a low tone, using the old theatrical good-luck wish.

She smiled back, gazing into his grey, translucent eyes, and gave him a knowing look. Without saying a word, she had conveyed her relief that he had broken this session up. He was aware she was already feeling grateful to him.

# Seventeen

As she walked towards Claridge's, Alicia was glad she was not filming today. It was Friday, the last day of September, and her day off. The weather was glorious. She was also happy she had agreed to have lunch with Constance Lambert. She really did need to talk to her friend and theatrical agent about a number of things.

The staff of the hotel greeted her warmly as she walked through the lobby and went into the Causerie, one of her favourite places.

Constance was already seated on a banquette and waved to her as she went in; a moment later Alicia was sitting down next to the older woman.

Alicia couldn't help thinking how chic Constance looked, but then she had great style and panache. Alicia said, 'Nobody does it like you, Constance. You're always so well put together, and I see you're wearing a Swann dress.'

'When am I not? And thank you for the compliments. By the way, I saw Cecily the other day, when she was at the shop in Burlington Arcade, down for her monthly visit, she told me. She also confided that she has reorganized her business and is only going to make couture clothes from now on. No ready-mades any more. I told her I thought it was a good move.'

'And I said the same thing when I was at Cavendon in August. What are you drinking, Connie? Champagne? I think I'll have a glass.'

Constance chuckled. 'No, it's ginger ale. I asked them to put it in a champagne flute because it seems to taste better. You see, I'm on a diet at the moment, but let me order you a glass of bubbly, darling.'

'Oh, I don't know, if you're not drinking—'

'Tell you what,' Constance cut in. 'I'll join you, to hell with the diet. I think I should toast you. After all, you've had a wonderful run these last few weeks; excellent dailies, so I hear.'

Alicia nodded. 'Yes, I know. I do hope I haven't offended Adam Fennell. He invited me to watch the rushes one night last week, and I said I couldn't. You know how I hate watching the daily takes. I don't want to see myself on the screen until the film is finally finished, cut and edited.'

'Why do you think you may have offended him?'

'Because I haven't seen him for several days, nor heard a word from him, and he's normally quite attentive to me.'

Constance frowned. 'I know you don't want to see the dailies, and I'm sure that's in your contract. I'll have to double-check later. What I do know is that he has raved about your performance so far to Felix, and even hinted about your being in the next film. No worries.' A thought suddenly hit her, and she said softly, 'Are you interested in Adam?'

Alicia stared at her, and felt a flush rising from her neck to flood her face. For a second, she was unable to speak, unexpectedly understanding how much she *was* interested in him. She merely nodded.

Constance smiled knowingly and beckoned to a waiter, ordered two glasses of Veuve Clicquot, then sat back, looking intently at Alicia. 'So, you want to know all about him? Is that it?'

'I suppose,' Alicia answered in a low voice.

'First things first. He's not married and never has been, to my knowledge. He's a bit older than you, in his late thirties, I think.'

A smile slipped onto Alicia's face. 'It's good to know he's not a married man. I avoid *them* like the plague. How long has he been in the picture business?'

'About ten years or so, not much longer. He's been extremely successful, worked his way up through the ranks rather quickly. He was with Korda. I don't know how that came about, but I believe Sir Alex mentored him for a time. Now he's out on his own. Felix says Adam's got the golden touch; that films he's involved with always take awards, and, more importantly, they're box-office hits.'

'I knew that, which is why I was happy to take this part.' Alicia hesitated for a moment, and then asked, 'Is there a woman in his life? Or wouldn't you know that?'

'I think I would, yes. You know what show business is like. There's always a lot of gossip. And I have to add this. When I've run into him at events over the years, he's always alone or with a group. I've never seen a woman on his arm, darling.'

'He's been very nice to me, Constance – charming, actually. He and Mario sent flowers the first day. That's sort of normal, since I'm the female lead. But the following week Adam sent me a little bouquet of white roses. There was a note. All it said was *Congratulations, Adam.* And he's popped his head around my dressing-room door several times, and merely said, "Hello, good work", or something like that. Then ever since I declined his invitation to see the rushes, he's not been around at all.'

Constance shook her head. 'It's meaningless. So far he's had nothing but praise for you. Maybe he's been at his office in London, and not out at the studio. Do you want me to dig around a bit?'

'Oh no! Don't do that! I'd be embarrassed if he knew I was asking questions about him . . .' Alicia paused when the waiter arrived with the champagne.

Constance picked up her flute and so did Alicia and they clinked glasses. Constance said, 'Here's to you, my darling, I think you're on to a big winner.'

Alicia gave her a cheeky look. 'I'm not sure if you're referring to the movie or the man.'

'I think I mean both, actually.' Constance took a sip of champagne, and went on, 'Look, are you really and truly interested in Adam? Going on a date with him? Seeing where it leads?'

Alicia nodded, and took a swallow of champagne. 'I know that only two months ago I was weeping over Brin, and the way he dumped me, crying my eyes out. And on your shoulder, no less. Still, I did get over him when I thought everything through at Cavendon. I suddenly understood that his behaviour had been horrible. Unacceptable.'

'And then you started working on the film, met Adam. And what?' Constance raised a dark brow eloquently.

'I liked him that first day at the studio. Then I found myself charmed by him. He does have a lot of charisma, and he's good looking . . .' Clearing her throat, Alicia added, 'For the last ten days, when I got home at night, I found I was thinking about him. *A lot.* And several times, when I ran into him accidentally on the sound stage, or the backlot, I felt . . .' She stopped and whispered, 'Attracted to him.'

'I can understand that. I think many women would feel the same way. He's quite a man. Listen, here's a plan. Why don't I have Felix invite him to dinner? Let's say next Friday, since you don't film on the weekends.'

'That will be all right with me, but would he accept?'

'If he's not busy he will. He's always accepted our invitations, and he has reciprocated in turn—' Constance broke off, and said, 'Oh my God! Don't move a muscle and don't turn your head. Adam is walking in here with another agent, Bob Griffin. He hasn't seen us yet, but he will when he sits down.'

Alicia could not speak. She just gaped at Constance, who took hold of her hand and muttered, 'My God, you're shaking like a leaf.'

Adam and the theatrical agent he was with sat down on a banquette at the other side of the Causerie. And Adam spotted them at once. He turned his head, said something to the agent, got up, and strode across to their table.

'How lovely to see you, Constance, and you too, Alicia. Mario and I are extremely pleased with your work, very impressed.' He smiled at her, his grey eyes focused on hers.

'Thank you. That makes me happy.' Alicia was surprised her voice was steady. It startled her that she could not look away from him.

Constance seized the moment. 'Felix and I were just talking about you earlier, Adam. We were thinking of inviting you to join us and Alicia for supper tonight. He was going to phone you. He probably has already. And now, how fortuitous that you're here. Are you by any chance free this evening?'

'Not until about eight thirty. I have friends coming for drinks at my flat at six thirty. Oh, here's a thought. Perhaps you would like to join me? Then the four of us could go to supper afterwards.'

'How wonderful,' Constance exclaimed. She looked at Alicia. 'That's all right with you, isn't it, my dear?'

'It would be lovely,' Alicia said and managed, finally, to tear her gaze away from Adam's face.

He now looked directly at Constance and inclined his head, offered her his biggest smile. 'All of this is just marvellous. You know where I live, don't you, Constance? You and Felix have been to my flat before.'

'Yes, we have. It's in Bryanston Square.'

He nodded. 'See you later, Constance, Alicia.'

He was gone in a flash, rejoining the agent on the banquette across the room, and started talking to him immediately.

Constance said, 'Wow, you really reacted to him! He did to you, too. I noticed that he couldn't take his eyes off you. Listen, this was such a lucky coincidence, Adam coming here for lunch, don't you think?'

'I do. Were you really talking about him this morning?'

'No. I just invented that on the spur of the moment, grabbed a chance to invite him. I'll fill Felix in later. Now let's look at the menu and order lunch, shall we?'

'I'm not very hungry, Constance. I think I was somewhat thrown when Adam suddenly appeared.'

'He excites you, doesn't he?' Constance murmured, knowingly.

'Very much,' Alicia whispered.

'I think I'll book a table at the Savoy Hotel for supper. Carroll Gibbons and his orchestra . . . *perfect.* You can be in his arms by ten o'clock tonight. On the dance floor, I mean.'

'*Alicia Stanton on the rocks.*' Victoria read the caption out loud, looked at the art editor of *Elegance Magazine* and laughed. 'Very clever, Tony. I love it.'

'And I was bowled over by your photographs, as you know. There's something awesome about the monoliths, and they're a great backdrop for the bouffant pink-tulle evening gown covered in gold sequins. Hard and soft . . . the huge stones make it pop out on the page.'

Still smiling, Victoria focused on the rest of the magazine spread, covering six pages, which Tony had just finished earlier that morning.

'I'm so glad Alicia wore the red silk dress and coat in the maze. A wonderful splash of vivid colour amid all the green hedges. I stood on a ladder, two paths away, to shoot it.'

Tony del Renzio nodded. 'I figured that out, love,' he answered, grinning at her. 'I hope the caption's not too corny. *In a daze in the maze.*'

'I think it's amusing. What did Melinda say?'

'She laughed, okayed the entire spread before she left for Paris an hour ago. She asked me to give you this.' He picked up an envelope on the desk behind him and handed it to her. 'I think it's your new assignment.'

'Do you know what it is?'

'Only vaguely. Read the note.'

Victoria did as he asked. Her eyes scanned the memo from the editor-in-chief:

*Dear Victoria,*

*You wowed me with your Alicia pictures. Congratulations. Tony has done you proud with his highly creative layout. I am planning a story on Christopher Longdon, Britain's greatest war hero. Do a little research on him. Plan a shoot. He's starting a charity for war veterans. It's going to be one of our more serious pieces. Think Hero. Bravery. Hero. We'll talk later.*

*Have a good weekend,*

*Melinda*

Victoria reread the note and then stared at Tony, 'Isn't Christopher Longdon in a wheelchair?' She frowned, made a *moue*, and added, 'He's paralysed, if I remember correctly.'

'Only partially, from what I understand.'

'This is one difficult shoot ahead of me, don't you think? I mean, a man in a wheelchair doesn't give me too many photographic options.' She felt uneasy, concerned already.

'I think you'll have to be inventive. That's not a problem for you, Vicki.'

Victoria turned away from the long worktable where the layout was spread out and sat down in a chair. Tony went and stood behind his desk, gazing across at her. 'Don't look so glum, ducks, you'll be able to manage. Apparently he's very charming.'

A sigh escaped, and Victoria now asked, 'Do you know where he lives? I have a feeling it's somewhere in the country.'

'No, actually, Christopher Longdon has a house close to Hampstead Heath. And listen, according to Melinda, there're plenty of people to help you, such as a physical trainer and an assistant, and both are men. She also told me there's a beautiful garden. So, plenty of possibilities, I think.'

'How does Melinda know so much about his household?'

'Christopher Longdon saved her brother's life during the war. They were friends and in the Royal Air Force together. She wants to help Christopher with the start-up of his charity,' Tony explained. 'She doesn't really know him well, but I guess she's checked things out.'

'Maybe she can introduce me to her brother. He might have some useful ideas for me.'

Tony shook his head, grimaced. 'Afraid not. Her brother, Ronnie, died last year. Never really got over his injuries.'

'Oh, how terrible. I'm sorry to hear that.' Victoria stood up, put the note in her pocket, walked towards the door. 'I'll do some research, do the best I can.'

'I know you will, ducks. That's why you're my favourite. You put such a huge effort into your work, which is more than I can say for most.'

'Thanks, Tony. And thanks for making my pictures look so good.'

Victoria walked down the corridor, mulling over the new assignment. She loved it here at the magazine and wanted to prove herself, make it a success. It was her big break. This brief troubled her, and she wondered how to make it work. It was a real challenge. Well, she liked a challenge, didn't she?

Once she was at her desk, she made a few notes about Christopher Longdon, and then wrote a list of possible sources who could help her. Charlie, more than likely, and also Elise.

They were all having dinner tonight, and she could talk to her then. Victoria's thoughts went to Lady Diedre, who knew everybody, and also Uncle Harry, who had been in the RAF.

The phone on her desk began to ring, and she picked it up instantly, 'Victoria Brown here.'

'It's Elise, Vicki, just checking that we're still on for tonight.'

'I've booked a table at Le Chat Noir, if that's all right with you?' She could hear the clatter and noise of the newsroom in the background.

'Great, but I can't make it before eight. I'm still writing a tough story.'

'That's when I booked it for. I guessed you'd be hard at it until then. Listen, before you go, do you know anything much about Christopher Longdon?'

'He's one of our greatest war heroes. Did over a hundred missions over Germany, or something like that, and he was very courageous. Why?'

'I've got to do a shoot on him for the magazine.'

There was a silence before Elise murmured, 'Gosh, that'll be tough. He's in a wheelchair.'

'I'll have to be inventive, Tony told me. So I will be. See you tonight, Elise.'

# Eighteen

When Victoria arrived at Le Chat Noir too early, she was seated at once by the new owner, Jean-Philippe. He was the son of the former proprietor, Jacques André, who had died last year. He and his mother now ran the restaurant together and were making a good job of it.

'We have *moules* tonight, Miss Brown,' he told her as he hovered next to the table. 'And also our Dover sole.'

'Thank you, Jean-Philippe,' Victoria answered. 'The *moules* always tempt me.'

He smiled and walked away, returning a moment later with water.

Victoria sat back in the chair, glancing around, wondering if there was anyone she knew in the restaurant, but they were all strangers. She straightened her skirt: it was a new one that she'd spotted in the window of a little dress shop near Greta's house, and she felt it made her look more sophisticated.

She pulled a small notebook out of her bag and glanced at the notes she had made earlier.

So far she knew that Christopher Longdon lived in a large house overlooking Hampstead Heath. He had been born in 1921, and had joined the RAF when the war started in 1939. Apparently he was one of the young fighter pilots who had helped to win the Battle of Britain in the air. This aside, he was among the very few who had survived the war, even though he flew his Spitfire every day. His plane had crashed several weeks before the Armistice was declared, which was when he was badly wounded.

She had heard this from Charlie, to whom she had spoken on the phone that afternoon. Charlie had only these few facts in his head, but offered to phone a friend who might be able to help. 'I believe Angus is a pal of Longdon's, or was,' Charlie had explained. 'They went to school together. Eton, I believe.'

Charlie had promised to phone her back tomorrow, and she knew he would. He was reliable. Putting her notebook away, she took a sip of water, wondering what kind of shoot this would turn out to be. How would she make him look heroic in a wheelchair? Wasn't that up to the writer? To the words that would tell his story movingly? She had no idea where to start, nor did she know anyone who could help her.

Paloma? Perhaps she would give Harry's wife a ring tomorrow and pick her brains.

'Here I am!' Elise exclaimed, appearing suddenly at the table, surprising Victoria with her stealthy arrival.

Victoria immediately jumped up and hugged Elise, who hugged her back. The two young women sat down, smiling across the table at each other. They had bonded years ago and were genuinely loyal and loving friends. Elise was wearing her usual office uniform of a blouse and tailored skirt, but the bright yellow colour of her blouse suited her dark hair and eyes and she looked as fashionable as ever, despite her long day.

Elise said, 'I *need* a drink. Shall we have a gin and orange? I've had a hell of a day, a crazy day.'

'And I'm facing a hell of a shoot. I need a drink as much as you.'

Jean-Philippe came over to greet Elise, and Victoria ordered their drinks.

'I really feel for you,' Elise began, settling back in the chair. 'I think Christopher Longdon is the most admirable man and, obviously, immensely brave. But this *is* a tough assignment, Vicki. I agree with you there. Here's the thing, I told my news editor about your assignment. He's a mine of information about people and he told me a couple of things. Christopher Longdon's not married. He was an only child and his parents are dead.'

'It's still not much to go on, but thanks anyway. We both know newspapermen always have the best information, so I spoke to Charlie today.'

At this moment the waiter arrived with their drinks, and Victoria waited until he had departed to start speaking again. 'He gave me a few details, but not much.'

The two women clinked glasses, said cheers and took a sip before Victoria spoke. She then told Elise everything she knew about the subject of her next shoot. 'Which amounts to nothing,' she finished.

'I'll do a bit of digging next week, see if I can come up with more facts,' Elise promised. 'However, I do think this is one of those assignments which will have to . . . *evolve*. By that I mean you might see endless things that will work, once you meet him. I'm sure some ideas will come to you then. You're in the dark at the moment.'

'You're right, Elise. Thanks for that!' Victoria exclaimed, her face suddenly lighting up. 'It's silly to have preconceived ideas, to be negative before I've even met the man. I shall give his assistant a ring on Monday morning. I'll explain I need to come and chat with Mr Longdon, that I have to do a sort of pre-shoot interview. That way I can take a dekko at the place, the garden, and the man himself. Hopefully, I'll find inspiration.'

'Knowing you, I bet this will turn out to be the best shoot you've ever done. A challenge suits you. Oh, and by the way, Charlie's coming to Greta's little shindig tomorrow night, and he asked if he can bring Alicia.'

'Oh I hope she comes! I want to tell her about the spread, Elise.

It's just marvellous, and she's really gorgeous in the clothes. Tony del Renzio showed it to me earlier today. The magazine goes to press tonight. The spread will be in the December issue. I can't wait for it to be on the newsstands.'

'Won't you have some early copies?' Elise asked.

'You're right, I probably will, and you and Greta will be the first to get one each, along with Alicia and Aunt Alice.' Victoria grinned at Elise and went on, 'Shall we look at the menu? Jean-Philippe told me they have *moules* tonight, and also some Dover sole, as well as their usual items.'

Elise rolled her eyes. 'Sounds delicious.'

'It's been such a funny week at work, a lot of negatives to develop, so much to do. And I haven't really had a proper meal for days,' Victoria remarked.

'The same for me. I seem to have been on the run mostly. Too many tough stories. Hey, but I'm not complaining, just explaining. I love being on a newspaper; it's like being in the centre of everything. You know what's going on everywhere, thanks to the tickertapes.'

'I know. And all the time.' Victoria lifted her hand when she saw Jean-Philippe and the girls ordered.

Once they were alone, Elise leaned forward and said, 'I need to talk to you, Vicki. I've not been feeling so good lately. I've been really blue, on and off. It worries me, because my mother suffered, you know.'

'You must talk to me. I'm your best friend,' Victoria replied. 'If not me, who else? Well, there's Greta, of course.'

'I prefer to talk to you, Vicki, but not at this moment. I shouldn't have brought it up now.' Elise pushed her glass away and gave a bright smile. 'Can we talk later, after dinner?'

'Whenever you want, I'm here for you.' Victoria reached out and squeezed her arm, offering her a loving smile.

'What are you wearing tomorrow evening, do you know?'

'Something simple,' Elise responded. 'Greta has only invited a small group, and it's not one of her fancy sit-down dinners. She's making a buffet. So I'll wear a plain silk dress.'

'So will I. You know what? I'm so glad it's the weekend. I've errands to do tomorrow, but Sunday I plan to sleep late.' She paused, leaned into Elise and said, 'Why don't we go to the pictures? I'd like to see *The Third Man*. It's had fantastic reviews.'

'That would be nice,' Elise responded, and then hesitated. 'But I might have to be on call to go into work on Sunday. Can I tell you tomorrow?'

'That's fine,' Victoria replied. 'Our dinner is on its way, thank goodness. I'm ravenous.'

Forcing herself to be more cheerful, Elise said, 'I'm so glad we made this date, Vicki. It's lovely to see you; it's been over a week.'

Vicki smiled, already fairly certain what Elise's problem was, at least part of it: she had no real personal life.

It was later, over coffee, that Elise finally began to confide in Victoria. 'I get terribly down at times these days, and I don't always know why. After all, I do have a job I love, and yet I suddenly find myself down in the dumps.'

Victoria nodded, answered her swiftly. 'Do you think you made a mistake? I mean, going to live in a flat on your own?'

Frowning, Elise shook her head vehemently, and sounded certain when she replied. 'No! I need to be out on my own, with a place of my own. After all, I'm twenty-eight and an adult woman.'

The way she said it made Victoria laugh. 'And I suppose I should be out on my own, too. Yet here I am, still living with Greta in her guest room.'

'You haven't found a flat, I know, but there's one to let around the corner from me, on Oakley Street. Perhaps you should go and look at it?' Elise made these words sound like a question.

'To be honest, I haven't had time to breathe lately, never mind go flat hunting,' Victoria responded. 'The new job has me running all over the place. Several times Greta has asked me to stay on, to share the house with her. She even suggested I could pay rent, if that made me feel better.'

Stirring her coffee, Victoria now said in a lower voice, 'I really think she misses you, Elise, and that she's also rather lonely, because I'm hardly there.'

When Elise did not reply, Victoria took a deep breath and plunged in. 'And *you're* lonely. I think that's probably why you get blue. You come home at night to an empty place, with no one to welcome you, no food to eat, because like me you don't have much time to shop . . .'

Her voice trailed off when she saw the miserable expression settling on her friend's face. Victoria wondered what to say next to make her feel better.

After a few moments, Elise said in a quiet voice, 'Are you suggesting I move back in with Greta?'

'I wasn't, not really, but why not?' Victoria smiled. 'Listen, we'll swap places. I'll take over your flat, and you can move back in with your sister.'

Elise started to laugh. 'No way. It took a lot of guts on my part to leave in the first place. I really do want a home of my own. I mean, what if I meet a nice man? I'd want to . . . entertain him. Having a flat means I have real privacy.'

'Don't get mad,' Victoria began cautiously and, speaking with care, she continued, 'I said that you are lonely, and you didn't respond. I want to put that another way. I think that perhaps you're depressed because you haven't got a boyfriend. And I do know you literally *ache* for one.'

Taken aback, Elise stared at her, aghast, and exclaimed, 'I don't think I *ache* for a man. However, I would like to meet someone, that's true.' There was an angry edge to her voice.

'I'm trying to be helpful,' Victoria murmured. 'Don't be cross.'

'I'm not, but since I use words to earn a living I like to be precise.'

Victoria remained silent, realizing that she had hit a sore spot. And she was aware she was correct. Elise's problem was that she needed to be involved with a man, actually in a *serious* relationship; that Elise wanted to get married, longed to have a baby, to start a family of her own.

'Sorry I snapped,' Elise said in a regretful tone a moment later. 'You're my best friend, and I know you are only concerned for me, not being critical. And you're right, if I'm honest. I do worry though, because I'm getting older by the minute.'

Victoria looked at her watch. 'Another minute gone! Hurry up, look around. Do you see a likely man? Go and grab him before someone else does.'

Elise's laughter bubbled up. She had to sit back in her chair to catch her breath. After a moment she said, 'There's really nobody like you, Vicki. You manage to pull me out of my dark mood. Thank you.'

'You don't have to thank me, I care about you. I'd do anything for you. I also know the reason why you wish to have your own flat. Luckily, I don't feel the same, not at this moment. I'm so busy with work, I'm rather relieved to camp out at Greta's for as long as she'll have me.'

'Then you'll be able to stay forever. She loves having you around, if only late at night and at weekends. And you're not facing the same problem as me.'

'What are you getting at?'

'You're only twenty-one, Vicki. You've got lots of time to meet someone, get involved, get married. I'll be thirty before I can blink.'

'Then I shall have to go on the hunt for you, Elise. Dig up a smashing chap from somewhere. Immediately. I shall now give every adult male I meet the once-over, keeping the beautiful Elise in mind. Leave it to me.'

# Nineteen

Adam Fennell stood looking at himself in the long mirror in his bedroom. As usual it was through critical eyes.

This evening he liked what he saw: the crisp white shirt, a blue silk tie, and a darker blue suit from the best tailor on Savile Row.

A lighter blue silk handkerchief was just visible in the top pocket of his jacket. Conservative, no flash, he thought, as he turned away from the mirror. He hated flash.

He had returned home at four o'clock. He was an early riser, generally at his office in Wardour Street or out at the studio by seven in the morning.

Leaving work early was mandatory. He needed a few hours to himself before his evening appointments. The first thing he did when he got home was strip off his clothes and take a bath. Cleanliness was of prime importance to him. Then he put on fresh underwear and a silk dressing gown and went into the library to look at the day's post on his desk.

An hour before going out he would don a newly laundered white shirt – always white – and one of his many impeccable suits. He never thought of himself as a dandy. He considered himself to be properly dressed and left it at that.

Adam glanced around as he walked through the large entrance foyer of his flat in Bryanston Square. He paused, making sure that the flowers on the antique hall table did not look too stiffly arranged.

He nodded to himself, pleased. Mrs Clay, his housekeeper, had obviously messed them up a bit after they had arrived from the flower shop, just the way he liked.

She was the best housekeeper he had ever employed, as concerned about absolute cleanliness as he was. There was never a speck of dust to be found anywhere.

He could not stand dirt, whether it was on himself, his clothes or in his home. He was clever enough to understand that this aversion sprang from his horrendous childhood and growing up in a hovel.

At the back of his mind was a fond remembrance of Jack Trotter lingering there, and he thought of it now. On that first day when he had met the publican of the Golden Horn, he had been given clean underwear, trousers and a shirt that had belonged to Jack's late son, and sent to boil a kettle and have a good wash in the flat above the pub.

Later, when he emerged, he had found Jack in the taproom of the public house. Jack had looked shocked when he saw him, had wondered out loud who would have guessed that there was quite a looker under all that grime.

After that, over the next year, Jack had teased him about his looks, warned him he better beware, that women would throw themselves at him when he was older. And they had.

Adam paused in the entrance to the sitting room, admiring it as he so often did. Everything in it was white.

The soaring ceiling and walls, the silk draperies at the two tall windows, the fabrics on the two sofas and the chairs placed around the room gave it a cool feeling. There was a white handmade rug in the middle of the polished parquet floor, which completed the pristine look and drew attention to the handsome fireplace.

What made the room so visually effective were the paintings hanging on the walls, splashes of vivid colour that enlivened the ice-white setting. Beautiful porcelain lamps, antique porcelain ornaments, and tall vases of white flowers were the ideal finishing touches.

As he walked in, looking around, checking that things were in place, he couldn't help wondering what Alicia Stanton would think of his room – the whole flat, in fact. He knew it was elegant. He had hired the best interior designer in London to make sure of that.

The thought of her being here later this evening excited him. He had wanted her for several years and was determined to have her. And eventually he had seen a way to get her. He had realized that she would be perfect for *Broken Image*, the new film he was making with Mario. Although he'd had to coax Mario into agreeing to hire her.

He had fussed over her a little at first, and then had pulled back, and it had worked. He was certain of that. She had been unable to tear her gaze away from his in the restaurant today. There had been that come-hither look in her blue eyes, and her desire for him was written all over her face.

Turning around, he walked back through the entrance foyer and went into his bedroom. Then he looked in the bathroom and was satisfied. In the last few minutes, Mrs Clay had cleaned up after him.

His bedroom was decorated in various shades of blue. There was a masculine, tailored feel to it, without the look of being overdone. Two carved antique chests of polished mellow wood were balanced by a small *bureau plat*, the elegant flat-topped French writing desk he liked. Standing on this were a French brass lamp, a leather blotter, and brass inkpots; that was all.

Adam stood in the middle of his bedroom, thinking about later. If everything went to plan, she would come home with him tonight, be here in his huge bed with him. He had to make sure of that. He had not seen her apartment and was not certain he would want to go there after dinner. Definitely not, he decided. She has to be here where I am fully in control.

Once more he returned to the entrance foyer and saw Wilson, his butler, walking towards him.

'Good evening, sir,' Wilson said, inclining his head. 'Cook has made the mixed canapés, as you requested, and Harvey and Molly *were* free to serve tonight. They're already here.'

'Then we're all set, Wilson. Thank you. And I assume you've put Dom Pérignon on ice.'

'I have indeed, sir.'

The first guests to arrive exactly at six thirty were Ellen and Reg Greene, who owned the public relations company which did publicity for his films. They were always on time, which pleased Adam, and were charming.

After affectionate greetings, he walked with them into the white sitting room, confiding that Alicia was coming later. As they took flutes of champagne off the tray Harvey offered, he added he truly believed she would steal the picture.

'That's not going to please Andrew Vance,' Ellen said. 'He thinks he's the greatest male lead around.'

'That's because he's blinded by his own vanity,' Adam murmured. 'He's also forgotten that James Brentwood *owns* that title.'

They then spoke about James Brentwood's success in Hollywood, and what a huge film star he now was throughout the world.

'MGM has seen to that,' Ellen remarked. 'They've done a wonderful job promoting him, but then aside from being a truly great actor, he's a cameraman's dream. He can also charm the birds out of the trees.'

Adam laughed. 'The camera loves him, that's true. I don't think there's any other male actor more photogenic, not even Errol

Flynn, Tyrone Power or Clark Gable. Mind you, the three of them are extremely handsome men.'

Out of the corner of his eyes, Adam saw the screenwriter, Margo Littleton, coming through the foyer, with her writing partner, Jeffrey Cox. Excusing himself, he went to greet them.

These were the two writers Adam had brought in to do the third rewrite and the shooting script. He admired them, thought they were the best in the business, and they always proved him right.

Margo and Jeffrey knew Ellen and Reg. Within a few seconds the four of them were chatting away, indulging in shoptalk.

Adam stood with them while Wilson moved around the sitting room adroitly, making sure everyone had champagne and that the waitress, Molly, was serving the canapés. The waiter, Harvey, followed with the Dom Pérignon.

At one moment, Adam excused himself, explaining he had a quick phone call to make, and hurried down the foyer to his bedroom. He wanted to be sure that everything was in order for later tonight, when he brought Alicia here to bed her. There was not a shred of doubt in his mind that this would happen, and he couldn't wait.

The large bed was set against the long back wall. It had not yet been turned down, but Mrs Clay would do that after they had all left.

He opened the drawer of his bedside table to double-check certain things were in place, and they were. He wanted everything he might need to be within easy reach.

When the designer had been restoring the flat, Adam had asked him to create two dressing rooms at each end of the bedroom. One had been for himself, and he used it every day.

The other was designed for a woman's requirements. He walked into this dressing area now and glanced around. Of course, it was spotlessly clean. There was a small bathroom, with a bath, a washbasin, a toilet and also his favourite innovation, a French *bidet*, which had had to be imported.

In the dressing room, which was painted pale blue, there was a mirrored Venetian dressing table with bottles of perfume arranged at one side and a set of combs and a hand mirror at the other.

Earlier this evening he had hung a loose kimono in the dressing area, and now he lifted the hanger off the hook and looked at the garment. It was pale blue, made of double chiffon, and it was brand new. He had bought it two weeks ago hoping for this night to come. His night of seduction.

This thought made Adam smile. Seduction wouldn't be necessary. She was already aching for him; he had seen that in her eyes a week ago on the backlot, and again today in the Causerie. The idea of the drinks party had come to him in a flash as he stood talking to her and Constance, and he had invited them to join him. He had then rushed back to his office after lunch and scrambled, inviting Ellen and Reg, Margo and Jeffrey. None of them had country homes; they were bound to be free on Friday night and they were. His improvisation had worked. They usually did.

The moment he had his group together, Adam had phoned Wilson, who had done his work efficiently after the call. Impromptu drinks at six thirty, suddenly announced, were not unusual, and Wilson knew how to make things run smoothly for his employer.

Adam was aware that Felix and Constance would be a little late, because they were going to pick up Alicia to bring her with them.

He glanced at his watch, saw that it was seven, and left his bedroom.

Walking up to Margo, he said, 'Oh, by the way, Felix and Constance are coming tonight, and they're bringing Alicia Stanton with them.'

'Oh, that's lovely, Adam, I do want to meet her again. When I saw her at Shepperton I was really impressed. I loved her comments about our improvements in the script . . .' Margo stopped. 'I think she's arriving now.'

Everyone knew each other since they were show-business veterans, and they instantly fell into conversation. There was a sudden nice buzz in the room, which delighted Adam.

Wilson made sure that Harvey and Molly moved around, filling up empty flutes with champagne, offering plates of canapés to the guests.

Adam noticed how easily Alicia held her own, moved elegantly through the small group, making certain to speak to everyone. But then she had been born into a great family of aristocrats, and her manners were impeccable.

Slightly amused that she shook his hand lightly, and immediately moved on when she arrived, he kept his distance. Obviously she did not want to display her feelings, and neither did he for that matter.

He stood at the other side of the room, yet found it extremely difficult to keep his eyes off her. Cleverly, she managed to avoid his gaze.

The way Alicia looked tonight was different. He had been momentarily stunned when she walked in; still was, if the truth be known. She looked more beautiful than ever, younger, almost girlish, and she appeared taller, rather willowy, a slender, reed-like creature moving with grace.

Within seconds he realized that when he saw her at Shepperton, on a sound stage or the backlot, she was wearing theatrical makeup, which was heavy, and her hair was arranged in a plain style to suit the character she was playing.

She was the Honourable Alicia Ingham Stanton now. *Herself*. Relaxed, natural, self-confident. He had not failed to miss how extraordinary her skin was, that special peaches-and-cream complexion some English women were known for. Her blonde hair shone in the lamplight; it was brushed out, fell in soft folds around her fine-boned face. The bloom is on the rose, he thought.

Like all the Ingham women, Alicia had wonderful blue eyes, and he knew the story about them always wearing clothes to match their eyes.

He smiled to himself, and glanced away, then walked over to Felix.

It hadn't surprised him at all that Alicia had kept to the tradition this evening. Her dress was pale blue, was well cut, had a plain top, long sleeves, and a full skirt that flared out around her shapely legs in the New Look fashion.

The fabric intrigued him. It was some kind of soft silk that literally clung to her body. He found it very sexy, couldn't wait to hold her in his arms on the dance floor at the Savoy, to feel that silkiness under his hands.

It was Constance who came to join him and Felix. She drew them both to one side, away from the others. In a low voice, she said to Adam, 'I know you're interested in Alicia, and I was wondering if you would like to take her to the Savoy for dinner alone. We wouldn't mind at all, would we, Felix?' Her husband nodded in agreement.

'No, no. I don't want you to do that, Connie,' Adam said at once, and firmly. 'It's much better if we all go out together. I don't want to . . . rush this.' He eyed Constance and then Felix, an amused look crossing his face. 'She's also interested in me.'

'You'll have to ask her about that. But I think it's a perfect match. What about you, Felix?'

'Ditto.' Turning to Adam, looking at him intently, Felix said, 'She's the best thing that could happen to you, and I think she needs someone like you.'

'Well put, Felix,' Constance said, and touched Adam's arm affectionately. 'Don't dillydally with this situation – show her you like her.'

'What has she said?' Adam asked swiftly.

'Let's just say she was asking about you when we were at lunch today.'

Adam's light grey eyes sparkled. 'I sort of guessed that. Look, I do want us all to go to dinner, that is the four of us. However, don't offer to take her home. Please allow me to do that, won't you?'

'If Alicia's happy, we are,' Constance responded.

Felix winked at him.

# Twenty

Alicia was glad that Constance had seated her opposite Adam at the table in the restaurant at the Savoy Hotel. For her it was preferable to face him rather than having him sit next to her. If he were close, it would be unbearable. She would be tempted to touch him – on his arm, his leg, it didn't matter where. She just longed to make physical contact, even to embrace him, put her arms around him. Of course she couldn't. Not yet.

Felix asked if they would like to continue with Dom Pérignon, and Alicia immediately shook her head. Constance declined also, and Adam merely said, 'You know I don't drink, so water will be fine with me.'

Alicia suddenly realized that he hadn't had a glass in his hand at his flat earlier. On the other hand, she had moved around a lot, trying not to be anywhere near him. Nor did she wish anyone to see her looking at him longingly. She believed she had managed quite well to conceal her interest in him. Now it didn't matter, because Constance and Felix knew her feelings about Adam Fennell: *she wanted to be with him.*

Sitting up a little straighter, tossing back her blonde locks, she gazed at Adam intently, her eyes opening wider. A small smile tugged at the corner of her mouth and she raised a brow, her eyes not leaving his face.

Adam gazed back at her, obviously sharing her feelings. After a long moment, he inclined his head slightly.

Alicia gave him a nod in return, her eyes even more intense.

A faint smile lightened his face. His grey eyes sparkled, and he sat up in the chair himself, thrusting his chest forward slightly. The deal sealed, he thought, and a look of pleasure crossed his face.

It was a look that thrilled her. And she offered him a wide smile that was warm, loving. To Felix, she said, 'I think I will have a glass of wine with dinner. I'm afraid I drank a lot of Adam's fine champagne, so nothing now, thank you.'

'Let's look at the menu,' Constance suggested. 'I'm a little hungry.'

Felix nodded, and beckoned the waiter. Glancing around the room he said, 'The place is full tonight, but then Carroll Gibbons and his Orpheans, as he calls his band, are still as popular as they were during the war. And they're as good as ever.'

Adam took a menu from the waiter, and scanned it, exclaimed, 'Ah, I see oysters! Well, of course, there's an R in the month. And Colchester oysters at that. They're for me.'

'I'll start with oysters, too,' Alicia murmured. Everyone ordered them, and then chose grilled sole.

'We're just old stick-in-the-muds,' Constance remarked. 'Not adventurous at all, at least as far as food is concerned.'

'I think it's a question of whether rationing will ever come to an end,' Adam remarked. 'I have always enjoyed really good English food, the kind they serve here. But I don't need much persuasion to go to a French restaurant or have an Italian meal in Soho.'

Alicia exclaimed, 'I love this song, "A Nightingale Sang in Berkeley Square".' Pushing back her chair, she looked across at Adam and said, 'Will you come and dance with me?'

Adam nodded, stood at once, came around and helped her out

of her chair, then took her arm. To Constance and Felix he said, 'You don't mind, do you? I wouldn't want to miss this treat.'

The Lamberts laughed, encouraged the two of them to take to the floor.

The minute their feet touched the dance floor, she was in his arms, holding on to him tightly. He slipped one hand down her back, placed it firmly around her waist.

She said, 'Is it really a treat?'

'No, it's a thrill. I've longed to hold you close to me.'

'I've wanted the same.'

He led her around the floor, holding her slightly at a distance, and then slowly he pulled her closer. So that they were face to face. Their bodies touched.

'Are we all right?' he murmured against her hair.

'We are.'

He placed his hand on her back, bringing her even closer, pressed her body into his. 'Is this better?' he whispered.

'Yes,' she whispered back, conscious how aroused he was. It filled her with excitement.

They had stopped dancing, just stood together in a tight embrace, swaying to the music, oblivious to the other dancing couples, aware only of their erotic feelings for each other.

At one moment he asked in a lowered voice, 'You will spend the night with me, won't you?'

'Yes.'

'It will have to be at my place. I'm expecting calls from Los Angeles early tomorrow morning.'

'But what about the staff . . .?' She left her question unfinished.

'They'll be gone by ten tonight. They don't work at weekends.'

'So you like your privacy?'

'I do. So, are we still all right?'

'Very much so.'

'That's a relief,' he murmured, and they began to dance again, although they remained locked in their tight embrace.

* * *

When they returned to the table, the plates of oysters had just been served, and Constance, always at ease socially, began to talk about the upcoming Royal Command Film Performance of *That Forsyte Woman*, to be held at the Empire in Leicester Square in November.

Adam, looking at Alicia, said, 'I do hope you can come with me? I've been invited to attend.'

A look of pleasure flashed across Alicia's face and she exclaimed, 'How wonderful! Thank you, I'd love to come with you.'

Adam smiled, began to eat his oysters.

Constance, always well informed, remarked, 'The King and Queen will be attending, and the two Princesses. But not Prince Philip, I'm afraid. He's on duty in the Royal Navy. Stationed in Malta.'

'That's a marriage of true love,' Felix interjected. 'And I hear that Princess Elizabeth will be going out to join him soon.'

'Who are the Hollywood stars coming to the Command Performance?' Alicia asked, turning to Constance.

'I know for certain that Errol Flynn and Greer Garson will be there, as stars of the picture, but not sure who else. Oh, Margaret Lockwood told me the other day that she plans to attend. Actually, a lot of English stars are expected.'

'Princess Elizabeth will outshine them all,' Alicia declared. 'She's beautiful, and one of the most glamorous women around. I love the clothes Hartnell makes for her.'

'Her sister's not bad either,' Adam pointed out. 'I think Princess Margaret is gorgeous too.'

'The Royal Film Command Performance is very important to us show-business folk,' Felix said. 'The money it makes funds the Royal Variety Charity, which, in turn, helps to care for elderly entertainers. We always support it, don't we, Constance?'

'We certainly do, but it's also a rather special evening. We get to see a new film, and I enjoy mingling with the Hollywood stars who come over for it. Last year we met Elizabeth Taylor, such a gorgeous young woman, and Alan Ladd, Myrna Loy and Robert Taylor.'

'And I met Vivien Leigh and her husband, Sir Laurence, at last year's do, and oh boy, was that a treat,' Adam remarked. 'She is a most fascinating woman.'

'Everyone fell in love with her when they saw *Gone with the Wind*.' Constance glanced at Felix. 'The whole world. How can she ever top that?'

'Oh I think she will,' Adam exclaimed, sounding sure of himself. 'She's a brilliant actress, and Larry will make sure she always gets good parts. Not to mention Alex Korda: she's a big favourite of his, that I know.'

# Twenty-One

There was a rosy glow from two small lamps on the antique table when Adam and Alicia entered the foyer of his flat in Bryanston Square.

He turned around and locked the door. When he swung to face her, she immediately stepped forward and put her arms around him. Automatically, he brought her closer. But after a long moment of holding her, Adam said, 'I don't want to start here, fumbling with clothes. I want it to be right.'

Stepping away from her, he took her hand and led her into his bedroom, where other small lamps created the same kind of low, welcoming glow.

As they went in together, Alicia saw the huge bed with pristine white sheets and large white pillows propped up against the headboard. It had already been turned down by the housekeeper before she had left, and the sight of it titillated Alicia. She couldn't wait to be in that bed with Adam beside her, making love to her.

Taking hold of her hand, he led her to the dressing room, opened the door and took her in. 'You can get undressed in here.'

There was a boyish grin on his face when he added in a lower tone, '*And hurry up . . . please hurry up*.'

He swung around in the doorway. 'I bought you a robe. Hoping this night would come. And now it has. Please wear it.' With those words he left her alone.

Alicia took everything in with one sweeping glance and saw how feminine the décor was. And she couldn't help wondering how many other women had used it before her. For surely she wasn't the first. To her surprise she experienced a rush of jealousy, then realized how silly she was being. She hardly knew him; there was no relationship.

Rapidly she undressed, looked at herself in the long mirror on one wall. She hoped her body would please him. She shook her head knowingly. She was well aware he wanted her just from dancing with him at the Savoy Hotel earlier. And there *would* be a relationship.

Standing in front of the washbasin, she took a facecloth and removed the bright red lipstick she favoured, recalling those pristine pillows. She noticed the bottle of Joy perfume on one end of the dressing table. She always wore it. It was her favourite. There was no doubt it had been put there for her. She sprayed it all over her body and reached for the robe. It was beautiful, obviously brand new, and made of double layers of chiffon. She slipped it on. It was styled like a kimono, had no belt, and felt lovely against her skin.

The very process of preparing herself, getting ready to couple with him, filled her with excitement, and there was a sudden throbbing inside her. She was growing damp just thinking about him, and what they were about to do.

When she went out of the dressing room, Adam was waiting for her, standing at the bottom of the bed. He wore a dark blue silk kimono, styled the same as hers. No belt, open fronted. Easy access to each other, she thought, walking towards him. She discovered her legs were trembling and she was tense with anticipation and overwhelming sexual desire.

They met in the middle of the bedroom. He took hold of her hand, drew her to him, slipped his arms inside her kimono, moved forward a few steps.

Their naked bodies were pressed close together. He slid his hands down onto her hips, pressed her against him. His hardness was unbelievable and Alicia looked at him, her blue eyes glazed with longing and lust.

Adam saw this clearly reflected in her face. And he felt the same. They were alike. He knew she would be sensual and erotic, would respond to him eagerly, would do whatever he wanted. This thrilled him. He bent his head, kissed her; it was a deeply passionate kiss, lingering.

She kissed him back, wanting him more than she had ever wanted any other man.

His tongue went in her mouth, entwined with hers, charging her up. Their tongues lay still, entwined again. His hands slid over her breasts, and he felt their softness. When he pinched her nipples, they hardened, and she shivered and pushed her body against his.

After a moment, Adam released her. He whispered against her ear, 'I won't hurt you, Alicia. I'll be careful, gentle, I promise.'

'I don't want that! I don't want you to be careful. I want all of you, every little bit. I want you to make love to me as you wish, do whatever you want.' She slipped out of her kimono, let it fall to the floor, reached for his, pulled it off his shoulders, dropped it next to hers.

Once she was back in his arms, she placed one hand on the back of his neck; with the other she reached down to touch him, needing to feel his flesh.

Instantly he gasped. 'Please don't, darling. I'll explode.' He took away her hand, led her across the room. And they lay down on the bed at last, exactly where they wanted to be.

Pushing himself up on one elbow, Adam gazed down at her, his translucent grey eyes shining. 'I've a confession to make. I've had a crush on you for two years.' That endearing boyish smile of his made her smile in return.

Alicia said softly, 'My crush on you hasn't been for that long, but it's equally meaningful. I want you, Adam, all of you. Touch me, please touch me.'

He kissed her neck and her cheeks and then her mouth. Lifting his head, he said, 'I want to devour you, fill myself with you. Yet I don't want to rush this night, our first together. I must savour you.'

Now he ran both his hands over her body, swept them across her thighs and over her legs, and let them rest there. The expression on his face was one of sheer delight.

'You're beautiful, Alicia, and your body is lovely, long and slender, your legs gorgeous. And these are voluptuous, just the way I like them.' He kissed her breasts, fondled them, bit her nipples, sucked on them, buried his face in them, filled with longing for this woman who so captivated him.

Alicia shivered, put her hand in his hair, stroked the back of his neck, a faint groan of pleasure in her throat. He filled her with bliss the way he touched her, loved her.

When he stopped and moved away abruptly, Alicia instantly opened her eyes. 'Is there something wrong?'

'No, we're all right.' He quickly checked the contents of the drawer in the bedside table, and then continued to kiss her, fondle her breasts. His sexual need of her was soaring higher. 'I can't wait much longer, Alicia, it's becoming urgent. Very,' he said.

'Touch me. You know I feel the same.'

He did as she asked, slipped his fingers between her legs, heard her long sigh. His massaging made her stiffen and tremble, and her gasps became sharper.

He realized she was delicately made; he also knew she was about to climax, and he wanted to be inside her when she did, because her joy would dim the hardness of him, if he took her precisely at that moment.

He genuinely did not want to hurt her, and understood what he must do. His voice was hardly audible when he murmured, 'I want to put a bit of balm on myself, and on you. For lubrication.'

'Do whatever you want,' Alicia was filled with growing euphoria, right on the edge of ecstasy.

He paused, felt her stiffen, and put his hand in the jar in the drawer. He smeared some of the balm on himself, then he began to massage her again, this time with the cream which smelled of lavender.

It took only a few seconds for Alicia to begin to tremble. And stiffen. She was about to go into spasms. He brought his mouth to hers and let his tongue linger. She put her hand down between his legs, slid her hand up and down. The balm made his skin feel like silk.

Taking her hand off him, he rolled on top of her, facing his body in the right position. He was quivering all over, and breathing hard, as he took her to him with suddenness, began to move against her. He lifted her body closer, his hands under her buttocks, and she cried out as he gave all of himself to her and with some force.

Alicia's arms and legs were around Adam, and he was holding her in a tight grip. They moved in unison, gasping and clutching each other, filled with lust and hunger and need. They were abandoned, wild, rolling around in the bed, floating together on a sexual high.

Adam, always a silent lover in the past, cried out with the sheer bliss of her, the sensuality, the need she had for him and his body, her raw lust, and the way she met every need he had, did exactly what he asked of her. They were transported, rapturous. Alicia cried out herself, ecstatic as Adam ravished her, made her his. And then he gave himself to her. And he was with the woman he knew was meant for him, and he felt a rush of satisfaction.

They clung to each other for a long time afterward, shaken by the intensity and passion of their lovemaking. They realized that they were already highly involved sexually, and on an emotional level as well, and that this was no passing fancy.

After a while, Adam said in a low voice, 'I didn't hurt you, did I?' This was asked in a quiet, concerned way.

Alicia said, 'No. Well, for a moment, when I first felt you inside me, I was a little jolted. But you didn't hurt me. Surprised me.' She turned onto her side, looked at him intently. 'Have other women complained that you hurt them?'

'A couple, that's all.'

'I'm sure you please most. You must have had a lot of affairs.'

Adam now swung his head, stared at Alicia. 'I'm a heterosexual man, thirty-eight years old. Of course, I've had affairs, but not as many as you're implying.' He frowned, shook his head, appearing perplexed.

Sensing he might be a little annoyed with her, she murmured in a warm voice, 'Sorry if I offended you. You see, you're the most marvellous lover; I've never experienced anything like this before, or anyone like you. You seem to be aware of every part of a woman's body, know how to arouse a woman, give her orgasms by the minute.'

He burst out laughing. 'Oh come on now, you're exaggerating! But never mind, thanks for the compliment.'

She laughed with him. 'No, you come on, tell me how you learned all about women and their sexual needs. And the most erotic parts of them.'

'My father was a doctor. He practised in Harley Street,' Adam explained. 'He treated aristocratic women, like you, Alicia.' Pushing himself up against the pillow, Adam continued his often-told story. 'My mother died when I was six. He never remarried, and brought me up himself, with a load of different nannies. We were very close. When I was fourteen my father decided I'd better know a few facts of life. Later, when I was a bit older, he literally gave me specific details about the intimate parts of a woman's body. And that's how I know what I know.'

'I understand.' Alicia also sat up and asked, 'So you grew up in London then?'

'I did, yes. For a long time we lived in Kensington. Later my father had a flat, right here in Bryanston Square. Smaller than this, naturally, and on the other side of the square. But you could say this area of London is home turf for me. I've never really lived anywhere else.'

'My family used to have a house in Mayfair, but Grandfather gave it up,' Alicia confided. 'Then my Uncle Miles had a house in South Street. A flying bomb hit it during the war . . .' She stopped abruptly, clearing her throat as tears unexpectedly welled.

Looking at her intently, Adam asked, 'What is it?'

'His sister, Aunt DeLacy, was in the house when the bomb hit. She was killed immediately, and so was Laura Swann, a beloved member of our staff.'

Reaching out, taking her in his arms, Adam consoled her, and eventually the sudden rush of tears were wiped away, and she relaxed.

After that they fell asleep, exhausted by their intense love-making. But when they both awakened in the middle of the night, it started all over again. They were still caressing each other at three o'clock. And they both decided the second time around was better. They also agreed they were meant for each other.

# Twenty-Two

Greta Chalmers glanced around the sitting room of her house in Phene Street, a look of pleasure on her face. There was a glow from the fire burning in the hearth and the soft light from the lamps in the room.

A short while ago, Victoria had put several small bowls of colourful hyacinths on end tables and lit a number of candles, which she had scattered around. The girls had done a lot to help her, and she was grateful. Her gramophone was playing a new Perry Como recording.

Lady Diedre had been the first to arrive. She had called earlier that morning and asked if she could come to the supper with Charlie. She was apparently alone in London this weekend. Her son, Robin, had gone back to Cambridge, and her husband, Will, was delayed in Geneva on business.

At this moment she was sitting on the sofa with Charlie, her favourite nephew, chatting to him intently.

Elise and Victoria were perched on the two chairs on each side of the sofa, both of them looking very pretty. Elise was in a new skirt that she'd made from a piece of dazzling print she'd spotted in Peter Jones. Her petite, curvy frame was shown to its advantage and dark green heels lent her height. Victoria was wearing purple, a favourite dress that clung to her willowy frame.

They were never far away from Charlie when he was here, his adoring sycophants; they hero-worshipped him and would do anything for him.

Greta admired the way he put up with their pestering with geniality and good humour. She thought he looked handsome tonight and wished he could meet the right woman. One day, perhaps.

She herself had never met the right man after Roy's untimely death. Although she hadn't given up hoping that she might have a relationship with someone eventually. Still, it didn't bother her that it hadn't happened so far.

For the last few days she had experienced a wave of genuine contentment washing over her. She was now Cecily's full partner in Swann, and, quite by accident, she had made them a nice amount of money over the past two weeks by deciding to have a big sale of all their old stock, both couture and ready-made.

Everything had flown out of the smaller shop, which they were closing, and the money made was an unexpected bonanza. She hoped it would mean they could continue to turn the business round and secure its future.

Customers who came to the sale bought handbags, perfume and other accessories, and sales had been very brisk. All her business success gave Greta an enormous sense of achievement and made up for any number of disappointments in her life.

The arrival of Greta's old friend, Arnold Templeton, and his younger brother, Alistair, drew Greta out of her chair and across to the doorway. She and Arnold had had a long and warm friendship and were best pals.

Leading the two men over to the drinks table that Victoria had set up, she poured them two glasses of whisky, and stood chatting to them both. 'How do you like your new job, Alistair? Arnold told me you've moved to a new law firm.'

'So far so good,' Alistair replied. 'The law has always fascinated me, as no doubt Arnold has told you.' He grinned at her, his hazel eyes twinkling. 'The new firm is more go-ahead, more of a challenge . . .' He broke off, staring at the pretty brunette walking in their direction.

Greta said, 'This is my sister, Elise. And Elise, you know Arnold, and this is Alistair, his brother.'

The two of them shook hands, smiling, and Arnold kissed Elise on the cheek. He had always liked her, grown fond of her over the years. It had been his idea to bring Alistair along tonight. He believed his younger brother was a good match for Elise, and when he had suggested this to Greta she had laughed, nodded, and shown him two crossed fingers.

Alistair edged closer to Elise and immediately struck up an easy conversation with her, asking her what she did for a living.

'I'm a journalist,' she answered, staring up at him, adding with pride, 'I'm a reporter on the *Daily Mail*, and I love every minute of being in a newspaper office.'

'I'm happy for you. I think it's so important to enjoy your job, since we all spend most of our time at work.'

'What do you do?' she asked, thinking he was rather attractive, very clean cut, with lovely eyes and the whitest teeth she had ever seen.

'I'm a barrister, and I love my job, too,' Alistair answered. They went on talking with some animation, and Greta glanced at Arnold. She then took hold of his arm and led him away, murmuring, 'Good shot on your part, Arnold. They seem to have hit it off.'

'I hope so. He's footloose and fancy-free. Yet I know he's longing to settle down. He told me the other day that dating is very trying at times. Apparently he hasn't found anyone he's liked enough to see twice.' Arnold grinned at her. 'And I think your sister is a gorgeous bit of stuff.'

'Gorgeous bit of stuff,' Greta repeated, looking at him aghast.

He grinned at her. 'Well, I suppose you meant it as a compliment,' Greta conceded, laughter surfacing.

There was a small flurry of excitement as four people came into the room. Greta hurried over to welcome them. The new arrivals were old friends of hers, whom she had known for a very long time. Johanna Newbolt and her husband Monty, Allegra Thomas and her fiancé Mark Allenby. Allegra was a columnist on *The Sunday Times*, and Johanna was an artist she often worked with for their magazine advertising.

After hugs and kisses, Greta led them across the room to the drinks table; she was followed by Arnold who helped pour the new guests glasses of wine.

'Thank you, Arnold,' Greta murmured, and glanced around. The sitting room was filling up. But three people were missing, she realized. Percy Cole, owner of the company who supplied them with their finest fabrics, and a good friend. And also Alicia and the associate producer of her film, Adam Fennell, had not shown up yet either.

Victoria came to join her, and said, 'Shall I pop downstairs and see how Zoe's managing?'

'That would be nice, thank you,' Greta responded. She smiled at Victoria and went on, 'You look lovely in the purple dress; that colour really brings out the green of your eyes.'

'Thank you, Greta. It's my favourite frock.'

When Victoria came back in, since Elise was still chatting away to Alistair, Victoria made a beeline for them, and took the other chair, next to Charlie.

Charlie asked, 'What about the Christopher Longdon story? Have you had any brilliant ideas?'

'Not really. But it did occur to me that he might agree to go to Biggin Hill, which is where he was based during the war. I thought I ought to get a picture of him with planes. What do you think?'

'Clever girl,' Charlie exclaimed. 'And Noel Jollion was stationed there too during the war.'

'Oh gosh, I remember that,' Victoria exclaimed, and then her breath caught in her throat and she stared at the doorway.

Alicia had suddenly appeared looking gorgeous in that fabulous blue dress. Standing next to her was Adam Fennell.

'Hello, everybody,' Alicia said. 'So sorry we're late.'

The entire room went quiet and everybody stared at the handsomest couple they had ever seen.

It took Greta only a moment to jump up and go over to them, smiling warmly, kissing Alicia who then introduced Adam.

Socially adept, Greta immediately shepherded Alicia and Adam over to meet her girlfriends and their partners. They all seemed awestruck by Alicia's beauty, and why not? The starlet looked spectacularly glamorous tonight.

Charlie stood up when he saw Alicia and Adam move on through the party and head down the room towards him. He knew at once that they were already involved, had become a couple. It was written all over his sister's face. He had not seen her looking so radiant in years. She was positively blooming, and there was a certain glow about her that enhanced her natural beauty. As for Adam Fennell, he looked like a nice chap, and was far younger than Charlie had expected.

After kissing Alicia's cheek and shaking Adam's hand, Charlie said, 'I must introduce you to our aunt.'

Diedre rose at once, as the three of them moved towards the sofa. Her smile was warm and loving as she embraced her niece, and then took hold of Adam Fennell's outstretched hand.

'This is Adam Fennell, Aunt Diedre.'

'Good evening, Mr Fennell,' Diedre said.

'It's a pleasure to meet you, Lady Diedre,' Adam answered.

Diedre stepped back, and went and sat down on the sofa, where Alicia immediately joined her. 'What a nice surprise you're here,' Alicia said.

'Will is delayed in Geneva, and I didn't feel like being alone. I asked Charlie to have dinner with me and he immediately invited me to come here with him.' Diedre chuckled. 'I did phone Greta just to be sure it was all right.'

'Goodness, you know you're always welcome everywhere, Aunt Diedre.'

'Thank you for the compliment, but sometimes it's a question of the guests . . . whether there's enough room or not.'

Alicia nodded and went on, 'Adam is the associate producer on my film. He's been rather kind to me.'

'I'm glad to hear it,' Diedre answered, looking at Adam Fennell, who stood talking animatedly to Charlie. There was something about him that put her guard up, but she was always resistant to that type of easy charm. She had noticed how they both looked at each other, and hoped Alicia didn't get seriously involved with him. Wait and see, she warned herself.

# Part Four

# Stepping into Reality

We have no more right to consume happiness without producing it than to consume wealth without producing it.

George Bernard Shaw, *Candida*

# Twenty-Three

Christopher Longdon sat up a little straighter in his chair when the door of his study opened and then closed. Standing there was a girl. A young girl, tall and slender, in a purple wool dress with a colourful print scarf tied around her neck.

There was only a fraction of hesitation before she walked forward. Her steps were swift, decisive, full of a kind of suppressed energy. He took in the cloud of soft brown hair around her face, which was heart-shaped with arched dark brows above the greenest eyes he had ever seen.

He had not expected a thing of such beauty to arrive here today, and a huge smile spread across his face when she stopped in front of his desk.

His smile was so infectious that she smiled back, stepped to one side of his desk and thrust out her hand. 'I'm Victoria, Mr Longdon. Hello!'

'Hello,' he said, smiling again and taking hold of her hand. As he held it tightly in his for the longest moment, Victoria felt something stir inside her. Her heart leapt. She was drawn to him, and it was a pull she'd never experienced before.

Realizing he still held her hand, he let it go, and said, 'I didn't expect you . . . What I mean is, I didn't expect someone like *you*.'

Observing her puzzlement, he explained swiftly, 'I thought a photographer of your calibre would be an older woman.'

Sudden laughter bubbled up in his throat. He couldn't help it, he let the laughter out. 'I suppose I imagined an older, sterner, tougher woman. Oh, I don't know . . .' He shook his head. 'Aren't we humans strange? Always having preconceived ideas about people . . . making judgements without knowing very much.'

Victoria, who had laughed with him, nodded, then said, 'Shall I sit down in the chair? It would be easier to do the interview?'

'I am being so rude, and of course you should sit down. Would you like coffee or tea? Water? Can I get you any refreshment?'

'No, thank you. The man who showed me in, Rory, asked me when I arrived, and I told him I was fine.'

Very fine indeed, Christopher thought. He said, 'Melinda sent me a number of tear sheets of your shoots, and I understood at once that you have a real imagination. Your photographs are daring and unique. God knows what you're going to do with me.' There was a mischievous twinkle in his dark brown eyes. 'I'm hardly a candidate for some eye-catching pictures, swinging from a chandelier.'

'I can't really agree with you there, Mr Longdon—'

'Please call me Christopher, and I shall call you Victoria, if I may,' he announced, cutting across her.

'Of course. My close friends call me Vicki . . .' She stopped abruptly, not certain why she had confided this.

'I rather like Victoria,' he murmured, and glanced down, shuffling several papers on his desk, wondering if he was actually flirting with her. No, that wasn't possible. He hadn't done that for years. Why? Because he hadn't wanted to encourage any woman to take an interest in him.

Breaking the silence, Christopher asked, 'How long have you been a photographer?'

'Since I was eleven,' Victoria replied, a small, amused smile playing around her mouth, her green eyes twinkling.

'Oh my goodness, are we still in the days of Charles Dickens? The days of child labour? Surely not.' He raised a brow, smiling at her, enjoying her.

'I grew up on Charles Dickens,' she responded. 'This is what happened. Someone gave me a Kodak camera as a present when I was eleven, and I discovered I loved taking pictures. Then a well-known photographer taught me everything she knew. She even helped me land my first job in London.'

'That was nice of her. Would I know of her?'

'Actually, you would. Her name is Paloma Glendenning, and since I've heard you love gardens, I'm sure you've seen her nature and garden books.'

'I have indeed, and they are marvellous.' He looked across his desk at her, smiled yet again. 'And how did you meet Paloma?'

'It's a bit of a long story, Mr Longdon . . . Christopher. I'm not sure you'd want to hear it.'

'I do want to hear it.' And I want to know all about you, he thought. Once again, he mentally chastised himself for being so interested in her; he had only just met her and she looked barely twenty, if that.

'All right then, Christopher, I shall tell you. But don't say I didn't warn you.'

'I won't. So, come on, I love a good story.'

'I'm not sure it's good, but it's certainly true. I was an evacuee during the war. You see my school in Leeds decided their girls should go and live in the countryside in Yorkshire. Safer. And far away from the big cities going to be bombed. I went to live in Little Skell village with Mr and Mrs Walter Swann. Their son Harry married Paloma Glendenning, the daughter of the famous actor, Edward Glendenning. Harry was in the RAF during the war.'

Pausing for a moment, clearing her throat, she then continued, 'Paloma had time to teach me about photography. I took a lot of pictures of their first baby, and, as I grew older, I helped her with her own work. She trained me and I assisted her when I could, in the holidays and at weekends. I learned a lot.' She stopped for a moment, and then continued. 'At the end of the war, Mrs Swann went to see the people at the Pied Piper Organization, and she discovered that my mother and grandmother had both died. So had my father, who was in the Merchant Navy on the Russian convoys. He went down with his ship.'

Christopher leaned forward over the desk, his face full of sympathy when he said, with genuine sincerity, 'I'm so sorry you lost your father . . . your parents, actually, and your grandmother as well. That was such a deadly war.'

'Thank you. They adopted me, Mrs Alice and Mr Walter, and I've called them aunt and uncle ever since. That made me very happy . . . to become a part of their family.' She smiled, her face reflecting her gratitude to the kind couple who had become her parents.

'And also them, I'm perfectly certain of that. So you grew up at Cavendon, then?'

'I did. Well, at Little Skell, one of the villages on the estate. Have you been there?'

'No, but a friend of mine lives close by. Noel Jollion. Do you know him by any chance?'

'Not very well. He was at Biggin Hill with you, wasn't he?'

'That's right. How do you know that?'

'Charlie Stanton told me. He's a friend of Noel's.' A wide smile spread across her face and eagerly she said, 'I did think of asking you to be photographed there. Would you mind going back to Biggin Hill?'

'No, not at all.'

'I know the sort of pictures I want, and which Melinda wants. I will have to put you with planes around you. I need the right mood. After all, you are one of our greatest war heroes.'

'Please, Victoria. I wasn't the only one. There were many other very courageous young men fighting that war—'

Christopher broke off as the door opened. Dora, the housekeeper, came into the room, excusing herself for interrupting. 'Lunch is served, Mr Christopher.'

For a moment he gaped at her, then looked at his watch. It was already twelve thirty. What had happened to the time? He stared at Victoria.

'Will you have lunch with me? Please.'

'I will.'

'Please set another place, Dora.'

'I already did, Mr Christopher.'

He looked at Victoria, and they both laughed, and he wheeled himself around the desk.

She did not try to help him in any way. Instinct told her he would resent it.

Victoria noticed immediately how beautiful the dining room was. It was a medium-sized room with a fireplace, but the instant, eye-catching image was of a glorious garden of vivid flowers set against a silver background that was plain silver above the flowers, all the way to the ceiling.

Since he hardly took his eyes off her, Christopher noticed at once the look of pleasure and surprise on her face. He said, 'It's silver wallpaper. I designed the flower garden myself, and had the paper custom-made. I see that you like it.'

'It's beautiful. I know from others how much you are involved with gardens and landscaping. Melinda told me you have a unique garden here. What a pity it's October now.'

'It isn't in full bloom, that's true, but we can go outside later. The trees are turning, glowing red and gold. You might get one shot out there.'

Christopher was sitting at the top of the table; Dora had put her next to him on his right. Now he turned to her, and said, 'It's minestrone first, and then fishcakes. If you would prefer something else, Dora is bound to have other dishes—'

'Oh no,' Victoria interjected. 'I love soup. In fact, I enjoy making soups, and fishcakes are also a favourite. I don't really like food which is too . . . fancy.'

He grinned at her. 'Then we are alike in that.' He paused for a moment, studying her. 'Do you write the story as well as take the pictures?'

'No, I don't. Shane Parker will be interviewing you. Oh, I see what you're getting at, Christopher. I mentioned the word *interview* earlier, and I should have said *talk* to you. You see Melinda prefers me to do the photography first. Then the art director makes a rough layout. Once Melinda's satisfied about the "look", as she calls it, the interview goes ahead.'

'I understand. You said *layout*, which indicates a lot of photographs?' A dark brow shot up questioningly. 'I'm not your best subject matter, you know that.'

Victoria was about to disagree, when Dora came in with a tray and put it down on a serving table. She brought a bowl of soup to Victoria, and then Christopher, and hurried away.

Victoria said, 'I think I can get several good photographs here in the house. In your study, for instance, dressed casually as you are now. You're right about the garden and the leaves turning – that could be colourful. And I hope to take two or three photographs at Biggin Hill.'

She gazed at him, half smiling, thinking that he was a nice-looking man, with large brown eyes, set wide apart, a broad brow, and a cleft in his chin. It was a strong, masculine face, and there was kindness there . . . in his eyes. Yes, that was it. His brown eyes were . . . warm, loving.

'You're staring at me, Victoria. Do I have a dirty mark on my face?' He asked this in a teasing voice, amused. He grinned at her.

She chuckled. 'I'm afraid that's a photographer's worst habit, staring at people, especially those they are going to photograph. I was just picturing you in your RAF uniform. Would you be prepared to wear it?'

'That's not a problem. I could also wear my flying suit as well, down at Biggin Hill. That's what we all wore in the war.'

When they had finished lunch, Victoria asked Christopher if they could go back to the study and he agreed. To her, this was an extremely personal room, with many photographs of him with his flying bods as he called them, and the medals he had been awarded.

She stared for a long time at the photograph of him with King George VI and Winston Churchill at Buckingham Palace, when he had received the Distinguished Flying Cross. Then she moved on to view the other memorabilia. She made a mental note of the hundreds of books on the shelves, deciding that this room told its own very special story about this remarkable man.

'What do you think then?' Christopher asked, wheeling himself over to join her. 'Will it work? This room?'

Turning, smiling at him, she nodded. 'It's full of you. And it will be a marvellous, intimate picture.'

Glancing away from him, focusing on a photograph on the other wall, she now said, 'Those are your parents, aren't they?'

'Yes. They're dead now, but at least they lived long enough to know I survived the war. My mother never stopped worrying about me flying.' Shaking his head, a half smile lingering, he went on, 'We were all so young, you know. Eighteen, for God's sake. None of us had even finished our formal education. And none of us were married. I don't think we ever thought about dying. We were very gung-ho, just up there doing our stuff, bringing down Jerry planes, getting back to base in one piece.'

'You *were* very young indeed, all of you. That photograph here,' she turned around, indicated a group picture in front of a plane. 'Baby faces. All of you look about twelve.'

'I know. Looking back it's hard to believe. A decade ago. It was another world.'

# Twenty-Four

After lunch, Christopher had introduced her to two of his closest companions: his personal assistant, Rory Delaney, who had been based at Biggin Hill during the war, one of the aides to Christopher's wing commander, and not in combat. He had worked for Christopher for the last three years, alongside Freddy Angier, the physiotherapist, who kept Christopher fit. Rory had promised to ring Biggin Hill to see whether they would allow some photographs to be taken there.

She and Christopher had now come out to the terrace overlooking the garden. Beyond the walls was Hampstead Heath. Although it was October, it was a beautiful day. The sky was blue, with puffy white clouds, the sun was shining and the weather was relatively mild. To Victoria it was what Aunt Alice called an Indian Summer day.

She could see how cleverly the garden had been landscaped, designed by Christopher – she knew from Melinda – after he had inherited the house from his parents.

Towards the end of the garden, near the wall, a number of trees were turning colour. In a few days they would be scarlet, gold and the honey tones of autumn. He was right. That area of the garden would be a perfect spot to have a few pictures taken.

Turning to Christopher, she mentioned this, and he agreed. Then she asked, 'How far is it to Biggin Hill?'

'It takes about an hour and a half, perhaps a bit less, depending on the traffic. It's not that far from London. Think in terms of heading towards Beachy Head and the coast.'

A moment later, Rory Delaney came out to the terrace and announced, 'I've spoken to Biggin Hill and you can go whenever you wish, Christopher. This week, next week.'

'Oh, I had hoped we could go there on Friday,' Victoria exclaimed, looking at Christopher. 'There's a bit of a rush on this shoot, because Melinda wants to get it into the magazine as soon as possible. To help your charity. We have a two-month lead time.'

'Friday is all right for me, isn't it, Rory? Do we have anything special?' Christopher asked.

'A lunch with your accountant, which can be cancelled.' Rory chuckled. 'It's yours to command, as far as Biggin Hill is concerned. The fellow I spoke to, a squadron leader, sounded really chuffed that you're going to be photographed down there. You're their . . . well, sort of their . . . *legend*.'

'You didn't speak to the base commander?' Christopher wondered out loud.

'No, he wasn't there. But I can promise you, on my scout's honour, that they will welcome you with open arms.'

Christopher turned to Victoria. 'I'm afraid our Irish friend here has kissed the Blarney Stone far too many times. He also has a tendency to exaggerate. On the other hand, he's the best wingman I have these days.'

Rory sat down next to Victoria and winked. 'They said a lot more laudatory things, Chris, but I'll skip those. Might go to your head.'

Victoria laughed. 'I'm sure they sang your praises, Christopher.'

They spoke a little longer about the shoot at Biggin Hill, and

Rory said he would handle everything for her, if she explained what she needed.

'Several planes out on the airfield, that's most important, and perhaps a few of the men who are based there. Also, I wondered if you might want to invite Noel Jollion, and perhaps a couple of other Biggin Hill chaps. How do you feel about that?' She looked at Christopher, wanting to see his reaction.

'It presents no problem. I'll see who I can rustle up, and I'll give Noel a ring. We have now agreed to do the shoot at the base this coming Friday. When do you propose to take the remainder of the photographs?' Christopher's eyes rested on her, admiring her beauty, thinking what a lovely person she was.

'I don't want to intrude on your weekend, but would you mind if I came on Saturday?' she asked, her eyes focused intently on his.

'Not at all, and you can come on Sunday as well, if you wish.' Looking over at Rory, he continued, 'You don't mind being here, do you?'

'At your service, as always, boss.' Addressing Victoria, Rory asked, 'How will you get there? Shall we pick you up on Friday morning, take you with us to Biggin Hill?'

'Well, I don't want—'

Interrupting, Christopher assured her, 'We have a lovely, very comfortable old Daimler. There's plenty of room in it, and a big boot for any equipment you have. I think it's best we all go together.'

'All right, and thank you.'

Rising, she turned to Christopher and said, 'I think I'd better be going now, I've taken up too much of your time already. Thank you for being helpful, and for a delicious lunch.'

'But you must stay for tea!' Rory exclaimed, having noted the sudden disappointment filling Christopher's face. He threw Victoria a knowing look.

She stared back at Rory and sat down again.

* * *

During tea on the terrace, Victoria talked to the two men about the charity Christopher had started. All she knew was that it would help veterans in many ways.

Christopher explained that his great-aunt had left him a small townhouse in Charles Street in Mayfair. Since he did not wish to live there, he had decided to gift the house to his charity and to use it as headquarters for the charity, and also as a club for the veterans.

'What a great idea that is, having a club for them. They can share experiences, socialize, talk; it's always good to discuss things,' Victoria remarked. 'When will the house be ready?'

Rory spoke up. 'It's in good condition and doesn't need any work done. We've already moved furniture out of three bedrooms, and are furnishing them as offices, for the people working on a permanent basis for the charity. So we're pretty well set.'

Christopher added, 'The reception rooms, the dining room and the library, all on the lower floors, do need a few masculine touches, but that's an easy job, just decorating. We want to get it rolling as soon as possible.'

'And we're looking for as much publicity about the charity as we can get,' Rory pointed out.

'Melinda indicated that to me, and I'll mention it to my friend, Elise Steinbrenner, on the *Daily Mail*. She might be able to write something.'

'Thank you, Victoria, that's very nice of you,' Christopher murmured, and sat back, a reflective expression on his face.

Eventually he said in a somewhat saddened tone, 'It's the strangest thing in the world to me – that the veterans of wars are never treated properly. It's a given throughout history that governments and the public seem indifferent to them and their suffering. And it's everywhere, not only in Britain. People are rotten to them, others oblivious.'

'I hadn't realized it was that bad,' Victoria said. 'How awful, and what a predicament for the men to be in.'

'I'm afraid it is. It seems to me that nobody cares about these brave *boys*, because that's what they mostly were. They put themselves in harm's way to fight for their country and to protect the people. And I'm not just talking about airmen, but soldiers and sailors as well . . . Our former fighting forces are not much appreciated when they return home from battle. In fact, they are the forgotten men. That's what I call them.'

Rory jumped into the conversation. 'Many of the men need a lot of help. Some are physically ill, or are suffering from the *shock* of war, and they are truly in pain.'

'That's one of the worst things,' Christopher said. 'The anguish they're left with, having seen their mates wounded and dying on those killing fields, often in foreign countries. We have a big task ahead, I know, but I do think my charity will work and that it will help them.'

Victoria had been listening attentively, had heard the passion and determination in his voice, noticed the sorrow etched on his face. And she understood that he was a most caring man who wanted to help those who were less fortunate, who were in difficult straits. She found herself touched by his goodness and compassion.

When she left the lovely old house in Hampstead, Christopher sent Rory with her to make sure she was put safely in a taxi. As they looked for one, Rory told her in a low voice, 'He's taken to you, and in a way I've not seen before. It's just incredible.'

'I like him a lot too. He's very special,' she answered, with a warm smile.

Rory merely nodded, but when a cab drew to a stop, and he helped her in, he muttered, 'Just don't mess with him – mess him up, I mean.'

Victoria gaped at him, flabbergasted by the comment. Before she could answer, Rory added, 'See you Friday at nine o'clock.' And he banged the door of the cab shut.

As she sat back against the seat, Victoria realized that Rory was being protective, and she understood exactly why.

The last thing in the world she would do was hurt a man like Christopher Longdon. He touched her deeply on many levels. In fact, he had bowled her over. She wanted to go back, and sit next to him, and . . . And what? she asked herself. Make him smile, make him feel happy, just be there with him. Those were the answers she gave herself.

'Thank you for fitting the gown on me,' Alicia Stanton said, smiling at Greta. 'I'm not in a hurry for it. The Royal Command Film Performance is not until November.'

'I know . . . It really suits you, Alicia,' Greta said, and then began to laugh. 'Blue again. But what can you do? The colour is perfect for you.'

'Adam chose it. Out of everything you showed us this morning, this was his favourite.'

Greta nodded. 'Anyway, you don't have anything in your wardrobe like this – bouffant, frothy. It's really lovely on you, very fashionable.'

Alicia sat down on the sofa in the main showroom, where Cecily's clothes were always fitted, and took a sip of the tea Aunt Dottie had just brought them.

'I was glad I didn't have to film today. And that Adam was able to come to the shop with me earlier. He had to make a plane to New York this afternoon; that's why he was in a hurry. He needed to talk to me, which is why I had to come back for the fitting.'

'So who's in charge when the producer is away on a trip?' Greta asked, sitting down, picking up her cup.

'The other producer, the line producer, and the director. Plenty of people. Although I think Adam is probably the driving force, the best of the lot. He's bringing this film in on time and has not gone over budget.'

When Greta remained silent, made no comment, Alicia looked at her closely and asked, 'Did you like Adam when you met him on Saturday?'

'I did, yes. I thought he was extremely personable, easy to talk to. In fact, everyone liked him. And I must say, he's awfully good looking. I wish my Elise could find a nice chap like him.'

'I thought Arnold Templeton's younger brother seemed rather struck by her. Certainly he was pretty much by her side all evening. And, by the way, thank you for letting us come to the supper, we really enjoyed it. And Adam got to meet you and some of the family.'

'My pleasure, Alicia. I want to tell you yet again that you were the epitome of glamour.'

'In a blue frock,' Alicia answered pithily.

A moment later Dottie arrived with Constance Lambert in tow. She said, 'When Mrs Lambert heard you were in the shop, Miss Stanton, I couldn't stop her from racing up here.'

They all laughed. Dottie went back downstairs, while Constance joined Alicia and Greta in the seating area of the Swann showroom.

'I bought one of your gold metal box bags, Greta. I think this new line is superb. Dottie's wrapping it now. And I hope I didn't interrupt anything.' She looked from Greta to Alicia.

'No, of course not,' Greta exclaimed. Constance was one of their regular clients and bought quite a bit from Swann. And she was much liked by the entire staff.

Alicia jumped up, went over to the clothes rack, and took the blue gown off the hanger. 'Look at this, Connie. I just bought it. For the Royal Command "do" in November.' She held it against herself. 'Do you like it?'

'It's perfect, darling. You'll steal everyone's thunder.' Constance stared at her for a long moment, and said in a lowered voice, 'It's all over town, you know. Everyone's talking about you and Adam being romantically involved, having an affair, et cetera, et cetera.'

'Good heavens! News travels fast. We were only seen in public together on Saturday. Four days ago, since it's now Tuesday. Wow!'

'Wow, wow, wow! That's what I'd say,' Constance cried, amusement echoing in her voice. 'Anyway, I understand it's lovely gossip, not bad stuff. People seem pleased for you both. All agog, actually.'

'Now I understand why everyone was careful around me at Shepperton yesterday, and constantly glancing at me.'

'They were probably envying you. Or envying Adam,' Constance replied.

When Greta walked into her house in Phene Street an hour later, she found Victoria sitting at the little table in the kitchen, making notes on a small pad. She was casually dressed in a soft indigo sweater and dark wool trousers, her long legs tucked under her. 'Hello, Greta,' Victoria said, looking up, smiling.

'Was your visit with Christopher Longdon successful? How did it go?' Greta asked, leaning against the doorframe.

'Very well. I found him to be extremely nice, helpful, welcoming. We sort of clicked – got on like a house on fire – and the time flew. I even stayed for lunch.'

Noticing the strange expression on Greta's face, Victoria asked, 'Why are you looking so surprised?'

'Does that often happen?' Greta sounded puzzled.

'No. But we actually worked hard at planning the entire shoot. Choosing what rooms to use in the house, whether to take any pictures in the garden, which is sort of finished now, but the trees are turning and are lovely. Also, we talked about Biggin Hill, where he was stationed during the war. In fact, we're going down there on Friday.'

Greta was amazed, and it showed. 'My goodness, Vicki, you obviously covered a lot of ground in a short time. What's he like?'

'Fabulous.' Her face was alight with enthusiasm. 'And very cooperative. He liked my idea of having him amongst planes out on the airfield, wearing his flying suit, surrounded by some of the airmen based there now. And he's going to phone Noel Jollion, who was also at Biggin Hill.' Victoria, confident about their plans, nodded. 'It's all going to work very well.'

'How wonderful for you, Vicki, that you were able to put this together so fast.' Greta paused, a thoughtful look in her eyes. After a moment, she said, 'He's in a wheelchair, isn't he?'

'Yes, but I never really noticed that . . .' She stopped, gave Greta a hard stare. 'His personality is warm, and he's outgoing, gregarious. The immense charisma takes over, I suppose.' Sitting up a bit straighter, she finished, 'Actually, I've never met a man like him.'

Greta's gaze remained closely focused on Victoria and she suddenly realized that the girl was glowing – radiant, in fact, her green eyes sparkling.

Oh my God, Greta thought, she's fallen for him. She decided to end the conversation right now. 'I'm going upstairs to have a bath, Vicki. See you shortly.'

# Twenty-Five

Later that week, on Friday morning at exactly ten minutes to nine, Victoria put her head around the kitchen door and said, 'Good morning, Greta.'

Greta smiled at her. 'And good morning to you. I see you're all ready for your trip to Biggin Hill. I must say you're very smart. That old Swann jacket looks good on you.'

Victoria nodded. 'I've had it for ages, but I love the back, the swing of it, and I think the cream works well with the blouse and black trousers, don't you?'

'Absolutely. You know, you could have been a model, Vicki, if you hadn't discovered your talent for photography.'

Victoria laughed. 'I prefer to be taking the pictures, not posing for them. Do you want to come out to say hello to Christopher and his crew?'

'I'd love to, and when you say *crew*, do you mean Noel Jollion and the other men who'll be in the pictures?'

'No, no, they'll be meeting us there. Noel's rather pleased to be a part of it, I think. By crew I meant his personal assistant, his physiotherapist, those people.'

Greta stood up. 'I'll just pop upstairs and get my jacket and bag. I'll be going to the office after you leave.'

'And I have to carry my camera bags to the door, so see you in a minute.'

Victoria kept her cameras and two large leather bags in a cupboard in the dining room, and she had just finished packing the cameras when Greta returned and stood in the doorway.

'You're lucky with the weather, Victoria. It's another Indian Summer day, just like it was on Tuesday. You will be shooting mostly outside, won't you?'

'With the planes, yes. But I thought I could get a really cheery shot in the Mess, with the group around Christopher holding pints of beer, or whatever. I want to catch something . . . convivial, very male oriented.'

A few seconds later Victoria and Greta walked over to the car, where Rory was standing; he opened the door on the side where Christopher was sitting.

Victoria immediately stepped forward, a huge smile on her face. She leaned into the car and kissed Christopher on his cheek, surprising herself more than him.

Standing back swiftly, she said, 'This is Greta Chalmers, Christopher. Greta, I'm happy to introduce you to Christopher Longdon.'

Greta thrust out her hand, unable to speak for a moment, stunned by the beauty of the man. There was no other word to use to describe him. He was strikingly good looking, very masculine, and his cheeks dimpled when he smiled, his dark brown eyes sparkling, very alive.

He said, 'Hello, Mrs Chalmers, Victoria didn't tell me you were coming with us. But you are welcome.'

'I'm so glad to meet you, Mr Longdon. However, I'm afraid I'm not tagging along. Although I'd love to. Duty calls. I have to go to work.'

She discovered she couldn't look away. He was extremely compelling in his slightly worn flying suit, with a white silk scarf tied around his neck. Now she remembered how all the fliers wore that scarf. And they had copied it.

Realizing she was staring at him far too long, she exclaimed, 'We copied the scarf, Mr Longdon! At Swann Couture, during the war. Because all the fliers like you wore them, and women wanted them.'

He nodded, then laughed. 'We wore them not to be dandies, but because in a Spit, a Spitfire, you turn your head a lot. The scarf was a precaution to stop our necks from chafing, as we constantly looked around for Luftwaffe planes on our tails.'

'We certainly sold a lot of them.' Turning to Victoria, Greta touched her arm. 'Have a wonderful shoot.' She looked at Christopher and smiled, 'It was a privilege to meet you, Mr Longdon.'

She said goodbye to Rory and walked back up the steps and into the house. No wonder Victoria was infatuated, and Greta was quite certain that she was. The man was charismatic; he had captivated *her* in only a couple of minutes. Injured though he was, he was bait for any woman.

Once Rory was in the driver's seat of the Daimler, he closed the inside window between the front and the back seats, giving Christopher his privacy, as he always did.

Leaning into Victoria, Christopher kissed her on her cheek, looked into her face, his smile as huge as ever. 'You kissed me first. So I am compelled to kiss you back.'

Victoria felt herself filling with happiness at being with him again. She relaxed, leaned back, content to be near him.

Christopher said, 'I thought it a good idea to wear my old flying suit. Rory asked the others to do the same, so we're all set to go when we arrive at Biggin Hill.'

'It *was* a great idea. I always prefer to do my outside shots while the weather is good. As Greta said to me earlier, it's another Indian Summer day. I hope it lasts.'

He inclined his head, and shifted slightly in the seat to look at her properly. 'Do you share the Phene Street house with Greta?'

'No. I'm just camping out there for the moment.'

'Don't you have anywhere to live?' he asked, a note of sudden concern echoing in his voice.

'Oh yes, I do. I have my own flat in Belsize Park Gardens, but something happened and I . . .' She stopped abruptly, realizing she was about to tell him about Phil Dayton. Clearing her throat, she continued quickly, 'Her sister Elise decided she wanted her own place, and she took a flat nearby. Greta was by herself, and lonely. Also, I felt a bit isolated in north London, and I was far from my friends in Chelsea and Mayfair. And the magazine office as well. So I camp out there a bit, and Elise is helping me to find a flat in the area.'

'It's nice of you to keep Greta company. I understand her predicament only too well.' A small smile lurked around his mouth. 'I also enjoy your company, Vicki.'

Her eyes widened slightly and she exclaimed, 'You called me Vicki, like my friends do. So are we now friends?'

'We are.' He paused, his eyes intently searching her face. 'If you'll let me.'

Victoria swallowed, her throat tight with emotion. There was a lilt of happiness in her voice when she exclaimed, 'It's a deal.' He gave her his hand, and she shook it, laughing.

He laughed with her, opened her hand, kissed her palm. 'Sealed with a kiss.' His eyes lingered on her. 'You must have done research on me for the shoot. So I'm sure you know all about me. But I don't know anything about you . . . except that you're the most adorable girl I've ever met.'

'What do you want to know?' she asked, thrilled by his words.

He studied her again. 'I think you must be very young. About nineteen?'

She shook her head.

'So how old are you?' he probed in a low voice.

'Twenty-one. I'll be twenty-two next March. But I've been

working since I left school. I might look young, but I'm an independent woman, you know. And you're twenty-eight, I know from the information I gathered.'

'Seven years difference. A very big gap.'

'I don't think so. Next question.'

He looked across at her again, his face hard to read.

'Are you in a relationship with anyone?'

'No, I'm not. Are you, Christopher?'

'Footloose and fancy-free. And have been for a long while. A moment ago you said something happened, when you mentioned your flat in Belsize Park Gardens. Then you rushed on to speak about Greta. So what exactly happened?'

'It's a long story—'

'I like your long stories,' he interrupted peremptorily. 'So tell me.'

'When I first went to London, I worked at Photo Elite, a famous agency. Paloma knows Michael Sutton, the owner, and she got me the job, a junior post, to get my foot in the door. Anyway, one of the young men working there became a bit of a pest, wanting to take me out. I wasn't interested.' She paused, and took a deep breath.

Christopher said, 'And so he persisted. I hope he didn't hurt you in any way.'

'No, he didn't. But he started to park his grey Vauxhall in my street, further along from Number Forty-Three. I'd obviously noticed his car, and it disturbed me. In the end I'd had enough. I got home and saw it and simply jumped in a cab back to Phene Street. I told Greta about it, and she insisted I stay with her that night – and I haven't got round to moving on yet. We both quite like the company. And then, through her, I got a job with *Elegance Magazine*. It was the perfect solution for me.'

'And what about this young man? Did you report him to the owner of the agency?'

'No, I didn't.'

'Why not?' Christopher frowned. 'He could still pester you from afar, you know.'

'He won't.' Victoria stared out of the window, her face set. 'Because once I'd given my notice to Photo Elite, I went to see Phil Dayton. I warned him that I would report him to Michael and the police if he didn't leave me alone. I frightened him off, I believe. If I'd told Michael about his behaviour, Michael could have given him the sack, and I would have made an enemy out of Mr Dayton.'

Christopher, already totally infatuated, experienced a rush of admiration for her. 'Clever girl,' he murmured. 'You did exactly the right thing. And so what happened to your flat?'

'I still have it, because I don't want to stay with Greta indefinitely. I'll go back there, but I've just been so busy. I've yet to find a flat in Chelsea.'

'I see.'

Christopher now fell silent. He settled back against the seat and closed his eyes. He was surprised by his attraction to this young woman who had come into his life so unexpectedly, taking him by surprise with her energy and naturalness. She was unlike any of the women he had known in the past. In fact, she was probably an original – they'd undoubtedly thrown the mould away when they had made her. He smiled inwardly at his thoughts. Her outgoing personality, her natural *joie de vivre* warmed his soul. It seemed to him that her nature matched his own.

Victoria had the same kind of happiness inside her that he did, and a positivity he had possessed all his life. It was a trait that had seen him through great trouble. They settled into a companionable silence. Without opening his eyes, Christopher felt himself relaxing. Her presence soothed him, made him feel calm, safe.

When they eventually arrived at Biggin Hill, Rory parked near the building where the Mess Room was located, then he went to help Victoria out of the car.

As he made for the boot, he said, 'I asked the base commander, on Christopher's instructions, not to have a welcoming committee standing out here. I suggested everyone wait for us in the Mess.'

'That was a good idea, the best way to handle things.' Victoria pulled her camera bag out of the boot, as Rory took the other one.

A moment later they were joined by Freddy and Bruce, who had parked the black van immediately behind the Daimler. After introducing them to her, Rory told Victoria that the two men would help Christopher to get out, once Bruce had taken the wheelchair out of the van.

As the two men went to get the chair, Rory called after them, 'Don't forget the crutches.'

Victoria stared at Rory, a surprised expression on her face. She frowned as she said, 'Can Christopher use crutches?'

'Oh yes, for a bit, anyway. His injuries were mostly on his left side. That leg's useless, but he can stand on his right leg for a short while with the help of crutches. He wants to do that in one of the group pictures.'

'I thought he was a paraplegic?' She sounded puzzled.

'He is, but only partially. He has an incomplete injury at a low level of his spinal cord: that's where the paralysis is located.'

She remained silent, digesting what he had just told her.

Glancing at her, Rory added, 'Christopher's upper body is very strong, especially his arms and his chest. Freddy has made sure of that. It enables him to do a lot of things.'

'Is Bruce also a physiotherapist?'

'Yes, and an expert masseur. They both keep him very fit.'

'Very fit indeed,' Christopher announced, wheeling himself over to the two of them. Addressing Victoria, he said, 'Shall we wait out here?' He looked towards the airfield. 'I see they've plenty of planes waiting, including some Spits.' He began to chuckle. 'What wouldn't I give to get into one and roar up there into the wild blue yonder, as the song goes.'

'I wish you could too,' Victoria said, and looked up at the sky. 'The weather's still all right, but there are a few clouds gathering.

I would like to get you and the men with the planes as soon as possible.'

'Then let's do it now, at once.' He turned his head and said to Rory, 'Will you go and get Noel and the other lads, please?'

'At once,' Rory answered, and dashed over to the staff building.

Victoria stepped closer to the wheelchair, and put her hand on Christopher's shoulder. 'Rory told me you can stand on crutches for a short while. Will you do that for a few shots?'

'I certainly will. Oh look, Noel's coming out with some of the lads I know, and oh my God, my former wing commander is with them. What a turnout.'

She smiled to herself on hearing these words. He was so modest. And of course it was a big turnout. He was Britain's greatest war hero. Over one hundred missions over Germany; a flight lieutenant who had saved his crew before himself many times over; who had made the ultimate sacrifice for them by forcing them to bail out first on his last flight. An unselfish and courageous gesture that had almost cost him his life as he went down with his plane.

# Twenty-Six

Cecily sat in front of the fire in the library, waiting for Miles to arrive home. He had gone to a special dinner in Harrogate to meet with some of the town council there. The evening was all to do with the Festival of Britain, which was already in the planning stage throughout the country, even though the Festival was not until 1951.

Because Miles was the Earl of Mowbray and a premier earl of England, he had been asked by the council to head up Yorkshire's participation in the upcoming plans for the Festival.

He had agreed. She smiled to herself, settling back against the cushions, enjoying this little period of peace and quiet.

Miles had agreed to a lot of things of late. Three months, she thought; it's only three months since he agreed to take the bank loan, putting practicality before his pride.

It had helped that it was a private bank, and he was dealing with the managing director, who was the son of the owner and was an old Etonian like himself.

There was a knock on the door, and Eric came in carrying a tray. 'I've brought a bottle of the best cognac, Your Ladyship,' Eric said, placing the tray on the table. 'It's His Lordship's favourite.'

'Thank you, Eric.' Reaching out she touched the bottle, glanced up at Eric, and nodded, 'Thank goodness the Fourth and Fifth Earls loved brandy and bought so much of it years ago. I couldn't believe the prices it all brought at the auction.'

A smile struck Eric's face, and he chuckled. 'His Lordship was all for the auction in the end, and, in fact, he enjoyed mucking around in the wine cellars with me, if the truth be known. I think he was more startled than me at the quantity of great wines, cognacs and liqueurs that were down there, and that had not turned like so many other bottles.'

Cecily nodded. 'I know. He said he believed his ancestors must all have been drunkards. I disagreed and explained that there wouldn't be so much stock left if that had really been the truth.'

Eric Swann, who was her father's cousin, leaned closer and said in a low tone, 'You've done this place good, Ceci. Always. And Cavendon's almost back on its feet, thanks to you. We're all proud of you. I just wanted you to know that.'

'Thank you, Eric, and thank you for everything you've done to help me, and Miles, make every little thing run smoothly.'

He inclined his head and departed, quieter on his feet than any butler she had ever known. Eric was family to her, but he never stepped out of place.

His comments tonight had been unusual, but she realized he had needed her to know that the Swanns of Cavendon thought very highly of her. Things here had improved enormously.

The bank loan had been a boon; the wine auction a huge success. The estate was on an even keel. Safe for them as well as the Inghams.

Her own business was finally on an upward arc, thanks to Aunt Dottie and Greta. Smaller offices, a reduced staff, and the unexpected revenue from the recent sale had helped to keep Swann steady. The money Aunt Charlotte had given her, plus Greta's investment in the company as her partner, had enabled them to go full swing into work on the collection for next summer. And what had happened today had been fortuitous.

The door opened and Miles interrupted her thoughts as he walked in. 'There you are, darling.' He strode over to the sofa, continued, 'You waited up for me. That's nice.'

She stood up and he took her in his arms, hugged her, kissed her cheek. 'You sound happy,' she said. 'The evening must have gone well.'

'It did indeed. And I must say I think this idea of the Festival of Britain is truly brilliant. It's going to do wonders for the country. In so many different ways,' Miles said. 'One of the most important things, as far as I'm concerned, is that the bombed-out cities are going to be rebuilt. Finally. Starting in January of 1950. The government wants the country to look good. Apparently they anticipate visitors from all over the world. And the Festival will be great for us, help Cavendon no end.'

'It sounds fabulous, and I'm happy you're happy.' Cecily sat down, picked up the bottle of cognac and poured a good measure into each of the brandy balloons. 'I've got some wonderful news, Miles.'

Joining her on the sofa, he accepted the balloon she offered and raised a brow. 'It must be awfully good news indeed if you're bringing out our rarest cognac.'

'The money from the sale of my two factories in Leeds went into the Swann business bank account today. And I want us to toast Emma Harte.'

Miles gaped at her, taken by surprise. 'You never told me she was involved,' he exclaimed. 'Did *she* buy them from you?'

'Only one, to use for her ready-made line, Lady Hamilton Clothes. The prices are reasonable and that collection still sells well. A friend of hers in the men's clothing industry in Leeds bought the other factory. So, here's to Emma.'

'To Emma Harte! Your good friend and saviour.'

'To Emma. My hero,' Cecily said, her eyes aglow.

They touched glasses and took a sip. Cecily continued, '*We've* managed it again, Miles – pulled off all sorts of deals, things that have kept Cavendon afloat. We're a good combination, aren't we?

A Swann and an Ingham usually do make it happen. Like our forefathers, Humphrey Ingham and James Swann.'

Miles laughed. 'Except they weren't married as we are.'

'Obviously not. However, they *were* joined at the hip. And then some. *Like family*.' She paused, then added, 'In fact, very intertwined.'

Miles took another sip of the cognac and put the balloon down on the table, staring at her. 'You say that in the strangest way. What are you getting at?'

'I want to show you something, and also tell you a story.'

'What kind of story?' he asked, suddenly intrigued, noticing the excitement on her face.

'A story Aunt Charlotte and I figured out. Separately first and later together . . . through the record books.'

'You're going to tell me secrets from the Swann record books? Isn't that forbidden?' It was obvious he was somewhat shocked.

'Supposedly. And I think they had their good reasons in those days, because there was a lot to hide at the beginning of our mutual family story. Genuine secrets.'

'The Inghams kept record books too, but I've never had time to look.' Miles shook his head. 'I left that to Aunt Charlotte, and she never confided anything.'

'I know. She told me she thought you weren't interested at all.'

'Aren't you breaking an oath? Telling me these Swann secrets?'

'I don't think so, because they're Ingham secrets as well.'

'Swanns make an oath to protect Inghams,' Miles muttered. '*Loyalty Binds Me*. Remember?'

'I do indeed. I took that oath. It is also the Ingham family motto. And I am now an Ingham, so I think I can confide in you. Anyway, does anybody care about those days these days?' she asked, starting to laugh.

'I suppose not. Tell me the story.'

'You know the facts about how Humphrey Ingham and James Swann worked together in the 1700s, the resulting earldom for Humphrey and all that, so I will go straight to the story. Come on, we have to go to the staircase portrait gallery.'

Cecily jumped up, offered her husband her hand, pulled him to his feet.

Miles was further intrigued as she led him up the main double staircase to the top landing, where they stopped in front of the first painting. 'You know who this is, don't you?' she said.

'Of course I do, silly girl. It's Humphrey, the First Earl, who started it . . . our line I mean. I know all of them actually.'

'Aunt Charlotte thinks your father looked like Humphrey. Do you?'

'As a matter of fact, yes. I always have. My father resembled him in certain ways. They had the same eyes, brows and forehead.' Miles glanced at her, seemingly still puzzled since he was frowning.

Cecily smiled knowingly and moved on. 'And this is Marmaduke, the Second Earl, and that's where the story really begins.'

'With Marmaduke? Humphrey's son and heir?'

'He was illegitimate.'

Flabbergasted, Miles shook his head. 'Oh come on, that can't be! How could he have been illegitimate? Humphrey was married to Marie, before he became an earl . . . She was his mother.'

'No, she wasn't. She couldn't conceive. However, Humphrey *was* Marmaduke's biological father. He was born here, and he was brought up here by Humphrey. And nobody ever questioned anything. James Swann saw to that: he took care of anything . . . *awkward*, shall we say? They were hand-in-glove, those two: partners in everything.'

'So there was never any question of Marmaduke's legitimacy?'

'None at all. Charlotte told me that in the Ingham records there is some sort of paper, an ancient birth certificate. Humphrey and Marie are listed as parents of the child, but Charlotte thinks it looks doctored.'

'Why are you so sure this is true?' Miles now asked.

'From working it out. Not together, but separately, as I just said. We came to the same conclusion. Take a look at Marmaduke again, Miles – a long, hard look. Tell me who he reminds you of?'

Miles moved closer to the portrait, then took out his glasses and peered at it again. '*Harry!* He looks like your brother. Well, I'll be damned.'

He let his voice trail off, swung his head and looked at his wife. 'Are you trying to tell me that the mother of Marmaduke was a Swann?'

'Yes. And it's true. Sarah Swann Caxton was James's sister, a young widow with two children by her late husband. But it was Humphrey she loved, and she bore Elizabeth first, before Marmaduke. Come over here, Miles. Take a look at Humphrey's only daughter.'

He did as she asked and knew at once she was correct. In different clothes and with a modern hairdo, the woman in the portrait could easily have been mistaken for Cecily at twenty or so. 'She's like you,' he murmured, swivelling to face her. 'And I notice the portrait is by Romney, a great portraitist at the time. Humphrey must have loved her a lot.'

'He also loved her mother. Sarah Swann Caxton was the love of his life, but he was married to Marie when Elizabeth was born,' Cecily explained.

'I wonder why Countess Marie put up with the situation? Any ideas, Ceci?'

'Here's the thing: she was seven years older than Humphrey. She couldn't conceive, and may well have felt terribly guilty. So she brought up his daughter as her own. A lot of women had to do a lot of things they didn't like in those days. It's called playing the game.'

'And Marmaduke as well. Oh wait a minute, *she* died in childbirth, didn't she? Marie, I mean. I remember my father mentioning that to me once.'

Shaking her head, Cecily replied, 'No. I told you, she couldn't conceive. Here's the thing, Miles. Some months before Marmaduke was born, Marie began to have a swollen stomach. So much so everyone believed her to be pregnant. Except she wasn't; she had a malignant tumour, more than likely cancer. And she did die, just before Sarah gave birth to Marmaduke.'

'What luck that was!' Miles stared at Cecily. 'That wasn't anything your ancestor James Swann could manipulate, that's for sure.'

'You're right. Let's go downstairs, darling, to the Long Gallery. I want us to look at the portraits of James Swann and his family. As you know, they're hanging there near the East Wing, where James and Anne lived all their lives. Apparently on Humphrey's insistence, from what I understand from the record books. He needed James with him at all times.'

'What are you inferring?'

'Nothing. Don't be daft! They were extremely close, intimate friends, bonded. Remember, it was pretty lonely out here in the eighteenth century, not any other aristocratic families around to socialize with. So the two of them were obviously reliant on each other. Also, they travelled the world together, and went to London on business all the time.'

'I get it,' Miles answered and zeroed in immediately when they reached the East Wing. He stood in front of the portrait of Sarah Swann Caxton, James's sister and mother of Humphrey's children.

A true Swann, by God! And another slightly different version of the Swann he was married to, whom he loved with all his heart.

Cecily came and stood next to him. He put his arm around her shoulders, held her close, and suddenly, unexpectedly, he choked up. How bound together she and he were, by history, by the past.

After a moment, he said softly, 'At the top of the staircase are the Inghams and down here are the Swanns. Think of it, Ceci: the two of us have their genes. We're a mixture of both families, you and I.'

'I thought the same thing the other day, Miles. It seems they found each other irresistible.'

'And still do,' he said, pulling her even closer to him.

'It never stopped, you know.'

'What do you mean?'

'The fornication continued over the centuries.'

'Are you serious? Is there more to this story?'

'Yes.' She hesitated, then said, 'Great-Aunt Gwendolyn, after she was widowed, had a long romantic love affair with my grandfather, Mark Swann. And they had a child, who died. But then they had another one, called Margaret.'

Miles peered at her, obviously so shocked he was speechless. Recovering himself, he said, 'No, not Great-Aunt Gwen. I don't believe you. Come on, admit it, Ceci. This is a joke.'

'No, it's not. Let's go back to the library and finish our cognac, and I'll tell you all about your great-aunt and my grandfather.'

Later that day, when she was alone in the upstairs sitting room off their bedroom, Cecily realized how differently she felt. About herself, Cavendon and Miles. About everything, really.

When Charlotte had confided important matters and events from the Ingham papers, things she had read in the Swann record books instantly clicked into place to make a whole.

It had been like fitting a jigsaw puzzle together. So much more now made complete sense, with her newly acquired knowledge about James Swann. In character, vision and brilliance, James Swann had been Humphrey Ingham's equal and had been treated as such. He had not been as rich as Humphrey because he did not own a business; he worked for a businessman who became an earl.

However, Humphrey had made sure James was enormously well compensated for his dedication and diligence. In fact, he had treated him like family. James and his wife had lived in the East Wing of Cavendon Hall all their lives. But then, with over a hundred and thirty rooms, there was an overabundance of space.

Yet, in a sense, Humphrey had turned them into kith and kin, and Sarah Swann had given Humphrey his only children. Family indeed, if you really thought about it.

How proud she was of James Swann. He had truly been the co-creator of Cavendon Hall, the estate, and the village of Little Skell, as well as contributing to the prosperity of the Ingham family.

The Swanns truly had a right to be living here, and this knowledge gave her an unexpected rush of joy. Cavendon was hers, too, and suddenly she believed that Aunt Charlotte felt the same way.

Before now, Miles had had no need to know, and anyway he had no real interest in his antecedents of long ago.

Miles had always focused on his father, the 6th Earl, and his grandfather, the 5th Earl, following their rules. All those other earls who had gone before were lost in the mists of time. Ashes to ashes, dust to dust, that was his attitude.

After his father's death, Aunt Charlotte had reminded Miles that the Ingham records were easily accessible to him. She had taken them both to the storage room behind the book-filled walls of the library. Miles had been aghast at the hundreds of labelled boxes piled high. She had seen him shudder when he saw them.

Now she remembered exactly what he had said to Charlotte. 'The past doesn't belong to me. It belongs to those who are dead. I'm alive and the future is mine. That's what I have to deal with. I have to preserve this place, take it into a new era.'

And he had done that. Cecily was proud of Miles. The odds had been against him ever since he had become the 7th Earl. He will succeed, she thought. He knows no other way. And I will be by his side. His wife and his stay. Bound together from the very start. Loyalty binds me.

# Twenty-Seven

Shifting white clouds raced across a bright blue sky and the sun was shining, but it was windy up on the moors at High Skell.

Victoria huddled into her camel-hair coat and readjusted her scarf, sitting down on the flat rock within the alcove created by the giant megaliths. This spot was somewhat protected.

She had come up there to think, to sort out her muddled thoughts, but at this moment, she was distracted by the view. Cavendon Hall and the park looked magnificent in the afternoon sunlight, and she only wished Christopher could see it. He liked natural beauty. But that would not be possible. He himself had joked that he couldn't climb rocks.

*Christopher Longdon.*

He was never out of her thoughts; she was infatuated with him. Actually, it was more than that. She had fallen for him. Hard. But what to do about him? And what did he feel for her? And, even if he liked her, and she suspected that he did, what kind of relationship could they have? She had been startled last Friday at Biggin Hill. When he stood up on crutches, to be photographed next to a Spitfire with Noel and his former wing commander, he had appeared to be steady on his right leg.

Not only that, she had noticed that he was tall, at least five eleven. But then she had only ever seen him sitting down until that moment.

Rory had said he was partially paraplegic, but she didn't know what that meant exactly, and she felt shy about asking Christopher.

On the other hand, there was a wonderful sense of ease between them, a compatibility she had never experienced before. They were alike in many ways. Perhaps she *could* bring it up with him.

At the sound of footsteps, Victoria glanced around and saw Alicia approaching. She was also wrapped up in a warm coat and with an Hermès silk scarf tied over her blonde hair. Raising a hand, Alicia waved.

Victoria waved back and stood up. The two women embraced and sat down together on the flat rock. Close up, Victoria was struck at once by Alicia's pallor, and she seemed taut, very tense. Her pretty features were strained and her face pale without her usual lipstick. Maybe she was missing Adam, who was still in New York. Alicia had mentioned that to her when she had arrived at Cavendon last night. She never filmed at weekends, and had arrived with Charlie.

After a moment, Alicia asked, 'How did your shoot go with Christopher Longdon?'

'Very well, actually. We went down to Biggin Hill, where he was stationed during the war. Noel Jollion came and Christopher's former wing commander as well. Plus a few other fliers. I got some fabulous shots.'

'Have you got any with you? I'd love to see some of them.'

'No, I don't. I only finished developing them on Tuesday, then they went to Tony del Renzio, the art editor. But I can show them to you next week, and I might even have the magazine proofs of your shoot as well.'

'Gosh, that would be wonderful! And I know Adam's dying to

see them.' Alicia sighed, and a sad expression settled on her face as she said this.

Victoria noticed at once. Leaning closer, she asked, 'Is everything all right with you and Adam?' When Alicia was silent, Victoria said, 'You look so sad.'

After a moment or two, Alicia responded: 'Everything's all right, I'm fairly sure of that. It's just that he's been a little angry with me. He tried to get hold of me the other evening, when he was first in New York. I was out with Charlie. He didn't believe me; he thought I was with another man. In the end, he accepted my story, which is the truth, Victoria. But I've realized something . . . Adam's got a jealous disposition, and he's possessive.'

'Perhaps any man would feel that way about you, Alicia,' Victoria murmured softly. 'You are very beautiful, you know, and a famous actress.'

Alicia gave her a long stare and began to laugh hollowly. 'Adam doesn't think I'm a famous actress: he says *he's* going to make me a big star.'

Victoria was so taken aback by this comment, she couldn't answer for a few seconds, and then she said pithily, 'Perhaps he's just trying to make himself seem more important in your eyes.'

'I always knew you were a smart girl,' Alicia exclaimed. 'As Mrs Alice would say, there are no flies on you.' Alicia let out a long sigh again. 'Men are difficult at times, and they're certainly not one little bit like women. We're as different as chalk and cheese. I sometimes think they're actually quite dumb.'

Nodding, Victoria said, 'Aunt Alice has another saying about men, and women, for that matter. She often told me not to forget that men are stupid and women are fools. And we probably are. But not all men are stupid.'

Victoria started to chuckle, and Alicia joined in. Like Victoria, she adored Alice Swann, who had always been devoted to her mother, Daphne, and to Alicia herself. Alicia also knew that Alice loved Victoria as if she were her own child.

The two women became quiet, were lost in their own thoughts

for a few minutes. Eventually Alicia turned to look at Victoria. 'So, talking of men, what is Britain's greatest war hero like?'

'Charismatic, good looking, warm and friendly. Very lovely, really. And he's kind. We got on like a house on fire.'

'It sounds like it,' Alicia remarked, staring hard at Victoria, instantly noticing the sparkle in her eyes, the radiance which suddenly filled her face. 'Oh dear, no! You've gone and fallen for him.'

'No, I haven't!' Victoria protested at once, not wanting anyone at Cavendon to know about her feelings for Christopher Longdon. 'I'm just trying to explain what an unusual man he is.'

'And not stupid like all the others?' Alicia said this teasingly. 'It's written all over your face, my girl.'

'What is?' Victoria asked challengingly.

'Your emotions, that's what. The hero has captivated you.' There was a moment or two of silence, and suddenly Alicia realized that Christopher Longdon was a man in a wheelchair.

Clearing her throat, not wanting to probe too much, Alicia began carefully, 'Forgive me if I'm wrong, but isn't Christopher Longdon a paraplegic?'

'Not exactly,' Victoria answered. 'Rory, his personal assistant, told me he was only partially paraplegic. Whatever that means.'

Alicia looked off into the distance, her eyes resting on the rim of the moors, her expression reflective. Finally, she turned to look at Victoria. 'Do you know if you can have a physical relationship with him?'

'I don't know, Alicia. I was actually thinking about it when you arrived. I came up here to go over everything in my mind.'

'As did I myself. We both know this place of old. I, from my grandfather, who often brought me here to see the view. And you came with Mrs Alice, for the same reason. But it does happen to be a perfect place to sort out your mixed-up thoughts.'

Alicia stood up. 'Come on, Victoria. I think you and I better have a little talk about the facts of life. In my bedroom, though, which is a much warmer place than up here in the wind.'

'I did take biology at Harrogate College,' Victoria volunteered, as she and Alicia walked away from the giant megaliths.

'And have you had any . . . practice?' Alicia asked.

Victoria remained silent.

'Have you ever made love with a man?'

'Well . . .' Victoria began and paused, then added in a low voice, 'not exactly.'

Whatever does that mean, Alicia wondered and groaned inside. Mrs Alice would be furious with her if she knew that Victoria was about to learn about sexual intimacy from her.

Victoria sat in front of the blazing fire in Alicia's bedroom, waiting for Alicia to come back.

She had gone down to the dining room in the South Wing to find a bottle of brandy and two glasses. 'We need warming up,' she said as she had disappeared a moment or two after they had entered the room.

Glancing around, Victoria nodded approvingly to herself. She had always admired this particular bedroom. The walls were painted the palest of green, and that colour made a perfect background for the green and pink draperies at the two windows and on the draped and quilted headboard. They were the only two colours in the room and they played well together. It was spacious and simple, not cluttered up with lots of bric-a-brac.

'Here I am, armed with the booze,' Alicia exclaimed as she walked in, closing the door with her foot. Placing the bottle and glasses on her Georgian desk in the window area, she poured two drinks and came over to the fireside, handing Victoria a shot glass.

'I couldn't find the brandy balloons,' Alicia said. 'These will have to do. Go on, just gulp it down in one swallow. That's the best way to feel the warmth from it.'

'I've not often had brandy,' Victoria told her, but swallowed half of it swiftly, then put the glass down on a nearby table, coughing. When she recovered, she said, 'That's got a bite to it.'

'It does the trick though.' Alicia sat back in her chair. 'I want to talk about *you* first, Victoria, so that I can advise you. And I do believe you need a bit of help in certain ways.'

Victoria nodded. 'I'll tell you anything you want to know. But you can't repeat our conversation to Aunt Alice.'

Alicia stared at her aghast, and exclaimed, 'Good God, I'd never do that! She'd be furious with me if she knew we were having such a conversation. And the same rule applies to you. Never give her an inkling that you've spoken about such a personal matter with me. Or anyone else for that matter.' Alicia ran her fingers through her blonde waves and shook her hair out. With some colour in her cheeks, she looked more like her old self.

'Of course I won't.'

'I'm going to ask you a few questions. You can just say yes or no, if you prefer.'

'That's all right, I don't mind explaining something if you don't understand.'

Alicia nodded and went on, 'Are you a virgin?'

'No.'

'But you indicated you'd not made love with a man, when I asked you on the moors.'

'I said *not exactly*, because it got botched up the first time. Martin Peek, the brother of my friend Christine, fancied me and I liked him a lot. We started having dates. It was when I was at Harrogate College. One night we went to a wood near Harewood and parked. We tried to make love in the back of his car. Then it all went wrong because . . . the . . . *thing* came off, and we stopped. Later he worried he'd made me pregnant.'

'He hadn't, had he?' Alicia looked at her keenly.

'No. But the frock might have been,' Victoria murmured, a small smile tugging at her mouth.

Alicia burst out laughing, and so did Victoria. Alicia then said,

'At least you've got a good sense of humour. Did you see Martin again?'

'Yes, when he was home from Cambridge. The *thing* was safe that time. But it was all over so quickly, and I didn't feel anything much. Maybe because I didn't love him?' These last few words sounded like a question.

'Maybe you're correct. On the other hand, I think he sounds awfully inept. How old were you?'

'I was almost eighteen, and Martin twenty-one. I never saw him again.'

'Is Martin the only man you've . . . *known* in that sense?'

'Yes.'

'Let's talk about Christopher Longdon and your feelings for him. Oh, and by the way, how old is he? Thirty or thereabouts?'

'He's twenty-eight,' Victoria answered.

'From the way you looked on the moors, and how you spoke about him, I suspect you have fallen very hard for him. And I know that feeling only too well,' Alicia said. 'There's nothing like true attraction. It is a mighty powerful emotion, that *pull* towards each other. The desire, the lust, the wanting. It overrides everything. Nothing else matters in the world but being with that special person.'

Alicia paused, shaking her head, and finished: 'It's ruined the lives of many a man, and woman, too. Mainly because it obliterates reason. Sexual fulfilment is all that matters. Actually, I think that kind of desire is . . . blinding.'

'That's how I feel about Christopher.' Victoria leaned closer to Alicia. 'I want to be with him all the time, close to him. I want to hold him, and well, I want *everything* with him.'

Alicia was quiet for a moment, thinking hard, and then she said, slowly and with care, 'I think we must discuss what it would mean if you became involved with him on every level. There would be great responsibility on your part, Victoria.'

For a split second Victoria looked puzzled. She frowned and asked, 'What do you mean *exactly*?'

'You are basically the one in control in this situation. You must think very, very carefully before starting a physical and emotional relationship with Christopher. He's a paraplegic, and also an extremely honourable man, a decent man. The whole world knows how brave he was in the war years . . .'

Alicia paused, and took hold of Victoria's hand. 'You must take this situation extremely seriously. You can't get involved with him and then just dump him, walk away, if you discover the situation's not to your liking.'

'I understand that very well, Alicia, I truly do. If I do get involved with Christopher, it would be forever. I would want to marry him, look after him, have his children.'

There was a long moment of silence. Eventually Alicia spoke. 'If he *can* have children. If he can have a sexual relationship with you. Can he? Has he ever discussed it?'

'Of course not!' Victoria exclaimed somewhat heatedly.

'How does he feel about *you*? Obviously the same, I'm quite certain of that.'

'I believe he's smitten with me, yes.'

'Has he ever touched you . . .' Alicia broke off, shaking her head. 'I sound like a member of the Spanish Inquisition, don't I?'

'No, you're trying to help me. Christopher has never laid a finger on me. He's kissed my cheek, held my hand, that's all,' Victoria said. 'I think his personal assistant, Rory, is aware of Christopher's attraction to me, though.'

'What makes you say that?' Alicia asked alertly, staring at Victoria.

'The first day I met Christopher, at the beginning of this month, I left his house in Hampstead just after tea. It was growing dark. Rory went with me to find a taxi. When I was getting in, he gave me a warning. He said something like – *Just don't mess with him, don't mess him up*. And I was startled, to tell you the truth.'

'That's what I'm also saying.' Alicia threw her a pointed look.

'Rory also told me that night that Christopher had taken to

me, and in a way he hadn't seen before. Rory seemed to think Christopher's reaction to me was unusual.'

'So we know he shares your feelings. But what about the partial paraplegia? I'm not understanding that.'

'Neither am I, really. When I heard Rory mention crutches at Biggin Hill, I asked Rory if Christopher could use them. He said he could. What I gathered was that Christopher has an incomplete injury at a low level of his spinal cord. That's what he meant when he said partially paraplegic. I just wish I knew a little more.'

'I agree.' Alicia sat back, swallowed the last of her cognac, her mind racing. Suddenly, she sat up straighter in the armchair and looked across at Victoria. 'I've just remembered something. I have a girlfriend who's married to an expert on paraplegia. His name's Abel Palmerston. I could ask Violet to help us understand better.'

Victoria immediately reacted to the name Palmerston. 'Is your friend's husband a doctor?'

'He is a specialist. A neurologist and very famous. Perhaps one of the best in the world. Why?'

'Because last Saturday, a week ago today, actually, I was photographing Christopher in his study. And, in between my shots, I heard him tell Rory not to forget to phone Mr Palmerston on Monday, to confirm his appointment. And now I've just remembered, a specialist is always called *mister* rather than doctor, isn't he?'

'Correct. Do you want me to phone Violet next week?'

'I'm not sure. And would she tell you anything about Christopher, if she finds out? I think doctors can't do that.'

'No, they mustn't reveal a thing. I was simply going to ask her about paraplegics, without mentioning any names.'

'Up on the moors I was contemplating asking Christopher myself. What do you think?'

'I would applaud that, and it's certainly a way to let him know you are serious about him.'

'I agree,' Victoria said. 'I want him to understand I am a serious person, an adult. Because I look young, he thinks he's too old for me, I suspect. Even though I've been working since I was eighteen.'

'When are you seeing him again?' Alicia asked.

'Sunday evening. You are still driving back tomorrow, aren't you, Alicia?'

'Yes, I am. I need to prepare for work on Monday. I'm filming every day next week. And I'd love your company. Charlie isn't coming back to London tomorrow. He's got his proofs to read.'

'There's something else I want to tell you,' Victoria said. 'I went to have supper with Christopher last Tuesday, before coming up to see Aunt Alice and Uncle Walter on Wednesday. At one moment Christopher asked me what I was doing the coming weekend, meaning next weekend. He asked if I was free. I said I was. He told me he wanted to show me a place he loved, because he believed I would like it, too.'

'Where is this place?' Alicia asked.

'It's a house in Kent. Where he grew up, near Romney Marsh. Shall I go?'

'Yes, you must. It's a marvellous chance to get to know him better. Anyway, who knows what might happen? You may very well get all the answers you need.'

# Twenty-Eight

He had returned in secret. Only his household staff knew he was back in London. That was the way Adam Fennell wanted it. He needed to be alone, to calm himself, and recover from the damaging effects of his trip to New York.

Not even Alicia Stanton was aware he was here. He groaned to himself as he remembered how ill-tempered he had been with her on the phone. He could kick himself for that bit of stupidity.

Marriage to Alicia was the next step. He had no doubt he would soon make her his wife.

A small smile slipped onto his face, as he looked at the framed photograph of her on his desk in the library of his flat. There she was, the aristocrat, the granddaughter of a premier earl of England, impeccable lineage, impeccable manners. Yet he could turn her into a trembling mass of sexual desire and need. His sexual prowess in bed was another way he bound her to him. She was always willing, very willing indeed.

Now he had some mending to do, having been irritable and accusatory on the phone from New York last week. And all because of Vince Ramsay. Vince was one of his backers who had unexpectedly turned him down when he had asked him to invest in

*Dangerous*, an Alfred Hitchcock-type thriller. And Rick Carrier had also declined. Their decisions had blown his plans out of the window.

In essence, they both disliked the script. Perhaps they were right. Maybe it did need more work. He would give it to Felix Lambert, ask for his opinion.

Adam trusted Felix; he was one of the old-timers he genuinely respected, and Felix had great judgement. He was also Alicia's agent. James Brentwood was a client as well. Adam had his eyes on Sir James; he hoped to snag him for another movie of his called *Revenge*. Hitchcock-style once again – Hitch was definitely 'in' at the moment. And to Adam he was the greatest.

In the end, Adam had managed to raise the money for *Dangerous* from Catherine Marron, a Broadway producer who had invested with him in the past. She fancied herself as a movie producer, and she fancied him. Bedding her was part of the deal. That was a small price to pay for her rather large investment in *Dangerous*.

An opportunist by nature, Adam was basically cold-hearted and calculating, although he was good at hiding these flaws in his character. His charm carried him along, as well as his plausibility and looks.

He brought his thoughts back to Alicia. With Catherine Marron in the bag as his main investor, he could concentrate on his future wife.

First, he had to apologize to her. He was very good at being contrite, and once he had her in his bed she would immediately forget about his anger. When he had not been able to reach her one night, he had accused her of being with another man. *Dumb*. He had been truly dumb. He knew that someone of Alicia's breeding would not like his behaviour. And Alicia's background was always in his mind. With marriage to her, he would truly rise to the top. Through her he could enter into the British aristocracy, become one of them.

He had planned to rise to the top ever since his childhood. It was within his reach. He would grab it. To do that he must take control of himself.

He had returned last night. Today was Monday, and Alicia was filming; he was well aware of her schedule. For her it would be a busy week. He would not go out to Shepperton Studios until Thursday. His plan was to surprise her, to surprise everyone, including Mario. And he would charm them all. He never failed.

Adam was not in good shape. His legs were bothering him again. He had bad cramping in his calves, and often felt crippled when he walked.

The trouble had started a few months ago. At the time he had remembered his father, as he did again now. That drunken lout had told everyone he suffered from rheumatism. Adam had not believed him, had blamed drink for his father's problems. Lately, he had wondered if his father had spoken the truth. Max, his masseur, had tried to convince Adam he did not have rheumatism. Max was proved right after he had been examined by a specialist, who told him he must walk more and take potassium.

Adam got up and went to his bedroom across the foyer. Opening a chest of drawers, he took out two boxes. Placing them on the bed, he looked inside them and nodded. A smile spread across his face. Some of Catherine's money had come in useful and she had also given him pleasure in her bed.

Wilson knocked on the door, came in, announcing that Max had arrived, and that he had sent him to the massage room. 'He said to take your time, sir. He has put the table up and prepared the room.'

'Thank you, Wilson. And don't forget, if there are any telephone calls, I am still in America.'

The clatter of the newsroom had always been music to Elise's ears, and she was truly happy whenever she was there. This morning was no exception. She was busy with a story about the Royal Command Film Performance, due to be held in November.

The King and Queen and the two Princesses were going to be present as well. No news about their gowns yet, but she would now phone Constance Lambert.

After they had greeted each other cordially, Constance said, 'How can I help you, Elise?'

'I'm doing a story on the Royal Command Film Performance, and I know it's rather in advance, but I wondered if you could talk to me about it for a few minutes, please?'

'You probably know this, but it's at the Odeon Theatre in Marble Arch on the seventeenth of November. The Royal Family are coming, but not Prince Philip, as he is stationed in Malta with the Royal Navy at the moment.'

'I have most of that. But since you're on the charity committee, I hoped you'd know which stars are planning to attend,' Elise answered.

'Well, of course, the dashing Errol Flynn, since he's the male lead in *The Forsyte Saga*, and I've been assured that Greer Garson will be there as well. She has the female lead. I think Errol will set a lot of hearts aflutter.' Constance chuckled. 'He's a handsome devil, if ever there was one. Anyway, I have a list here, just a minute.'

'Take your time,' Elise replied. 'I have my pencil and pad at the ready.'

A moment later, Constance said, 'All right, Elise, here we go. The names of the British stars I know are going to be there are Margaret Lockwood, Anne Todd, James Mason, Phyllis Calvert, John Mills and his wife, Mary Hayley Bell. They usually attend because they are huge supporters of the Royal Variety Charity, which benefits financially from the big premiere.'

'I think it's probably too early to ask about the gowns the female stars will be wearing, isn't it, Constance?'

'I think so. Oh, by the way, Alicia Stanton is coming with her producer, Adam Fennell. You can say Alicia will be wearing her favourite colour, blue, and will be in a ball gown made of tulle, designed by her aunt, Cecily Swann.'

'Oh gosh! I am stupid. I should have asked my sister, instead of bothering you. Do you think Princess Elizabeth and Princess Margaret will be in Norman Hartnell gowns?'

'More than likely. He's their favourite, and he does design the kind of glamorous gowns Princess Elizabeth, in particular, loves. Why not give Mr Hartnell's showroom a call?'

'I will, thanks for that tip, Constance. And thank you so much for all this. I can now write a good introductory piece.'

'My pleasure, Elise.'

Elise spent the entire morning working on the story, focusing on the glamour of the big event, the presence of the Royal Family, and the top Hollywood stars who would be there on the opening night. She was editing the piece when her phone began to ring. Picking it up, her eyes still on the story on her desk, she said absently, 'Hello? Elise Steinbrenner here.'

'Hello, Elise, how are you?'

'Alistair!' she exclaimed, recognizing his voice, suddenly totally focused as she sat up straighter in her chair. 'How are you feeling?'

'Much better, thank you,' he answered, happy he was getting such a warm response.

'Where are you? Still with your parents in Surrey?'

'I'm back in good old London town because I am really that much better. Well again. Almost my old self. Whoever would have thought that appendicitis could cause such havoc?'

'It can be very serious, you know,' Elise replied. 'Especially if peritonitis sets in. People have died from having their appendix removed. But this is good news. Hey, back at work for you, I hope.'

'I'm taking another week off, and then it's back to the old grindstone.'

There was a momentary pause before Alistair said, 'First, I want to thank you for coming to the hospital and cheering me up. And secondly, I want to make good on my promise to take you out to supper. If you still want to come out with me, that is.'

'You know I do, Alistair. We sort of clicked when we met at my sister's house, that's what I thought, anyway.'

'We did. Then I had to go and collapse a few days later at work, and get rushed into Emergency. Listen, are you free tonight, by any chance?'

'I am. As it happens, I finish early. Around five thirty.'

'I know you like Le Chat Noir, because my bossy big brother gabbed about how much you enjoyed it. Shall I take you there?'

'I'd love that. Arnold has heard me raving about Le Chat Noir, because there's something very inviting about it, and it's just great fun. You'll like it, I know.'

'I'll book a table right now. Shall we say seven? Or is that too early?'

'It's perfect.'

'See you later, Elise.'

'Yes, you will, Alistair.'

After hanging up the phone, Elise sat back in her chair, the story she was editing forgotten for a moment.

Finally, at last, they were going to get together. She had really taken to Alistair that night at Greta's supper, at the beginning of October. He had chattered to her all evening, stayed by her side, and asked her if he could phone her the following Monday to make a date.

And then he hadn't rung her, and she had been disappointed, felt foolish, and even a bit angry. She had shoved thoughts of him to one side, pushed her head into her typewriter and got on with work. Work had always been her saviour.

A day or two later, that same week, Arnold had phoned her at the newspaper to explain that Alistair had been taken very ill and was in hospital.

After Alistair had been operated on for appendicitis and was recovering, Arnold had phoned again and asked her if she would like to go with him to visit his brother.

She had agreed at once, and had been happy when she saw how pleased Alistair was to see her. In fact, he hadn't stopped smiling at her for the entire time she had been there at the hospital that day.

I was right about him, she thought. I knew he was decent and sincere when we first met. We clicked that night. And I hope we can stay clicked. A slow smile crept on to her face.

# Twenty-Nine

Whatever was going on in her personal life, Alicia was a quintessential professional, and her work always came first.

She had the clever knack of being able to pigeonhole things and to focus on the most important matter at hand. In this instance, her part in the film.

And so she had managed to push away her anger with Adam, bury her hurt that she had not heard from him in days. Since their row, in fact.

But then she knew that nobody else had received any communication from him either. Even Mario, the producer and his partner, seemed baffled by Adam's silence.

She told Charlie this now, as they sat together in the bar of Siegi's Club on Charles Street in Mayfair. 'Anyway, I've had a busy few days, and work has been a solace,' she added. Picking up her glass of champagne, she clinked it against Charlie's, and said, 'Here's to you, darling, and your new book. I know it will be a great success.'

'And may I say that I'm sure your film will be a big hit.' After a sip of the champagne, he continued, 'It was such a relief to get the proofs back today, and now I can start thinking about my next one.'

'Good heavens, Charlie, so soon! You're a glutton for punishment.'

'I have an idea I'd like to pursue, and I want to talk to Aunt Diedre about it. But let's get back to Adam Fennell. Look here, I don't think his silence is indicative of anything really serious, like a breakup between the two of you. First of all, he's in New York on business, and then there's the time difference.'

'I agree with you.' Alicia fell silent for a few seconds, and then shook her head, pursed her lips. 'It's just that he behaved in such a childish way, sounded so jealous and possessive.'

'Ah well, my dear, that's men for you. Or, should I put it this way, that's a man in love with *you*. And I think he *is* rather serious.'

Alicia frowned. 'You do?'

'I'd bet my bottom dollar on it, kiddo,' he murmured, using the lingo of their youth. 'I have to admit, I do like Adam a lot, and I think you fit well together.'

'He'd preen if he heard you say that,' she shot back in a sarcastic tone.

Charlie looked at his sister carefully, and after a moment, he remarked, 'You sound as if you think the idol has feet of clay. Are you off him? No longer enraptured?'

Her brother sounded so dour she had to laugh, and answered quickly. 'No, I'm not off him, nor disenchanted. I guess I'm just a bit ticked off that he didn't believe me, when I said I was out with you. Doesn't that show lack of trust?'

'A little bit, I suppose, but then remember he was probably frustrated he couldn't speak to you, when he'd been longing to do so. All day, perhaps. Mmmmm, well, let's face it, men in love can become quite irrational.'

Alicia gave Charlie a warm smile and picked up her drink. 'This is the only glass I can have this evening, Charlie. I have a very big scene tomorrow and I've got to look good, sound right, and do my stuff.'

'I've no fears about you. In fact, now's my chance to tell you that my hat's off to you, the way you've worked so hard since you were twenty. You're a fabulous actress, and *now is your time.* I think you'll have all the accolades you deserve with this one.'

'Thank you. And what I'm really proud of is that I've hardly ever been out of work. And, like you, I have supported myself. I've never asked our parents for financial help, and neither have you.'

'That's true. And I prefer it that way. How are they? Have you heard anything lately?'

'I had a letter from Mother last week, wishing me luck with the film. They seem to be in good shape at the moment. Things have smoothed over since the row in the summer, though she never mentions coming back. It seems that she meant what she said.'

Charlie nodded. 'I was speaking to Dad the other day and he more or less indicated they would be staying in Zurich until the spring.'

'I think Cecily might be upset if they don't go to Cavendon for Christmas. But what can you do?' She shrugged, glanced at her watch. 'Can we go upstairs for dinner, please, Charlie? I don't want to make it a late night.'

'Absolutely.' He swallowed the last of his champagne and together they left the bar and went upstairs to the dining room. Within minutes they had been seated and were looking at their menus.

After a moment, Alicia stared at Charlie over the top of her menu, and said, 'I bet we're going to eat the same thing.'

He grinned. 'We usually do, don't we?'

'I'm having potted shrimp, then steak Diane.'

'Ditto, darling.'

Charlie ordered their food and another glass of champagne, but Alicia settled for water. Wanting to get off the subject of Adam, she asked Charlie what his plans were for Christmas.

'Talking about our parents a moment ago has left thoughts of Christmas lingering in my mind,' Alicia began. 'From what you told me they are staying in Zurich. Dulcie and James are in Los Angeles. However, they might make it back if James finishes his current film.'

'I'll tell you honestly, Alicia, I don't want to go to Zurich,' Charlie confided. 'You know how much I love our traditional Christmas at Cavendon. I'm a bit of a stick-in-the-mud, I suppose, and I'll be at home in Yorkshire. What about you?'

'Adam said something to me about going to Beverly Hills, and that really is a problem for me, for the same reason as you. I prefer to be at Cavendon. Also, I don't want Aunt Cecily and Uncle Miles to feel deserted by all of us,' Alicia said.

'I agree. Aunt Diedre, Robin and Uncle Will will be there, and so will Aunt Charlotte, of course.'

'And what about our siblings? Any ideas about them?' Alicia asked.

'Thomas and Andrew will definitely go to Zurich. After all, they work in Dad's company, run it for him now. But Annabel will be at Cavendon, I'm sure,' Charlie said.

'I feel badly I haven't seen her lately. Have you?' Alicia said, thinking of their youngest sibling.

'I went to the art gallery the other day and took her out for a quick lunch,' Charlie replied. 'She's the most self-contained and independent person I know. She's determined to do her own thing. She still loves playing the piano, I know that, but after Alex Dubé died, so did her ambition to be a concert pianist.'

'Sad, that. She is wonderfully talented, and I've always thought of Annabel as a musical prodigy. Do you think our mother put her off? Persuaded her *not* to try for the concert stage?'

Charlie shook her head. 'I don't know, but I don't think so. Annabel's a pragmatist. She told me a long time ago that she wanted to earn her own living. Her other passion has always been art; you know that she loves being Dulcie's sidekick, running the gallery in Conduit Street.' Charlie grinned and added, 'And, like you, she spoke about Christmas when we had lunch. I suppose it's on all of our minds.'

'Well, let's face it, it's not that far away,' Alicia murmured, wondering if Adam would create problems if she didn't go to Los Angeles. She pushed that thought to one side. I'll deal with that another day, she decided.

Charlie saw the waiter headed their way. He said, 'Here comes our potted shrimp. Alicia, why are you looking so puzzled? Or is it troubled?'

'Ah nothing, forget it . . . I was just wondering if Adam might be difficult about Christmas.'

'Invite him to Cavendon. He wouldn't want to turn that down. Nobody would.'

The following morning, Alicia was picked up early by the studio car and was on her way to Shepperton by six o'clock. It was Thursday, and the big shoot of the week. Not in length of time, but of importance in the storyline. As often happens, the scene was being shot out of context. When the film was edited, it would be at the end.

Alicia thought of that as she settled back in the car, and silently thanked God for their continuity girls who kept a check on everything.

Very purposely, she had put Adam out of her mind. Instead she was concentrating on Victoria and wondering what would happen this coming weekend down in Kent.

The two of them had enjoyed driving back to London together, and Victoria had told her about the club and the work Christopher wanted to do with veterans.

What was so marvellous was that the charity would benefit soldiers and sailors as well as airmen.

A good man, Alicia thought, and she found herself relaxing – understanding, all of a sudden, that the famous war hero could be trusted to do the right thing. He was a man of honour and integrity.

She had told Victoria that she was in charge, but now Alicia changed her mind. It was Christopher who would be calling the shots. He knew all the ramifications, realized what he was capable of, and what being with a woman would entail. Just as he was aware that any woman who took him on would be faced with enormous responsibilities. He would make the right decision for them both. Instinctively, she knew that, no matter what, Victoria was safe with him.

Once she was in her dressing room at the studio, Alicia took off her coat and headscarf and went straight to Makeup, where Anna Lancing was waiting for her.

They had worked together for a long time, and after their usual jocular greetings, Alicia sat down in the chair and allowed Anna to go to work on her face. They never spoke when Anna was applying cosmetics. She needed a face that was immobile.

Alicia let her thoughts drift, moving from Victoria going to Romney Marsh to her mother in Zurich, whom she missed, then to Cecily battling it out, in one way or another, at Cavendon. Alicia would be there again for the weekend, fully intending to clean out her closets, as she had promised her aunt she would.

Cecily kept a hamper at one end of the staff dining room next to the kitchen. It was there for the family to leave clothes they no longer wanted. The discarded items were eventually sent to the Salvation Army in Harrogate, who gave them to needy families. It was a tradition that had been started years ago, and Cecily insisted on maintaining it, determined not to let Cavendon drown in faded remnants of the past.

Thinking of clothing had Alicia zeroing in on the Royal Command Film Performance, which was not too far off now. She mentally went through her own jewellery, wondering what to wear with the blue tulle ball gown. She had a few nice pieces to choose from, some from her father and some from her Great-Aunt Gwen.

Thinking about the Cavendon jewellery made her appreciate how hard it must be for her mother, to see such change sweeping through her home, the old way of running things overtaken by the pressing need to pay the bills.

When her makeup was finished, Alicia went next door to Hair, and then back to her dressing room. Marriette Tufton, her long-time dresser, was waiting for her, and within minutes she was in her costume and fully ready to go out to the sound stage.

Once she arrived, she was greeted by the technicians as she carefully stepped over wires and avoided equipment, making for the set where she would do her scene.

The director, Paul Dowling, came to welcome her, as did her leading man, Andrew Vance. The three of them stood talking for a few moments, and then Andrew led her over to the set.

Alicia had a special talent that, in a way, gave her an advantage over other actors. She had an extraordinary memory, a photographic memory, in fact. She knew her words by heart very quickly. They were so solidly embedded in her memory that she was totally free to concentrate on her acting. The words just flowed out of her naturally.

A technician shouted: 'Camera. Lights.' And then Dowling called out: 'Action!'

The set was decorated as a country kitchen. Alicia and Andrew were standing in the middle of it. She began to speak first, softly, her manner gentle, full of kindness, as she told Andrew, her lover in the film, that she was going back to her husband and family. That they must now separate. She was leaving him.

Andrew, a very good actor himself, reacted instantly. He appeared stunned, then tearful, became angry, went back to being tearful.

Suddenly the shouting started. The anger erupted once more. The words became harder, nastier, harsher, and louder. There were tears. She screamed when he grabbed hold of her roughly. She struggled, freed herself.

And then, finally, there was the anger-filled exit as Andrew stalked out of the kitchen in a fury. Alicia was left alone in the kitchen, tears rolling down her face.

Alicia was certain the director had got it in one take. To her surprise, Paul put them through their paces again, then a third time, and a fourth, before he was totally satisfied.

Finally the director called, 'Cut. And print.'

Before Paul could say words of praise to his two actors, some of the crew began to clap, and then, from a distance, a voice cried, 'Bravo! Bravo!'

Everyone glanced around, mystified.

It was Alicia who saw him first. There he was, Adam Fennell, walking out of the shadows from the back of the sound stage, coming onto the set, as resplendent as usual. Crisp white shirt. Perfectly tailored dark blue suit. Ironed from head to toe, she thought.

He had a smile as big as a week on his face as he walked directly to her, put his arms around her and kissed her on the mouth.

She found herself succumbing to him. She kissed him back, and passionately so.

Around them the crew went wild. Whistling, cheering, clapping. For a moment she thought they would never stop. It was their genuine excitement, seeing the magic and the make-believe of film spilling over into real life. That was what they did, didn't they? Create make-believe and magic. Unexpectedly it had become reality.

When he finally let go of her, Adam took her face in his hands and stared deeply into her eyes. He said, in a low, contrite voice, 'I'm sorry, so very sorry. I got caught up in business, distracted by it. But I did do it, Alicia. I've secured the money for your next film, my darling.'

He smiled at her, touched her cheek, and walked away, heading for the director.

Startled by his words, Alicia's eyes remained on him as he spoke to Paul. He had been raising the money for *Dangerous*. She felt a little thrill of joy. She continued to watch him as he then went over to Andrew, obviously congratulating her leading man. And then he talked to the cameraman and the entire crew, actually, laughing, showing them he was a grateful producer. She looked around, suddenly wondering where Mario was, but she couldn't see him anywhere.

It works, she thought. Adam's combination works, and he knows it will. It's the charm, that hail-fellow-well-met attitude. He might be their boss, but he's also their pal. A good mate who shows his gratitude.

And she loved Adam for making them feel good. And the anger slipped away and the hurt healed and she was full of admiration for him.

# THIRTY

As soon as she emerged from her dressing room, he whisked her out to his car, and on the way back to London, he told her he was taking her to supper to celebrate. And then he piled praise on her, congratulated her, told her she could win an Academy Award for her performance in this film.

He promised he would make her a big star, no matter what. He also told her several times how much he loved her, and in a way he had never loved any other woman before in his entire life.

Adam was well known around town, and was greeted with great cordiality by the maître d' at the Grill Room of the Dorchester Hotel.

They were seated at one of the best tables, in a quiet corner, and he ordered a bottle of Dom Pérignon at once. He then sat back in his chair, beaming at her.

She smiled back, reached out and took his hand, which was resting on the table. 'Thank you for putting together the deal for *Dangerous*, Adam. I do appreciate it, truly. And I'm very excited.'

'You're going to be even more excited when I tell you that I have bought another script for you. It's called *Revenge* and, in many ways, I think it's the better script of the two. It reminds me of *Notorious*. Did you see that film?'

'I did. It came out a couple of years ago, and starred Ingrid Bergman, Cary Grant and Claude Rains.'

'And it is probably the best film Hitchcock has made, so far in his career. He directed and produced it and it was released in the summer of 1946. I've seen it a dozen times. I think of it as a spy *film noir*. *Revenge* is not the same story, obviously, but it could be a *film noir* – and really put us both on the map.'

She laughed, shaking her head. 'Don't be so modest. You *are* on the map.'

A waiter poured the champagne. Once they were alone, he toasted her lavishly, leaned across the table and whispered, 'I can't wait to have you in my bed, ravishing you. I do love you so much, my darling Alicia. You do feel the same way, don't you?'

'Absolutely! Of course I do. Why would you think otherwise?' She gave him a long, lingering look, and added, 'Shall we leave now? Forget about supper?'

He laughed. Was obviously amused. 'The staff are still at the flat. I always prefer us to be alone when we're together. And we have the whole weekend to give each other pleasure.'

Alicia's smile slipped, and she exclaimed, 'Oh! Adam, I have to go to Cavendon tomorrow! I promised Cecily I'd help her with some chores this weekend. I can't get out of it.'

He gaped at her, anger rushing through him. His face stiffened. And then he immediately let it soften, took control of himself when he said, 'I do understand, but hell, I've been away for days and missed you so much, wanted you desperately. I just have to look at your beautiful face to become aroused. As I am right now.' He leaned back in his chair, a sad expression clouding his handsome features.

Being observant, Alicia had seen his face stiffen, but she had mistaken it for disappointment, not annoyance. Now, she said in a sudden rush of words, 'Why don't you come with me tomorrow? We can drive up there and have the weekend together.

Anyway, I want you to meet the rest of my family. Please say yes.'

He said slowly, 'I'll say yes if you will say yes.'

'To what?'

He did not answer her. He slipped his hand into his jacket pocket and brought out a small red leather box, placed it in front of her. 'Say yes to this, my darling, I'll be very happy.'

He had surprised her, there was no doubt about that. She recognized the Cartier box at once. When she opened it, she gasped. Sitting there was the most dazzling diamond ring, a single stone with a baguette diamond on each side.

'Oh Adam, it's simply gorgeous . . .' The ring had taken her breath away.

A smile tugged at his mouth. 'Will you marry me, Alicia? Will you become my wife?'

She didn't hesitate. 'Yes, I will.' A smile of genuine happiness flooded her face, and she took the ring out of the box, and sat staring at it.

'Please let me put it on your finger.' Adam stretched out his hand.

Alicia gave him the ring; he slipped it on the third finger of her left hand. 'I'm thrilled that you're going to be my wife. We'll be together always, my darling. And yes, I will come to Cavendon tomorrow.' In a lowered voice, he asked, 'Will I have to have a room of my own? I suppose so.'

She nodded her head. 'Yes, you will. But I'll slip in to visit you, don't worry about that.'

'I'm really looking forward to finally seeing Cavendon. I've heard so much about it – one of the great stately homes in England, isn't it?'

'Yes, although I only ever think of it as my home, the place where I grew up.'

'Who else will be there?' Adam asked, as always curious.

'Maybe my brother. You know Charlie, you met him at Greta's.'

He nodded, then beckoned to a waiter. Looking at her, he gave her his most engaging smile. 'Shall we order something to eat?

You must be hungry, you worked so hard today. And God bless you for that, darling Alicia, and for your glorious talent. What an extraordinary actress you are. Soon to be my wife.'

Alicia looked radiant, her worries gone. Adam did love her – and he wanted to marry her. Suddenly, the future looked glittering.

After supper they returned to his flat in Bryanston Square. The staff had left by ten o'clock, and it was the small rosy glow of the lamps in the foyer that welcomed them.

Leading her into his bedroom, and then to the dressing room, Adam said, 'Hurry up, please hurry up,' and opened the door for her.

Once alone, Alicia stood looking at herself in the mirror, remembering to take off her bright red lipstick and makeup. She undressed with speed, as aroused as he already was.

Tonight was going to be special. Perhaps the most special night of her life. She had become engaged to the man she loved, who loved her to distraction. He always made that patently clear.

The blue chiffon kimono was hanging there for her, and she slipped it on, went into the bedroom. He was waiting for her and hurried forward, pulling her close to him. Their kisses were as passionate as ever, and once they were on the bed, wrapped in each other's arms, their wild abandonment began. Tonight it seemed to them that their lovemaking was more intense than ever, and it carried them into the early hours of the morning.

His sensuality knew no bounds, and he brought her to ecstasy with his usual expertise; she responded to him with ardour, filled with a mixture of desire and adoration.

To Alicia, there was no man like him in the whole world, and when he whispered against her ear, 'I can't wait for you to be my wife,' she clung to him, bursting with happiness. He belonged to her, and she to him.

* * *

They arrived at Cavendon on Friday afternoon at three o'clock, well in time for tea. Adam had hired a car and driver, and they had made good time on the road from London.

Cecily greeted them in the grand foyer and welcomed Adam cordially, and then Alicia took him upstairs to the spacious suite of rooms, decorated in shades of pale grey and white, which she had chosen for him.

At once Adam admired it, smiling at her, silently thrilled. Finally he was where he belonged. In a great house on a great estate and about to become a member of a family of enormous wealth and distinction.

'I'm just going to tidy up, before tea,' Alicia said. 'Any moment Eric will be bringing your suitcase.'

Swinging around, Adam nodded. 'Shall I wait for you here?'

'Yes, I'm only a few steps away.' Taking hold of his hands, she led him from the sitting room into the adjoining bedroom, showing him around, pointing out the bathroom. 'You'll find everything you need in there.'

As they walked back into the sitting room, she said, 'I'm glad you're here, Adam. I'm sure you'll enjoy it.'

'Are you going to wear my ring and tell them you're engaged?' he asked.

'Naturally I am.' Holding his hand, she pulled him out of the room, took him across the corridor, and opened a door. She said, 'This is my room, should you need me.'

'That is a given,' he answered, his boyish smile surfacing.

# Thirty-One

The old farmhouse was called Seamere. It was not far from Aldington, close to Romney Marsh. On the drive down to Kent, Christopher told Victoria that his parents had bought it years before he was born, and had furnished it with old pieces they had found locally.

Now, as the ancient Daimler slid up the long driveway through a thickly wooded area, Christopher spoke. 'Vicki.'

Victoria turned to look at him; as always he had a smile on his face.

He said softly, 'This place is very important to me. I spend a lot of time here . . . I hope you'll love it as much as I do.'

'I think I will.' She felt that rush of longing, the need to be closer to him, in his arms, and kept herself steady. Until he made a move she must remain self-contained and in control of her emotions. She was well aware they could run rampant. To love someone and not be able to say it was pure torture.

Leaning closer to her, he kissed her cheek, then said, 'I have chosen a room I think you'll enjoy . . .' He broke off and chuckled, 'Well, here we are at last!'

Victoria saw that the Daimler had entered a large courtyard.

Freddy drove right into the middle of it and braked. The black van, driven by Bruce, parked behind them.

'Go on, Vicki! Jump out! Get your first view of Seamere,' Christopher said, that hint of earlier laughter still in his voice.

She did as he told her, got out of the car and stood looking up at this house which meant so much to him. And caught her breath, startled by its unique beauty.

The farmhouse was not exactly Elizabethan, yet it had a distinct Tudor air about it. Long and low, it was perfectly proportioned, with a sloping roof and many windows.

Suddenly, there he was beside her in his wheelchair. Looking up at her, he asked, 'Well, what's your verdict?'

She put her hand on his shoulder. 'It's beautiful. I could live here forever, Christopher.'

I hope you mean that, he thought, and swivelled his head at the sound of running steps. Victoria followed the direction of his gaze.

A tall, well-built man was hurrying towards them. He wore a fisherman's sweater, corduroys and an old tweed jacket. There was a cheery smile on his ruggedly handsome face as he said, 'I'm Alex. Alex Poniatowski, Miss Brown. Welcome.'

'I'm glad to be here, Mr Poniatowski.'

'Please, call me Alex.'

In response she said, 'The whole world calls me Vicki.'

Alex nodded and went to Christopher, gave him a huge bear hug. Their mutual affection for each other was apparent.

Alex now said, 'We'd better go inside. It's growing colder, and the dark will be down on us shortly. Remember, you always want to be here at that special time, Christopher.'

Striding forward, pushing the wheelchair, Alex headed for the house determinedly. Victoria understood why he was doing this when she saw that there were several stone steps in front of the huge front door. The wheelchair had to be pushed up manually.

She knew who Alex was. Christopher had told her about him the other day. He was his senior personal assistant. Alex ran the veterans' charity, handled the public events Christopher had to attend, and managed his business affairs in general.

He was a Pole who had fled his native country just before the Nazis had devastated it, turned it into rubble, destroyed its elite. Once in London, he had joined the Polish Division of the British Army.

He and Christopher had become friends during the war, introduced to each other by a mutual friend.

Victoria was aware that Alex had worked for Christopher since 1946, and was devoted to him.

Once they were inside the house, Victoria's photographer's eye quickly took in dark beams, white walls, polished wooden floors, a few paintings on the walls. She also realized it was a smaller house than she had thought from the outside.

Alex was standing, waiting for her in the large front hall. He said, 'Christopher has gone to his library.' He turned around and indicated the corridor. 'It's down there. I'll have Bruce bring your luggage. Do you want the housekeeper to unpack for you?'

'Thank you, but I can do it myself. I haven't brought much.'

'Christopher will show you your room later. There's something he wants you to see. Now. Something outside. Better hurry.'

She rushed down the corridor and, at the first open door, she looked in. It was indeed a library. There were deep blue walls and hundreds of books. Several lamps had been turned on, and a fire blazed in the hearth.

'I'm down here, near the window,' Christopher said, on hearing her arrival.

'Yes, I see you.' She walked down the room, her ballet pumps silent on the wooden floor. There were no carpets in the Hampstead house either. Of course. Nothing to impede the wheelchair.

The window Christopher had referred to was, in fact, French doors, which were open. Immediately outside, there was a terrace facing the gardens.

She stepped outside to join him and discovered there was already a chair for her there, a bucket of champagne, and two glasses on a small table.

'Shall I pour?' she asked.

'That would be grand, my lovely.'

After handing him a flute, she took her own glass and sat down next to him.

'Alex told me to hurry. That there was something you wanted me to see outside. What is it?'

'There's a change at this time down on the Marsh. I have always thought it to be a magical moment. Then later, after supper, if it's a clear night, you will see the lights of France. But now we must wait and I'll explain it to you.'

There was a pause. 'I can't tell you how happy I am that you're here, just next to me, Vicki.' He smiled at her then pointed.

Christopher said, 'Seamere is built on a rise, so it's a little higher than the gardens. If you look closely, you'll see that they slope downward.'

Victoria did as he said, stared ahead, then nodded. 'Yes, I see they're almost level here, gradually drop away.'

'Then there are several acres of flat land, as you'll notice and, beyond, miles of low-lying Marsh, some of which is below sea level. That's why the sea looks as if it's up high in the sky.'

'You're right! It does. A visual illusion. The mists are rising over the Marsh now, Christopher. Oh yes, it is magical!' She turned to face him, her eyes sparkling.

'It was my father who explained this to me when I was a child, and I still enjoy sitting out here when the mists rise up, float around, remembering the old stories he told me about the smugglers, for which the Marsh is notorious, and other romantic, ancient tales.' Reaching out, he took hold of her hand. 'This was something I wanted to share with you, Vicki.'

'I'm happy you did. I want to share *everything* with you,' she murmured, putting emphasis on the word everything.

He picked up on this immediately and said, 'Another reason I wished you to come here for a few days was for us to get to know each other better. Be under the same roof together, see how we tolerate each other on a daily basis.' A faint smile touched his mouth. 'Later, I wish to talk to you about a few other things. Now, I hope you won't mind if Alex joins us for supper. As I'm sure you've gathered, we are close friends, and I rely on him.'

'I don't mind at all, I'm your guest here.'

'We do spend quite a lot of time together, Vicki, he and I, and that won't change.' He paused, staring at her intently, his expression quizzical.

She smiled at him. 'As long as I am with you also.'

'I hope you will be. You'll meet Vita and Joe shortly. They live here, run the house for me, look after everything, and Vita is a good cook. She's making leek-and-potato soup first, hot not cold, and then a fish pie, which is delicious. I know you like fish.'

'All the English do, don't they? After all, we grew up on an island, we didn't have much choice.'

He grinned. 'Let's have another bit of bubbly before dinner, shall we?'

Rising, she filled their glasses and sat down again, glancing at him. 'I've never seen you drink much alcohol. Actually, I thought you were almost a teetotaller.'

'I suppose I am. I feel I must always have my wits about me, since I'm in this chair a lot, navigating myself. But tonight is very special to me. To have you here in the place I love the most gives me such a thrill. To share it with you, see your reaction. Tomorrow I'll give you a tour of the house, take you up to the bedroom I had as a child.' Noticing the puzzled look on her face, he explained, 'I installed a lift when I came back at the end of the war.'

A short while later, Christopher wheeled himself back into the library and out into the corridor. He paused, waiting for her. 'This is your room here,' he said, indicating an open door. 'Go in, have a quick look, Vicki.'

As she walked in, she realized how attractive it was – comfortable and not overdone. Opening off the small hall was the bedroom. A four-poster bed took pride of place; the room was a mixture of soft, faded yellows and creamy tones.

She moved on, went through an open archway, found herself in a small seating area. A fire burned in the grate, and there were French doors opening onto the terrace.

A repeat of the same pale colours gave the two areas a flowing feeling, and she noted the comfortable chairs, a sofa, a small desk and shelves of books. And her suitcase standing there.

When she returned to the corridor, she touched his shoulder, her face full of smiles. 'It's perfect. Thank you.'

He nodded, remained silent, but his dark brown eyes sparkled with pleasure as he went down the corridor.

'I hope you're hungry,' he said as he reached the foyer and continued on down another, shorter corridor. 'I'm ravenous,' he announced, rolling himself into a medium-sized dining room where a fire burned and lamps had been turned on. The candles were burning brightly on the table, adding to the rosy glow.

Wheeling himself to the round table, he said, 'Sit next to me here, my lovely, and Alex will be on my other side. Oh, here he comes now.'

Alex came in, smiling and cordial, and sat down next to Christopher. Victoria noticed that he had changed his clothes. He was wearing a dark blazer, checked shirt and woollen tie, with grey trousers.

Christopher had not changed, but he was already in a smart tweed jacket, a pale blue shirt and darker blue tie.

She couldn't help wondering if she should have changed, but there hadn't been time. There was nothing she could do now, and hoped the pale green knitted dress was suitable for supper in the country.

Alex was asking her if she liked her room, when Vita, a middle-aged woman, came in to greet Christopher and to welcome Victoria to Seamere. After exchanged greetings, she hurried off, explaining she would now serve dinner.

Christopher said, 'She may seem a bit standoffish at first, Victoria, but it's simply shyness. Her husband Joe is much more garrulous. They were here with my parents and have worked at Seamere for years.'

'I thought she was very nice,' Victoria responded, and stopped short as Vita promptly returned, pushing a tea trolley. This she left out in the corridor and brought the soup bowls in one at a time.

'The soup's delicious,' Victoria said, and went on between spoonfuls, 'I love the colours of my room, Alex.' And then, looking at Christopher, she added, 'Seamere is tranquil. So relaxing after the rush and push of London. No wonder you want to be here all the time.'

Alex said, 'Like Christopher, I can't wait to return. There's something addictive about this funny old farmhouse, and all the folk tales about the Marsh and its mysteries. And the Kentish countryside is so beautiful. You might like to go for a stroll in the woods tomorrow or down to the sea.'

Before Victoria could respond, Christopher said, 'Perhaps you'll walk Victoria around and show her the bluebell wood, Alex. Not that they're out at this time of year.' He glanced at Victoria. 'But you'll see them in the spring, won't you?'

'If I have anything to do with it, yes, and I will pick the bluebells,' she shot back, laughter in her eyes.

He looked at her and winked, which took her by surprise.

Vita *was* a good cook. Victoria realized this as she ate the fish pie, which *was* as delicious as Christopher had boasted. There were shrimp, cockles and mussels, strips of haddock, pieces of cod, and bits of onion and celery, all mixed together in a light creamy sauce. The fish casserole was topped by a crust made of thick mashed potatoes which had been browned in the oven.

They talked about Kent for a short while longer, and then Christopher began to ask Alex questions regarding the progress of the veterans' charity.

Victoria listened. She also drifted with her thoughts from time to time, thinking of the advice Alicia had given her, wondering if she should act on it or not. Alicia's suggestions had been a bit daring. What if her actions shocked him? When she had mentioned this possibility to Alicia she had smiled, pointing out that Christopher was more than likely a sophisticated man, not one to be easily shocked. Still, I have to think it through some more, Victoria told herself.

# Thirty-Two

'What are those bright lights flashing over there?' Victoria asked.

She and Christopher had returned to the library after dinner, where Vita had served them coffee. Now they sat together looking out of the French doors, closed because the night had turned colder. But the fire blazed behind them and the room was very cosy and there was still a view to be seen.

'It's the beams from the Dungeness lighthouse,' Christopher told her. 'And look to the left and you'll see a line of twinkling lights. That's the coast of France; we're very close to the English Channel. I'm not sure if you realized how close, Vicki.'

'No, I didn't.' She stood up, put her face nearer the glass, and said, 'Goodness, I do see the lights . . . they're glittering stars.' Returning to her chair, she smiled and said, 'Thank you again for inviting me here for the weekend. I'm enjoying it so much.'

'That makes me happy. I had my reasons for wanting you to come to Seamere. Well, I told you that earlier. I must talk to you about several . . . serious things, Victoria, and I'd prefer to do that tonight. It's important.' When she did not respond, he said, 'Is that all right with you? It's not that late, only about eight thirty.'

'Yes, of course it is. And I know the time. We did have an early dinner.' He sounded so solemn she was suddenly worried.

'I think it might well be a long chat, so I'm going to suggest you change into something comfortable, perhaps trousers and a jumper. And unpack. During that time Freddy or Bruce will come and help me get ready for bed. That way I won't have to disturb either of them later, and you and I can simply relax in front of the fire with a brandy, and talk uninterrupted.'

'Can you get into bed alone?'

'Yes, with the crutches. No problem, don't worry yourself about that.'

'Shall I go and find one of them?' she asked, standing up.

'No, that's not necessary. I have a device in the bedroom. I press it and it buzzes them. See you in fifteen minutes. How's that?'

She nodded and left. His words, so serious, had triggered fears in her. Was he going to tell her something terrible? Something she didn't want to hear? About himself? About his health? Pushing these dire thoughts away, she quickly unpacked her suitcase, hanging up her few clothes, slipping her underwear into a drawer, and then going into the bathroom to unpack her toilet bag. She washed her hands, brushed her teeth, and then her hair. In the bedroom, she took off the dress and jacket she had worn all day and hung them up.

Victoria loved Cecily's wide, floating trousers, and Greta had given her a pair made of navy blue crepe de Chine. She paired them with a simple white shirt and slipped her feet into a pair of navy pumps.

Returning to the bathroom, she stared at herself in the mirror, decided she looked presentable and sprayed herself with Ma Griffe. Glancing at her watch she saw that she had taken exactly twenty minutes.

Within a second she was walking back into the library and found Christopher sitting in his wheelchair in front of the fire. He was wearing a dressing gown, and his feet were bare.

She sat down in the chair facing him and said, 'Here I am. And I'm all ears.'

He sat studying her for a moment or two before saying in a light voice, 'Don't look so glum, I'm not going to tell you anything bad. Not too bad anyway.'

Her hackles went up, and she exclaimed, 'I knew it was going to be—'

He cut her off. 'Not *bad* in the way you think. I just want to talk to you very honestly, get a few things out, mull them over with you. Honestly, you're not going to be upset by what I'm going to say. All right?'

She was so relieved she couldn't speak. Her throat had been choked up for the last few seconds. She simply nodded her head. Finally she relaxed in the armchair.

'We haven't known each other very long, you know—'

She interrupted him when she said, 'Since October the fourth and today is the twenty-first.'

Trust a woman to know the exact date, he thought, although he was amused by her preciseness. He inclined his head. 'I don't think time matters, actually, when it comes to emotions. I believe everyone knows when they've met their soulmate. Don't you agree?'

'I do.' She took a deep breath. 'Am I your soulmate?'

'I believe you are.' He hesitated. 'I have certain worries, Victoria. I'm not like other men; I'm disabled, for one thing.'

'Are you telling me you can't have an intimate relationship with me?'

'No, I'm not, because I can. In fact, I went to see my neurologist last week, and he gave me a thorough going-over. His name's Abel Palmerston, and we're good friends, besides being doctor and patient. And Abel completely reassured me. He also told me he believes I could father children.'

'So there aren't any problems. Everything is normal, isn't it?'

'In that sense, yes. But I worry about you, Vicki,' he said. 'Worry that you might get bored with me, fed up because I'm stuck in this chair, and that you might feel obliged to stay with me because you don't want to hurt my feelings. I wouldn't want that.'

Victoria sat back, her thoughts swirling around in her head. She remembered Alicia's words, how she had told her to seduce him, to get it over with, to prove to him that he could get an erection because she, Vicki, aroused him. She had even told her what to do to make that happen.

'I'm in love with you, Christopher,' she finally said. 'And I have been since the first day I met you. Are you in love with me?'

'I am. Very much so, and from the moment you came floating into my study like something from a wonderful dream. And we've told each other that, haven't we? Without saying those exact words.'

'We have.' She looked at him, and took her courage in her hands. 'So why are we sitting here discussing it? Why aren't we in your bed making love? Instead of wasting time.'

He couldn't help it, he started to laugh, loving her all the more for her honesty, her straightforwardness. He certainly knew where he stood with her, and this pleased him – reassured him, in fact. He loathed duplicitous women, being so ethical himself.

Victoria was fully aware that she often amused him, made him laugh, and she used that talent frequently. Now she was relieved. She jumped up, rushed over to him, knowing that the tautness, the tension between them was suddenly, and finally, broken. Because they had spoken out at last, admitted that they were in love with each other.

She bent over the chair and kissed him on the mouth. He put his arms around her. She felt his muscles, the strength of his arms as he pulled her closer, kissed her in return and with passion.

After a moment, she disentangled herself, and said, 'Think of it this way. We're about to have a practice run. And if it doesn't work, it won't matter. We can simply try again.'

As she had known he would, he began to chuckle, and took hold of her hand, kissed her fingertips. 'Thank God you came into my life, my darling girl.'

'And I'm here to stay.'

Christopher said, 'Go to your room and put on whatever it is you sleep in, and come back in a few minutes. I'll be in bed, waiting for you. My bedroom is through that door.' He indicated the end of the library. 'Oh, and lock the library door when you return.'

In her room, she changed into a flimsy pink nightgown and matching peignoir that was feminine, pretty and rather revealing. She was following Alicia's advice once more. Taking off her earrings and watch, she placed them on a small dressing table in the bathroom, sprayed herself with Ma Griffe yet again, and left, closing the door behind her.

When she entered the library, she saw that Christopher had turned off most of the lights. Only one burned near the fireplace, which still flamed brightly up the chimney. She locked the door, as he had instructed, and called out, 'I'm back. May I come and join you?'

'I'm waiting for you, Victoria. Come on, my lovely.'

Pushing open the bedroom door, she went in, and then stopped abruptly. The room wasn't what she had expected. It was almost sterile, with pristine white walls, and it was empty except for a modern version of an old-fashioned brass bed, his wheelchair, and a white-painted chest under a window. His crutches were propped against a wall.

Christopher lay on the bed, with two pillows behind his head, and she was momentarily dazzled by him. How truly handsome he was, with his thick brown hair, sparkling brown eyes, and the cleft in his chin.

He had pulled the sheet up to his waist, but he was naked. She noticed how broad his chest was, as were his shoulders. She already knew the strength of those strong, well-muscled arms, and understood how hard Bruce and Freddy had trained him.

Desire rushed through her, and she walked over to the bed, taking off her peignoir as she did, knowing how revealing the nightgown was.

Christopher was unable to take his eyes off her. The shape of her full and rounded breasts, her slender hips and long legs were visible through the flimsy fabric, tantalizing him. He wanted her. Now.

She paused at the edge of the bed, pulled off the nightgown, let it fall on the floor, and climbed into bed.

She slid over to him.

Filled with yearning, he pulled her closer, wrapped his arms around her, holding her tightly. He was overcome with happiness at the feel of her silky skin, her breasts against his chest. How he loved her. He would cherish her forever, keep her safe, let no harm come to her.

His hands roamed over her body; he bent his head, kissed her breasts. Her hands were on the nape of his neck, in his hair, and she was moaning quietly as he fondled her breasts, sucked the nipples.

When he ran one hand down her thigh, slipped it between her legs, she trembled under his touch, arched her back.

Victoria was soaring with ecstasy. Finally she touched him, stroked him, thrilled he was as aroused as she was. She felt wonderful, her love for him spilling out of her. He was hers. She would never let him go.

Christopher stilled her hand all of a sudden, and said against her cheek, 'Please stop. I'm too excited.'

'I want you inside me,' she murmured.

'I'm afraid I have to remain on my back,' he said in a low voice. With hardly any effort at all, he stretched his right arm over her body and pulled her onto him. Moving her slightly with both hands, he managed to position her where he needed her to be.

When he entered her, she let out a small cry of pleasure, then began to move against him, knowing he could not. She kept increasing her speed until they were both soaring. They clung together and cried out with the joy of it, and when he could no longer hold back he spasmed and again cried out, and she said his name over and over. They were joined. As one. As they both knew they should be. Soulmates forever.

'If that was a practice run, I can't imagine what the real thing will be like,' Christopher said against her hair.

Victoria began to laugh. 'Even better, I suppose. And I can't tell you how thrilled I am your neurologist was right.'

Christopher smiled to himself, thinking of how helpful Abel had been, and also a bit *risqué*, offering all kinds of suggestions. He said, 'What are we going to do, Victoria?'

'About what?'

'Haven't we just commenced a romantic liaison? Is it to be kept a secret?'

'It's hardly a secret here. I'm sure everyone knows I'm in your bed.'

'So am I. And I wasn't meaning here. I was thinking, in particular, of Alice and Walter Swann. What will they think and say when they hear about us?'

'I'm sure they'll be happy, if I am happy.'

'I don't know about that,' Christopher said, sounding doubtful. 'After all, look at it from their point of view. You're only twenty-one, just starting out in life, and here I am, a war-weary chap of twenty-eight going on twenty-nine, and a disabled man at that. They won't be as happy as you think.'

They lay in his bed, side by side, covered by the bedclothes, snuggled close together. Pushing herself up on one elbow, Victoria frowned as she looked down at him, and said, 'You might be disabled, but you're all man as far as I'm concerned. And a hell of a man at that. They'll be fine with it.'

'No, they won't. They'll think you're saddling yourself with a cripple.'

'Please don't say that, Christopher!' she cried, her voice rising. 'They're not like that at all. They're not bigoted.'

'It's nothing to do with bigotry. It's to do with their love for you and wanting the best for you. And you're awfully young, darling.'

'In numbers, yes, but not in character or intelligence. Alicia thinks I'm very grown up for twenty-one. An adult, she calls me. Don't forget I've been working since I left school. And plenty of girls my age are married.'

'Maybe I should marry you quickly, Vicki. Do an Edward the Fourth.'

'What's that? An Edward the Fourth?'

'Edward became King of England at eighteen. He was a glorious specimen. Tall, handsome, blond, and a womanizer to boot. And so his mentor, the Earl of Warwick, promised him to the King of France for his daughter, wanting a good marriage for his protégé. However, Edward met a beautiful Englishwoman called Elizabeth Woodville, and he fell in love. She wouldn't sleep with him, so he married her in secret.'

'And Warwick was angry and so was the King of France. You're talking about the Wars of the Roses. The rival branches of the House of Plantagenet – the Yorkists and the Lancastrians.'

'Clever girl.'

There was a silence. She leaned her head against his shoulder. 'It will be all right in the long run. Life somehow takes care of itself.'

'I suppose so.'

She said, 'I don't want it to be a secret, Chris, honestly I don't.'

There was another moment of silence, and then he asked, 'Why did you just call me Chris?'

'I don't know . . . I felt like it, felt like making you feel better. Why?'

'The only person who ever called me Chris was my mother.'

'Oh, do you mind? That I did?'

'Don't be silly. I love it, and you can call me anything you want. I love you, Vicki.'

'And I love you, Chris.'

Victoria fell asleep not long after this conversation, but Christopher remained awake, his mind turning and twisting.

His thoughts were about Victoria. He had not really expected to meet anyone like her, and certainly not to fall in love with someone as young and beautiful. In the years since the war, he'd come to terms with his injuries, and had stopped himself from thinking about marriage, and a family, throwing himself instead into his charity work, his garden.

Suddenly his priorities were changing. All he could think about was Victoria, and whether he could marry her. He wanted to look after her, protect her. He would go and see his solicitor next week, once they had returned to London. He would make a new will, make sure she was a beneficiary. He simply had to protect her, and that was one easy way to do it. And he would leave Seamere and the Hampstead house to her.

This solution made him feel better about keeping her safe. Yet, at the forefront of his mind, were thoughts of the Swanns. They might have many objections to him, and he wouldn't blame them. After all, she was like a daughter to them.

On the other hand, she was twenty-one and of age. Still, he didn't want to come between her and these two loving people who had taken her in during the war and brought her up.

The answer came to him suddenly. He would ask Victoria if he could go with her to Cavendon within the next few weeks and meet them, let them get to know him. He could talk to them, make his intentions clear. Ask properly for her hand in marriage. He was a pretty decent chap, wasn't he? Maybe they would accept him.

He reached out and touched her tenderly, this girl he loved so much and for whom he would give his life.

# Thirty-Three

'Everyone likes Adam,' Cecily said as she and Alicia folded clothes for the Salvation Army, sitting at the long table in the staff dining room.

'I know. He was a great hit last night at dinner. He can talk about almost anything, which makes him an asset in social situations, and he's charming.'

Glancing at her, Cecily remarked, 'You look beautiful, Alicia dear, positively glowing. It's easy to see you're in love with him, and he obviously adores you. Is it serious?'

Alicia's mouth puckered up in a smile; she put her hand in her cardigan pocket and took out the Cartier box, handing it to Cecily.

'Oh my God, what a whopper this is!' Cecily took out the ring and put it on her finger, stretched out her hand, admiring the ring. 'Wow! It's really quite beautiful.'

'It's not too big, is it? Not vulgar?' Alicia asked.

'Anybody who tells you this ring is vulgar is displaying their green-eyed jealousy. And no, it's not a bit vulgar. Big, yes, but certainly very wearable. He's got good taste. And why is it in your pocket and not on your finger?'

'I wanted to wait until Charlie was here to tell him in person, and I need to telephone Mother and Father. But I'm glad that *you* know first that we're engaged, Ceci. And I'll wear it tonight. Who'll be at dinner?'

'The same as last night, the four of us: Aunt Charlotte, Diedre and Will. And I invited Harry and Paloma. Ten with Charlie, who's supposed to arrive sometime today.'

'I told Adam not to bring a dinner jacket. Miles hasn't changed the rule Grandfather made, has he? Without telling me?'

'No. And he won't. I am delighted that your grandfather banned it during the war, because he decided it was silly and frivolous to wear a tuxedo, to get dressed up when men were dying for their country. And I know all the men in the family are rather relieved they don't have to wear one. However, I always like to wear a nice frock.'

'And so will I. I thought Miles, as the head of the family, might wish to announce that Adam and I had just become engaged. He will, won't he?' Alicia looked at her aunt beseechingly.

'Of course.' Cecily sat back in the chair and stared off into the distance, her expression thoughtful. Finally she asked, 'How are your parents? Is Daphne all right?'

'Charlie spoke to our father recently and seemingly they are both well. My mother wrote a note, wished me luck, weeks ago now, when I first started the film. But they don't know I've become engaged because it only happened on Thursday. I'm planning to telephone once Charlie's here.'

'Hello, Mummy, can we come in?'

Cecily swung around at the sound of Gwen's voice. She stood in the doorway, holding her cat, Cleopatra.

'Yes, come and join us, darling.'

The eight-year-old ran forward, kissed her mother on the cheek, and then her cousin.

Alicia said, 'Your little cat's looking rather well-groomed today, Gwen. Have you been brushing her again?'

'Yes. Mummy says I have to, because that way I remove a lot of her top hairs.' Sitting down at the long table next to Cecily, she immediately noticed the diamond. 'Oh Mummy, what a lovely ring! Is it new?'

Laughing, Cecily took it off and put it back in the red box which she gave to Alicia. Smiling at her wartime baby, as she always thought of her, Cecily said, shaking her head, 'Not mine. It belongs to Alicia, and she's just become engaged. But it's a secret until tonight, when Daddy's going to announce it. Understand?'

'I won't tell anyone.' She grinned at her cousin. 'I like keeping secrets. Sometimes Mummy tells me her secrets.'

'And let's remember they *are* secrets,' Cecily warned, giving her a cautionary look.

Christopher sat in his wheelchair in the doorway of his childhood bedroom, watching Victoria walking around it.

She was interested in seeing everything, kept turning to look at him, making comments, smiling from time to time, enjoying herself as she discovered more about him.

When she went over to the rocking horse, she pushed it lightly and then stopped it. Grinning at him, she suddenly threw one leg over it, got on and started to rock. Since she was wearing trousers, she was able to do this easily.

Laughing, amused by the things she did, he began to clap.

'I love this horse,' she cried, waving to him.

'As I did too,' he answered, waving back; he was filled with sudden happiness just because of her presence.

Even when the horse had stopped rocking, she continued to sit on it for a few seconds, her eyes scanning the room once again. 'It really is a boy's Ali Baba cave of treasure,' she said. 'I love your posters of aeroplanes. You wanted to fly even then. And the display of your toys and books on the shelves tells me so much. Oh, and the dear little teddy bear on the bed, as ragged as they all become. Does he have a name?'

'I'm afraid not. I called him Teddy, which was not very original. Did you have a teddy bear? Did it have a name?'

She didn't answer for a moment, frowning, looking odd, and then she said quietly, 'Yes, I did have one. I called him Cuddy, my version of cuddles, because I cuddled him a lot.'

She got off the rocking horse with agility and grace and went over to him. 'Thank you for sharing this room with me, Chris. Now, do you want to take me to see the bluebell woods?'

Although he was a little surprised, he made no comment. He wheeled himself to the lift, and she followed behind him.

Christopher could not see her face, but he knew there had been a curious change in her demeanour after the conversation about his teddy bear. She had unexpectedly appeared withdrawn. He had not seen her like this before.

On the other hand, he was pleased she had mentioned the walk to the woods. He still had certain matters to discuss with her, and he wanted everything to be talked over and decided this weekend. Being outside gave them total privacy to say anything they wanted to each other.

When she had left his bed this morning and gone to have a bath, to get ready for breakfast with him, he had given Abel Palmerston a ring. As he had promised he would.

His neurologist had been delighted to know that his diagnosis had been accurate, and that Christopher had been able to 'perform his manly duties', as Abel called them.

Christopher soon found Freddy, who helped him to put on a thick quilted vest over his tweed jacket without getting out of the chair. He then wrapped a thick wool car rug around Christopher's legs. 'That should do it,' Freddy said, and Christopher thanked him.

Freddy looked over at Victoria. 'It's coolish, Miss Brown, even though it's sunny.' He took a green Barbour jacket out of the cupboard and helped her into it, and then handed her a red woollen scarf. 'You'll need these.'

She smiled, said, 'Thank you.'

* * *

As usual, Victoria walked beside him. They did not speak, but their silence was companionable. It was a bright day, with a sparkle in the air and a hint of winter in the light breeze.

'It's better to take this main path,' Christopher said, indicating the wide dirt clearing which led into the woods. 'Joe has made it smoother over the last few years, and it's better for my chair.'

'Are you sure you don't want me to push you?' Victoria ventured, noticing the path looked bumpy, if smooth in other areas.

To her surprise, he said, 'Perhaps you should. The boys and Alex usually do that. Thanks for thinking of it.'

'No problem.' Victoria went behind him and took hold of the wheelchair, pushing him. And pushing her sudden sorrow away. She had managed to stamp on it as a child: she must stamp on it now; not spoil this time with him because of the past.

Christopher said, 'Listen, Vicki, I've a confession to make—' He cut himself off, did not speak for a moment, wanting to find the right words. He finished, 'I'd promised to call Abel this morning, so I did. He was very pleased. He told me he was thrilled that I'd performed my manly duties.'

'I'll say you did. You were so passionate we might have made a baby.' She came to a standstill, bent over him and kissed his cheek. There was a wistful tone to her voice.

Taking a deep breath, he said, 'I thought you seemed a bit sad, even sorrowful, when we left my bedroom. What happened in there?'

'I don't want to talk about it now, if you don't mind. But I will tell you. Soon.'

'Whenever you feel you can.'

'You called this the bluebell wood. So, where are the bluebells, Mister Longdon? Vanished overnight, have they?' she teased.

He chuckled. 'If you're at Seamere next spring, I guarantee you'll see carpets of blue between the trees. Will you be here?'

'Absolutely. Hopefully. And one day pushing a pram. Not that I'd mind pushing you forever.'

He laughed with her, then said, 'You know, I wanted to ask you last night, but I was so excited and desperately longing for you, I forgot. So here goes now. Did you use a diaphragm?'

Startled though she was for a moment, she managed to say evenly, 'No, I didn't. Because I didn't . . . I wasn't sure what would unfold.'

'I see. Then perhaps I must take precautions.'

'I don't think so, Chris.' Vicki looked at him and took a deep breath. 'If we're serious about this, I want your baby, Chris, scads of your babies.'

He did not respond. Instead he told her, 'In a moment, this wide path branches left and right. Turn right, and we'll come to a small clearing. There's a seat there where you can sit, and we can look across the Marsh to the sea.'

Within a few minutes, Victoria was exclaiming about the view. The woods were on even higher ground than Seamere, and she could follow the flow of the land as far as the eye could see.

'Oh, Chris, what a lovely spot this is,' Victoria exclaimed, sitting down on the iron seat. 'It's very clear today – the sea is high in the sky.' She turned to look at him and smiled.

He took her hand in his and held it tightly. 'I want to make you happy, Vicki, and keep you safe. If you don't want us to use contraception, then so be it. I shall have to do an Edward the Fourth, if you get pregnant.'

'Agreed. You see how easy it is to solve our little problems,' she answered, sounding triumphant.

'I want to talk about the Swanns. I still don't think they will be overjoyed about us being together, planning to marry.'

'You have to trust *me* on this, Christopher. I know them so well, and they'd never go against my wishes. Because they would want to be sure I'm happy after my terrible—' She stopped short and very abruptly, shook her head, as if annoyed with herself.

Christopher knew she had been about to blurt something out

and had just stopped herself in time. He didn't want to force it out of her, because he respected her. She would tell him when the time was right, when she felt comfortable confiding in him.

Scrutinizing him intently, Victoria said slowly, in a voice that shook, 'I . . . I was . . . when I was a small child, I was abused. My . . . mother abused me.'

He simply stared at her, speechless, appalled by her words. After a long moment, he said, 'I can hardly bear to think of what she might have done to you, Vicki. Never mind the reason why. You're a beautiful woman; you must have been a most beautiful child. And why? Why?'

'She locked me in a small cupboard when I was two, three and four. Under the stairs. I couldn't get out because it was latched on the outside. I was afraid. And shook a lot, and it was very hot. If I made a sound, she would hit me . . . then later she would punch me, or sometimes hit me with her belt.'

After pausing and taking several deep breaths, Victoria continued, 'My grandfather was a solicitor. Well-to-do. When he died, we went to live with my grandmother at her house in Headingley. My mother was afraid of her mother and so she stopped hurting me. A few years later, my grandmother had a stroke. She wasn't able to protect me any more.'

Victoria unbuttoned the Barbour, pushed her hand into her jacket pocket and found a handkerchief. After blowing her nose and wiping her tear-filled eyes, she said, 'Aunt Alice saw the fading bruises when I first went to live with her and Uncle Walter.'

'And she asked about them. And finally you had someone you could tell,' Christopher said in a low tone, filled with anger about her wicked mother, understanding Victoria's hurt and sorrow.

'I didn't, actually. Once the war was over, I was so terrified of being sent back to my mother, I finally told Aunt Alice about my abuse. When she visited the Pied Piper Organization they told her my mother and grandmother were dead and my father lost at sea. So they *could* adopt me.'

'Couldn't your father have prevented her from hurting you?' Christopher asked in a low-pitched, miserable voice.

'He was always in the Merchant Navy, not there. I never really knew him.' Unexpectedly, Victoria started to weep, and she pressed the handkerchief to her eyes, mumbling, 'Sorry, so sorry, Chris.'

He rolled his chair around the end of the garden seat so that he sat facing her, taking her hand in his. 'What a horrendous thing to have happened to you, my lovely Vicki. I'm sure Alice Swann was as furious and horrified as I am now. And what you're trying to say is that because of the unconscionable abuse you suffered as a child, they'll let you marry whomever you wish. Is that it?'

She nodded her head and held onto his hand and tried to smile through the tears. 'And when I looked at your teddy bear, I remembered Cuddy, and how he had been a comfort to me in the cupboard. And one day, because I'd made a noise when *he* was there, the man, she threw Cuddy away.'

'Oh my God, no! What on earth was this harsh, vindictive woman thinking of?'

'The man she was with. The many men she was with in my childhood. They came and went, and she locked me up so they wouldn't see me. Wouldn't know I even existed.'

He reached out his arms to her, tears in his eyes. 'Come and sit on my knee, Vicki, so I can hold you. Come on, darling, please. I want to hold you tight and never let you go.'

That night, when Victoria went into the dining room with Christopher, his teddy bear was sitting in her seat with a red ribbon tied around his neck. There was a card attached. She opened it, read it, and a radiant smile flooded her face. Her eyes filled with love for this most extraordinary man. The note was simple. It said:

*Dearest Victoria,*
*Now we both belong to you.*
*Kisses from Chris and Teddy*

'Thank you, Chris, thank you so much. I will keep you both very safe for the rest of my life,' Victoria murmured, touched by this gesture on his part.

'I know you will. And I will look after the two of you. I'm going to marry you, Victoria Brown, with your parents' blessing.'

The countryside had never meant much to him. He was not bothered about nature and he did not like animals. The city streets were his natural habitat.

But nonetheless, Adam Fennell paid a great deal of attention to the land he walked across on Sunday morning. He had gone out for a stroll; the weather wasn't cold and he felt the air would do him good. Also, Alicia was still busy packing and labelling clothes for the Salvation Army.

Thousands of acres. A great working grouse moor in fantastic condition. *Money*. They spelled money in capitals. And then there was the great stately home, a treasure trove of priceless paintings, art objects, valuable antiques. There was the collection of jewels in the vaults, tons of silver, and a wine cellar bursting with vintage wines. The Inghams were one of the most important aristocratic families in England. And he was about to marry Alicia Ingham Stanton. He would live here, be amongst all this splendour.

He thought of Jack Trotter and the Golden Horn and wondered what Jack would say about his climb up the ladder to success if he were alive.

A smile spread across Adam's face, and then he laughed out loud. He had learned a lot about business and other things from Jack. Rosie popped into his mind, and very vividly so. She had been ten years older and had taught him everything she knew about sex and how to give a woman thundering pleasure. But otherwise he had had no other tutors. Just the publican and a barmaid. The rest he had taught himself. In order to fit in, he'd invented a much smarter background for himself, one in which his parents were conveniently dead.

A flock of birds rose up into the blue sky, and Adam glanced at them soaring higher. Like he was. He walked on, heading towards Cavendon Hall.

Alicia had told him that the best shortcut into the house from the park was through the library, so he headed for the terrace that ran along the back of the house.

As he climbed the steps, he suddenly felt the calf of his right leg knot into a cramp, and he almost fell, but managed somehow to stay upright.

There was a wrought-iron garden seat on the terrace, standing against the wall between the two French doors. He limped over to it and sat down, and began to massage his leg, quietly groaning in agony.

A moment later he heard a noise in the library and shrank back on the seat, not wanting anyone to see him disabled in this way. What if it was Alicia?

Someone opened one of the French doors and said, 'There, that's better. What this room needs is a little fresh air, Aunt Charlotte.'

He recognized the voice. It was Cecily Swann, the Countess of Mowbray. Attempting to stand, to leave before he was spotted, Adam felt his left leg cramp up and cursed under his breath. He fell back on the garden seat, massaging that leg now, remembering that Max, his masseur, had told him not to forget to take potassium.

The Countess was speaking again. Adam sat up straighter, listening alertly.

'I told Miles some of the secrets, Aunt Charlotte.'

'That's surprising, Ceci! What did you tell him actually?'

'You're not angry, are you?'

'Of course not. Did you tell him about Marmaduke?'

Cecily laughed. 'Yes, I did. And Sarah Swann. I couldn't resist. Anyway, I felt I ought to tell you that I had confided in him.'

'And what else did you reveal?'

'The story of Great-Aunt Gwendolyn. After all, she is dead.'

'You didn't say anything about Daphne, did you? Oh, I do hope not, Cecily. You can't reveal anything about her troubles, not even to her brother.'

'I didn't. I never will. I spoke to Miles about earlier generations only. Nobody cares about *them* these days.'

'People do care about the living, though. Where is that particular record book? For the years 1913 to 1914? You've had them all out lately.'

'They're all back in the trunk in the attic.'

'Are you sure it's locked? Perhaps you should go to the attic and check.'

'Please stop worrying, Aunt Charlotte. Who on earth would be interested in those old record books?'

'You never know,' Charlotte murmured. 'And now I think I shall go and freshen up. It's almost noon.'

'And I must go and find my little Gwen.'

After a moment, Adam heard the library door close, and he relaxed, replaying their conversation in his head. Daphne had been in some sort of trouble a long time ago – when she was still a girl. It was obviously such a big secret that the old aunt was genuinely worried about it leaking.

Adam stood up and limped along the terrace, having decided to enter the house through the front door. But wild thoughts were whirling around in his head. Alicia had been born in January 1914, that he knew. Was there something secret about Alicia's birth? Could she be illegitimate? No, that couldn't be. On the other hand, anything was possible.

After all, it was good old Jack Trotter who had taught him that knowledge is power. Jack had drilled it into him, in fact.

*Wow.* Now that I have information like this in my hand, then

I'm in clover. There was no one he could question, that was obvious. However, he could read the record book. Which was in the trunk. In the attic. All he had to do was get to it – and presumably to open the lock.

He must plan everything carefully. The way he had always done. The way he had built the life he dreamed of.

# Part Five

# Different Perceptions 1950

You can never plan the future by the past.

Edmund Burke,
*Letter to a Member of the National Assembly*

# Thirty-Four

Alicia sat at the desk in the conservatory at Cavendon, making notations on a pad regarding the script for *Dangerous*. Notes that would help her with the part.

She had just finished reading the first rewrite by Margo Littleton and Jeffrey Cox, and it was certainly an improvement on the original.

Putting her pen down, she sat back in the chair, staring out of the window. It was a cold, dreary sort of day, the sky leaden, the trees bereft of leaves. A typical February day.

*February*, she murmured under her breath. How can it be February of 1950, with the country heading to a General Election once again? Where have the last few months gone? They had just flown by, disappeared in a flurry of work, of finishing the movie, having the wrap party, and a rather rushed Christmas and New Year. Then Adam going off to New York to see his backers, coming back moody and distracted. She had long suspected he might be having problems with them. When she suggested this, he had practically bitten her head off. Not like him. He was mostly warm and loving. And occasionally a bit erratic. She also knew now how possessive he was of her. And jealous.

She thought about what Charlie had said in October of last year: Adam was a man in love and his behaviour was normal. But was it? A number of incidents flitted through her mind, and then she pushed them away. Why dwell on them? His better traits far outweighed his little outbursts. She thought of these as childlike tantrums, best ignored.

There were notes she had made about another script called *Revenge*, which she had read last week. Opening the desk drawer, she shuffled through papers and soon found the notes.

As she took them out she caught sight of a piece of her mother's stationery. It was white with a blue edge and had the family crest engraved at the top of the sheet. Pushing the drawer closed, she shook her head, filling up with unexpected dismay.

She still felt extremely hurt that her parents hadn't bothered to come home to see her and meet Adam. Even though they might not want to return to Cavendon, they could have visited her in London for a few days.

When she had phoned them to tell them she had become engaged, they had congratulated her, yet they hadn't invited her to bring Adam to Zurich either.

Was her mother still harbouring resentment about what she called the commercialization of Cavendon by Cecily? Or offended that she and Charlie came up here most weekends? Perhaps their parents viewed this as disloyalty on their part. All were possibilities.

Alicia loved her mother and father and had placed Daphne on a pedestal as a child. She thought her mother to be the most beautiful woman in the world, and her father the knight in shining armour, protecting their mother and them.

And yet, now when she looked back, there had been other little things over the past year – a certain coldness in her mother at times, lack of attention, small slights, a decided preference for her brother Charlie, undoubtedly her mother's favourite. Alicia understood that, understood the mother–son syndrome, and was not troubled by it. Neither were her other siblings.

She loved Charlie too, admired and respected him. They had been close since they were small, and this had never changed.

They were comrades in arms, as Charlie liked to call them, battling their way through the Ingham clan, finding their own places, standing tall, fully aware they were members of a distinguished family. They knew all about loyalty and duty and what was expected of them.

Sometimes, when she was little, and her mother had scolded her, or been inattentive, Alicia had run to her grandfather, Charles Ingham, the 6th Earl.

They had bonded; the small child and the older man had become even closer over the years of her growing up. They understood each other, were on the same wavelength, and she had been devastated when he had died.

'My ilk,' he would say to her, putting an arm around her as she stood by his chair. 'And I'm so glad you're of my ilk.'

Alicia sighed. She understood why the changes that had come to Cavendon were hard for her mother to accept. The Ingham family had had its share of tragedy, but it had stood firm under her grandfather's steady hand, through war and scandal. Life now was different; the old ways had gone, the two world wars changing British society forever. Even as a young woman, Alicia remembered a different Cavendon, one of a fleet of servants and white tie for dinner.

Putting aside her thoughts of her family, Alicia read her notes and realized from her jottings how much she had loved this script on the first reading. Months ago Adam had told her he thought it could be a *film noir*, in Hitch's style. And she agreed. Alfred Hitchcock was his favourite director, and hers.

The clicking of heels on the stone floor of the conservatory made her look up from the script. Cecily was hurrying towards her, a smile on her face.

'Here you are. I've been looking for you all over. I've just had a letter from Dulcie, and she and James and the children will be going to New York in March, finally sailing home to England.

For good,' Cecily said. 'Apparently the film is finished. They've put their house up for sale. And they're busy packing.'

'Oh I'm so happy, Ceci, thrilled to have this news. I've missed them so much, but then we all have. And you're sure it's for good?' Alicia raised a brow.

'Absolutely. James misses the theatre, as you well know, and he wants to tread the boards again. That was the way Dulcie put it. Good news, right?'

'It is. Felix and Constance are no doubt pleased. They miss him a lot. Just think, they discovered James when he was about fifteen or something like that.'

'I know what you mean. He's almost like a son to them.' Cecily shivered. 'It's a bit chilly in here, Alicia. Come to my little parlour. We can have a cup of coffee or tea and chat for a bit.'

The sketches of clothes were the first thing Alicia noticed when she walked into Cecily's parlour, which she used as an office, located next to the dining room.

'Ceci, these are wonderful!' she cried, rushing forward. She stood gazing at the drawings, struck by their uniqueness, their enormous stylishness.

'I'm glad you like them,' Cecily said, joining her. 'They're some of my new designs. We're putting these six dresses into work this week.'

'They're very different, eye-catching, and I like this new length, just that bit longer, but so graceful, and you know I adore evening gowns with bouffant skirts.' She turned, her eyes sparkling. 'Adam told me he would like to buy some new clothes for me. From your next collection.'

'How nice of him, and very generous. He's such a lovely man. We're really happy for you, Alicia,' Cecily said. 'And what a contrast he is to Bryan Mellor. So much more charming and personable. Whatever happened to Bryan?'

'Not a word since he went off to do that tour,' Alicia said, shrugging, obviously indifferent and over him completely. 'Seems he runs out when things get serious.'

'Is Adam coming for the weekend?' Cecily asked, walking over to the fireplace, standing with her back to it, warming herself. 'That was another reason I was looking for you.'

'Yes, he is. He's been back from New York for a week now and he is much more rested. These trips are killing, what with the time-change and all that.'

'I can well imagine. Diedre and Will won't be here. They're going to Geneva for the weekend.'

Alicia stared hard at Cecily and asked, 'Have they ever heard from my parents? Or gone to see them when they've been in Switzerland before?'

'Not to my knowledge, Alicia. In fact, no one has heard much from Daphne and Hugo. Certainly not me.' Cecily frowned. 'You look troubled all of a sudden. Is something wrong?'

'I was thinking about my parents earlier, wondering why they've never bothered to come and meet Adam.'

'I realized that, and so does Miles. But I don't think Daphne feels too friendly towards us. Me, in particular. And she won't come to Cavendon for a long time, in my opinion. She didn't come for Christmas, which would have been a good time to put an end to this difficult situation.' Cecily let out a long sigh, shaking her head and looking baffled.

'She probably thinks Charlie and I are being disloyal because we're siding with you.' There was a pause before Alicia added, 'Do you think my mother might be ill?'

'It has crossed my mind, and Miles has brought that up to me, as well. Have you mentioned this to your father?'

'Not exactly. Anyway, he would never tell me, or any of us. He's so adoring of our mother, totally devoted. He tries to protect her from everything.'

'I know that. When he met her, it was love at first sight – adoration, in fact. And that's the way it's been ever since,' Cecily remarked.

'Nothing will change. But if she is ill, I think it would be important to tell his children, don't you?' Alicia sat down in a chair, throwing Cecily a quizzical look.

'Well, yes, of course, you ought to know,' Cecily agreed. 'But Hugo is very stubborn. Try not to worry too much about them, Alicia. If your mother were really and truly ill, he would inform you. I do know when she left she was worn out, very tired.' Cecily crossed the room and sat down on the sofa. 'Cavendon has been her passion all of her adult life, and keeping it looking beautiful her true vocation. The changes we've had to bring in were very hard – very upsetting to her. She overdid it, I believe, and exhaustion can be debilitating.'

There was a knock on the door, and Eric came in. 'Would you like any refreshments, Your Ladyship? Miss Alicia?'

Cecily smiled at him. 'I was about to ring for you. I'd love a cup of coffee. What about you, Alicia?'

'The same please,' Alicia answered, looking across at Eric, who gave her a warm smile and disappeared.

'God knows what I would do without him,' Cecily confided in a lowered tone. 'Eric has kept this house running like clockwork. He's certainly given me time to grow into the extra duties Daphne used to cover, but still have time for designing and my business. He's a treasure. And so is Peggy. Now, what was I saying?'

Not wanting to focus on her parents again, Alicia now decided to open up a new subject and asked, 'What do you think about Christopher Longdon?'

'That he's a marvellous man!' Cecily exclaimed. 'My parents were extremely surprised when Victoria told them she was getting engaged to him, but the minute they met him they fell under his spell. In fact, we all did. He asked my father formally for her hand.'

Alicia smiled, so proud of Victoria and how she had handled it all. 'And that spread on him in *Elegance Magazine* was fantastic,' Alicia remarked. 'I think Victoria really outdid herself. I was rather touched by some of the photographs she took, especially the one in his childhood bedroom with his old rocking horse and teddy bear. She told me it was a last-minute shot and that they managed to squeeze it in.'

'There's no question that she's a talented young woman, and the pictures she took of you are beautiful, Alicia. That was another outstanding spread in the magazine. Miles and I, we're so pleased you did it at Cavendon and not in London. Good publicity for us for the house tours this spring.'

A moment later Eric returned with the tray of coffee. Placing it on a side table, he filled the cups and passed them to Cecily and Alicia.

After thanking him, Cecily said, 'Mr Fennell will be coming this weekend, Eric, but not Lady Diedre and Mr Lawson. I also think Mr Charlie will be here.' She glanced at Alicia. 'He will, won't he?'

'Yes,' Alicia answered. 'As a matter of fact, he'll be driving up with Mr Fennell.'

Once they were alone, Cecily said, 'Christopher Longdon has been rather helpful to Miles. He's sent several veterans to see him, and Miles and Harry recently hired them. They and their families have just moved into empty farms in Mowbray, and Harry will train them to run the farms. Much-needed work for them and certainly very helpful to us.'

Alicia nodded. 'I think the veterans' charity Christopher has started is so marvellous; it's just rotten how our former soldiers are treated. I sent the charity a cheque and so did Adam.'

'That was good of you, darling.'

Cecily sat drinking her coffee, her thoughts on Alicia. She was such a kind and loving person, always wanting to help others when she could.

Cecily would never forget how devoted her niece had been to the 6th Earl, her grandfather, as he was growing older. A memory came rushing back, of Alicia returning to Yorkshire to be with him, instead of going to Berlin on the family trip.

Alicia had explained that she had promised to spend time with him that summer, and she had kept her promise. Nineteen thirty-eight, Cecily thought. It had been in 1938. So long ago now.

Later that week, on Friday afternoon, Charlie and Adam arrived at Cavendon at three o'clock, well in time for afternoon tea in the yellow drawing room.

This was a tradition Adam loved, enjoying the relaxing atmosphere of it: the food, the bonhomie. Minding his manners as usual, he had brought his hostess a present, which he put on the hall table for Cecily to open later. It was a large box of her favourite chocolates from Fortnum & Mason.

Alicia was relieved to see that he was in a happy mood and had obviously had an enjoyable journey with Charlie, who was also in good spirits.

Annabel had come up the evening before, and Alicia had pumped her youngest sibling about their parents, newly concerned about it. But Annabel was seemingly just as mystified as Alicia. Yes, their mother's behaviour was odd, but no, she didn't think their mother was ill. The twins visited regularly and had not mentioned anything out of the ordinary, Annabel had confided.

Now Annabel was playing the piano for Aunt Charlotte when Alicia, Charlie and Adam went into the yellow drawing room. Miles and Cecily were the last to arrive.

'Where's Gwen?' Alicia asked Cecily, glancing around. 'She told me earlier she would see me for tea.'

'She's down in the kitchen with Cleopatra. The cat's not feeling well, she says,' Cecily explained. 'But it's not anything serious, I'm sure.'

'Harry thinks she might have eaten something she found outside that's disagreed with her,' Miles interjected. 'The cat will be fine.'

Aunt Charlotte said, 'Thank you, Adam, for sending me that lovely book on great cathedrals of the world. It was so thoughtful of you. I'm enjoying the many gorgeous photographs.'

'My pleasure, Aunt Charlotte,' Adam responded, smiling at her. Then, looking across at Annabel, who was still playing, he turned to Alicia and said, in a low voice, 'Your sister is extremely talented. She ought to be on a concert stage.'

'Yes, she wanted to do that once,' Alicia whispered. 'I'll tell you later.'

# Thirty-Five

Adam Fennell was in his element.

He was thrilled to spend most weekends in this grand stately home, waited on by servants, in his own mind playing the lord of the manor.

The real lord of the manor, Miles Ingham, the 7th Earl of Mowbray, had welcomed him cordially and liked him a lot. The entire family liked him, much to his great satisfaction.

This place suited him. He was where he belonged. And where he would live for the rest of his life. With his beautiful Alicia. He had hoped that this weekend they could have set the wedding date, but she had been reluctant to do so until they had been to Zurich to see her parents. He knew she'd been hoping that Daphne and Hugo would fly over for Christmas to meet him.

It had been a carefree weekend, and last night the dinner had been festive. But then the family always seemed to make Saturday nights special, full of enjoyment for everyone.

For the last few months, Adam had been creating a routine for himself, getting up sometimes in the middle of the night, going downstairs to the library, where he would sit and read a book.

The second time he did this disappearing act, Alicia soon came looking for him. He had explained that he was suffering from insomnia, needed to move about the house, read a bit in the library in order to finally go back to bed and fall asleep. She had said she understood and had never come to look for him again.

Now at last Adam felt sure of himself, confident that he could finally go up to the attic safely, open the trunk with his set of burglary picks, and read the record book for 1913.

The more he thought about it, the more he was certain that this was the relevant year. *The summer of 1913*. Nine months before Alicia's birth in January of 1914. There was obviously a huge and perhaps dangerous secret connected to her birth, because Aunt Charlotte had been so concerned about that particular record book.

Adam had got on in life partly through being endlessly curious, some might say nosy, needing to know everything about everybody. And he had not forgotten the conversation he had overheard months earlier when he was out on the terrace, massaging his cramped leg.

Since Cavendon was a huge house, he had done a lot of roaming around for weeks on end, poking about in many rooms without drawing attention to himself. In fact, he had never stopped snooping surreptitiously.

He pushed himself up on his elbow and looked down at Alicia. She was in a deep sleep. Not surprising. She had told him how exhausted she was before kissing his cheek and saying goodnight.

He glanced at his watch. It was one o'clock. The perfect time to go up to the attic. The entire household would be fast asleep by now. He did not drink, but the Inghams did, and a lot of wine had been consumed by them during and after dinner.

Slipping out of bed, Adam found his dressing gown, put his feet in his slippers and left Alicia's room quietly. He crossed the corridor to his bedroom, where he had left the lamps on when he had gone to Alicia.

He went straight to his briefcase in the walk-in closet, took the key for it out of a jacket hanging on the rod and opened the briefcase. There they were – his set of burglary keys and picks, plus a flashlight. These he put in his dressing-gown pocket and left the room.

Adam made his way to the short hall, crossed into the West Wing in a few steps, and opened the door which led up to the attic. He knew his way, knew exactly where the trunk stood, because he had done dry runs several times in the last few months.

Deciding it was all right to turn on the attic light, he did so, bent over the trunk and picked the lock swiftly in his usual experienced way. Finally, he lifted the lid, and within seconds he was holding the black leather book. The white label on it had the years written across it in black ink: 1913 and 1914.

Opening the book, he began to leaf through it swiftly, but discovered it was written in a peculiar way. Far better to take it back to his room than endeavour to read it up here, he decided. Closing and relocking the trunk, he turned off the light and went back down the stairs.

Much to his horror, his right leg suddenly cramped up, and as he tried to ease it with his right hand, he slipped, falling halfway down the stairs. Somehow he managed to break his fall by clinging to the bannister with his right hand. His left clutched the record book to his chest.

Adam lay very still on the stairs, listening, wondering how much noise he had made. Not a lot, he decided and, continuing to listen for a moment, he realized the house was quiet. There was total silence around him.

Finally, the cramp stopped. Pushing himself to his feet, he went on down the stairs and opened the door. As he stepped into the corridor, he found himself staring at Aunt Charlotte, whose bedroom door faced the one going up to the attic.

There she was, staring back at him from the doorway, obviously as shocked as he was. She looked from his face to the book in his hand, recognized it, and opened her mouth to say something.

Instinctively, Adam rushed her, pushing her back into the room, closing the door behind him with his foot.

'What are you doing with that book?' she demanded.

He did not speak, simply pushed her once again, until she was in the middle of the floor. He gripped her arm tightly with his right hand.

She tried to grab the book, almost got it, then unexpectedly it flew out of his hand, skidding across the rug. Struggling with him, endeavouring to shake him off, Charlotte staggered slightly, almost losing her balance.

Adam immediately took advantage, pushed her even harder with both hands. She fell backwards and hit her head on the brass fender. He gasped when she opened her eyes and stared up at him, tried to speak. Cautiously, he bent over her. But her eyes had closed.

Was she dead? He had no idea. What he did know was that if she lived she would expose him. All of his plans, made so carefully over several years, would be ruined. He would be ruined. *Finished.*

Bending over her more closely, Adam grasped the lapels of her woollen dressing gown and lifted her up. He noticed her eyes remained closed. He suddenly let go of her and she fell back; her head struck the fender hard once more.

Where was that record book? His eyes scanned the floor and finally he saw it underneath a chair. He ran over and grabbed it, took it over to a chest near the door.

Returning to Aunt Charlotte, he picked up her limp arm, found her wrist, felt for a pulse. There wasn't one. A small sigh of relief escaped. He was safe.

Adam took the record book off the chest and went out into the corridor. In his haste to get back to his room in the South Wing, he did not notice that the door to the back staircase at the other end of the corridor was slowly closing.

It was Peggy Swift Lane, the housekeeper, who discovered Aunt Charlotte's body on Sunday morning. When she knocked on the

Dowager Countess's door at nine o'clock, and then walked in as she always did, Aunt Charlotte's body was in her direct line of vision.

She ran forward, understanding immediately that something terrible had happened. Bending over Aunt Charlotte, she realized that she was dead. Just to be sure, Peggy touched her cheek lightly with one finger. It was cold.

Tears welled in Peggy's eyes, and she stifled a sob. She had known Charlotte Swann Ingham since she was a young girl, working here as a maid at Cavendon.

Straightening, Peggy hurried out of the room and ran down the corridor, took the back staircase. Once she was in the pantry behind the dining room, Peggy motioned to Eric, whom she could see in the dining room, where most of the family were having breakfast.

Looking down the room at Peggy, Eric noticed her stricken face and nodded to her. A moment later he was in the pantry, asking her what was wrong. She told him. A look of sorrow swept across his face, and he gasped, then instantly took control of himself.

'I'd better ask His Lordship to leave the table,' he murmured. 'Wait out there in the corridor. Better still, go to the library.'

Steadying himself, Eric walked down the dining room and spoke to Miles quietly. 'There's an urgent matter, Your Lordship. Could you please leave the table and come with me?'

Miles looked up at Eric, saw the seriousness on his face and nodded. He excused himself to the others and left the room.

'What is it, Eric?' Miles asked once they were in the small hallway. 'Obviously there's something terribly wrong by the look on your face.'

'Yes, m'lord. There's been a dreadful accident, involving the Dowager Countess. Please, m'lord, could you come to the library? Peggy is waiting to speak to you. She will give you the details. I don't know them. She just came downstairs to tell me.'

Instantly Miles felt a rush of apprehension, and he almost ran to the library, where Peggy was standing stiffly in the middle of the room, looking shocked and bereft.

'What's wrong, Peggy?' he asked, hurrying to her, followed by Eric, who stood to one side, wanting to know himself what had actually happened.

'It's the Dowager Countess, Your Lordship. I went to wake her this morning, at nine as always, and I found her on the floor near the fireplace. She's had a terrible accident . . .' Tears welled and Peggy struggled to keep her voice steady. 'She must have fallen when she got up during the night.'

Miles felt his chest tighten and swallowed hard as his throat thickened. He knew that Aunt Charlotte was dead, even though neither of them had been able to actually say those words.

In as steady a voice as he could muster, he asked, 'Aunt Charlotte is dead, isn't she, Peggy?'

'Yes,' was the only word Peggy could get out. She had begun to shake, and the tears ran down her cheeks.

Eric, also shaken, was as white as bleached bone. He said, 'Should I go and ask Lady Cecily to join us, Your Lordship?'

'Yes, you'd better do that, Eric, and with your usual discretion. Once Her Ladyship has been told, the four of us will go upstairs.'

As Eric hurried off, Miles looked at Peggy, frowning, 'None of the maids will go into Aunt Charlotte's room yet, will they?'

'Oh no, Lord Mowbray. Never. I have always personally looked after the Dowager, ever since she married your father, excuse me, the Sixth Earl.'

Miles nodded and walked over to the window, looked out, blinked back the tears. Charlotte had so loved his father – all of them, actually. He and his sisters had been like her own children.

He heard Cecily's high heels clicking against the marble floor of the grand hall even before she came into the library, and he hurried across the library to the doorway.

Eric was ushering her in, and then he closed the door behind them firmly, stood next to it.

'Something's happened, hasn't it?' Cecily said, rushing to Miles, noting the mistiness in his eyes, the gravity of his expression.

'Yes, Ceci, it has. This morning, when Peggy went in to awaken Aunt Charlotte, she found her lying on the floor near the fireplace. She must have fallen during the night . . . a terrible accident.'

'Oh no,' Cecily said, clutching his arm, her voice suddenly breaking. 'She's dead. She is, isn't she, Miles?'

'I'm afraid so, darling.'

Cecily turned to Peggy, 'You're sure she's dead, Peggy? Did you touch her?'

'Yes, Your Ladyship. She was ice cold.'

'Rigor mortis has probably set in already,' Miles said, his voice thick. 'Let's go upstairs. Leave the others to finish breakfast.'

Once they were in the bedroom, Miles went and knelt down next to Aunt Charlotte's body. He felt her wrist. No pulse, obviously. Why had he done that? Just to be certain, he thought. Just to be certain. We never wanted you to leave us, he said to her in his head.

Cecily joined him, knelt down next to Aunt Charlotte and touched her cheek gently, then rested her head against his shoulder. Tears were damp on her face.

Miles touched Cecily's shoulder and then he stood up, looked across at the bed, and went over to Eric and Peggy. 'It's quite obvious what happened. She got out of bed during the night, tripped and fell.'

Eric nodded. 'She wasn't showing her age, but she did tell me her legs ached at times, m'lord.'

Miles let out a sigh, nodded. 'Eric, would you please ring Dr Ottoway, at his home in Mowbray. Tell him what's happened. Ask him to come here as soon as possible. Give him my apologies for not calling myself, but I must inform the rest of the family about Aunt Charlotte's death.'

'Yes, Your Lordship. I'll go and do that immediately.'

Cecily said, 'What about Aunt Charlotte? We can't leave her lying here on the floor, can we? Surely not. Shouldn't we lift her up? Among us, we could do it, and put her on the bed.'

'But of course we must do that!' Miles exclaimed. 'How thoughtless of me. She'd hate it if anyone saw her in such an undignified position on the floor.'

# Thirty-Six

Before going downstairs to inform the family of the tragic death of the Dowager Countess, Miles and Cecily went into the small sitting room which opened off their bedrooms.

Cecily rushed into his arms immediately, and they held each other tightly, trying to be comforting. They both wept, filled with sorrow about their beloved Aunt Charlotte. She was another Swann who had devoted her life to the Inghams and to Cavendon.

Charlotte had loved two Ingham men: she had married one, Miles's father, and been a mother to his children after his first wife had left him.

In a sense, Charlotte had been a mother to the many Swanns who lived in the surrounding villages, and she was the matriarch to both families, a situation which had never occurred before.

Finally they drew apart, and Cecily said, 'I hate it that Aunt Charlotte was alone, Miles. I do wish someone had been there with her, holding her hand.'

'It was probably a quick death,' Miles replied softly, his heart heavy with grief. 'She must have stumbled, fallen, hit her head on the edge of the fender. But I know what you mean, darling, and now we must plan a funeral to honour her and celebrate her life. Her long life, eighty-one years: such a grand age, Ceci.'

'Yes, it was. And a life she so much enjoyed and lived to the fullest.'

Miles said, 'Well, we'd better pull ourselves together. I have to go down and tell the others what's happened. We both did a hasty disappearing act and they must be wondering why by now.'

'I think you're right.' Cecily found a handkerchief in her jacket pocket and wiped her eyes. 'Once everyone here knows, I must ring my parents.'

'I know that. And I must phone Dulcie, Diedre and Daphne. I doubt that Dulcie can make it back from Los Angeles in time, but Diedre will return at once from Geneva, that I know. As for Daphne, I can't hazard a guess. My sister is rather strange these days.'

'Will you hold the funeral in three days, Miles? Not wait for Dulcie and James?'

'That is the Ingham tradition, Ceci. We bury our dead in three days. And then have a week of mourning together. The immediate family, that is.'

'Let's go downstairs before I really start crying.'

Miles took hold of her hand and whispered, 'Be brave, Ceci.' He kissed her cheek. 'We will have each other, thank God.'

When they arrived in the doorway of the dining room, everyone stared at them, worried looks on their faces. It was Charlie who asked, 'What's happened, Uncle Miles? Something bad, I suspect.'

Miles nodded. 'Yes. Let's go into the library so that I can explain.'

Miles and Cecily walked across the great hall and into the library. The others followed behind.

Miles now remembered how his father had always gone and stood in front of the fireplace when he had something important to announce, and so he did that. I'm following the tradition, he thought. Then he asked Cecily to sit in the chair nearest to him.

Once everyone was seated, Miles said in a low, serious tone, 'I'm afraid I have some very sad and distressing news to impart. Aunt Charlotte seemingly had an accident during the night. I'm so sorry to have to tell you that she died.'

There was a loud unified gasp and a voice cried, 'No! No!'

Miles realized it was his niece, Annabel, who had spoken, and who was now starting to cry quietly, hunched over in a chair.

'What exactly happened?' Charlie asked, his eyes suddenly moist, his voice wobbling.

'It looks as if she got out of bed during the night and had a bad fall,' Miles explained. 'It was Peggy who found her near the fireplace this morning. Our supposition is that she hit her head against the edge of the brass fender. I have sent for Dr Ottoway, who will be here shortly to examine her body and provide the necessary death certificate.'

Charlie nodded, tears welling again. He groped for a handkerchief in his pocket. 'I think I'd better telephone my mother and father in Zurich, don't you, Uncle Miles?'

'I do indeed, Charlie. Speak to them, break the news gently and explain that I will call them later. I must ring Diedre in Geneva and Dulcie in America. And do ask your parents to come to the funeral.'

Annabel was still weeping, patting her eyes constantly with her hankie. She was obviously so upset, and so Cecily got up, went to comfort her niece. 'I loved Aunt Charlotte,' Annabel whispered to Cecily, holding onto her tightly, endeavouring not to start sobbing. 'She always wanted me to play the piano for her, and I counted on her for so many things. She was like a grandmother to me. I shall miss her so much, Aunt Ceci.'

'We all will, darling,' Cecily answered. 'And now we must be brave, bury her with honour and dignity as she deserves.'

Alicia was in shock, her face pale, her eyes bright with tears. Her voice shook when she asked, 'When will you have the funeral, Uncle Miles?'

'In three days,' he replied quietly.

Startled, Alicia exclaimed, 'But Dulcie and James will never make it here in time.'

'I'm sure they won't. However, that is the Ingham family tradition. Three days. And it still holds. It will always hold. I must get in touch with all of our children, the family's children, at university and boarding school, and tell them to come home at once.'

Charlie, wanting to be helpful, said, 'Is there anything else I can do for you, Uncle Miles?'

'Yes, Charlie, there is. You could telephone the local undertakers for me, before you ring your parents. Explain what has happened and tell them we need their services. Thanks for offering, Charlie. I'm grateful.' He also knew it was good to keep everyone busy, so they didn't wallow around too much in their grief.

'What can I do?' Alicia asked, wiping her fingertips across her damp face, pulling herself together, reminding herself she was an Ingham woman. A woman warrior.

'I think Cecily and Alice might need help with the flowers for the church.' Miles glanced at his wife.

'We will, Miles,' Cecily interjected. Then, looking into Annabel's face, she went on, 'Annabel, can you advise Uncle Miles about the music for the church service? You and Aunt Charlotte shared your musical tastes and favourites.'

'Yes, I will,' Annabel answered. 'And I would like to play the piano in the church for the service.'

'Can't I do anything?' Adam asked. 'Everyone seems to have a job. But not me.'

Miles said, 'Perhaps you and Alicia can make a list of who will be attending the funeral, other than the Inghams and the Swanns. For example, Felix and Constance Lambert loved Aunt Charlotte and will want to come, I'm sure. Perhaps you would contact them for me.'

'We will do that, of course,' Adam answered. 'And I want to offer you my condolences, Miles. I'm so sorry that Aunt Charlotte died. She was such a lovely lady.'

* * *

Dr Ottoway arrived with one of his nurses, and Cecily took them upstairs to Aunt Charlotte's bedroom. After explaining how Peggy had found the Dowager Countess on the floor near the fireplace, earlier that morning, she left them to do the examination.

Going to her little parlour, she phoned her mother and very gently broke the news to Alice. She heard her mother choking back her tears, and asked, 'Do you want me to come to be with you, Mam? For a while?'

'No, no, Cecily, I will walk up to Cavendon. I want to see Charlotte before the undertakers remove the body. When will they arrive?'

'I don't know. Miles asked Charlie to phone them. Why don't you and my father come up now? We can be together, have a bite of lunch later.'

'I couldn't eat a thing . . .' Alice stopped short, and she began to sob.

'I understand, Mam,' Cecily replied in a quiet voice. 'I will be here waiting for you and my father. Just come, so we can be together, comfort each other. Miles has told the staff. He's with Harry now.'

After hanging up, Cecily went down to Eric's office, just a few steps away from the kitchen. He looked up as she knocked and walked in, straightened in the chair, and stood at once.

'Are you all right, Eric?' Cecily asked. He was a Swann, her cousin. She went and sat down in the chair near his desk. 'This has been a very difficult morning for you.'

'For us all, Your Ladyship. She was my favourite aunt, and she was always so good to me when I was a boy.' He swallowed hard, and added, 'It's the suddenness of it, the shock. It knocks you flat. She'll be missed around here, I can tell you that.'

'I know.' There was a moment's pause and Cecily stared at him intently. 'We Swanns must always hold together, stand firm together, and be courageous.'

'I know. We do. We are.'

'We've been through a lot together, you and I, Eric, and we've always pulled through.'

He nodded knowingly, and said, 'I've told Percy, and he's passed the word around the three villages. There will be a big turnout. His Lordship will have to use the church down in Little Skell. It'll be a morning funeral, that's the Ingham tradition. Can we do a wake for the villagers in the church hall? That's the tradition, too.'

'I'll ask Miles, and I'm sure he'll agree to the wake. My mother will have the Women's Institute members make the food.'

'Will we have any overnight guests, m'lady?'

'That's one of the reasons I came to see you, Eric. To my knowledge three guests. Mr and Mrs Lambert, representing Sir James and Lady Dulcie, and Miss Chalmers. But that's just a guess on my part. I'll know more later. We'll serve a light lunch here for our guests and the family.'

Tears suddenly welled up and Cecily shook her head, looking bemused. 'I can't believe I'm planning this funeral with you. I just had tea with Aunt Charlotte yesterday. It doesn't seem possible she's gone.'

Cecily was crossing the great hall, going towards the library, when she saw Dr Ottoway and his nurse walking down the main staircase.

When he reached her, the doctor said, 'I would like to see His Lordship, Lady Mowbray. Would you be kind enough to take me to him?'

'Of course,' she answered, and glanced at the nurse.

Dr Ottoway said, 'Could Mrs Frayne wait here please, Your Ladyship?'

Cecily nodded, smiled at the nurse and indicated a chair where she could sit.

Leading the doctor into the library, Cecily hurried over to

Miles, who was at his desk. 'The doctor has seemingly finished his examination.'

Miles nodded and stood, turned to the doctor. 'Please, Dr Ottoway, let's go and sit over there near the fireplace.'

The doctor said, 'I believe your supposition about the Dowager Countess falling to be correct, Lord Mowbray. It is the only thing that could have happened.'

'I understand,' Miles replied. 'It was an unfortunate accident.'

'Yes, it was. Two weeks ago the Dowager Countess came to see me for a general check-up. At that time she told me she sometimes felt dizzy, and she also complained of being a little unsteady on her feet, that her legs felt tired. I did examine her for vertigo at that time, but she didn't have it. I think these minor symptoms had a lot to do with her age.'

'I agree with you,' Miles said. 'And yet she didn't show her age in any other way. She was as mentally alert as I am, and full of energy almost every day.'

'I know that, Lord Mowbray,' the doctor replied. 'Weakness of the legs and occasional dizziness can't be detected by anyone other than a doctor, Your Lordship.'

'I do want to thank you for coming so promptly, Dr Ottoway. I am most appreciative, as is Lady Mowbray. We would like you to attend the funeral on Wednesday morning with your wife. If you can spare the time, of course.'

'Mrs Ottoway and I will be there, m'lord. And I want to offer you and Her Ladyship our most sincere condolences for your loss. I know how much you are going to miss the Dowager Countess – such a fine woman.'

'Thank you,' Miles and Cecily said almost in unison.

'I believe the Dowager's death to have been caused by a blow to the side of her head due to a fall. As she'd been to see me recently, I am comfortable that the symptoms she described are consistent with a dizzy turn and a fall. Here is the death certificate.'

* * *

Little Skell Church was filled to the rafters. Everyone from the village and nearby High Clough and Mowbray had assembled early.

Alice Swann had invited Genevra and the entire Romany family to come, and they joined the other villagers at the back of the church.

Intermingled in the front pews were the Inghams and the Swanns, along with the Jollions, who were now related by marriage through their niece Paloma, Harry Swann's wife. Victoria sat next to Harry, and on her other side was Christopher Longdon in his wheelchair in the aisle. He had met Aunt Charlotte several times, and they had become friends, so he had asked to come.

Greta Chalmers, Aunt Dottie Swann Pinkerton and her husband, Howard, occupied a pew on the other side of the main aisle. Seated with them were Felix and Constance Lambert, and many members of the local aristocratic families.

In the front row were Miles, Cecily, and their children, David, Walter, Venetia and Gwen. She sat next to her aunt, Lady Diedre, her aunt's husband Will and her cousin Robin. Then came Charlie Ingham Stanton. His sister, Alicia Ingham Stanton, the twins, Thomas and Andrew, and their youngest sibling, Annabel, filled out the row. Adam Fennell was sitting next to Annabel at the end.

Adam was well put together as usual. Crisp white shirt. Black suit and tie. And he looked composed and in control. But a buzzing had started in his head. He felt he might be having one of his attacks that seemed to make life difficult. He hoped not.

For a moment he was unaware of what was going on around him. This was because he could hear Jack Trotter's voice at the back of his head, murmuring that he must be careful not to let his little fits take over. *You must be strong, lad. Seize control of yourself. You're clever. You can make it big . . . Seize control . . .*

He would do that now. But he couldn't understand why everyone was saying Aunt Charlotte had fallen. He hadn't wanted her to expose him. All his plans would evaporate if she did . . .

Annabel was saying something to him.

Taking a deep breath, focusing totally on Alicia's sister, he pulled himself together. 'Sorry, Annabel, I missed that.'

'I was just explaining that I have to go. People are still coming in, but I have to go and play now.' She smiled, stepped out of the pew, went down to the piano to one side of the altar. Within moments she was playing a hymn he vaguely knew: 'Jerusalem'.

Settling back against the wooden pew, Adam did as Jack said. He took control of himself. Glancing around, he was truly amazed to see so many people.

Cecily, her mother Alice, and Alicia had decorated the church with flower arrangements. Harry had insisted on helping them because he and Charlotte had always been involved in the gardens of Cavendon and the indoor decorations for special occasions. What they had created was breathtaking; they had outdone themselves on the altar. The arrangements behind and around the coffin, and on top of it, were magnificent.

Once everyone had settled down, Annabel stopped playing, and the vicar spoke for a few seconds.

It was Miles who gave the eulogy; he touched on different aspects of Charlotte's life, and how vitally important she had been to all of them. But he knew that he should not go over his allotted time, for others had begged to speak.

When Miles stepped down from the pulpit, it was Cecily's father, Walter Swann, who spoke next. Charlotte had been his cousin and he spoke of her devoted family ties, how she cared for every Swann on the estate. Harry, Cecily's brother, was the next Swann to stand up. After a touching remembrance of her, he told a few amusing stories about their gardening adventures, and there was laughter through the tears.

When it was Charlie's turn to speak, he did so in glowing terms about their matriarch. He then went on to explain that his mother, Lady Daphne, who had been very close to Aunt Charlotte, was so distressed by her unexpected death that she had become too ill to travel from Switzerland to Cavendon. He and his siblings were representing her and their father, Hugo Stanton.

At Miles's request, Charlie also mentioned that Lady Dulcie, her husband Sir James, and their children were absent because they were in Los Angeles. They had not been able to make it in time for the funeral.

Finally, it was Cecily who went up to the pulpit. In her clear and loving voice, she spoke of Charlotte Swann as her mentor, the woman who had put her on the right road and had helped her to reach for, and catch, her dream. Also the first Swann woman to marry an earl, before Cecily, joining the two families together in marriage. She then said she wanted to recite Aunt Charlotte's favourite psalm before Annabel played her favourite hymn, 'Amazing Grace'. It was the Twenty-Third Psalm, 'The Lord Is My Shepherd'.

As Miles looked up at his wife, listening to her lilting voice, he remembered that his sister Diedre had recited the same psalm at the funeral of Great-Aunt Gwendolyn during the war. Another great matriarch, he thought, and now it is my darling Cecily who must step into their shoes. And I know she will fill them, make them both proud.

# Thirty-Seven

Alicia felt so tired, almost unable to move. She sat in a chair near the fire in her bedroom, still wearing her dressing gown, sipping a cup of lemon tea.

She wondered if she was coming down with something, perhaps the flu, then realized that her exhaustion came from the events of the last few days.

The funeral yesterday had been trying for the entire family. Grief-stricken, shocked and sorrowing though they all were, they had had to stand up, ramrod straight and looking pleasant, as they greeted their many guests and all those who had come to mourn Aunt Charlotte. Even entertaining their luncheon guests had proved to be a strain of sorts.

A loud knocking on her bedroom door made her jump. Startled, Alicia put down the cup of tea and rose. She was walking towards the door when it opened and Adam stalked in looking grim.

She stared at him, amazed to see that he was dressed in a navy blue suit, white shirt and tie, and looked as if he was about to return to London.

He gaped at her, obviously flabbergasted to see her in her dressing gown. 'Why aren't you ready?' he demanded in an annoyed voice. 'I told you to be ready by eleven! And it's already eleven thirty. I've been waiting downstairs for half an hour.'

'Please calm down and lower your voice. Please,' Alicia answered in a steady tone. She was not accustomed to being spoken to so harshly, but she did not want a violent altercation to erupt.

Glaring at her, Adam said in a slightly quieter tone, 'How long will it take you to get dressed? In other words, what time can we leave?'

'I'm not leaving, Adam, and I have told you that several times in the last few days. The Ingham tradition is that we mourn our dead for a week after the funeral. The immediate family, that is.'

'Do you want me to stay then?' he asked, his manner abrupt.

'No, I don't. You can't anyway. You're not family.'

'Not family!' he shouted, losing his control. 'I am your fiancé! We are engaged. I *am* family.'

'I'm afraid not. You will be when we are married, but not until then. That's just the way it is around here. Lots of rules and regulations, dating back hundreds of years. We still live by them.' Alicia held herself very still.

He did not respond. He just stood there glaring at her, and she recognized that he was fuming inside. He had quite a temper, if provoked, and a lot of things seemed to do that lately. She stepped back, drawing closer to the fireplace.

Adopting a soothing tone and a calmer manner, Alicia said, 'I will be back in London next week, and we can spend the weekend together at your lovely flat in Bryanston Square. Just the two of us.' She smiled and added, 'You'll enjoy that, won't you?'

Adam heard Jack Trotter's voice at the back of his head. *Calm it, lad. You don't catch flies with vinegar*. He wished that buzzing in a corner of his mind would go away. He tried to take control of himself, but his anger burst through. 'I need you in London with me. Tonight! And you knew that. I am seeing the new backer, Terrence Vane, and he's expecting to meet you. Get dressed at once, we must be going.'

Adam sounded so furious that she took another step back.

Alicia was staring at his face. It was bright red with his fury, and those translucent eyes she liked so much were as cold as grey ice. Hard, unforgiving.

She was suddenly afraid of him; she drew closer to the hearth and knocked over the stand holding the poker and tongs. They made a clattering sound as they fell.

The noise seemed to break Adam's angry attitude. He shook his head, smiled at her, walked over to her, and touched her arm lightly.

'I'm so sorry, Alicia,' he said in a more conciliatory tone. He shook his head once more. 'I didn't mean to speak to you so rudely, so loudly. I'm afraid I'm somewhat charged up about Terrence Vane wanting to back *Revenge*. And he really was excited about meeting you tonight. Never mind. I'm sure he'll understand about poor Aunt Charlotte, and that you are currently in mourning.'

'I think he will,' she said lightly, endeavouring to be nice, yet wishing he would leave.

Adam stepped forward, put his arms around her and held her close. Then he kissed her on the mouth.

A shiver went through Alicia, and she gently extricated herself as soon as she could. 'Make a date with Terrence Vane for next Friday, and I will be there,' she promised him.

'That's my good girl,' he said, beaming at her.

No, not your girl at all, she thought. Not any more. Alicia said, 'Why don't we take him to Zigi's Club. I'm a member, you know.'

Alicia's bedroom overlooked the front entrance of Cavendon Hall. She went over to the window and, parting the curtains, looked out. She saw Adam's chauffeur-driven car disappearing down the driveway and was filled with relief.

After picking up the poker and tongs and righting the stand on the hearth, she returned to the chair and sank into it gratefully.

Her enormous relief that he had gone did not surprise her at all. His behaviour had troubled her for some weeks, and his presence in her family home for the past six days had been unbearable at times. She had never spent such an uninterrupted period of time with him before.

He had overstepped the mark on various occasions, been over-familiar with some members of her family, and behaved in a way that alarmed her sometimes. Furthermore, his possessiveness of her was suffocating, his jealousy unwarranted, and his erratic behaviour both troublesome and unnerving. And then there were his outbursts of temper.

A shiver ran through her as she thought of his rant only fifteen minutes ago. She had actually been frightened of him. For the first time, admittedly, but nonetheless fear had flared in her, making her step away from him, put distance between them.

Her mind went back to his arrival last Friday. He had been all kindness and charm, got on well with those at tea, and later at dinner. They were accepting of him, friendly.

Deep down, she knew that her aunt, Lady Diedre, did not like him at all. Not that her aunt displayed her dislike, she was far too well mannered. But instinctively Alicia had known that Diedre was not a fan of Adam Fennell.

That night they had made love, and he had been as passionate and sensual as usual, and she had responded to him. But the following day she admitted to herself that her sexual desire for him was on the wane.

She examined this now, wondering how she could have gone from sky-high sexual yearning and wanting him all the time, to this unexpected lessening of her need. Was it the beginning of indifference? Was it because he was possessive and difficult? Had those traits diluted his sensuous charms?

Quite suddenly, Alicia saw him as he had been a short while ago – his face bright red with fury, his translucent grey eyes as cold and hard as ice.

It struck her that he was not who he appeared to be. The charm was a front which disguised a difficult, troubled, and complicated man, and, very simply, they were not temperamentally suited for each other.

Adam Fennell was not right for her. She saw that very clearly now with objective eyes. Looking back to the week she had started the film, last September, she remembered that she had been emotionally fragile because of her split with Bryan Mellor.

Obviously, Adam had spotted this, and homed in on her with his kindness, his small gifts, his caring, and his obvious admiration for her.

Their sexual attraction for each other was real, almost overwhelming, and had developed with speed and genuine need. She had to admit she had been his willing partner in their wild, passionate, and fulfilling lovemaking in his bed.

A deep sigh escaped her. Then she pushed herself to her feet, went into her bathroom to get ready for the day. She looked down at her beautiful ring and twisted it around her finger. And she wondered how to break off with him, and discovered she had no idea.

Just before lunch, Alicia went into the blue and white sitting room and was happy to see Cecily was already there with her mother, Alice Swann. The older woman looked tired and drawn, and Cecily was pale, her face sombre.

Hurrying forward, Alicia greeted them both affectionately and sat down on the sofa next to Alice, taking hold of her soft hand. 'I'm so glad you're still here, Mrs Alice,' she said to the woman she had been named for. 'It's comforting to be with family in sad times.'

'Indeed it is, Alicia. It's always those who are left behind to grieve who suffer the most, and having family for support is so important,' Alice answered, patting her hand.

Looking intently at Alice and then at Cecily, Alicia said, 'I just wish my parents had been able to come. Especially my mother. She was always so close to Aunt Charlotte.'

'I know,' Alice responded. 'And I agree with you. It was Charlotte who saved her life, who supported her through some difficult times—'

'And as you did, too, Mam,' Cecily cut in swiftly. 'I haven't forgotten what you did. You hardly ever left her side when she was . . . ill that time.'

Alice smiled at her daughter, nodded, then went on quickly. 'Because of her closeness to Charlotte, I can only think that Lady Daphne is genuinely far too upset to travel, as Mr Hugo said.'

There was a moment of silence. Alicia glanced at Cecily and threw her a knowing look. 'Unless my mother is actually ill. By that I mean with some sort of *real* illness. I noticed things last year, before she went to Zurich with my father.'

'What things?' Cecily asked, looking surprised and frowning.

'Sometimes I noticed that her hands trembled. And she could be forgetful. I'd ask her about a date we'd made, and she seemed surprised. I could tell she was trying to remember, sorting through her mind, I thought.'

'You're not suggesting she has the onset of dementia, are you?' Alice Swann asked, sounding alarmed, staring at Alicia. 'Please don't tell me *that*.'

'I am telling you the truth about my mother's behaviour, Mrs Alice. But I'm not for a moment suggesting dementia, or Parkinson's disease for that matter. Frankly, I just don't know why she behaved like that. Charlie and I have discussed it several times and he thinks she was, very simply, truly stressed and exhausted when they left last summer.'

'I hope to God you're right!' Cecily exclaimed, and sat back in her chair, a worried expression on her face.

Her mother looked reflective for a few moments, and then she turned to Alicia. 'I know how busy you are, Alicia, preparing for the new film, but do you think perhaps you and Charlie should go and see your parents in Zurich?' she suggested gently. 'If only for a day? Find out for yourselves if Lady Daphne is genuinely ill. Might it not put your minds at rest? And it would be a comfort to her at this sad time.'

'I could go, I suppose, if Charlie is free. I wouldn't want to go without him.'

Cecily said, 'But what about Thomas and Andrew? I thought the twins went to see your parents all the time. Haven't they said anything about your mother's health?'

'They say she's all right, just tired, glad to be in Zurich. And away from Cavendon. But they're not a reliable source of information.' Alicia made a *moue* and finished, 'Remember, they're men, never pay attention to anything. And they work for our father, run the London end of his company. They'll hear whatever he tells them; they won't question it.'

At this moment, Miles came in with Cecily's father, Walter Swann, along with Miles's eldest son and heir, David, and his younger brother, Walter. David, who was now twenty, had come home from Oxford for the funeral, as had eighteen-year-old Walter, who had just started at the university.

After greeting everyone, Miles said, 'Let's go to the dining room. I saw most of the others lingering in the great hall, talking with Diedre, Will and Robin.'

Alicia fell in with her family as they left the sitting room, so glad to be alone with them. And she realized, at that precise moment, how much she had always been aware of Adam's presence, monitoring what he did and said.

Once they were all seated, and Eric had poured the white wine, Miles raised his glass and said, 'As we start our week of mourning for Aunt Charlotte, I want to say how pleased I am that this rule was made so long ago. Because it gives us a chance to comfort each other for a few days, come to grips with our sorrow, and remember Charlotte with love in our hearts. And then we can go back to our normal lives, surrounded by that love of family, and we can be at peace.'

They all lifted their glasses, and Gwen said, 'Can I toast with my water, Daddy?'

Smothering the laughter bubbling, Miles said, 'Of course you can, Gwen. That's most suitable.' He looked at her intently and added, 'And you're certainly not getting any white wine, so you can forget about that.'

The whole table laughed, and noticing that Gwen looked somewhat disappointed, Diedre, who was sitting next to her niece, asked, 'How is your little cat, darling?'

Gwen beamed at Diedre. 'She is better. When she sees the vet tomorrow I'm sure he'll pronounce her fit. I've looked after her very well, Aunt Diedre.'

Cecily said, 'Yes, you have.' Then she promptly changed the subject, started to speak about the turnout for the funeral yesterday, and what a tribute it had been to Aunt Charlotte.

Alicia was seated between Will Lawson, Diedre's husband, and her younger brother, Andrew. After chatting to both of them through the first course, she fell silent.

Lost for a while in her many whirling thoughts, she responded when spoken to, but for the main part Alicia remained the observer. Eventually, as her gaze went around the table, she saw her family in a different way today. She was looking at them through extremely objective and critical eyes.

There was nothing much to criticize and so much to admire, she decided. As her attention settled on Cecily's father, Walter, for a split second she saw Harry in him. And also in his namesake and grandson, Cecily's eighteen-year-old. She smiled inwardly when she turned to her favourite, her brother Charlie.

Although she knew there was a deep sadness inside him, he was being his usual cheerful self, chatting to every member of the family who were seated near him.

He looked good, she thought – rather handsome, in fact, with his soft wavy hair and sparkling eyes. He was wearing a black blazer and a white turtleneck sweater, a favourite ensemble of his. She often teased him about it, saying he looked like a

German U-boat commander, and he always had the good grace to laugh.

She looked at each of the men at the table in turn. Instantly she noticed they were simply dressed in their old tweed jackets and sports coats, some with woollen ties. Miles was dressed in a pale blue shirt with a darker blue silk Ascot tied around his neck, and a navy blazer. There was nothing pretentious or slick about any of them.

Alicia suddenly remembered a remark Diedre had made on Friday night, a remark she had accidentally overheard. Now she made up her mind to ask her aunt about that remark, and her opinion of Adam Fennell. Later. After lunch.

# Thirty-Eight

Alicia caught up with Lady Diedre as she walked across the great hall with Gwen, holding the child's hand, half bending, listening attentively to what she was saying.

'I'm sorry to interrupt, Aunt Diedre, but I do need to speak to you. If you're busy with Gwen, could we make a time for later, please?'

Turning around, Diedre saw the worried expression in Alicia's eyes, and she instantly looked down at Gwen and said, 'Do you mind if I join you in the staff dining room in a few minutes, Gwen darling?'

'That's all right, Aunt Diedre.' Looking up at Alicia, Gwen asked, 'Will you come too? To see Cleopatra, now that she's so much improved.'

'Course I will, darling,' Alicia agreed. 'Fifteen minutes and then we'll both come down, won't we?' She looked at Diedre, who nodded in agreement.

'Are you all right, Alicia?' Diedre asked, once the child had walked on, her eyes riveted on her other niece. 'What's this about?'

'I am all right – never better, actually. But I do need to make some decisions that are important and I need your advice. And

I really will come down to see the cat,' Alicia finished and grinned.

Diedre smiled. 'Well, where shall we go to be really private? The others have gone to the blue and white sitting room for coffee, as you know. But that doesn't mean Miles won't walk into the library if he needs something.'

'Would you mind coming up to my bedroom, Aunt Diedre? We can chat there.'

'Good idea, come on then, darling.' As she finished speaking, Lady Diedre headed for the staircase and the South Wing.

As she followed her aunt up the stairs, Alicia couldn't help thinking what great legs Diedre had, and a wonderful figure. Not bad for fifty-six, she thought admiringly.

Once they were seated in the two armchairs in front of the fire in Alicia's bedroom, Diedre said, 'All right, let's get down to brass tacks. Why do you need my advice?'

'I'll get to that in a moment. First, I want to ask you a question. I heard you make a remark to Uncle Will on Friday. It was something like "all Brylcreem and cologne and not much else". I wasn't eavesdropping. I simply accidentally heard it. Were you speaking about Adam?'

For a moment, Diedre considered lying, saying it wasn't about Fennell, then instantly changed her mind. It was her duty, as an older family member, to tell Alicia the truth, and it was also her way. She'd always been a straight talker.

'I'm sorry, Alicia. Yes, I was referring to Adam Fennell. "Brylcreem and cologne" indeed. It was rude of me, but to my mind he's an empty suit. There's not much else there.'

'I've always known instinctively that you didn't take to him, that you don't like him,' Alicia murmured, sitting back in the chair.

'No, I don't, and neither does Will.' She stopped herself. 'Very simply, Fennell's not good enough for you.'

'Thank you for being so honest with me, Aunt Diedre. He's begun to irritate me a lot, and he is erratic—'

'In what way?' Diedre interrupted, a brow lifting as she sat up straighter, very alert.

'He seems to be in control most of the time, and then he goes off in an erratic way, gets flustered. It's usually to do with his business. The financial part, losing a backer, or something like that.' Alicia paused, a troubled frown on her face. She was unconsciously fiddling with the engagement ring on her finger. 'Anyway, to get to the point, I'm going to break off with him.'

Diedre let out a huge sigh of relief. 'I'm so pleased to hear that and I know Will's going to applaud this decision on your part. He thinks he's slick, an opportunist, and he's asked me several times to tell you to be careful, not to rush into marriage.'

Diedre sat staring into the fire for a few seconds, and then turned to Alicia, took hold of her hand. 'There's so much at stake here, Alicia. Your whole life, in fact. You can't get stuck with a man like that. And you certainly don't need the hassle of getting a divorce and all *that* entails.'

'No, I don't. I must admit I've only myself to blame. At first I was very taken with him; there was an enormous pull . . .'

Alicia broke off, shrugged. 'It was intense for both of us . . .' Again she stopped, shaking her head. 'I'm not sure how to explain that overwhelming attraction.'

'You don't have to, Alicia. I've experienced that myself,' Diedre replied. 'And many years ago, just before the war, your Aunt DeLacy became involved with a man called Peter Musgrove, who was similar to Adam Fennell. Film-star looks, snappy dresser, a bit of a dandy. I couldn't stand him, but she was enamoured of him. At the time, I believed it was that same pull you're talking about now.'

'And what happened to this man Aunt DeLacy was so attracted to?'

'She managed to extricate herself. Eventually. And then he was called up, went off to fight in the war. The thing is, Musgrove was from a very good family; he went to Eton, all that stuff. He also helped DeLacy with the gallery. He was a great art dealer himself, sent her clients. But . . .' Diedre paused again, staring into the flames. She finally looked at Alicia and said, 'He was common. As common as muck, a phrase often used around these parts by the locals.'

'Is that what you think about Adam Fennell?'

'I do. Common as muck, whatever his background, and wherever he comes from. You've made the right decision. Now, do you need my advice about something else?'

'I do, Aunt Diedre. Do you think Charlie and I should go to Zurich? To see our parents? To find out exactly what's going on, especially with our mother?'

'I do think it's a good idea. I've rung up your father several times in the last six months, and made it seem normal, just asking if Will and I could go and stay with them for a weekend. Hugo puts me off by saying Daphne's still shattered about what he calls "the mess at Cavendon".'

Diedre took a deep breath, blew out air, then shook her head. 'It's like talking to a brick wall. You know as well as I do that your father blocks the way, hates my interference. They seem determined to have nothing to do with any of us who still spend time here.'

'When Charlie or I have asked the twins what's happening, they say everything's fine, but they're like trained seals, you know.'

Alicia said this in such a droll way that Diedre couldn't help laughing. After a moment, clearing her throat, she said, 'If you decide to go, don't tell them you're coming.'

'We won't.' Alicia stood up. 'Shall we go and see Gwen's cat, as we promised?'

'Oh yes, we'd better do that. Otherwise we'll never hear the end of it. If ever there was a true Ingham warrior woman, it's Gwendolyn. Our nine-year-old has a rod of steel through her spine, just like her forebears.'

* * *

Later that day, just before dinner, Alicia went along the bedroom corridor in the South Wing and knocked on Charlie's door, calling, 'It's *moi*.'

A moment later, he flung the door open, pulled Alicia into his arms and hugged her tightly. 'I'm so happy one of our ancestors had this idea about a week of mourning. It really helps to be with kith and kin, doesn't it?'

'Indeed it does,' Alicia said, following Charlie into his bedroom. Except for his jacket, he was ready to go down to dinner, as she was. 'I came up to tell you something,' she began, and then hesitated, before saying in a firm tone, 'I've decided to break off with Adam. I've realized I don't want to marry him . . . that it won't work.'

She sat down in a chair. Momentarily taken aback, Charlie stood staring at her.

'I'm surprised. And yet I'm not,' he said, after a long, thoughtful pause. 'I like Adam, he's got a certain charm, and he's well mannered. And rather clever in the film business. But in the last few days here, there were moments when I got an odd feeling about him . . .' Charlie let his sentence trickle away.

'What do you mean?'

'I thought that buried under all that charisma and bonhomie there might be a bit of a temper, and, occasionally, I wondered if his mind had drifted off somewhere. It was like he wasn't paying attention to me when I was speaking, that he wasn't focused.'

'All true. You *know* we had this hot-hot-hot love affair. But all that . . . *stuff* has begun to wane. I am going to tell him next week when we're back in London. After that, I think we should go to Zurich to see what's going on with Mother. I've been speaking to Aunt Diedre. She agrees.'

Charlie said, 'What exactly did she say?'

Alicia told him, and then repeated Diedre's opinion of Adam Fennell.

'I certainly trust *her* judgement about anybody. After her long career at the War Office.'

'You will go to Zurich with me, won't you, Charlie?'

'Nothing could stop me. Of course I will.'

# Thirty-Nine

In his usual precise and efficient way, Adam Fennell had made special plans for his supper with Alicia. Her week of mourning had finished, and she had returned to London last night.

Since it was Friday, and needing to be totally alone with her, he gave his staff the weekend off, telling them they could leave at five in the afternoon. His housekeeper had assured him there were plenty of cold dishes in the refrigerator, which he would enjoy if he was hungry.

He had come home very early from his office, bathed and changed into fresh clothes as usual. Now he sat at the desk in his library, thinking about their reunion. He had been angry with himself at different times this past week. How dumb he had been to quarrel with Alicia. And to lose his temper. That, most especially, had been ridiculous on his part. Control. I mustn't lose my control. Not ever with her.

At the back of his head, he heard Jack Trotter's voice: *Play it nice, lad. Always nice. Tantrums never work.*

And that was what he had done all week. He had sent her flowers. Phoned her every day. His manner had gone from apologetic and contrite to warm and tender.

She had responded in a lovely way, had been nice as always. And it was she who had suggested that they meet tonight; she who had suggested their rendezvous should be early. Five o'clock.

Now he smiled at himself, full of confidence and self-assurance. He had managed to make everything all right. And she obviously couldn't wait to see him. He also knew that within minutes of greeting her warmly, he could lure her into his bed.

Once there, she would be his. He would have complete control of her. He knew how to arouse her, how to tease her, how to withhold what she wanted until she was crying out, eagerly, begging him for it. *Ah, yes, Rosie, the barmaid at the Golden Horn, had taught him well. And so had Jack Trotter.* The buzzing in his head started all over again. He wished it would go away.

Stay calm, he told himself. Stay calm. Be controlled. Don't become erratic. Keep your temper. He took a deep breath, went across the hall into his bedroom, entered his dressing room, stared at himself in the mirror.

And smiled. He looked the best he had ever looked. She would not be able to resist him.

A few minutes later the bell rang, and he hurried through the hall and opened the front door, a smile on his face.

'Hello, Adam,' Alicia said, smiling back. 'I'm afraid I'm a little earlier than I said I would be.'

'The earlier the better, darling,' he replied, taking her arm, drawing her into the flat.

As he did so he could not help noticing that she was wearing a tailored suit and a silk blouse, not one of the clinging dresses he loved on her.

Then he reminded himself she had several of those here. And she wouldn't be needing clothes anyway. He bit back a smile, thinking of the weekend ahead of him.

Adam pulled her into his arms in the middle of the foyer and kissed her on the lips. After a moment she gently drew away from him, and said, 'Adam, can we go into the library for a moment or two? I need to speak with you about something rather important.'

She sounded so serious, he looked at her swiftly, his gaze intense. But she was smiling and seemed perfectly normal.

Nodding, taking hold of her arm, he led her into the library. She immediately sat down in the chair facing his desk, so he went behind his desk, sat opposite her.

A frown settled on his face. He asked, 'Why this sudden formality? What is this about?'

Alicia reached into her handbag and took out two red Cartier boxes. Placing them on the desk in front of him, she said in a steady voice, 'Adam, I'm so sorry to have to tell you this, but I cannot marry you. I am returning your ring and the diamond earrings you gave me at Christmas.'

He gaped at her, scowling, rendered totally speechless as he attempted to digest her words.

She said, 'I'm so sorry to break off our engagement, but I can't marry you, Adam. You see I know it won't work, it really won't. It's best this way – to part on friendly terms.'

Fury rushed through him as her words sank in. He jumped up, went around his desk and stood over her, glaring down into her face.

'You cannot break off our engagement! I won't let you humiliate me, make a fool of me in front of the whole world. Everyone knows we're engaged. We're *the* couple, and you know it. *I won't let you do this to me.*'

He was shouting now, and she saw the cold look in his translucent grey eyes, the hardness on his face, the tight set of his jaw, and she recognized that anger was bubbling up inside him. She knew she had to get away.

Somehow she managed to slide off the chair, clutching her bag, and stepped away from him before he could stop her. She felt better on her feet. *Safer*. There was a deadly look in his eyes now, and she noticed he was shaking with rage.

'I must go now, Adam,' she said, trying to edge past him into the foyer. But he blocked her, grabbed her arm very tightly and hissed, 'If you leave me, I will break you. I will ruin your career. Ruin your life. Nothing will ever be the same again for you.'

Alicia was in complete control of herself, and she answered in a stern tone. 'You cannot do either. Please don't attempt to frighten me. I am an Ingham, and Ingham women are fearless.'

'Ingham. Always the bloody Inghams. Who the hell do you all think you are? *You* are the daughter of a whore. *Yes*, a well-known whore.'

A sardonic smile slipped onto his face. 'Hugo Stanton is not your father. Nobody knows who your father is, Miss Alicia Hoity-Toity Ingham. Wait until I give this story to the newspapers. I can just see the headlines. Here's one of them: "Alicia Stanton is the daughter of a tart".'

He laughed in her face. 'I'm going to teach you a lesson you'll never forget, you fucking bitch. You're not going to do this to me, shame me, make me a laughing stock.'

'I don't know what you're talking about. It's all nonsense. Of course Hugo Stanton is my father.'

'No, no, he isn't! Ask your mother. And, in the meantime, if you want me to keep your scandalous past a secret, you have to pay me. Pay me a lot. But first I am going to have a huge taste of you.' He laughed. 'You know you love it. Just like your mother.'

Before she could dodge out of his way, he grabbed her arm, dragged her out of the library and across the foyer to his bedroom.

He pushed her down on the bed, threw himself on top of her, endeavouring to kiss her, one hand pulling up her skirt.

Alicia struggled desperately, managed to slap him hard on the face. Instantly he pulled away, startled. She pushed her knee into his crotch, and he shouted out in anger and sudden pain. He leaned over her, a steely look in his eyes. Swiftly she brought up her right arm and her clenched fist and hit him on the jaw, stunning him. In her haste to get off the bed, she slipped and fell onto the floor. Alicia was in good shape; she picked herself up and rushed out into the foyer. Only to be caught by him a moment later.

Standing facing her, holding her by both arms, his grip strong,

Adam said in a cold, controlled voice: 'I have your secret. I can release it to the world. Or I can forget it. But you have to pay me. I want twenty thousand pounds. Yes or no? It's your call.'

Alicia looked into his face, her eyes narrowing, and she knew at once that her suspicions about his backers disappearing had been correct. He was out of money. Needed it badly.

Taking a deep breath, she said, 'I don't have twenty thousand pounds. I won't pay blackmail.' Playing for time, she said, 'But perhaps Charlie could help me out.'

Adam began to laugh, suddenly enjoying this negotiation. 'Then let's give him a ring, shall we? I'm sure he's in London. Little brother is never far away from you. I've often wondered about that strange relationship you have with him.'

Ignoring the ridiculous taunt, Alicia replied, 'You're correct about him being not far from me. He's outside, actually. If you open the door, you'll see him.'

Adam, knowing there was no way she could leave his flat, let go of her and walked over to the front door. She had spoken the truth. There was Charlie, leaning against a car, smoking a cigarette.

'Come in, Charlie,' Adam called. 'Your big sister needs your help.'

As Charlie walked in and closed the door behind him, his journalist's instinct kicked in. He took in everything in one sweeping glance around the foyer.

They both looked a bit ruffled, as if there had been a struggle, and the atmosphere was very strange. He was filled with relief that Alicia was obviously unharmed, leaning against the doorframe of the library. But she looked very pale and scared.

He noticed that Adam was controlled, but he sensed that fury was brewing inside him. Charlie saw it in those icy grey eyes and the rigid set of his mouth.

'So why does my sister need my help, Adam? Alicia wishes to break off the engagement. Accept that; be a gentleman about this situation.' Charlie walked forward as he spoke.

'Oh, I will. I will indeed. But I've just informed your sister that

I will ruin your family for what she's just done to me. You see, I know a secret – the big secret of Cavendon.'

'Really? Do you wish to share it with me?' Charlie looked from Adam to Alicia, who raised a brow and shook her head.

'It's all nonsense, Charlie,' she said. 'He's mad, crazy.'

Ignoring her comment, Adam continued, 'I not only wish to share it with you, I will share it with the world. *You* won't like the headlines, that I do know.'

'And the big secret is?'

Adam told him.

Charlie laughed, shaking his head, and laughed again.

Adam said, 'Your mother got pregnant in the spring of 1913. She never told anyone who the father was. She was just seventeen and very promiscuous. So she probably didn't know which man it was. Then onto the Cavendon stage walks Hugo Stanton, the long-lost cousin come home. The cousin who wants to be back in the fold. A sudden, very quick marriage to the Lady Daphne within a few weeks of his arrival, surprising many Inghams. Baby born in January 1914, supposedly premature. They called the baby Alicia.'

'None of this is true! Where did you get this stupid story from?' Charlie demanded, his anger apparent.

'Bryan Mellor. He said one of the family told him in confidence about Alicia's birth when he was courting her.'

'This is ridiculous, Adam. And do you honestly think any newspaper in Fleet Street is going to print this outrageous story? I'm one of them, for God's sake, and well liked by my colleagues. Furthermore, they'll know it's a load of rubbish.'

'There's always a scandal sheet and a reporter with his hand out. I'll get it printed. And the whole world will know what trash the Inghams really are.'

Charlie remained silent, his mind working. He was suddenly recalling odd bits of gossip he had heard amongst family members over the years. His father's sudden arrival at Cavendon. His parents' swift marriage after only a few weeks of knowing each other. The so-called premature birth.

He knew his mother was not promiscuous, and that his parents had truly fallen in love. Still, he knew the world was a dangerous place. Did he dare take a chance and walk away with Alicia safely on his arm? Blackmail, he thought. Adam's out to blackmail us, and he might not stop. But can I take a chance with our reputation? And with Alicia's? Mud slung sticks a bit: that he knew for sure.

'How much do you want for your silence?' Charlie now asked in a steady tone. He was furious inside. Not only with Adam, but with himself for succumbing to this hideous man's request. Nonetheless, he felt he had no choice.

'Twenty thousand pounds,' Adam said, a triumphant note in his voice.

'I don't think we ought to do this, Charlie,' Alicia exclaimed, staring across at her brother. 'It's blackmail. And the story's not true.'

'What you're saying is correct, Alicia,' Charlie answered. 'On the other hand, he's correct in that there will be a scandal sheet that will run with it. And mud sticks. It's important for us to protect the family name. Are you with me on this?'

She simply nodded. 'I must get my handbag.' She ran into the bedroom where she'd dropped it and returned a moment later.

While she was gone, looking at Adam, Charlie said, 'I won't pay what you want. I can't. I will give you four thousand. That's it.'

'I'll pay half,' Alicia said.

Adam said, 'I want the cheques now. And don't think of cancelling them on Monday. If you do, I'll go to the newspapers. And you'll face the headlines.'

'We struggled, Charlie. I fought him off. He tried to rape me,' Alicia said, and leaned against her brother in the back of the chauffeur-driven car. 'Actually, you would have been proud of me. I landed a good right hook on his jaw.' She was shaking a little, her voice weaker than usual.

'I am proud of you. God, I'm relieved that we'd agreed I would be waiting for you outside. And that you're all right,' Charlie answered, his jaw set.

'I'm a bit bedraggled and shaky, but happy that we got that over with.' Alicia smoothed down her hair. She frowned. 'Unfortunately, we've made ourselves a bad deal, you know. He's a blackmailer.'

'And a mentally sick man, in my opinion,' Charlie said, reaching to put his arm around her and hold her closer. 'Thank God you came to your senses about him, saw him for what he was. I'm afraid we were all fooled; we fell for his charms.'

'I was beginning to understand that he was running out of backers. I'm absolutely sure he needs money.' She bit her lip. To think she had been engaged to the man.

'Let's be thankful I managed to get us on the flight to Zurich at the last minute. Adam won't be able to find either of us this weekend, and you'll be safe. We'll be landing late, so we'll have to stay at the Baur au Lac Hotel tonight, which will give us a chance to think about this and how to deal with him, then go and visit our parents tomorrow morning. You didn't tell him where we were going, did you?'

Alicia shook her head. 'No, I only spoke about the engagement. What a relief. As Aunt Charlotte used to say: '*it was meant to be*.'

'God winked,' Charlie said.

Later that evening, on the flight to Zurich, Charlie suddenly said, 'If Fennell does need money desperately, four thousand isn't going to get him far.'

'I know. But I gave him back the diamond engagement ring, and the diamond ear clips. They're very valuable. From Cartier. He'll sell them, and he'll attempt to get new backers for *Dangerous*, and the other film, *Revenge*.'

'So you think he'll stick around London?' Charlie asked.

Alicia nodded. 'More than likely, he's created quite a front for himself.' An involuntary shiver swept over her, and she said, 'I just want him to stay away from me.'

Charlie leaned closer to his sister and murmured, 'That's why I paid the blackmail money. I knew he would go to the newspapers, find one scandal sheet who'd use it. He's that bad. And a desperate man will do anything to survive. I couldn't take a chance by walking away, Alicia. I just had to get us safely out of his flat.'

'I know. I also know blackmailers always come back, Charlie. Be prepared.'

# Forty

'I know the original reason we were coming to Zurich was to discover the truth about our mother's health,' Charlie said. 'And you know how weird Father is about that.' He pushed his coffee cup away and stretched out his artificial leg. 'We have another reason to be here now, and that is to ask them about your biological father. Is it Hugo or not?'

'Charlie, what are you saying? You don't believe that the hateful Fennell stumbled onto something genuine, do you?' Alicia asked, alarm making her voice rise. 'Surely it can't be so.' She gazed at her brother, her eyes widening. 'You don't think it could be the truth, do you?' Her breakfast sat in front of her, untouched. All the drama had robbed her of her appetite.

Charlie did not answer for a moment. The two of them sat in the beautiful dining room of the Baur au Lac Hotel, overlooking the gardens and the lake. Finally, he turned to his sister and said, 'No, I don't believe it's true – but, to be honest with you, I've heard bits of odd family gossip over the years.'

Sitting up straighter in the chair, looking extremely worried, Alicia took a deep breath and asked, 'Do you mean about our mother? Our father? Or me?'

'Not you, never. And the gossip hasn't been about who your father is; rather it's been about the quickness of it all, those many years ago.'

'Could you please fill me in, Charlie? *Please.*'

'There's not much to tell, other than this. Hugo Stanton came back to Cavendon in 1913. He had been living in America, where he worked with an important real-estate tycoon, Benjamin Silver, and made his fortune. He also married the boss's daughter, so to speak: Loretta, his first wife—'

'You mean our father was married before?' Alicia sounded aghast, and gazed at Charlie in disbelief.

'Yes. But I was told by Aunt Charlotte never to mention it. Apparently our mother didn't like it to be known that there had been a wife before her.'

'So what happened to Loretta?'

'After her father's death, Hugo and Loretta moved to Switzerland. She was very ill with tuberculosis, and she died. Hugo inherited her fortune, bequeathed to her by her father, and the villa. Our father became very wealthy indeed.'

'You mean our Villa Fleurir was Loretta's villa first?'

'I believe so, yes.'

'Phew!' Alicia shook her head. 'Why did a first wife have to be kept a secret?'

'God only knows, and he won't split,' Charlie answered. 'Anyway, let's go back to Hugo's arrival at Cavendon. Apparently, he took one look at Lady Daphne the day he arrived and that was it. A *coup de foudre*, the French call it – struck by a bolt of lightning, I believe we would say. Apparently he asked our grandfather's permission to court her, and the Sixth Earl talked to Daphne, and she agreed to a courtship. And wham, they discovered true love – and, let's face it, their union has endured.'

'But what's so wrong about that? Why would anyone gossip about that?' Alicia asked, sounding mystified.

'They got married very quickly. In a big rush, really. Some family members, especially the women, wondered why it was such a hasty marriage. It would look like a shotgun marriage, they said.'

'Perhaps they thought she'd been a naughty girl and slept with Hugo and was pregnant.'

'That is a possibility, yes, especially since you were called a premature baby.'

'I was?' She frowned. 'Why haven't you told me any of this before?'

'Because none of it mattered. It only came up because of something I'd said about the Villa Fleurir here in Zurich, and Aunt Charlotte corrected me. Then the story about Loretta came out. It was nothing specific. Honestly.'

'And I've never been called a bastard?'

'Don't be so silly, of course not. And I honestly believe you and I have the same biological father.'

Alicia sat quietly for a few moments. Her mind was whirling.

'Then I suppose we must ask. If nothing else, to close down this blackmail threat. You will let me bring it up, won't you, Charlie? I really do have to hear it from their lips.'

'I know you do, and you certainly will.'

'I've hired a car and driver,' Charlie told Alicia as they walked through the lobby of the Baur au Lac. 'I don't want to be dependent on our parents, and their getting a car for us, and all that organizing they're prone to do.'

'I'm glad you did. Now, before we go outside and get into that car, let's go over our modus operandi once again.'

'Good idea,' Charlie agreed. 'After we've asked about Mother's health, and the usual, I am going to be the one who says we've come to Zurich to ask them some questions, because of certain rumours you've heard about your birth. Okay?'

Alicia nodded. 'Then you stop there, and I ask my father if he is my father. Or am I a bastard?'

'You don't actually mean to say exactly *that*, do you? Use that awful word.'

'Not really, but I may. It might be necessary, to shock them. You know they live in their own dream world. They exist for each other. I'm surprised they ever had children.'

Charlie burst out laughing. 'That's what happens when you spend most of your life making love.'

Alicia grinned. 'Do you remember when we were little and we couldn't understand why they were always in bed? You told me you thought they needed a lot of sleep because they were older than us.'

'I do, yes. So come on, let's go and face the lions in their den.'

When Charlie and Alicia arrived at the Villa Fleurir, it was Anna, the housekeeper, who opened the front door to them. She exclaimed in surprise and shook their hands, starting to speak.

Before she could say anything, Charlie brought a finger to his lips, '*Shush*. They don't know we're coming.'

Anna nodded, still smiling, and opened the door wider. To Charlie, she said in a low tone, 'Your parents are sitting outside. It's such a nice day.'

A moment later, when they walked out onto the loggia to greet Hugo and Daphne, their parents were totally astonished.

So much so that Lady Daphne, absolutely speechless, remained seated. Hugo jumped up at once, hurried forward. He hugged Alicia and Charlie, and asked, 'Why didn't you let us know you were coming?'

Charlie said, 'We wanted to surprise you, Father, and you too, Mother.'

By this time Lady Daphne had risen, and she was full of smiles as she went to kiss Charlie and then her daughter. 'You look lovely, Alicia, and so spring-like in your pink suit.'

'Thank you,' Alicia murmured, and followed her parents, who were returning to their chairs.

Charlie and Alicia sat down on a loveseat opposite them, and exchanged pleasantries with their parents while Anna fussed around bringing fresh coffee and Swiss pastries. No one mentioned Cavendon; they stuck to talking about Alicia's films and Charlie's work.

Alicia couldn't get over how well Daphne looked. Relaxed, rested, her beauty in full bloom, even though she was now in her early fifties. Well enough to travel to Charlotte's funeral, Alicia thought, unexpectedly fuming inside, wondering why her mother had ducked it. Charlotte had been such a close friend to her mother. Well enough to have come to Cavendon for Christmas. She found she couldn't bring herself to join in any more conversation, her emotions threatening to spill over.

There was a natural pause and it was Charlie who spoke first.

He said in a level, easy tone of voice: 'We wanted to come and see you anyway, wondering how you were. It's been such a long time since we saw you. But we also do have another purpose.' He looked from his mother to his father, and continued. 'We would like to ask you a couple of questions, because Alicia and I have heard some disturbing rumours – comments, if you will – about Alicia's birth.'

Alicia, watching her mother intently, saw how taken aback she was by Charlie's remarks. Also, how her gaze flicked immediately to her father. Hugo, obviously as surprised as Daphne, said, 'I'm not sure I understand you, Charlie. What kind of rumours?'

Before Charlie could answer, Alicia felt her emotions overwhelm her and exclaimed, 'I've been told you're not my biological father. Is that true?'

The shock flooding Lady Daphne's face was palpable, and Hugo's loving expression had changed to one of absolute horror. Neither of their parents spoke; they simply gaped at them.

'It's a lot of nonsense,' Hugo finally answered vehemently, shaking his head. 'I *am* your father, Alicia.'

Alicia stared at her mother, and said in a demanding voice, 'Is

Hugo telling the truth? Is he my father? Or did you have a lover who made you pregnant?'

Her gaze went to Hugo, and she continued in the same hard voice, 'And then *you* came along, the knight in shining armour, and married her swiftly to save the Ingham name. Is that the way it really was, *Father*?'

All the colour had left Hugo's face. He was extremely pale and trembling slightly, when he exclaimed angrily, 'Whoever it is who has told you this is lying. *I am your father.*'

Although Alicia had grave doubts about Fennell's story, and had come to Zurich with an open mind, believing Hugo was indeed her father, there was something about her mother that now annoyed Alicia.

Her mother's apparent good health? The fact that she hadn't come to the funeral? Or was it that look on her face?

Alicia frowned, stared hard at Daphne, and saw a certain guarded quality there. Perhaps that was it. She looked so pleased with herself and unaffected by the world around her, it seemed.

'I want the truth from you, Mother. I think I deserve to know who fathered me.'

After a long silence, Lady Daphne began to speak, waving her hand at Hugo as he tried to interrupt her.

'Listen to me, Alicia, and try to understand what I am saying. When you plant seeds in a garden, that's an easy task. But once the seeds begin to grow, you have to tend them, nurture them, look after them, cherish them even, and—'

'I don't want to know about gardens,' Alicia cut in harshly. 'Tell me who planted his seed in you?'

Charlie said, 'Please, Alicia, calm down! Don't become so angry when you don't know anything at all. Be nice.'

'It's all right, Charlie,' Lady Daphne said quietly. 'I shall tell your sister what she needs to know. It is her right.'

Taking a deep breath, she plunged in. 'I was seventeen. Young, innocent, inexperienced. I had no boyfriends. But I did have a friend called Julian Torbett, who lived nearby. One spring afternoon I went over to visit him, but he had gone out. I returned to Cavendon through the woods. I was halfway home when I felt something hit the middle of my back. It was as if a huge sack of potatoes had struck me. I fell forward, hard, hit my face on some rocks, and then rough hands turned me over. I was staring up at a huge man, bundled in thick clothes. His face and head were wrapped in a dark scarf. I could hardly see his eyes even. He tore my jacket and blouse. And then he raped me. Before he left me, he told me that if I ever told anyone I was raped in the Cavendon woods, he would have my mother and Dulcie killed.'

Lady Daphne paused, her voice cracking slightly, and took a deep breath. No one spoke. They knew she had not finished her story.

At last she said, 'I lay there unable to move. I felt bruised and broken. He had handled me so roughly, and I was in total shock. A short while later, gentle hands were touching my face, saying my name softly. I realized it was Genevra, the gypsy girl. She helped me to straighten my clothes the best she could, then led me out of the woods, half carrying me, in fact. It had started to rain, and she wiped my face with her scarf and patted my hand, soothed me. Before she left me, she said I should tell everyone I had fallen. She repeated that several times. Later, I realized she had been witness to my assault.'

Charlie was aghast and he glanced at Alicia and then at Daphne. He said, 'What a horrendous thing to happen to you, Mother. However could you bear such a shocking and heinous assault? How did you manage to recover?'

'With the help of Alice Swann and Charlotte. Only the Swanns knew; no one else – not even my parents. But when I realized I was pregnant, they had to be told. Again it was Alice and Charlotte who saw me through that ordeal. Charlotte also came up with a plan to take me abroad to have the baby. But that didn't become necessary. Because Hugo Stanton, my father's cousin, came back to Cavendon after a long absence. He fell in love with me, as I did with him. And that's the full story.'

Lady Daphne sat back in her chair; tears glistened in her blue eyes and she groped for a handkerchief in her pocket.

'Not quite the whole story,' Hugo said, his voice now firm and confident. 'I did fall in love at first sight with the beautiful Lady Daphne, and sought Charles's permission to court his daughter. He asked her, and she agreed to my courtship. However, she did tell me about the rape, and what had happened to her in the woods at Cavendon. She thought I should know that she was carrying another man's child. She also explained that she would not give up the child for adoption, because it was hers – an Ingham.'

He looked across at Alicia, and finished softly, 'She loved you even before you were born, Alicia, and she wanted you, and I knew she would never let you go. You were her child. Please understand that. And I agreed the child she was carrying would be *ours*.'

Alicia sat stone still. She was stunned, and she couldn't help saying, 'But why didn't either of you tell me the truth? When I was old enough to know. I would have understood.'

Hugo said, 'Perhaps you would have – you're very intelligent, a true Ingham in every way. But why burden you with it? Why burden your mother with reliving it?'

Standing up, Hugo went over to Alicia, took her hands and pulled her to her feet. Gazing into her face, so like her mother's, he confided, 'Only a few minutes after you were born, I held you in my arms, and I saw the tiny little puffs of blonde hair, the blue eyes, and I fell in love all over again. *With you.* I've loved you all your life. You know, darling, any man can so easily and quickly plant his seed in a woman. But it's what he does after the child is born that makes him a true father. A good father. Or a bad father. I have tried to be a good father to you, and I think I succeeded. I hope so.'

Alicia saw the bright tears in Hugo's eyes, and she welled up herself. She took a step forward and went into his outstretched arms. They stood there together, holding onto each other tightly until their tears finally stopped.

Once Alicia was calmer, Hugo released her. She walked over to her mother, sat down in a chair, reached out, took Daphne's hand in hers. 'I'm sorry I spoke so rudely, so harshly. I really am. And now that I know your story, I think you must have been very brave to go through what you did. I have just two questions, if you would answer them.'

'I will try, darling.'

'Who was the man who did that to you?'

'I knew that it was Richard Torbett, the brother of my friend Julian. But I never told anyone, except your father. And he kept my secret.'

'Is he still out there? Is he alive?'

'No, he's not alive. Your father happens to know he was killed in the trenches in France in the First World War.'

Alicia simply nodded her head, and continued to hold her mother's hand very tightly, beginning to understand so much about her parents and their life together.

# Forty-One

Charlie walked along the corridor to the Features Department at the *Daily Mail*, where Elise Steinbrenner now worked, and knocked on Elise's door before walking straight in.

She was sitting at her desk; she looked up and smiled brightly when she saw him. 'Hello, Charlie.'

He grinned at her, and asked, 'How are you, ducks? Liking the new job, I hope.'

'I do, and I don't know why you call me "ducks".'

'It's an affectionate term, maybe Cockney, and I like it, don't you?'

'Since it's you saying it, yes.'

Charlie sat down in a chair, and said, 'I need your help. Urgently. Are you busy with a special feature at the moment?'

'Jimmy has given me a series to do. About different aspects of the upcoming Festival of Britain next year. The building work that's going on now, like the South Bank, the repairing of the bomb sites in cities, that sort of thing. But I can help you. What do you need?' She had swivelled her chair and sat staring at him, her eyes questioning.

'I'd like you to do some research, look for anything you can find on Adam Fennell and—'

'Alicia's fiancé?' she exclaimed, cutting in. 'Why him?' Elise stared at Charlie, her expression puzzled.

'He's no longer her fiancé. She broke off her engagement to him this past weekend. Keep that under your hat, will you, please? For the moment, anyway. Fennell hasn't accepted it very well.'

'Do you think he might be troublesome? He seemed like a nice enough chap when I met him at Greta's house.'

'He's so charming he could sell ice to the Eskimos, as the saying goes. Although I prefer the expression "charm the pants off any woman". I think he might be a bit of a Lothario. I also suspect he's . . .' Charlie stopped, grimaced, and finished, 'A bit touched in the head. I don't know how dangerous, mind you, but you never really know about anyone, do you?'

'No, you don't. You and I see a lot, since we're journalists. We're not crime reporters, but we are on the inside of everything. And it's a dangerous world out there.'

'To be correct about this, perhaps you ought to tell Jimmy Maze you're helping me out,' Charlie suggested.

'It's not a problem, honestly, Charlie. Jimmy's nice, easy-going and he likes me. That's why he got me moved up here to work in Features. And he'd do anything in the world for *you*, Charlie.'

'This is what I need. As much as you can get on Fennell. Where he comes from. Where he went to school. And university. How he got started in the film business. Who his backers are. In the past, and now. I do know a few things. For instance, he worked for Sir Alexander Korda for a couple of years. Then again, he often goes to New York. If anyone asks you why you're doing a story on him, say it's because *Broken Image*, his latest movie, is coming out in a few months' time. That's your basic cover.'

'I get it. Just in case Adam Fennell smells a rat?'

'Correct.'

'I'll start here, in the Clippings Library, look in the folders, see what's already been written about him.'

'Thanks, Elise. If you have to go out anywhere, take cabs, make your life easier. I'll cover your expenses on this, obviously.'

Rising, he walked across the room, kissed her on the cheek, gave her a cheery grin and went back to his own office.

Seating himself at his desk, Charlie thought about Fennell and the cheques he and Alicia had given him. There was no doubt in his mind that Fennell would come back, asking for more. Blackmailers were like that. Even if Charlie had it, he wouldn't give Fennell any more money. But he didn't have it. And neither did Alicia. They now had to go into their savings to pay their bills.

He glanced at his watch. It was noon. He must leave immediately, take a cab to the Savoy Hotel and the Grill Room. That was where he was meeting Inspector Howard Pinkerton of Scotland Yard. Uncle Howard to them all, and married to a Swann, Aunt Dottie, who worked with Cecily and Greta Chalmers.

Charlie had asked for a quiet corner table in the Grill Room of the Savoy Hotel, and the maître d', who knew him well, had been most obliging. He had arrived in the courtyard of the Savoy at exactly the same moment Howard had been alighting from his cab. They had laughed about their good timing as they shook hands, and went into the lobby together.

Now they were seated at that quiet corner table, each enjoying a dry martini, and catching up on family matters and on Charlie's career as a historian.

'I'm certainly looking forward to reading your book on Dunkirk,' Howard said. 'I think that's going to be a big seller. Very timely: five years after the end of the war. Anyway, cheers again, Charlie, and lots of luck with the book. Now, you said you needed to tell me something important. So out with it. How can I be of help?'

'Do you mind if we order first, Uncle Howard? The story's a bit . . . complicated, shall we say.'

'That's fine with me, and I know what I'm having. Their wonderful roast beef on the trolley.'

'And to start?'

'Smoked salmon, please. I can't resist.' Charlie beckoned to a hovering waiter and gave their order, choosing the same as Howard. Turning to him, he asked, 'Would you like wine with lunch?'

Howard shook his head. 'One martini for me. That's my limit. It's my day off, but I don't like to drink too much at lunchtime.'

'I'm with you there.' Charlie took a sip of the martini, then again turning slightly on the banquette, he looked intently at Howard and said, 'I know you're not a Swann, but you're married to one. I would like to have the same confidentiality the other Inghams have with the Swanns. Can you do that?'

Howard nodded. 'I know you had to ask that, Charlie, but it goes without saying that I'll keep all of your secrets. I had that arrangement with Great-Aunt Gwen, you know. Or perhaps you don't know. And she and I solved many Ingham family problems together. So, what's this all about?'

Charlie filled him in regarding the broken engagement, the strange behaviour of Adam Fennell, and the suspicion both he and Alicia harboured about Fennell's mental state. Then he explained that Fennell had come up with a preposterous story about Alicia's birth and Hugo not being her biological father, careful to make it sound incredible. He then mentioned Fennell's threat about giving the tale to a scandal sheet to blacken the Ingham name. 'Headlines galore' was the way Charlie put it.

Finally, taking his courage in both hands, Charlie confessed that he and Alicia had paid Fennell off with cheques to make him go away.

Howard had listened with intense concentration; even after hearing about the blackmail payment, he had remained silent. Now he was running all the information through his well-trained mind. After a few swallows of the martini, he said, 'I do wish you hadn't done that. Paid him off. But you did, so that's that. He may very well come to you again. Blackmailers usually do. If he does, make a date with him, and let me know. I'll be there and I'll soon scare the hell out of him. So, *why* did you pay him, Charlie?'

'I know how damaging newspaper stories can be, especially in a sleazy scandal sheet. I'm also aware that mud sticks, no matter what, and could really damage Alicia's profile. And there was gossip years ago, when my father returned to Cavendon. We all know the legendary story of how he fell in love with my mother instantly, and she with him. And that they married very quickly – too quickly for some, I'm afraid. They probably thought Hugo had made her pregnant.'

'I know all that, and I suppose even a bit of old gossip can be blown out of proportion, made to seem like something else entirely. The papers certainly love an aristocratic scandal. Or anything about an actress like Alicia. So let us focus on Fennell. What do you know about him?'

Charlie laughed hollowly and exclaimed, 'Not very much. In fact, I would go so far as to say nothing at all. Other than that he's charming, plausible, good looking, a bit of a dandy, and apparently he's been rather successful in the film business. Alicia fell for him, and we all took to him, and look where we are now.'

'The victims of a clever con man, I suspect.' Howard shook his head. 'I'll be at the Yard the rest of the week, and I'll do a bit of digging, see if I can find anything on him. Anything criminal, that is.'

'That's very good of you, Uncle Howard, thank you. I just want to protect Alicia.'

Glancing at Charlie swiftly, Howard threw him an odd look. 'Do you think Fennell is dangerous?'

'I don't know. However, he can act very strangely. And he has a nasty temper.'

'Tell me everything you can think of about him, give me a profile of him. You're a brilliant newspaperman, you can do that more easily than most.'

Charlie filled him in as best he could. Between courses he wracked his brain, endeavouring to remember every little detail he had noticed about Adam Fennell, however small or insignificant it might seem.

Eventually he stopped and said, 'That's about it, Uncle Howard.'

Howard looked at him for a moment. 'You've just given me the profile of a psychopath,' he announced grimly.

'A psychopath!' Charlie repeated, immediately looking worried. 'Oh my God.'

'Where is Alicia? In London?'

'No, she's at Cavendon.'

'Tell her to stay there. I want to know a lot more about Fennell. I'll put a tail on him. Where does he live?'

Charlie told him, then asked, 'You don't think Alicia is in danger, do you?'

'No, I don't, not at the moment anyway. Nevertheless, it's best to be careful.'

Alicia and Cecily had just met for tea in the yellow sitting room, when Gwen came in carrying her cat, Cleopatra.

'If you don't put that cat down and let her *walk*, I shall send her to the Cat Orphanage,' Cecily announced, staring at her nine-year-old. 'And where will that leave you?'

'At the Cat Orphanage with Cleo. Where is it?' Gwen asked.

'Don't be cheeky, Gwen, you know I don't like bad behaviour, rudeness!' Cecily said quietly. 'You're damaging the cat.'

Gwen stared at her mother, looking alarmed. 'What do you mean?'

Before Cecily could answer, Alicia took over. 'A cat or a dog is like a human being in many ways. We have legs, and they have legs, and we must all walk. If we don't, we get stiff, and our muscles get weak, and soon we are helpless,' Alicia explained. 'Now, you don't want Cleo to be a helpless little thing, do you?'

'No, I don't. I love her, Alicia.'

'Then put her on the floor. Anyway, she shouldn't be on your lap when we're eating. That's bad manners.' Alicia glanced at Cecily.

'Well said,' Cecily responded, and smiled to herself as Gwen placed the cat on the floor, somewhat reluctantly. 'Look, you see, she's now running away!' Gwen cried, and made to get up.

Alicia prevented her little cousin from leaving the chair. 'Stop being so silly, so possessive of the cat. She's got to run and jump and be happy. Holding her tightly next to your body is making her *unhappy*.'

'Oh.' Gwen stared after the cat, which raced around the room, then jumped up onto the top of the sofa and sat staring at them.

'You see, she hasn't left,' Alicia said. 'She's here, watching you, because she loves you, too.'

This made Gwen smile, and – much to Cecily's relief – her daughter sat properly in her chair when Eric came to serve tea.

'When is Uncle Miles coming back from London?' Alicia asked Cecily between sips of her tea.

'Tomorrow morning, in time for lunch. He and Harry have gone to see Christopher Longdon about hiring some more veterans. There are still several empty farms on the estate, you know.'

'Uncle Miles told me the two families who are already here have become really good at their jobs.'

'They have indeed. It's made a big difference to our agricultural output, Alicia.'

Turning to Eric, who was offering her sandwiches, Cecily took one, and thanked him. 'You can leave the plate here, Eric,' she said pleasantly. 'We'll help ourselves, and leave the pastries as well, please.'

'Yes, m'lady.' He smiled in his genial way and left the room.

Gwen pulled a piece of paper out of her pocket and said, 'I made the shopping list, Mummy, as you asked me to do. Shall I read it out to you?'

'If you must,' Cecily murmured, thankful that Alicia had spoken up about Gwen's constant hugging of the cat. It infuriated Miles, the way she took it everywhere with her.

'I need two white cotton blouses, two pairs of white socks. And a new pair of slippers. Oh, and Daddy needs new slippers. His are worn out.' Gwen put the paper back in her pocket.

Puzzled, Cecily stared at her daughter and frowned. 'No, they're not. His slippers are fairly new.'

'No, they're old,' Gwen said, shaking her head. 'I saw his slippers. It was the night Aunt Charlotte died . . .' Gwen stopped speaking abruptly, remembering she shouldn't have been up in the middle of the night.

Cecily frowned. 'What do you mean, about the night Aunt Charlotte died?'

Gwen bit her lip, looking slightly fearful, and said in a low voice, 'Please don't be angry, Mummy, will you? Say you won't.'

'I won't be angry, just tell me about Daddy's slippers. Come on, darling, don't be silly. I won't be angry.'

'It was because of Cleo. You know my little cat was poorly then. And I kept going to the kitchen to check on her, up and down the back staircase. One time, when I was going down again, I was kneeling on a step, pulling the door closed, and I saw Daddy coming out of Aunt Charlotte's room.'

There was total silence for a few minutes before Cecily said, 'I understand, Gwen. Let me ask you a question. Did Daddy see you?'

'No, and I didn't see him. Just his slippers. Then I closed the door and ran down to the kitchen.' Gwen paused, nodding her head, adding, 'And they were *old* slippers,' she insisted.

Alicia started to say something and stopped, looking across at Cecily. 'I feel a bit strange,' she murmured. 'Do you think Gwen could go and ask Eric for a glass of water? I'm sure he's in the dining-room pantry.'

Cecily nodded, aware that something was wrong. Alicia was extremely white, and there was an anxious expression in her eyes. 'Gwen, please find Eric and ask him to bring a glass of water for Alicia.'

'Yes, Mummy,' the child said, and ran out of the room.

'Whatever's the matter, Alicia?' Cecily asked, staring at her niece. 'You're as white as a sheet. Do you feel unwell, faint?'

For a split second Alicia couldn't answer, and then she said in a low voice, 'It was Adam Fennell leaving Aunt Charlotte's room. You see, he took those old slippers out of the hamper for the Salvation Army.'

Cecily gaped at her, incredulity settling on her face. 'You can't be serious. Why would a man like Fennell take old slippers? Whatever for?'

'Because of the family crest embroidered on the front. When I saw him wearing them in his bedroom I was furious. He wouldn't put them back in the hamper. He kept them.'

'I would have been as angry as you. Collecting trophies, was that it? Wanting to be like an earl. Oh my God! Now I understand. What was Fennell doing in Aunt Charlotte's room? In the middle of the night?' Cecily was shocked when she realized what this could mean, what the implications were. She felt a tightness in her chest. 'Where are the slippers now, Alicia? Do you know?'

'Probably in the bedroom you assigned to him. I warned him not to take them out of this house,' Alicia mumbled, and she sat back, feeling overwhelmed by this new development.

Cecily nodded. 'Are you thinking what I am?'

'Yes, I am. He might have hurt Aunt Charlotte. Maybe her death wasn't an accident at all. Perhaps he killed her.'

At this moment, Eric returned with a glass of water on a tray. After giving it to Alicia, he spoke to Cecily.

'Mr Charlie is on the telephone in the library, Your Ladyship. He wishes to speak to you and also to Miss Alicia.'

'Thank you, Eric.' Looking over at Gwen, who had followed Eric into the yellow sitting room, Cecily said, 'We'll be back in a moment, darling. Finish your tea.'

'Yes, Mummy. Can I have a cream bun?'

'Yes,' Cecily said hastily, and hurried out after Alicia, followed by Eric who had retrieved the glass of water and now placed it on a side table in the library. He said, 'I'll look after Lady

Gwen, Your Ladyship,' and he turned to head back to the sitting room.

'Thank you, Eric.'

Cecily dashed across the library floor and sat down in the chair at the desk. 'Hello, Charlie. It's Cecily.'

'Hello, Aunt Ceci, I just wanted to ask you if Uncle Howard can come up to Cavendon tomorrow? There's been a strange development about Adam Fennell.'

'Of course Uncle Howard can come. But why?'

'Could I speak to Alicia first, if you don't mind? I need to tell her something rather important.'

'She's right here.' Cecily stood up, handed the receiver to Alicia and pressed her down into the chair.

'What's happened, Charlie?' Alicia asked, anxiety echoing in her voice.

'Adam Fennell doesn't exist. There is no such person,' Charlie told her.

'What do you mean? Please explain, Charlie.'

'I've had Elise Steinbrenner checking him out. There wasn't much in our Clippings Library, just pieces about his films, his career. So, being a good reporter, Elise decided to go over to Somerset House, where every birth, marriage, and death is registered. It's possible to purchase a copy of any of those certificates, and anyone can do a search there—'

'And there is no birth certificate for Adam Fennell? That's what you're saying?'

'I am. I had lunch with Uncle Howard today, filled him in about Fennell's behaviour, his blackmailing us. Although it was his day off, he decided to go to his office at Scotland Yard. He wanted to check out Fennell, look for his name attached to any form of criminality. He couldn't find a thing. But the fact he isn't who he said he was has made Uncle Howard suspicious. He wants to come up to Cavendon tomorrow, see if he can find out a bit more from you.'

'I understand, and just listen to this.' Swiftly and very precisely,

Alicia told her brother about Gwen's late-night meanderings and the old slippers.

'My God, this information certainly changes things! Could Fennell have hurt her? But why would he have been in Aunt Charlotte's bedroom in the first place?'

'Aunt Cecily and I haven't figured that out yet. Anyway, speak to her, Charlie. Tell her what you've just told me.'

After handing the phone to Cecily, Alicia moved closer to the side table and picked up the glass of water. She felt sick, had developed a pounding headache.

Sitting down in an armchair, she closed her eyes, her heart aching. What if Fennell *had* killed her aunt? It was her fault. She had brought him into the midst of her family. How could she ever forgive herself? But why would he kill Aunt Charlotte? For what reason? There wasn't one, in her opinion. Alicia knew that unless she found the answers to these questions, she would never have peace for the rest of her life.

# Forty-Two

Cecily went back to the yellow dining room, leaving Alicia speaking to Charlie on the phone in the library. Gwen looked up when her mother came into the room. 'I didn't mean to upset you about the slippers, Mummy.'

'You didn't upset me, darling. In fact, you've been very helpful. And thank you for that.'

Within minutes, Eric appeared with a fresh pot of hot tea, and clean cups and saucers. A moment later, he was pouring the tea for Cecily, explaining, 'Miss Clegg apologizes for not saying goodbye, but she was running late, Your Ladyship. She has left Lady Gwen's homework in the children's playroom upstairs.'

'Thank you, Eric, and thank you for the hot tea. You might look in on Miss Alicia, and ask her to join me, would you please?'

'I will, m'lady.'

Gwen said, 'I like Miss Clegg more than Mrs Plumpton; she's better.'

Cecily looked at her daughter and asked, 'In what way?'

'Miss Clegg is cleverer, and she speaks clearly, tells me things in a way I can understand. Anyway, she's a good teacher and younger.'

Cecily nodded and glanced at the door as Alicia walked in, looking more pinched and whiter than ever.

Eric was right behind her, and he immediately poured a cup of tea for her, and asked her if she needed anything else.

She shook her head and thanked him.

After informing Cecily that he would be in the butler's pantry near the dining room if she needed him, he left.

Alicia said, 'That was a shock, hearing there wasn't such a person. It totally took me by surprise. I was reeling for a few minutes.'

'Have you spoken to Felix and Constance about that person?' Cecily asked, guarding her words with Gwen present in the room. 'Perhaps they might know more than us, and yes, I'll say it was quite a surprise. Actually, it was a huge shock. Have we all been blind, deaf and dumb?'

'I have, and it's certainly all my fault. I shouldn't have introduced him here.' Alicia looked at Cecily and her eyes brimmed with tears. Finding her handkerchief, she blew her nose and took control of herself, not wishing to break down in front of her youngest cousin.

'Can I leave now, Mummy?' Gwen asked. 'I want to look at my homework. And can I take Cleopatra with me? *Please.*'

'Yes and yes, and again, thank you. I shall buy your father a new pair of slippers, so you can be relaxed about that problem.'

Gwen laughed as she ran out, calling the cat to come with her.

Once they were alone, Alicia said, 'I think I must tell Felix and Constance that I've broken it off with Adam Fennell, don't you?'

'Yes, I would if I were you. Better get your story out first, before he tries to say he broke it off with you. And now we are finding out strange things about him, I'm glad you did call it off.'

'So am I. Charlie told Uncle Howard that Fennell blackmailed us, because Charlie thought he ought to be absolutely truthful. Since he'd asked for Uncle Howard's help. He told me Uncle Howard said Fennell was a con man.'

'I suppose Uncle Howard didn't like hearing *that*, about your generosity. Cops never approve if someone pays blackmail. What I don't understand is how Adam Fennell knew anything about the attack on Daphne so many years ago.'

'He told us that it was Bryan Mellor who mentioned it to him, and that Mellor got it from a member of the Ingham family.'

'But nobody knew about Daphne being raped when she was seventeen, Alicia: honestly, they didn't. Just my mother and father, and Aunt Charlotte. Only three Swanns, and later I knew because they needed me to make clothes for her, clothes that concealed her pregnancy. Oh, and of course, her parents knew.'

'What a terrible thing to happen to my mother, and at Cavendon, her own home.' Alicia's eyes filled again and she patted her face with her hankie.

'I'm so happy you went to see your parents, Alicia, and what a piece of luck that you'd already planned the trip to Zurich, because of your worries about your mother's health.'

'I told Charlie that, and reminded him what Aunt Charlotte always said: *it was meant to be*, when something odd happened. His comment was that *God winked*.'

Cecily nodded. 'I've heard that expression before. Because some people don't believe there's such a thing as a coincidence.'

'I know. Do you think Fennell might have realized the Swann record books were kept in the attic?' Alicia asked. 'In a sort of logical way, without really knowing. Like a good guess.'

'I don't know. But even if he did, he couldn't get into the trunk, it's locked . . .' Cecily stopped and immediately jumped up. 'Speaking of the trunk, I feel I must go and check it right now. Do you want to come with me?'

'Yes, I do.'

A few moments later, the two women were in the bedroom corridor of the West Wing, and going up the attic stairs together.

After turning on the ceiling light, Cecily hurried over to the trunk, relief flowing through her when she saw that it was locked. Peering more closely at the lock, she suddenly realized it looked scratched. She straightened, and said to Alicia, 'Wait here. I'll be back in a minute. I'm going to get the key to the trunk.'

'Is something wrong?'

'The lock looks scratched, as if someone has tried to force it open.'

When she returned a few minutes later, Cecily knelt down in front of the trunk and fitted the key into the lock. It took a moment for her to get the trunk open; she nodded to herself, muttered to Alicia, 'I think the lock's been tampered with. There, I got it to open. Finally!'

Cecily lifted the lid and eyed the top layer of record books, and knew at once that someone had been inside the trunk.

She had her own special way of placing them in certain sequences, and they were slightly out of kilter. Her heart missed a beat, when, for a second, she couldn't see the relevant book. And then she found it, placed at the front of the trunk, underneath two layers of other books. She never put it there. It was always at the back, under only one layer of the others.

She handed the book to Alicia and stood. 'I can't swear that Fennell was in this trunk, but someone was, and they certainly knew how to pick a lock. The record book was put back, thank God, although it was in the wrong place.'

Alicia said, 'I can't imagine how Adam Fennell knew about the record books. Or the trunk in the attic. I never discussed anything with him, or with Bryan Mellor.' She looked down at the black leather notebook in her hands. 'Would it be worth asking Uncle Howard to test this for fingerprints, do you think?'

'I do. Be careful how you carry it.' Locking the trunk, Cecily put the key in her pocket and followed Alicia down the attic stairs, then stopped at one moment. She said, 'Go down to the corridor, close the attic door, and go into Aunt Charlotte's room. And close that door. Listen carefully, Alicia.'

'What are you going to do?'

'I'm going to walk down the stairs stealthily. I want to know if you can hear me.'

'Clever idea.' Alicia did as she was asked.

Cecily crept down the stairs, slowly, carefully, as anyone might who was trying not to be heard, and then she faked a slight stumble. She waited a moment before going down the last few steps.

Alicia came out of Aunt Charlotte's bedroom. 'Did you fall? Or fake a fall? I did hear a bit of noise.'

'Good to know. Because I occasionally saw Fennell rubbing the calf of his leg, as if he had a cramp, and that's what I did. I faked a cramp.'

'He didn't want anyone to know,' Alicia said. 'He thought people might think of it as a disability. But I caught him rubbing his calves often. Do you think that's what happened?'

'I just don't know. But look at the two doors: they face each other exactly. And there's another thing, Aunt Charlotte was reading late, as she usually did. In the attic, I remembered that I'd seen an open book and her glasses on the bed when we went into the room after Peggy found her. Perhaps she was awake and reading when Fennell was up there, and heard him on the stairs.'

'If he was,' Alicia said.

'And you've never seen anything at all with another name on it, Alicia?' Inspector Howard Pinkerton asked as he sat with Cecily and Alicia in the blue and white sitting room at Cavendon. 'No letters, legal papers? What about a passport?'

'No, because I've never travelled abroad with him. Never travelled at all, actually, except to come up here. But he must have a passport, Uncle Howard, because he goes to New York quite a lot.'

'Charlie mentioned that yesterday, and I checked immediately with the Passport Division. There is no passport application in the name of Adam Fennell. It *is* an invented name, and I wish I had a way of finding out who the heck he really is.'

'What about his fingerprints?' Cecily asked.

'I have nothing to compare them with. Nevertheless, I did want my boys to try to get fingerprints from the bedroom and bathroom Fennell used here, and now from Aunt Charlotte's room, at your suggestion.'

Cecily carefully placed the record book in front of him. 'And then there's *this*. It's the Swann record book for the years 1913 and 1914, and, if Fennell's touched it, his prints will be there. The only other prints will be mine, Alicia's and Charlotte's.'

'I understand. In the meantime, I want you both to know I have people checking up on Fennell everywhere, finding out everything they can about his work, his social life. From what I'm learning, he sprang into the centre of the film industry as if from another planet. No one had heard of him or known of him until that day. About ten years ago. He's the mystery man.'

'He told me that he was from London and had lived in Bryanston Square, on the other side, as a child, and that his father was a doctor. A widower, who'd brought him up. He said he had never lived anywhere else . . .'

Alicia stopped speaking, staring out of the window, her head tilted on one side, as if she were listening to something no one else could hear.

Howard exchanged a questioning look with Cecily and raised a brow; Cecily merely shrugged and shook her head, seemingly as baffled as he was.

Finally, Alicia brought her gaze back to Howard and said slowly, 'I have a very good ear for voices and accents, perhaps because I'm an actress, and in the inner recesses of my mind there is an odd echo in Fennell's voice. The voice that comes out when he's angry or frustrated. He shouts and yells, and in doing so another voice emerges. It has an underlying accent, I detected.'

Alicia paused, took a drink of water, and finished, 'I think he might have been brought up in the North of England, probably Manchester.'

'That's some talent you have, my dear.' Howard looked at her admiringly. 'I'll have his picture sent up to the Manchester City Police. You never know, he might not have a record, but occasionally a cop recognizes a face, the face of . . . a person of interest, shall we say? That's something to go on, and, of course, we have the slippers. That Lady Gwen saw them on someone's feet at one o'clock in the morning is some sort of miracle. Observant little girl, I'd say. And, according to the death certificate from the doctor, Aunt Charlotte died around that time.'

'That's correct,' Cecily answered. 'And I can drive you over to see Dr Ottoway, if needs be.'

'That would be a good idea,' Howard answered. 'Now, let's go upstairs again. I'd like another prowl around, and we can see how my lads are doing, taking all those fingerprints.'

They went into the bedroom Fennell had used. Howard's colleagues had already covered the entire room taking fingerprints. He opened the cupboard door and immediately saw the slippers again, and looked across at Alicia, who wouldn't come into the room, just stood in the doorway. 'I can't bear the stink of his cologne,' she had confided in Cecily.

'And you say he only wore them in this room?' he asked Alicia.

'Yes. I wouldn't allow him to do otherwise, or take them to London. He stole them, that was the way I saw it, and he had also embarrassed me. By the way, I've just thought of something, Uncle Howard. I believe Eric saw him taking those slippers out of the hamper.'

'I'll have a chat with Eric later. I'll get one of my boys to bag the slippers. I have to take them away.'

He was looking at Cecily as he said this, and she nodded, 'That's fine. We'll do everything we can to cooperate with you.'

Howard peered into the cupboard. 'He left some shirts here, two, and a jacket.' Immediately Howard began to feel in the pockets and, after a split second, he exclaimed, 'He left his pen.'

'I don't believe it!' Alicia cried. 'Please show it to me. If it's the pen I think it is, it will be the best source for fingerprints, because he wouldn't allow anyone to touch it. He loved that pen. It has a special nib, and he was so fussy about it. He himself filled it with the ink.'

'Then it's a jewel,' Howard answered, took out a clean white handkerchief, and holding it he carefully lifted the fountain pen out of the inner top pocket of the dark jacket.

Walking across the room, he held out the handkerchief and showed her the pen.

'That's it. I am certain there will be only one set of fingerprints on it. Fennell's.'

'Then this will be my source, knowing they're his and only his. My team can compare the fingerprints from the rooms here and identify Fennell's by using the pen.'

'This is a lucky break,' Cecily said. 'Now, let's go up to the attic and look at the trunk.'

Four weeks later, Elise sat with Charlie and Howard Pinkerton at a corner table in Le Chat Noir. Charlie had invited them to dinner to thank them for their help and to sum up all their findings. In the background, a piano played and the little restaurant was buzzing with chatter and laughter.

'Not that we know very much about Fennell and who he really is,' Elise said. 'But we are now aware he's a possible murderer, a suspect in Aunt Charlotte's death.'

'I already have a warrant for his arrest, so we can question him on suspicion of murder, if we do find the bastard,' Howard said. 'And Elise, you've been a fantastic help, finding out as much as you did. You've made my job easier.'

'I second that,' Charlie interjected. 'You're one hell of an investigative reporter. Thank you. I just want to say that I don't know how you've managed to finish the great series on the Festival of Britain. Jimmy Maze told me he's thrilled with it.'

Elise beamed at them both and, looking across the table at Charlie, she added, 'I got up at four o'clock in the morning to work on my series, then I went trotting around to interview those friends, so-called, of Fennell's. You know, he's been very clever. No one suspected him of being a fraud. Just the opposite.'

Charlie nodded. After a sip of his Chardonnay, he continued, 'I couldn't believe it when you told me Fennell's flat was empty, and that it was only a rental. He must have done a moonlight flit, as we call it in Yorkshire.'

'Or his man Wilson did it,' Elise suggested. 'The first time I went to Bryanston Square, Wilson was there, as you know. He told me Fennell was abroad. But the second time I called, the flat did look as if it was closed down, dustsheets around.'

Howard said, 'When one of my boys went to see Wilson, at your suggestion, Elise, the landlord said the flat was up for rental again. The butler had obviously moved very fast. Fennell probably realized we were after him.'

'Same with the Wardour Street office,' Elise reminded them. 'One day the receptionist was there telling the same story, the next she was also gone. The office was closed.'

'Obviously Fennell plays everything close to the chest,' Charlie said. 'Because Felix and Constance Lambert were stupefied when they heard on the grapevine that Fennell had closed his office and gone abroad.'

'Constance told me they'd had enormous respect for him. They are heartbroken that Alicia and your family have been conned by him, that he caused so much trouble for you.' Elise shook her head. 'God knows where he is.'

'Not in New York,' Charlie announced. 'I just spoke to my friend, Oliver Kramer, a few hours ago. He's a very good freelance journalist, and he's been doing a bit of snooping around for me. Tonight he told me Adam Fennell has not been seen in Manhattan lately. Not since before Christmas. And now it's the end of March.'

'Perhaps he might never come back,' Elise said softly, looking at Howard.

'That's a strong possibility,' Howard replied. 'But if I do find out where he is, Scotland Yard will seek to have him questioned and possibly extradited back to Great Britain. He's now a suspect in a murder investigation.'

'I understand,' Charlie murmured. He was reflective for a moment or two, before continuing, 'Aside from wanting to see you both, to thank you, I must add that I think now is the time we must step away. In my opinion, there's nothing else we can do. What are your thoughts, Elise? Howard?'

'Ladies first,' Howard said, glancing at the young reporter, giving her a warm smile.

'I agree with you, Charlie.' Elise's intelligent face looked thoughtful for a moment. 'But let me just say that I'm always here if you need me.' She smiled at him.

Howard nodded in agreement. 'We should stop; you're correct, Charlie. We've done everything we can. For the moment. Life is funny in my line of work. You never know what might turn up. You think you have a cold case, and then suddenly it becomes hot again.'

'Seemingly, Adam Fennell has disappeared into thin air. On the other hand, something odd could happen to reveal his whereabouts,' Charlie said.

Howard grinned. 'It's happened before in my years at the Yard.' He pushed his whisky glass away from him and leant back in his chair. 'Anyway, changing the subject, I was thrilled to read all those wonderful reviews Alicia received for *Broken Image*. The critics are raving about her.'

'And the film is doing well,' Charlie answered. 'It's cheered her up. She's been awfully despondent about Aunt Charlotte's death and introducing Fennell into the family. Guilty feelings, of course. Miles and Cecily, all of us actually, have given her a lot of support. And the producer of *Broken Image*, Mario Cantonelli, has offered her a part in a new film of his. And he's no fan of Fennell's, by the way.'

Elise smiled. 'Alicia told me. But Mario's certainly a fan of hers, and she has the lead again in this new production. She'll start filming later this year. *Prophecy*, it's called.'

'I'll prophesy this,' Howard said. 'Alicia will be fine. She's an Ingham and Ingham women win. They always come through every rotten thing that happens to them. And with flying colours.'

Charlie laughed. 'That's a good way of saying it, Uncle Howard.'

Elise looked at Howard and then at Charlie, and announced shyly, 'I have some news of my own. I'm getting engaged to Alistair. We're going to be married in the autumn.'

Both men looked surprised, and before Charlie could stop himself, he exclaimed, 'But what about your career in Fleet Street? It's meant so much to you.'

'Alistair doesn't mind if I work for a few years, Charlie. Until we want to start a family.'

'Congratulations,' Howard said, and Charlie repeated the same word.

'Greta is giving an engagement party for us in two weeks, in the middle of April. I do hope you will both come, and Aunt Dottie.'

'Wild horses couldn't keep me away,' Charlie exclaimed, grinning at her.

'You know very well we'll be there.' Howard squeezed her arm affectionately. 'Dottie has hinted that there was something in the wind, something special about to happen.'

'My other good news is that Alicia has agreed to attend the party, thanks to Cecily, who persuaded her. Because we all know she hasn't been going out,' Elise murmured.

'Things are getting back to normal with her.' Charlie lifted his glass, and so did Howard.

In unison the two men said again, 'Congratulations, Elise,' and clinked their glasses against hers.

# Forty-Three

Greta Chalmers was doing a quick tour of her house in Phene Street before the guests arrived. This was her routine check-up to make sure everything was in its place and looked beautiful.

Because Christopher would have to remain downstairs in his wheelchair, Greta was paying special attention to the library, located across the hall from the dining room.

The library was rarely used since her father's death, but it had been thoroughly cleaned earlier in the week. Carrying a slender glass vase holding only three pink roses, Greta moved a photograph slightly on a bookshelf and put the vase in front of it.

At that moment, the doorbell rang; it was Arnold Templeton with his brother Alistair. After greeting them both, she took them upstairs to the sitting room, where a waiter served the two men drinks.

'I'll be back in a minute,' Greta said. 'And Elise will come down shortly, Alistair. She's just finishing dressing.'

Alistair grinned at her. 'I know we're early, but I couldn't wait to get here, to see her. And thank you for giving us this engagement party, Greta.'

Arnold looked at his brother, and said in a joking tone, 'And don't forget to thank *me*. After all, I introduced you to Elise.'

There was laughter and a bit more brotherly teasing, and then Greta hurried back downstairs. She returned to the library, lighting the votive candles on some of the bookshelves. After she glanced around one more time, now satisfied, she walked down to the kitchen, popped her head around the door. 'Everything all right in here, I'm sure,' she said.

The new caterer, Minnie Harris, nodded. 'I'm on time. And I haven't burned anything yet, Mrs Chalmers.'

Greta laughed, appreciating the young woman's humour. When the doorbell rang again and people walked in, she was surprised to see Cecily, Miles, Alicia and Charlie arriving together. She ushered them inside, sharing warm greetings with them, and said, 'Please go up to the sitting room.'

As the Inghams trooped upstairs, the door opened and Victoria walked into the hall and went to hug Greta. She was wearing a beautiful floral dress with a full skirt that flared out around her long, slender legs, and her face was full of happiness. On her ring finger, her emerald engagement ring caught the light.

There were only two steps into the house from the street, and Alex Poniatowski managed the wheelchair expertly, bringing Christopher into the hall. The two men greeted Greta, who bent to kiss Christopher on the cheek and shook Alex's hand. She'd got to know them both over the past months and she loved their camaraderie. Somehow Alex, with his easy-going nature and quiet strength, didn't get in the way of Christopher and Vicki. 'Come into the library,' Greta told them. 'Everyone is going to be coming in here shortly, since we're eating across the hall. Now, what would you like to drink?' The two men asked for whisky, but Victoria declined. Greta stepped into the dining room where another small bar was being serviced by a waiter and ordered the drinks.

Returning to the library, Greta said to Victoria, 'Cecily and Miles are upstairs with Charlie and Alicia, if you wish to go and say hello.'

Victoria looked at Greta knowingly and nodded. Turning to Christopher, she said, 'I'll be back in a moment. I know Alex is longing to meet Alicia Stanton.'

'Oh come on, don't make a big fuss,' Alex exclaimed, nonetheless looking pleased.

Christopher began to laugh and said, 'Alex, you're blushing.'

Victoria and Greta left the two men sipping the drinks the waiter had brought them, and stopped to confer briefly in the hallway. 'Alicia might not like him,' Victoria said in a low voice. 'She's really off men, after that awful Fennell. She's confided in me a lot lately.'

'Cecily asked me to make sure we introduce Alex, just to see how Alicia reacts to a new face. That was the way she put it. Nobody's matchmaking, Victoria. Cecily and I just want to make Alicia understand there's a big wide world out there.'

'A world full of men, hey?' Victoria laughed merrily.

'And some nice men, which I think Alex is, and obviously not everyone is like that hateful Fennell,' Greta shot back. 'But don't bring her down now. Let's wait until just before supper. I've seated her next to him at the table. Also, perhaps we should give everyone time to relax.'

'I'll just go up and greet them,' Victoria murmured. 'Is that what you want me to do?'

'That's right.' Greta looked at the front door and spotted Aunt Dottie and Uncle Howard coming in, followed by Victoria's sculptor friend, whom everyone thought was a model because she was so beautiful.

After hugging the last arrivals, Victoria took hold of her friend's hand. 'Come upstairs. I've got a lovely surprise for you.'

A moment later, Victoria was greeting Miles, Charlie, Cecily and Alicia before introducing her friend. She said, 'This is Phoebe Bellamy, everyone. I think some of you already know her, because her sister is married to Harry. But I don't think you've met her, Charlie.'

Everyone was smiling because Charlie was staring at the tall girl with long auburn hair and freckles all over her face. He appeared to be mesmerized by her.

Charlie had never seen anyone quite as beautiful, and he was silent for a moment longer, before saying, 'Are you the famous Phoebe who was knocked off her bicycle by Harry Swann at Cavendon years ago?'

'That's me,' Phoebe answered, laughing. 'But I'm not famous like you, Charlie. I love your historical books, by the way.'

'Do you really? Shall I get you a glass of champagne, Phoebe?' he asked, his face full of smiles.

'I'd love it,' she answered. 'I'll come with you, shall I? Help you to carry the drinks.'

As they walked across to the bar together, Cecily looked at Alicia and said, 'Hopefully, we might have found a suitable girlfriend for Charlie at last.'

It happened after supper, when a small group gathered together for coffee in the library. Christopher sat in his wheelchair, Alex stood beside him, talking to Alicia, who was also standing with her back to the bookcase. Victoria, Charlie and Phoebe were sitting on a large sofa on the other side of the room.

Everyone was happy, very jolly, and the dinner had been a smashing success. Spring leg of lamb from Cavendon, new potatoes and peas from the kitchen garden there too, brought down specially by Cecily and Miles, and a whopping great trifle, which Elise had said was the trifle to end all trifles. There had been many toasts, jokes, a lot of teasing, and much laughter. A wonderful time had been had by everyone.

The other guests who couldn't fit into the small library had gone upstairs to the sitting room, where coffee and liqueurs were being served.

Victoria looked across at Alicia, saw that she seemed to be getting on well with Alex. The two of them were chatting amiably and laughing a lot, when Alicia stepped back, drawing closer to the bookshelves.

Her blonde hair was longer now, and as she moved her body, tossed back her hair, it became entangled with the three roses in the glass vase. As she tried to free her hair from the roses, she knocked the glass vase onto the floor, then drew her hair around her neck and pulled out the three roses, with Alex helping her.

When he picked up the glass vase and straightened up, he found himself staring at a framed photograph on the shelf, which until that moment had been hidden by the vase of roses.

Alex drew closer, stared at the picture and exclaimed, 'Why is that man in this photograph with you and the Inghams?'

Alicia followed his gaze and gasped, wondering why that picture was still here in Greta's house. It had been taken at Cavendon the first weekend Fennell had visited them.

She gaped at Alex and said, 'Do you know Adam Fennell?'

'So that's what he's calling himself now, is it?'

Charlie, who had heard this exchange, was on his feet instantly. He stepped over to the bookshelf, said to Alex, 'What can you tell us about him? He's caused us a great deal of trouble.'

The room was suddenly silent, and Charlie said to Alex, 'Let's find a private spot. Come on, Alicia.'

Victoria said, 'What's the matter? Is something wrong?'

'No, no, it's nothing, Vicki. I think Alex might be able to help us, that's all. Be back in a few minutes.' Charlie took the framed photograph off the shelf and stuck it under his arm.

The three of them left the library. Charlie said, 'Let's go into the dining room. No one's in there now. I need you to speak to Uncle Howard, Alex. I'll get him, and Elise as well. Alicia, take Alex in there, please. I'll join you in a moment.'

She simply nodded, went on into the dining room, which had been partially cleared. Alex hurried after her, asking, 'How do you know that chap? He's bad news.'

'Charlie will explain,' Alicia muttered, stunned that Alex

Poniatowski knew Fennell; knew his real name, by the sound of it.

Once Charlie brought Elise and Uncle Howard downstairs, he closed the door firmly behind them. 'What's Adam Fennell's real name, Alex?'

'Fred Hicks. How do you know him? He's the worst, a real con man. And God only knows what else.'

Taking a deep breath, Alicia said, 'He was the associate producer of my last film. We became involved, got engaged. For a few months he was my fiancé, but I broke it off recently.'

'I can only say it's your good luck to have done that. He's a criminal.'

Howard said, 'How do you know this chap Hicks?'

'I was in the Polish Division of the British Army during the war, and I had a very good friend, Giles Saunders, who was in the regular British Army. A career officer. We knew each other through our families. Anyway, I met this chap, Hicks, through my friend Giles, because they were in the same platoon for a time. He'd cheated us both in various ways, and just when we were about to do something about it, he killed an officer and went AWOL.'

'He murdered an officer?' Howard stared at Alex. 'Was he ever caught and charged? What about the Military Police? Didn't they catch him? Arrest him?'

'They're still looking for him, I believe. Giles would know, he's still in the army, and now with the Military Police, in fact.'

'Then you must let him know at once,' Howard said.

'I will. But where is Hicks? Do you know? Or has he gone on the run again?'

'He's disappeared into thin air,' Charlie said, and handed the photograph to Alex. 'Are you certain that this is him?'

'I am. He looks different, younger than he did in 1940, oddly enough, and his hair is slicker. He's become a bit of a dandy. Despite the many changes in his appearance, I know it's him. And we have to deal with him, don't we? Before he causes more trouble. Now, tell me why you're after him?'

'It's like this,' Howard said. 'Charlie was worried about Fennell, who was angry with Alicia when she broke off with him. Charlie thought he might be dangerous and he was threatening her with blackmail. So we met, he told me various things, and I decided I should get involved. I am explaining this so you understand this is now an *official* Scotland Yard investigation, and not a family check-out by Uncle Howard.'

'I understand, Inspector,' Alex answered, realizing the gravity of the situation.

'You cannot discuss anything I tell you with anyone. It's highly confidential.'

Alex nodded. 'I realize the need for that. You have my word.'

'To continue. I went up to Cavendon to talk to Alicia and took my fingerprint boys with me. Just in case. You never know when you might need them.'

'Did you want to compare them with someone's?' Alex asked.

'I didn't have anyone's. Not at first. It was a lucky break that Fennell forgot his favourite fountain pen. We got a beautiful set of his prints off the pen, and there were no other prints on it. Later, when we compared the prints from the pen to those from other rooms, we knew exactly where he'd been in the house.'

'The pen nailed him,' Alex said. 'You could check which rooms he had been in quite easily.'

'Exactly,' Howard replied. 'Charlie suspected Fennell had discovered a family secret from a leather record book kept in a trunk in the attic. Cecily says someone broke into the trunk, read the record book and then put it back. She thinks Aunt Charlotte, who always read in bed, might have heard a noise and gone to look in the corridor. You see, the door to the attic is opposite her bedroom.'

Charlie nodded. 'We think she saw Fennell with the record book. That's our conclusion.'

'Yes. We all believe that, in fact. She would have objected very strongly, and they may have had a struggle. In any case, Aunt Charlotte ended up dead, I'm afraid,' Howard finished.

'What the family originally believed was that she had had an accident, had fallen in the night and hit her head on a brass fender,' Charlie added.

Alex looked at Howard intently. 'Do you think he bashed her head in with something?'

'It's possible. We found Fennell's prints on a chest and on a wooden chair in her bedroom, Alex. So he was definitely in there. We also found his prints on the record book.'

'So he's murdered for a second time,' Alex exclaimed. 'I'll get in touch with my friend at the Military Police tomorrow morning, first thing. I think the two of you should meet.'

'Thanks, and I will inform Interpol.'

Charlie said, 'Good. Perhaps we'll get a bit closer to the truth.' He turned to Elise. 'If there's nothing you want to add from your research, we ought to get you back to your party. Alistair'll be wondering what's going on. Right, Elise?'

She smiled. 'Yes, though I just want to say that this bit of important news has been the icing on the cake. I just hope all our hard work pays off.'

Elise was surprised that nothing much had happened regarding the Fennell investigation in the last couple of weeks.

She, Charlie and Howard were no wiser than they had been before Alex Poniatowski told them Fennell's real name. They were all frustrated.

One good thing had happened, though, again thanks to Alex. He had suddenly remembered about ten days ago that Fred Hicks had once had a brother called Andy who had died.

Alex had suggested to Howard that Fennell might have stolen his brother's identity when he left the army. He needed a birth certificate in order to get a passport, and he couldn't use his own because he had gone AWOL.

She knew that Howard had immediately informed the Military Police, who were still hunting for Fred Hicks, and Interpol as well. Once more, it was a waiting game.

In the meantime, Elise had been busy with her work on the paper; she was also redecorating her flat, which was where Alistair and she would live after they were married in September.

They had made that late date so that their wedding didn't clash with Victoria's. She was marrying Christopher in May.

Elise sat up straighter in the chair, suddenly realizing she had a fitting at Swann in Burlington Arcade at five o'clock today. Cecily had designed Victoria's gown and hers as her wedding gift to the little evacuee her parents had adopted as part of the family. Elise was the only bridesmaid, with little Lady Gwen and Paloma's daughter Patricia as the flower girls.

She was picking up her bag and reaching for her jacket, when her door flew open and Charlie rushed in, looking excited. 'They've found him, Elise! Interpol has found Fred Hicks, aka Adam Fennell, and he's—'

'Been arrested?' she cut in, her eyes shining. When Charlie nodded, she exclaimed, 'Thank God for that. Now we can all breathe easier, and most especially Alicia.'

'We can indeed,' Charlie agreed. 'But Interpol hasn't arrested him, Elise. They found his dead body in a back street in Naples. Shot execution style, with a bullet in the back of his head.'

Elise was flabbergasted. 'What else did Uncle Howard tell you?'

'He doesn't have too many more details at the moment. He's awaiting a full report. He's going to call me again in a few hours.'

'Why on earth was Fennell in Naples?' She frowned. 'That's an odd place for him to be.'

'Not at all. According to Uncle Howard, Interpol had been tipped off by an informer that a man called Josh Miniver, an Englishman, was dealing drugs with the Cosa Nostra, the Italian Mafia. Seemingly, Fennell double-crossed the *capo di tutti capi*, the tsar of a vast criminal empire in Italy. Bad judgement on his part. Interpol recognized who the chap called Miniver really was, because they had Fennell's picture to go on.'

'They also identified him by his fingerprints, didn't they?'

Charlie grinned. 'As Alex said, nailed by a fountain pen. Apparently, Fennell was hooked up with some Italian countess in Rome, and living the high life.'

'Just imagine . . . he called himself Miniver, no doubt because of all those wartime films starring Greer Garson. What a dope.'

'And a psychopath, according to Howard,' Charlie replied. 'For Alicia, it's a new beginning, I hope.'

# Forty-Four

Lady Daphne had finally come back to Cavendon with her husband, Hugo Ingham Stanton. They had arrived on Monday 15 May, and the last two days had been easy and affectionate, with no mention of Daphne's angry departure the previous summer. Her brother, Miles, and Cecily had been welcoming.

In a sense, it's like I've never been away, Daphne thought now, as she walked around the new gardens Harry had been working hard on.

They looked beautiful. Every single thing looked beautiful. And the rooms she had so lovingly decorated and cherished had been left untouched. Nothing had been touched, and for that she was truly grateful. Her hard work over the years had not been lost, had not been in vain.

Glancing at her watch, she realized she should make her way to the walled rose garden in Cavendon Park. She had asked Cecily to meet her there at three o'clock. 'Just for a little chat,' she had said to her yesterday. 'I have a few things to share with you.'

Cecily had accepted at once and had added, 'You've made my mother so happy that you decided to come to Victoria's wedding,

Daphne. And I'm happy, too, that you're here.' Daphne had been grateful for her sister-in-law's grace and warm welcome.

The moment she and Hugo had arrived, they had been struck by Victoria's beauty. In the past year, the girl Alice loved like a daughter had matured, become a young woman.

The little evacuee, so shy, so wary, had blossomed like a flower in Harry's gardens. Her time in London had polished her and brought out her sparky character and confidence. And here she was, about to marry one of Britain's greatest war heroes in ten days' time. God bless her, Daphne thought. She's always been a good girl, thoughtful and kind.

When Daphne went down the steps into the rose garden, she noticed that some of the early spring roses had already bloomed, and their scent was so familiar she almost started to cry; so many memories here in this garden, everywhere at Cavendon.

She had been born here, grown up here, lived all her married life here. And then she had run away from it all. She should never have abandoned this place, or the people who lived here. She had been wrong. She must make it right.

Daphne saw Cecily coming down the steps and waved. Her heart tightened when she noticed the touches of grey in that glorious russet hair, the fine lines around Cecily's eyes. Not many, just a few, and she looked wonderful for her age. Cecily had celebrated her forty-ninth birthday in the first week of May; Daphne herself was in her early fifties, and she didn't look so bad either. We've weathered the years well, she and I. And we've been through so much together. I hope she can forgive me for the way I behaved last year.

The moment she sat down next to her on the garden seat, Daphne knew that Cecily harboured no animosity towards her. She was smiling and there was the glow of friendship in her eyes.

Daphne said, 'Look, I brought this to show you, Ceci.' As she spoke, she showed her the linen shopping bag, opened it, and ruffled the envelopes inside.

Cecily stared at her, a surprised look on her face. 'Are those the notes and cards I sent you over the months you've been away?'

'Yes, and I read every one, and wept, and loved you more and more, and grieved because I'd treated you badly. I'm sorry, Cecily, that I judged you so harshly.'

'I never knew whether you'd received them or not, because you never replied. But I hoped you had. You're not giving them back to me, are you?' Cecily's voice had suddenly risen, was touched with alarm.

'Of course I'm not,' Daphne exclaimed, pulling the linen bag closer to her. 'I reread them all the time. I just wanted you to know how important they've been to me, and still are.'

'Diedre and Dulcie are thrilled that you're here, and they can't wait to see you this weekend,' Cecily said, her voice warm and loving.

Daphne nodded, sat back against the seat and looked around the garden, and then up at Cavendon, the great house on the hill.

Turning to face her sister-in-law, she said, 'It's lasted for almost two hundred years, and that's what you're doing, endeavouring to make it last longer, keep it safe forever. I understand that now.'

Cecily nodded, and frowned slightly when she saw tears glistening on Daphne's lashes. She was about to speak, when Daphne took hold of her hand, brought it to her lips and kissed it lightly, affectionately.

After a moment, Daphne said, 'I've come back to Cavendon . . . to die. If you'll let me stay.'

'Daphne! Daphne! Whatever are you saying? What do you mean?' Cecily cried, filled with sudden fear on hearing these words. Her throat thickened, and she shook her head. 'Please tell me what you mean?' Her voice was broken with tears.

'I have cancer. It's very bad, Ceci. I have about six months at the most, and I do want to die here. This is my home, where I've lived always . . . please say I can stay.'

'Oh my God, Daphne, of course you can stay! I thought you'd come back to stay forever. I would never keep you away; you've helped to make Cavendon what it is. You belong here. Oh, please, tell me we can get new doctors for you. We must try to cure you. I don't want you to die. Oh, Daphne, Daphne, I love you . . .'

Tears were sliding down Cecily's cheeks. She was in shock, could hardly believe this conversation was happening, and she began to shake.

Daphne moved closer to her and put her arms around her. 'There's nothing anyone can do, Cecily. We've seen the best doctors in Switzerland. None better anywhere, I'm sure . . . The facts are the facts, and I must accept them.'

Cecily was heartbroken, unable to stop weeping. Daphne held her close, trying to soothe her, comfort her, calm her – this woman she had known all her life. Eventually, the sobbing stopped, and Cecily tried to pull herself together.

Sitting up, releasing Daphne, Cecily found her handkerchief and wiped her eyes. 'How long have you known?' she asked, once she was feeling steadier.

'I began to feel unwell last year, and about last October we went to see my doctor. He told me, and put me on the best medicine, and it worked for a while. But not any more.' Daphne paused, swept her hands across her damp face. 'That's why we didn't come at Christmas. I just felt too ill.'

'But why didn't you tell me? Or Miles?' Cecily looked deeply into her face. 'We would have come to see you and Hugo. You must know how much we love you both. You're our family, and differences should never get in the way of our feelings for each other. We must stand together in adversity.'

'I didn't want to burden you.'

'Is that why you stayed away from Aunt Charlotte's funeral?' Cecily ventured softly.

'It is. I felt unwell again, and it was better just to remain in Zurich. I'm sorry, perhaps I should have told you then. Please forgive me.'

'Daphne, darling, Daphne, there's nothing to forgive. Not about anything. And you will stay here by my side and I will look after you, take care of you. I promise. And truly there's nothing to forgive, because you've never done anything wrong.'

'Thank you, Ceci. There is something else we must discuss, and this is very serious. No one must know I have cancer, and that I'm dying. No one at all.'

Cecily was startled by this statement, and exclaimed, 'But I must tell Miles; he's your brother, the head of the family.' She shook her head vehemently, her face troubled.

Daphne took a deep breath and plunged in. 'I honestly don't want anyone to know. Only Hugo and you. I don't want everybody worrying, fussing, and sympathizing with me. I want to live the last months I have on Earth as if I am in normal health. I don't want my children to know.'

'Oh Daphne, I'm not sure it's right to keep this from them.'

'Cecily, listen to me. This is the one last wonderful thing you can do for me. And that is to protect me. Let me have those few happy months. *Please*.'

Cecily's eyes filled up, and she could only nod.

Daphne continued, 'When you were a girl, probably about twelve, I think, you took the oath. The ancient oath to protect any Ingham with your life.' When Cecily was silent, Daphne said, 'You did, didn't you?'

'Yes. I swore the oath. Loyalty binds me.'

'There you've said it again. Promise me you will protect me by keeping my illness a secret.'

Cecily couldn't speak. She didn't even nod. After a moment, she finally said, 'I think Miles ought to know. He'll keep your secret. You know he will.'

Daphne looked at her for a long moment and then she smiled, 'I'll make a deal with you, Cecily Swann Ingham. All right?'

Cecily said, 'What kind of deal?'

'Ah, I see the negotiator in you,' Daphne replied, and smiled again, wanting to be cheerful, to lighten the sorrow of this moment. 'You will keep my secret, won't you? Hugo has promised to keep it. And then, after the wedding, so as not to spoil anything for your mother or the bride, I will tell Miles myself. Do you agree?'

'Yes. I understand what you want. We mustn't let this terrible news of your illness ruin Victoria's marriage to Christopher. You have my promise. And I want you to know that I am here for you, whatever you might need.'

'Cheerfulness, Cecily, and a happy attitude. Nobody should be able to guess. And we'll have to be on our toes. You know they're all very sharp and clever, our children.'

'That is true, they are,' Cecily said, and asked, 'You will tell Miles once they've gone on their honeymoon, won't you?'

'You have my word, my oath. Loyalty binds me.'

Alicia was beginning to feel better. The arrival of her parents at Cavendon had cheered her up immensely, and the news of Fennell's 'execution', as Charlie called it, had destroyed the lingering fear she had been harbouring about him.

Charlie had called it a new beginning, and she hoped it was. She still had feelings of guilt at times, because she had been the one who had brought Adam Fennell into the family.

Alex Poniatowski had introduced her to a psychiatrist, who had been able to help her deal with this guilt, and it lessened her anxiety. And not one member of the family had ever blamed her.

Alex was on her mind today because he would be coming to the wedding on 27 May. He was to be Christopher's best man, exactly one week from today at the church in Little Skell village.

She looked up as Victoria came into the blue and white sitting room, looking pretty in a red and white striped cotton frock.

She hurried over. 'Hello, Alicia,' Victoria said, and kissed her on the cheek. Sitting down in a chair, she went on, 'It's so lovely of you to have this coffee morning with me.'

'It's my pleasure, and I'm glad you agreed to come early,' Alicia said. 'I have a present for you, as well as the traditional bride's little gift from her girlfriends.'

As she finished speaking, Alicia handed her a decorative shopping bag. Inside was something wrapped in tissue paper. When she pulled the package out and took off the paper, Victoria was holding an old, rather worn blue leather box.

Opening the lid, she gasped. 'Oh, Alicia, they're beautiful. But I can't take this string of pearls; they're far too valuable.'

'Yes, you can. I want you to have them. Aunt Vanessa gave them to me years ago when I was your age. And now they're yours . . . to wish you a wonderful marriage, and to say thank you for helping me get through these last few weeks. I appreciate all the love and kindness you've shown me. And your cheerfulness and positive attitude has helped me.'

'Thank you, Alicia, I'll treasure the pearls always.' After a moment, Victoria ventured in a careful voice, 'Well, what about Alex Poniatowski? Do you like him? What's happening between you?'

'Friendship, at the moment, Vicki. You know all about the psychiatrist he introduced me to, and I'm getting some good advice, and feeling more relaxed.'

'Christopher told me that Alex had a bad time just after the war. He'd joined the British Army. He had plunged into the fighting, knowing he was helping to destroy the Third Reich, and was fighting for freedom and democracy. And then, later, after the war ended, depression and survivor-guilt hit him,' Victoria said.

'That's what Alex told me himself, and the fact that he couldn't get the image out of his head of his family being brutally killed when the Nazis wiped out the elite of Poland. And, actually, we have bonded in a certain way, if you want the truth.'

'I want you to be happy, Alicia, and maybe it will become . . . more romantic. Perhaps you will fall in love with Alex.'

Alicia laughed. 'Mrs Alice asked me about him. Whether he was a suitor or not? And I said I thought maybe he was, but he was keeping quiet about it. Perhaps giving me time to mend.'

'That sounds just like Aunt Alice. She wants everyone to get married.'

'I asked her if she had any advice for me, and she said this: "Wait. And see."' Alicia smiled at the younger woman. 'And I will.'

A moment later Elise came into the room, followed by Annabel, Alicia's younger sister.

Within seconds the young women were chatting and laughing together, excited about the wedding next Saturday. They would all be back at Cavendon for the entire weekend.

Eric came in with Peggy, and they served coffee and small cakes, and then left them alone to look after themselves.

A moment later, Cecily arrived and said, 'Here I am. Sorry I'm late, and I can't really stay. I just want to give you this, Victoria.'

Cecily handed her a square-shaped package and sat down next to her, smiling as Victoria opened it.

There was a box inside the wrapping paper, and when Victoria lifted the lid, she saw a pair of lovely old hair combs made of tortoiseshell.

'Something *borrowed*,' Cecily said. 'They're to pull back your hair at the sides, so your wreath of creamy white rosebuds sits right on top of your head, holding your veil.'

Victoria put the combs in her long hair immediately, and said, 'Thank you so much. Do you mean like this?'

Cecily nodded. 'Yes, I do. And they're perfect. But *borrowed*.'

Annabel handed Victoria a small box. 'This is something *blue*. I bet you can guess what it is.'

Victoria cried, 'A blue garter.' And she saw she was correct when she opened her gift. 'Thank you, Annabel.'

'And here's mine,' Elise said. 'They're *new*.'

Victoria found a pair of silk stockings in the paper parcel Elise had passed to her. 'Thank you, Elise; they're very sexy, don't you think?'

'And this is from me.' Alicia put a silver-coloured paper envelope on Victoria's lap. 'It's something *old*.' The lace-trimmed wedding handkerchief inside the silver envelope was delicate, truly lovely. Victoria handled it carefully and thanked Alicia.

'The only way you can actually have that with you, when you get married next week, is to tuck it through the blue garter on your leg. Or pin it to your knickers,' Alicia announced, sudden laughter surfacing.

They all laughed happily with her.

Victoria, ever the practical one, told them, 'I shall pin it to my knickers. I want Christopher to see how great my leg looks when I'm wearing a blue garter. Like one of those Can-Can girls in Paris.'

Cecily rose and said, 'I can't stay for coffee, I'm afraid. I'm taking Lady Daphne to Harrogate. We're going shopping. See you all for lunch later. It's going to be a lovely weekend, with us all here together. Like old times.' Cecily was beaming when she left.

Alice Swann was relieved when the sun came out on Saturday afternoon, the twenty-seventh of May. It had been cloudy all morning, and she had worried that it would rain. But the wind had blown the clouds across the sky above the moors. It had become a radiant day for Victoria's wedding.

Staring at herself in the cheval mirror in her bedroom, Alice nodded. She thought she looked rather smart in the elegantly tailored yellow silk dress her daughter had designed for her. It was from Cecily's new limited collection, which was promising to be a success.

She walked across the upstairs hall and went into Victoria's bedroom, where Cecily was helping the bride with her veil. It was made of cream tulle and held in place by a circle of creamy white silk rosebuds.

'You look lovely, Victoria,' Alice said. 'Turn around, please, so I can see the front of the dress.'

Cecily nodded when Victoria looked at her questioningly.

'That's it, Victoria. You're ready. And you're a very beautiful bride.'

'Thank you,' Victoria murmured, and slowly turned so that Aunt Alice could see her.

Alice nodded and tears came into her eyes when she saw her little evacuee, now a bride. She blinked them back. 'Christopher will never forget the way you look today. Simply angelic.'

Cecily smiled at her mother. 'I cut the bust high in the Empire style, and let the fabric fall down into soft pleats at the front. The square neckline and long sleeves add a sense of the Tudor period. What do you think?'

'You've outdone yourself, Cecily,' Alice answered, and peered at the dress. 'Why does the cream silk seem to sparkle?'

'The fabric has very tiny crystal beads sewn all over it, here, there. I just wanted it to be different and special.'

Suddenly Walter appeared in the doorway of the bedroom. 'I think you and Cecily better be going to the church, Alice. It's almost time for me to walk Victoria over.'

Victoria had chosen the church in Little Skell village for their wedding, close to the house belonging to Walter and Alice, in the village that had taken her to its heart as an evacuee.

Alex Poniatowski was relieved she had made this choice; he was able to wheel Christopher up the church path quite easily and into the church without any trouble with the chair.

As they went down the centre aisle, Christopher said, 'What a marvellous church this is, Alex; very old and beautiful with the coloured stained-glass windows. And somebody's gone mad with the flowers.'

He laughed, loving everything that was happening to him today. Who would have thought this would ever come to pass? He was about to marry an extraordinary young woman who had stolen his heart and who made him incredibly happy.

I'm the luckiest man in the world, he thought. I survived a horrific plane crash, lived to tell the tale, and I'm now a bridegroom. His handsome face was radiant with happiness.

When they arrived at the altar, Christopher said, 'I think it's going to be quite a crowd, don't you?'

'Yes. The Jollion family, Harry and Paloma and their brood. And so many Swanns and Inghams I've lost count. A big bunch, with your friends, too.'

'Cecily told me that the entire three villages turn out for weddings, and throw confetti, rose petals and rice. Very traditional.'

'And very English, which is what I like,' Alex answered.

There was sudden activity at the back of the church as Christopher's little band of ushers arrived: Harry, his RAF friends, Noel Jollion and Rory. They looked smart in their morning suits, and each of them wore a white rose in the lapels, as did Christopher and Alex.

'First the ushers, and now here comes the bridesmaid, Elise, in rose, and those adorable little girls, Patricia Swann and Lady Gwen, also in pale rose.'

'I hope she hasn't got the cat with her,' Christopher said, and laughed when he saw Alex's expression. 'I'm joking,' he said.

Christopher ached for Victoria to arrive, and kept his eyes focused on the back of the church as the pews started to fill up with people.

When Victoria arrived on Walter Swann's arm a few minutes later, the ushers moved out of the way so that they could stand right at the back. Victoria had asked Harry to do that. She didn't want Christopher to get a glimpse of her until she walked down the aisle, and was pleased that, at this moment, she and Uncle Walter were not visible.

Victoria breathed in, smelling the fragrance of the roses and the other flowers, which was intoxicating, obliterating the mustiness of the old stone walls. Everywhere candles flickered; many of them were long tapers, which made everything appear magical, dreamlike, to her.

Suddenly the organ music started, making her jump. Startled, she clung to Walter's arm. He glanced down at her. 'All right, love?'

'Very all right, Uncle Walter.'

There was another rush of excitement as more and more people arrived, and Victoria spotted Lady Daphne with Mr Hugo, Alicia and Annabel. Then came many of the men from Biggin Hill, and some of Christopher's other RAF bods, as he called them. The sight of them will please him, she thought; make him even happier.

For a moment, she felt as if she were drifting away, felt a slight dizziness, and then her head cleared, when Walter said, 'This is it, Victoria. Down the aisle we go, my darling girl.'

They moved slowly, elegantly and in step, Walter guiding her. All kinds of thoughts rushed through her head and she let them go at once. Thoughts of her childhood had no place here today. They were dead and gone, those old, horrific memories. Christopher's love had erased them, she knew that.

The future was ahead of her. With this extraordinary man who loved her. She smiled to herself when they drew closer to the altar, and she looked at Christopher's astonished face as he finally saw her.

It was the same look he had given her when she told him she was pregnant with their first child. Only two other people knew she was carrying his baby: Aunt Alice and Cecily. That was why she had designed an Empire-style gown to hide the bump.

A husband and a child, she thought. The two people I love the most in this world. They will be my world. I will look after them both, and love them forever.

And then she was there, standing next to Christopher's wheelchair. Alex stepped aside, and Walter put her hand in Christopher's. He simply gazed at her with tears in his eyes. She was crying too, but she blinked as the wedding ceremony began and looked at the vicar.

Victoria didn't really hear anything, except Christopher's voice and her own, and she felt the tears stinging for a moment as they uttered the same important words: 'I do.'

Suddenly, David and Walter came forward, carrying cushions, on which were laid their gold wedding rings. These were taken off the cushions, and then they gleamed on their fingers . . . and the organ music started, floating up into the rafters of the church.

Alex was motioning to her and she bent down and kissed Christopher, and then walked alongside him, as Alex pushed the wheelchair. The organ music changed, and they moved along to the sound of the famous melody, 'Here Comes the Bride'.

When they arrived at the back of the church, Christopher said, 'We're married, Vicki. I can hardly believe it, my lovely.'

Her eyes were still moist when she bent over him and kissed him on the mouth. Against his ear she whispered, 'And you will be a father in the not-too-distant future.'

He looked up at her and said, 'My life is just beginning, Mrs Longdon.'

'And so is mine,' she answered. And she meant every word.

# ACKNOWLEDGEMENTS

I am always a bit sad when I finish a book because I have to say goodbye to so many people who have been with me on this journey: my characters. They are real people to me before they step on to the page, and my friends by the time the book comes to an end. And I am always reluctant to let them go.

Fortunately, I usually have another group of people waiting in the wings, ready and willing to walk out on to the stage, to have me bring them to life and tell their stories. In other words, I have a new adventure ahead of me.

Once a book is finished, others become involved. I owe thanks to a number of people: to Lonnie Ostrow of Bradford Enterprises who helps in various ways, from research to skilfully getting my edits and changes onto the computer; and to Linda Sullivan of WordSmart, for producing a perfect manuscript without errors. A beautiful typescript is a treat for me.

My editor at HarperCollins, Publishing Director Lynne Drew, is the most wonderful sounding board for me, full of ideas and suggestions which help to make the new book better. I cannot thank Lynne enough for everything she does for me, and for always being there. I must also thank Charlotte Brabbin, Eloisa

Clegg and Penny Isaacs, who has been my copy-editor for many years. Thanks also to Kate Elton, Executive Publisher, Elizabeth Dawson, PR Director, Oliver Wright, UK Sales Director, Roger Cazalet, Associate Publisher, Lucy Vanderbilt, Group Rights Director and Charlie Redmayne, CEO. They are a marvellous group to work with.

My husband Bob has always been involved in my writing, from the moment I have the first idea for a novel until I write the last page. His love and caring, enthusiasm and encouragement are unmatched, and keep me going strong even on difficult days with storylines and characters. The movies Bob has produced of my books are superbly cast with big stars, and are both dramatic and captivating. I owe the biggest thank you to him for being such a loving husband and partner in all ways.

Barbara Taylor Bradford is proud to support the National Literacy Trust, a charity dedicated to improving literacy across the UK. Barbara is passionate about improving life chances, particularly among women, to ensure everyone reaches their full potential. To find out more about Barbara's involvement, please go to: www.literacytrust.org.uk/barbarataylorbradford.